ALSO BY BRITTANY N. WILLIAMS

Saint-Seducing Gold
(The Forge & Fracture Saga, Book 2)

THAT SELF-SAME METAL

The Forge & Fracture Saga

BRITTANY N. WILLIAMS

AMULET BOOKS • NEW YORK

Library of Congress Control Number for the hardcover edition: 2022028492

Paperback ISBN 978-1-4197-5865-2

Text © 2023 Brittany N. Williams
Sword artwork courtesy Ezepov Dmitry/Shutterstock.com
Book design by Chelsea Hunter
Map by Jamie Zollars

Excerpt from *Saint-Seducing Gold (The Forge & Fracture Saga, Book 2)* © 2024 Brittany N. Williams

Printed and bound in U.S.A.
10 9 8 7 6 5 4 3 2 1

Amulet Books are available at special discounts when purchased in quantity for premiums and promotions as well as fundraising or educational use. Special editions can also be created to specification. For details, contact specialsales@abramsbooks.com or the address below.

Amulet Books® is a registered trademark of Harry N. Abrams, Inc.

ABRAMS The Art of Books
195 Broadway, New York, NY 10007
abramsbooks.com

For Grandma who's always been with me

and Tito who's just arrived

———○———

In loving memory of Mommy, Sonia, and Sherman.

Thank you for always believing in me. I know you'd love this one.

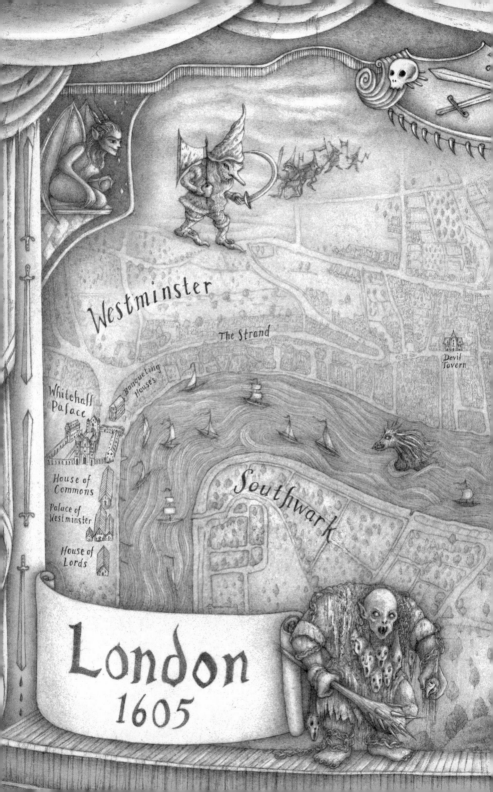

Westminster

The Strand

Devil
Tavern

Whitehall
Palace

Banqueting
Houses

House of
Commons

Palace of
Westminster

House of
Lords

Southwark

London
1605

Shakespeare's
House

Goldsmiths
Row

Joan's
House

St Martin
Ludgate

St Paul's
Cathedral

Tower of
London

Nonesuch
House

London
Bridge

Bear
Garden

Globe
Theatre

Clink
Prison

St Mary
Overies

Tabard
Inn

CHAPTER ONE
Rotten in the State

ou two need to count before you accidentally take each other's eyes out."

Joan Sands watched the two boys practicing in front of her and struggled not to breathe too deeply.

A chill wind blew through the weathered tapestries covering the gaping windows. Shadows floated and shifted as the candles danced with the breeze, their light the only thing keeping the darkness at bay. The draft carried the moldy aroma of damp fabric across the open room.

Joan scowled as the stench filled her nose, so strong she could taste it.

The Banqueting House at Whitehall Palace stank to high heaven and not even the wide-open main entertainment room could save them from the rank smell. Joan would've held practice outside in the nearby courtyard but for the day's heavy rain.

The hall, made of brick and timber and canvas, had been a source of pride for King Henry VIII—rest his soul—back in 1540, but it had barely made it to 1605 intact. Rumor said that King James absolutely hated the building.

Not that Joan blamed him. She swore a hard enough gust would send the whole thing tumbling down. Besides, who wants to entertain royal guests and courtiers in a place that smelled like a soggy alehouse?

She willed herself to get used to it. She couldn't stop up her nose without blocking her view of Samuel Crosse and Nick Tooley butchering the fight she'd taught them months ago.

Behind them, the other members of the King's Men set properties in their places—pillows, daggers, a fake vial of poison, and the like—and unpacked costumes. The acting company always eagerly anticipated the summons to perform for their royal patron—King James himself. His Majesty's favor gave them the protection of being members of his household, the clout of serving the king, and the money that being so powerfully employed afforded. If the king called, so would the company appear, no matter how much the musty old banqueting hall smelled like old, soggy potatoes.

Every so often, one of the men would glance Joan's way and chuckle. All the actors in the company knew Joan never forgave the sloppy execution of a stage fight, and each was grateful to not be currently under her scrutiny.

Samuel and Nick had both fumbled so badly through the movements in that morning's rehearsal that Joan demanded they drill the fight in the empty playing space. She'd see they got the moves right before they performed for King James and the court. Or before the boys accidentally ran each other through.

Samuel yelped as Nick's blade sliced across his knuckles.

"Sorry!" Nick shouted.

The latter looked more and more likely.

"Hold," Joan called, shaking her head as Nick and Samuel stopped fighting. She walked over to Samuel, who had his injured fingers in his mouth.

"Are you bleeding?" Nick tugged anxiously at his ponytail; his blade pointed safely toward the ground.

Samuel frowned and looked at his hand, blond brows drawn together on his pale forehead. "No," he said.

Joan's eyes followed Nick's length of hair from where it was tied at the base of his neck and swept around past the smooth column of his elegant throat. It draped over one broad shoulder, slithering down in an inky black fall. The barest glimpse of a rich brown collarbone peeked out through his open shirt. His skin was as dark brown as her own, only with undertones of red instead of gold. His hair straight and silky where hers was a lush spray of soft coils and curls. But that she could trace that path with her fingers and know the feel of his hair.

She shook herself when she realized she'd been staring, her entire face going hot.

"Be glad it only hurts." Joan took the sword from Samuel, who smiled at her knowingly. "Being a full beat behind can cause much worse."

He laughed. "Yes, yes, of course. Well, will the master show me how it's done?" He grinned and stepped back, arms wide in a flourish.

Joan rolled her eyes at him and squared herself up with Nick. "Come on, then."

"Ah, please be gentle with me, Joan." Nick stood tall, bringing his sword up in a salute.

Her heart raced as her gaze instantly caught on the thick fan of lashes surrounding his deep-brown eyes.

She needed to focus.

Joan touched her fingers to the blade, felt the metal sing to her. It whispered its secrets, gave Joan its name—Alala. The cold surety of the steel grounded her. She commanded the sword to dull even more. The metal shifted under her fingers; the change subtle enough that no one watching could have noticed what Joan had done.

This was a secret she would not share.

Joan cleared her throat. "Half speed this first time, then full." She tightened her grip on the sword and saluted him back.

"In your skirts, Joan?" Samuel snorted. He looked her up and down appraisingly. "Really?"

She cut her eyes at him. "There's no need to trouble myself with changing for this simple a combination." She smacked the flat of the blade against the fleshy back of his thigh, grinned when he yelped. "Do try to pay attention so you don't embarrass the whole company in front of His Majesty and the whole court."

Nick and Samuel both guffawed but listened, Samuel stepping off to the side to watch and Nick taking his first position. She smiled to herself. It was always easier working among the apprentices. These two boys at seventeen were only a year her elder, and, for all his talk and bluster, Samuel always listened to Joan's directions. The older company members were another story—especially a certain white-haired sharer. Augustine Phillips only pushed himself to a point. He and Joan never seemed to agree on what that entailed, but, as one of the men whose money paid for their costumes, props, and her instruction, Phillips's desires always prevailed.

Joan shook her head and slipped into the first stance, feet wide, left forward, right back, rapier held in front of her ready to strike. Her mind went quiet as her focus zeroed in on the impending fight. The blade hummed in her hands. Nick had the first move.

He swung his sword around and brought it down directly over her head. Joan caught his blade on hers, knocking it away with her guard. The move left him wide open and she faked an elbow strike to his face.

He grunted and threw himself backward, giving an extra flourish because they were moving so slowly.

Joan stifled her grin. She swept across, as if to slice open his belly, and Nick jumped back out of the way. He jabbed at her hip. She parried. He sliced at her opposite arm. She brought her rapier up to block just as he swung his sword back around and pretended to slice into her gut. The death blow. End of fight.

"At speed?" Nick said as they shifted back to their starting positions.

Joan nodded. "Keep watching, Samuel."

"Yes, teacher," he droned.

Joan ignored him.

Nick swung for her head. She blocked, shunting his blade away and elbowing him in the "face." He grunted, stumbled back a few steps. Joan pressed forward, slicing at his belly. He dodged, stabbing at her hip. Blocked. His sword swung for her arm. She brought hers up to parry and met only empty air as he tapped the flat of his blade against the side of her bodice. He flexed his shoulder and jerked his hip to make it look like he drove his sword deeper into her side. Joan dropped her rapier and fell toward him, selling her "death."

Joan looked up and their eyes met. Their faces were so close, she could see the hints of gold swirling in his brown irises. All she needed to do was lean up and—

"Hm, I'm not sure I have it as yet," Samuel said, leering at them. "Would you two go at it again? Although, if you need a moment alone with Nick, Joan, I can . . ."

Joan's face exploded with heat. She stepped away from Nick, doing her best not to look at him. She picked up her fallen sword and tossed it at Samuel—point down, of course—keeping her expression neutral.

"Laugh if you'd like, but mess up again . . ." She let the threat hang in the air, leaving Samuel to dread what dastardly and exhausting punishment she'd come up with should he fail.

Samuel laughed harder but Joan could see the fear in his eyes. "Aye, teacher."

Good.

"Now let's see it once more." She stood back and folded her arms, pretending that her heart wasn't still racing.

———|———

Later, Joan wandered around the playing space with her hands full of dulled swords that she herself had mended and prepared for the King's Men's impending royal performance.

It wasn't the most profound use of her skills, but it was a consistent one, and that was enough for now.

"Which would you say is worse?" James—Joan's twin brother and of no relation to the king, though they shared a name and an attitude—strolled up behind her, waving a handkerchief in front of his nose. "The chill or the smell?" He was set to perform this evening just like Samuel and Nick, though you'd never know it from his calm behavior. James never panicked before a play, and none of them ever understood how he managed it.

His soft features matched Joan's own, from the curve of their broad noses to the gentle slope of their cheeks to the roundness of their wide brown eyes. But while James kept his dark, curly hair cut short, Joan let hers grow—the spiraling strands long enough to reach her waist when stretched.

James still wore the yellow jerkin he'd chosen this morning—he'd picked a matching yellow skirt, bodice, and sleeves for Joan, as was his practice—but he'd exchange it for an elaborate white gown to play Juliet for tonight's play.

"Can we say the smell and this chill both are equally bad?" Rob Gough said, his dark brown face twisted into a scowl. He already wore his wig but not his costume. The flowing red curls looked odd without the gown he'd wear later, but somehow it didn't seem ridiculous on him.

Joan shook her head. James and Rob could wear nearly anything and look fantastic. As apprentice members of the King's Men, both boys played the women's roles in the company's plays. English ladies were forbidden by law to perform themselves onstage in such "vulgar" displays.

No. More specifically, the law didn't allow women to speak lines onstage. The women of court often danced in their own masques—elaborate spectacles of music and fantastical costumes—in this very building. And there was even a troupe of female acrobats set to perform sometime this evening. So, while the female body was allowed space, the same couldn't be said of the female voice.

And wasn't that the most unfair thing.

"At least you two could spend most of the day outside," Nick said, joining their small group. Joan jumped at the sound of his voice, swords clattering together loudly as she struggled not to drop them. "Joan, Samuel, and I have been breathing in the stench for hours."

She tried to slow her breathing. This was ridiculous. She'd spent the better part of the day with Nick, why should his presence now make her anxious? She needed to collect herself.

James gave her a look. She ignored it. Because she was busy holding swords.

Very important business—

Nick smiled at her, his full lips quirking a little higher on one side as they always did before he slid into conversation with Rob. Joan suddenly found that she enjoyed this lopsided grin the most.

Nick's glorious black hair hung loose around his shoulders this time, thick and shiny and nearly reaching the small of his back.

Joan's curly hair wound about her head in an elaborate series of twists and braids held in place by yellow ribbons and fine silver thread. Had it been loose, the damp air would have the strands shrinking themselves closer and closer to her head. She wondered if Nick's hair would be as soft as hers, if it would slide through her fingers like silk.

"Sister"—James bumped against her shoulder and held out a handkerchief—"careful, you're salivating."

Joan went bright red and smacked him with the hilts of the swords.

Through some supernatural twin connection, James had sensed that the boy they'd known for three years suddenly made Joan's heart pound whenever he so much as looked at her. And now her brother refused to give her a moment's rest whenever Nick was near.

"Nicholas," he crooned, "doesn't my sister look splendid in yellow?"

Joan's heart plummeted to her feet as Nick turned to look her over. His gaze swept over her, from her finely braided and pinned hair, down along her broad nose and full lips, past her slim shoulders. His eyes lingered on her modest bosom, accentuated by her tight bodice, then skirted away.

Joan wanted to melt into the floor. She wondered what it would feel like to be an only child.

She only needed one free sword to find out.

"Two things," Samuel said as he strolled over. "One." He held up a finger. "Master Phillips suggested I come make it look less suspicious that all the brown folk are standing together like it's some kind of meeting."

Joan rolled her eyes but blessed Phillips and his paranoia for saving her further embarrassment. She glanced across the great hall to where the white-haired old man stood watching them, all pale face and bushy white brows and beard.

Rob and James exchanged a look and Samuel shrugged apologetically. "If you were holding a meeting, I expect I would have been invited despite my fair complexion."

Nick burst out laughing. "What a foolish old—"

James pinched Nick into silence, a gesture Nick returned in kind.

Joan shook her head. Nick wasn't wrong. Phillips's suspicious beliefs about her, James, Rob, and Nick were surprising given what the old man was hiding from the rest of the company.

Rob rolled his eyes. "Why is Master Phillips always like this?"

Joan clenched her back teeth together and kept her mouth shut. Despite his prejudices and stubborn nature, she liked Master Phillips. He was the actor under whom her brother served as apprentice and was generally kind. But sometimes he just—

Well, it needn't be said. They all understood.

She, James, and Rob were all Black and of a similar complexion, Rob only a bit darker than the twins. Nick, while not Black, could thank his distant ancestors from the east for his rich brown skin. Then there was Samuel, with the barest hint of a tan on his pale face and bright golden-blond hair.

Though the whole lot of them had been born here in England to English parents who had English parents, only Samuel never had to combat questions about his heritage.

Or petty suspicions.

"Two," Samuel said, continuing his message, "Joan, I'm to ask you to deliver this token of esteem"—he held up a sparkling necklace—"to one of the lady acrobats over in their tiring-rooms."

Joan sighed heavily but handed Samuel the swords. His knees buckled under the sudden weight before he got his bearings. James snickered.

Joan rolled her eyes. They always forgot she was stronger than them. No matter how many times she'd proved it.

Samuel huffed and held the chain out for Joan to take. As soon as the metal touched her hands, she knew what it was: gilded tin. Cheap but done well enough to fool someone less savvy.

And Joan knew metals better than nearly anyone else.

"Which lady is this meant for?"

"I was told you should use your refined eye and give it to the lady you think it suits best."

James nodded with a grin. "Joan does know beautiful women."

"And men," Samuel said and wiggled his eyebrows at Nick.

"I do," Joan said, thrusting her chin high despite her mounting embarrassment. "Does your sister still ask after me, Samuel?"

Samuel's grin turned lewd. "Oh, she pines, Joan. Shall I bring her by the playhouse again? She'll be sad to know she has competition now."

"What competition?" Nick asked suddenly.

The other three boys burst into laughter and Joan used the distraction to race for the door.

It was best to leave before their innuendo dug even deeper into her thoughts and feelings.

The halls that wound through the rest of the Banqueting House connected rooms and smaller sections in a twisting labyrinth that erased all sense of direction or time. Everything became dark-painted wood beams that pressed in on you from all sides, flickering candles, and a rush-strewn floor that hissed with every step. The contrast with the wide-open main hall was stark.

Joan would never say she was afraid to walk the narrow expanse, but the trip was never her favorite.

She was halfway to the rooms reserved as a tiring area where the women changed and prepared for their performance before she realized she had the tin necklace clenched in her fist. She relaxed her hand.

The chain lay in a crumpled and crushed mess, more a lump of tin than cheap jewelry.

Wonderful.

Joan glanced around the empty hall before holding the twisted necklace up in the air. She focused on the knots, on the places where the links fused together.

Joan huffed, annoyed that she'd let her anxiety and nerves trigger her powers like that. Thankfully, she could fix her mistake just as easily.

She coaxed them to unbind themselves, to straighten back into the easy linked chain. As the metal ran over her fingers, it sang and grew warm to the touch.

Done. The necklace looked unblemished. She sent the links curling around themselves, creating a delicate spiral pattern in the cheap metal.

She draped the chain gently over her fingers and breathed deeply. She felt the metal go cool and quiet against her skin then realized she had no idea which of the elder acting company members had sent the trinket to woo a lady acrobat.

Joan could narrow the suspects down to the two most obvious culprits, but if she chose the wrong one, she'd be subjected to his incessant whining. She'd have to double back to ask them outright.

Damn.

"Should you be doing that here in the open?"

Joan flinched and threw her arm back in the direction of the man's voice. Her head whipped around and she stopped her fist just before it connected with the familiar brown face of her godfather.

"Bless your quick reflexes, Joan," Baba Ben said, eyes wide.

Joan dropped her hand to her side, cheeks hot and heart racing with embarrassment. "Sorry," she mumbled.

"Are you apologizing for nearly backhanding me, or for using the powers Ogun blessed you with out in a place where you could be caught?"

Joan knew the folly in answering truthfully so she murmured, "Both?"

"Are you asking me?"

"No . . ."

Baba Ben sighed, his slim shoulders slumping. "Joan, this of all places is not a safe location for us to show our magic."

Joan nodded, her face blazing hot. She knew this. Not only did the religion they practice fall outside of the legally mandated Protestantism, the spirits Joan and her family venerated—the Orisha—blessed the faithful with magical abilities. Blessings the law and King James would see as witchcraft and an abomination punishable by death.

And here she was, on the very grounds of the royal palace of Whitehall, in a building soon to be full of members of the king's court, using her magic openly to fix a cheap trinket—and a mistake of her own making.

"And," Baba Ben said, "I think you forgot to say a certain something—"

"Maferefun, Ogun," Joan mumbled quickly.

She always forgot to say the words of gratitude to Ogun, the Orisha of iron, her head Orisha.

Baba Ben shook his head. "Be mindful, Joan. Without Ogun's blessing, you have no power over metal. You wouldn't have been able to fix that little necklace."

Or mangle it in the first place, honestly.

But he was right, and thanks was so simple to give.

"You cannot be so careless with the Orisha." He grabbed her shoulders, leaning down to look her in the eye. "These rituals, our practice, are here for a reason."

"I know."

"You and I are the only living children of Ogun. He chose us, and the least we can do is show him we're grateful for his blessings." He straightened, a frown darkening his face. "And this should be the last time I have to remind you. Understand?"

Joan nodded, her gaze skittering to the floor. Baba Ben's disappointment always cut her, and she faced it so often because of this. She knew she'd likely face it again, because as natural as it felt to use her magic, connecting with Ogun still felt foreign. And how could she explain that to the man who'd been communing with Ogun since before Joan had been born?

Joan felt the anxiety tensing her shoulders and took a breath to calm herself. There was no need to mangle the necklace again by getting worked up.

She was wrong. She'd have to learn and adjust or face the consequences.

Then it hit her.

"Baba Ben, what are you doing here?" She stepped back, really taking her godfather in.

He wore an elegant brocade doublet, his linen shirt peeking through the matching slashed sleeves. A green velvet floppy cap accented with a long pheasant feather sat atop his head, covering his kinky white hair. Shining silver thread wove through the fabric, catching the light as he moved.

That thread was Baba Ben's signature, put into every garment he made in his tailor's shop.

"I have business with the king," he said, grinning.

Joan frowned. "Business?"

"Yes, business." Baba Ben glanced around then beckoned her closer. "Do you know of the Pact between we mortals and the Fae?"

Joan shook her head.

"Nearly two millennia ago, Ogun helped broker a deal between the people of this land and the Fae determined to do them harm. It therefore falls on we children of Ogun to ensure that the ritual to keep it in place is performed with each new king or queen of England." Here Baba Ben frowned, the expression casting deep creases along his face. "I've tried to meet with King James to reestablish the bonds for the last few years with no success. I've felt something fraying with these past two All Hallows' Eves and I fear what will happen if the ritual isn't performed before the end of this third. Thankfully, an acquaintance was finally able to arrange an audience for me, which is why I look my best."

Joan's mind raced. Ogun had helped bind the Fae nearly two thousand years ago? Sometimes the depths of what she didn't know about the Orisha seemed boundless.

"What is the ritual, Baba?"

He smiled and touched her shoulder gently. "That we will discuss when you're more spiritually mature. Yes?"

Joan sighed but returned her godfather's smile. "Of course, Baba." She added this to the long list of things she'd only find out when she was "more spiritually mature," whenever that would be.

"I saw him come this way," a gruff voice said from somewhere down an adjacent hall. The thump of several heavy boots followed soon after. "How hard can it be to find a blackamoor in a feathered cap?"

Joan's heart dropped.

Guards.

Baba Ben spun her, shoving her back into the hall. She slipped around the corner, her feet catching in her skirts and hit the ground hard. She bit down on her lip to keep from shouting and tasted blood. Joan strained her ears to hear anything.

The boots thundered closer, the sounds of a struggle, shouting, the loud smack of a slap, a grunt of pain.

"Why are you arresting me?" Baba Ben said, his voice raspy.

Joan clamped a hand over her mouth as the clanking of manacles echoed down the hall.

"I have an audience with His Majesty," Baba Ben shouted.

"Oh, of course," a nasally voice replied—one of the guards. "I'm sure the king is just waiting around to talk to a common Negro."

The group of guards burst into loud laughter. The thud of flesh hitting flesh again and again. A cough then a low groan.

Joan felt tears burn her eyes.

This couldn't be happening. Not to Baba Ben.

"Take him away," said one of the officers.

She had to see. She needed to know what was happening. She pressed her back against the wall, leaning over to peek around the corner.

Two guards, their faces pale in the candlelit hall, hauled Baba Ben none too gently, the shackled man's feet stumbling across the floor. A third hung behind as they dragged their prisoner away.

The man barked out a loud laugh once he was alone. Then his pale skin seemed to melt off his body, leaving behind a woman with golden-brown skin and a bald head.

Joan gasped.

That woman's transformation meant only one thing.

She was Fae. But it didn't make sense because she didn't glow. All Fae looked illuminated to Joan—to all who'd been blessed by the Orisha—but this woman—

She turned, and Joan threw herself backward and out of sight.

Whoever—whatever—that woman was, she'd infiltrated the royal guards. That made her seriously dangerous.

Joan didn't know if she'd been seen. If the guards or that woman found her now, her fate would surely be the same as Baba Ben's. She couldn't risk that.

She slipped her shoes off, grasping the hard soles to keep them from clacking against the floor. Silently as she could, praying with every shift of a muscle, Joan eased to her stockinged feet, and ran.

CHAPTER TWO
On the Windy Side of Care

lames crackled merrily in the fireplace, warming the entire bedroom in the early morning creeping cold. The bells at St. Paul's Cathedral chimed six o'clock as the sky brightened with the first hints of sunrise.

Joan sat on the floor in front of the fire, wide awake, her knees pulled up close to her chest. Her eyes felt heavy and her head hazy, but she'd given up lying in bed sometime around the chime of three bells.

How could she sleep when memories of yesterday with Baba Ben haunted her dreams? With that looming sense of dread pressing down on her chest?

Her godfather hadn't completed his ritual with the king, not after being arrested. The pact he spoke of must've broken, and that meant that the Fae were free to do—what? She'd seen the fear in his eyes. What was coming?

She held out her hand, an iron disk forming in her palm. She laid it against her knuckles and let it tumble along her fingers: index then middle then ring then pinkie and back again.

Her door swung open and James stumbled in, bleary-eyed and still half asleep. He headed straight for her wardrobe. He mumbled something that almost sounded like words then abruptly turned to glare at her. "What are you doing on the floor?"

"Couldn't sleep," Joan said. She propped her chin on her knees, watched her iron disk tumble across her fingers. "No point staying in bed when I was wide awake."

She heard James sigh and felt him drop to the floor beside her. He pressed their shoulders together and Joan leaned her weight against him.

"Something's wrong," she said. "Baba's ritual, it was important."

"Did they say why they arrested him?"

Joan shook her head. "They just grabbed him." She hugged her legs closer, remembering the sound of her godfather being beaten. "There was a woman—"

"A lady guard?" James snorted.

Joan elbowed him, hard, and he mumbled an apology.

"There was a woman *pretending* to be a guard. She transformed, like she was Fae, but she didn't glow."

James jerked away from her, eyes wide. "What?"

James was blessed by Oya—the Orisha of the wind and death. He saw the Fae just as Joan, Baba Ben, and their parents did: always surrounded by a light as if they'd swallowed the sun.

Except the woman yesterday—

She'd looked like any other human, and Joan had no idea how or what that meant.

A grin spread across James's face. "This is excellent. That Fae woman was probably behind Baba Ben's arrest. Fae are mischievous but not malevolent. He likely offended her somehow, and this is her way of inconveniencing him."

Joan frowned.

James was right. The Fae were known to make mortals uncomfortable on occasion but never to cause severe harm. That foreboding still sat heavily in her chest.

"The ritual—" Joan shook her head. "Baba said if it wasn't performed yesterday, something bad would happen. What if that woman is part of it?" She hugged her knees even closer. "Something's changed, I feel it. Don't you?"

James took a deep breath, then let his shoulders slump as he exhaled. "Something is amiss. Whatever it is, death lurks closer than usual."

Joan felt a shiver run down her spine.

As a child of Oya, James was never wrong about death. Ever.

"Get up," James said as he pulled her to her feet. "Get dressed. You've had no sleep and we're due at the playhouse soon. Remember what Father always says."

Joan nodded, shaking out her legs as she stood. "One problem at a time." She called her little iron disk back into herself, the metal disappearing into her palm. Their parents had already said they would find where Baba Ben was being held today, and there was nothing Joan and James could do until they had him back.

She'd rest her mind on that for now.

She took a deep breath to clear her head, stretched, then headed straight for her window to throw open the curtains. Muted light slithered across the floor as the sun filtered through the glass panes.

Their house had five levels, its height and location on Goldsmiths' Row a clear sign of the wealth her father earned as well as his trade. Joan and James had run of the top floor with the best views. Their large bedrooms faced each other with a small hall between them. Their parents' rooms occupied the next floor down. Below that sat the kitchen, the dining room, and a small guest bedroom. The receiving room and her father's office took up the floor just above where his workshop and the storefront for his shop sat at street level.

Every day, Joan would look out from her high-up room and see all the way to the tower of St. Paul's Church. But this morning, fog draped the city, blocking her usually spectacular view. She could barely see the top of their neighbor's house across the street.

Well, that did nothing to lift her mood.

She huffed and walked over to lean against her tall wooden bedpost. James kept shuffling through the clothes in her wardrobe, frowning in deep concentration.

"What color today?" Joan said.

"Green." James said from deep within the wardrobe, his voice muffled as he dug for something in the back. He found whatever he was looking for and pulled himself free with a grunt. "Green complements our complexions and our brown eyes."

Joan caught the bodice and heavy skirt James tossed to her. He threw the matching sleeves directly into her face. Joan squeaked—half startled and half pained—and scowled. She vaguely remembered tossing the sleeves to the back of her wardrobe sometime two weeks past.

Or maybe more. She didn't keep track.

That must've been what had him digging so hard.

Satisfied, James stumbled toward the door, just barely more awake than when he'd come in to pick out her clothes. Her brother, bless him, did poorly in the mornings.

"You know you could sleep in longer if you let me pick out my own clothes."

James whipped around to face her. "And let you spend every day in brown wool like some drab frump?" he said, completely scandalized. "Never."

Joan frowned. He wasn't wrong about her gravitating to plain brown wool in spite of all the more richly colored clothes her father bought for them, but still—

"You're far too pretty for that." He turned back to the door. "And I like for us to match. I'll be back to help lace you."

Joan barked out a laugh as her brother strutted out of her room. She turned to the mirror leaned against one wall and held the bodice up against her chest.

Light and dark green swirled together in an intricate repeating pattern. It really did complement her brown skin and eyes. She wondered what Nick would think when he saw her today.

Wait, where had that thought come from?

She caught her own eye in the mirror and blushed. Why was the tall boy on her mind first thing in the morning?

She knew why.

And she knew why it was pointless, how it didn't fit into her plans for her future.

In the mirror, her blushing face turned melancholy.

She sighed and turned to go wash up, dropping the clothes on her bed as she passed.

Outside, the fog was just starting to thin as the sun crept higher in the sky.

Joan closed her curtains anyway. Best not to risk giving someone a glimpse of her while she dressed. Or to remind herself of all she couldn't see through the thick morning haze.

┼

Joan rushed down the stairs, past the landing for their parents' floor, and down to the dining room.

Her mother and father were likely up by now and already sitting down to strategize about Baba Ben's arrest and eat whatever Nan Hall, their maid, had prepared for breakfast.

"Mother," Joan called as she ran into the room. She held a green ribbon looped through three gold beads in one hand. "Can you help me—"

The table sat empty. Nan slipped out of the kitchen, a plate loaded with bread and sausage balanced in each hand, her light brown skin flushed from the heat. Her dark coils of hair were tucked tightly underneath her white cap, a few loose curls slipping free to dangle in her youthful face.

Her rosary hung round her neck. Nan only dared wear the polished wooden beads within the safety of the Sands home. Because if they could trust Nan to keep the Orisha secret, she could trust them with the secret of her Catholic faith.

"Morning, Nan," Joan said frowning. "Where are Mother and Father?"

Nan grinned at Joan and sat each plate down in front of an empty chair. "G'morning, love." She dusted her hands off on her crisp white apron and jerked her head toward the table. "Your parents had to step out for . . . business, but they'll return soon enough. Mistress Sands used her"—Nan flapped her hand at the wall—"ways."

Joan's frown deepened as she sat down.

When Nan said "ways," she meant magic.

Joan's mother was a child of Elegua—the Orisha of crossroads and doorways—and he'd blessed her with the power to open doors to travel between any two places. Bess Sands never used the ability lightly because it always left her tired and unable to leave her bed for nearly a day afterward. If she'd used it now, it meant her parents had gone far away.

"Oh," Nan said, "Master Sands said he left something for you to finish in his workshop, if you're able."

Joan sat up. "A pwojec—" she mumbled through a mouth full of bread.

Nan shot her a look. Joan flushed, chewed, and choked as the food got caught in her throat. She took a gulp of apple ale and coughed. Nan shook her head and offered no sympathy.

Joan cleared her throat and tried again. "A project?"

"Mmm. He said it was suited to your skills."

Her heart raced. "Is it a pendant? Another salt stand? A chalice?"

Nan cut her eyes at Joan, who immediately clamped her mouth shut. She squirmed in her seat, pulling the soft center out of her bread and eating it without tasting it.

Her father rarely asked her to help him despite her abilities with metal. What Joan could accomplish by magic, Thomas Sands could nearly match by the skill of his own two hands. Nearly.

"Joan, we need to go!" James thundered down the stairs. He snatched the sausage from Joan's plate. "Morning, Nan. Do you have our lunch?" He scrambled across the hall to the kitchen, tearing bits of meat off with his teeth and chewing loudly.

Joan rolled her eyes and slid his full plate from his side of the table to hers. Nan sighed and followed James into the kitchen.

He then bolted back into the dining room, dropping two fabric-wrapped pouches into his bag. "Joan," he said, mouth full, "we need to go!"

"You go ahead," she said. "Father left some work for me. I'll catch up."

James squinted at her. "Don't be late," he said before running down the rest of the stairs.

"Take the foils and things with you!" Joan shouted after him. She heard a clatter of metal down in the workshop as James grabbed the dulled swords for today's performance.

The bell over the shop door clanged harshly as he ran out into the street.

Joan snorted out a laugh and set about finishing off her brother's breakfast. When she was done, she took up both empty plates and walked them over to Nan in the kitchen.

"Nan, would you like me to—"

Nan took the dishes and flapped her hand at Joan, shooing her out of the room.

Joan grinned and bolted out the kitchen, fists gripping her skirt as she ran down the stairs to the ground floor. She swung herself around the banister.

The early sunlight streamed in through the windows at the front of the shop, bouncing cheerily off the polished wood shelves lining the walls. Joan slipped past the long showcase table at the center of the room and headed straight for the door at the back. Her fingers closed around the steel knob. The metal sang at her touch as she swung the door open.

Her father's large worktable took up most of the back room. Tools covered the surface in tidy rows and clusters—hammers, pliers, files, and dollies each nearest the projects they'd be best used for. The forge sat against the far wall, cold and ready to be heated to blazing for the day's work.

It would stay that way until Henry, her father's apprentice, arrived to open for the day. Which was fine. Joan needed neither fire nor tools to forge.

Joan slipped around the table and hopped onto her father's tall stool. Whenever she came here alone, she'd take his seat, pretending she was the brilliant goldsmith running the shop.

Would that she could be. But this place would go to Henry when her father died. Joan would not want for money—she'd likely be married to some merchant's son by then, probably a grocer—but it wasn't about the money.

This work called to her. Bringing beauty out of a cold lump of metal, breathing life into it sang to her heart. But the thought of her owning the shop felt so improper, she couldn't even bring herself to ask her father. They already granted her so many allowances by letting her work at the playhouse. What would they say if she declared that she wouldn't marry and was instead taking control of the shop?

That would likely be the end of her freedom.

Her only other option was to marry Henry and hope she outlived him. A widow could inherit a man's business where a daughter could not. But Henry was—

Nick's smiling face leapt into her mind unbidden.

Henry wasn't who she wanted but she could make do with him for what she needed. Couldn't she?

Joan sighed. Across the table and shoved off into a corner lay a wooden tray loaded with tangled balls of chains and necklaces. She raised an eyebrow at the mess.

Henry's work.

Her father's apprentice was passable at goldworking but absolutely terrible with delicate pieces. Joan knew this. Her father knew this. Henry knew this.

Joan was skilled enough to become the next Nicholas Hilliard—a world-famous goldsmith fashioning gold items by royal request.

All Henry could do after three years under her father's tutelage was tie necklaces into knots.

And yet . . .

She scowled at the beaten and marked worktable, unclenching her fists. Anger did nothing but make her lose focus.

Joan shook her head and slid the tray toward herself. She laid her hand over the ball of twisted metals. One by one they slithered out from one another to form orderly rows. She shoved it back into the corner for the men to find later and finally noticed another tray.

This one held a painted canvas, four gold rounds, and a note. Joan pulled it across the table.

Joan—

A gentleman wants a golden pendant in his lady's likeness. I trust you to make it extremely flattering.

She eyed the painting, taking in the artist's less than generous depiction of the pale, blond woman. "I'm sure he won't mind if I take a few liberties." She grinned and cracked her knuckles.

Then she set to work coaxing beauty from a lump of metal and a mediocre piece of art.

CHAPTER THREE
Heavy Is the Crown

oan sprinted through the street, heavy skirt gripped in tight fists. Her sides strained against the stays in her bodice as she huffed and puffed. But she couldn't stop.

There wasn't time.

She'd spent too long working in her father's shop shaping and curling the gold to her will until Henry arrived to open the shop midmorning. Then she'd tucked herself into a back corner so he couldn't watch her work—who knew what he'd do should he find out about Joan's powers. She was still working when Nan brought down Henry's lunch and the bells at St. Paul's rang for one o'clock.

That caught her attention. Today's performance at the Globe would start at two o'clock. But no one would care if she wasn't around for the beginning of the play, so she thought she had plenty of time to get across the river. That is until she noticed the crown she'd repaired for that day's performance perched cheerily on a stand across the room. The very crown Phillips had to wear when he appeared in the very first moments of the play.

She'd grabbed the thing and bolted out the door. She ignored Nan's shout of "Joan, your hair" as she ran past her.

Let her curls fly and bounce around her head, there was no time for any artful arranging.

Her shoes skidded on the gravel as she rounded the corner and slipped down a side street, kicking stones up at the people moving at a more leisurely pace. They may have time to stroll and take in the wares of the harkers who lined the streets of Southwark, but Joan did not.

She threw a hand up to slip around a pale woman with a basket of carrots perched on top of her head. "Pardon—"

Someone shouted back at her; something uncomplimentary about her complexion most like, so Joan ignored it.

Or at least tried to.

She really should have, but—

She could feel the heat of rage swarming in her cheeks. Slowed her pace to turn and shout back.

The gilded tin crown in her satchel clanged against her thigh.

No time.

She huffed and sped back up. Her long, kinky hair flopped around her face in tight, unruly coils. Joan blew one out of her eyes with an exhausted puff of air just as the rounded white walls and brown beams of the Globe came into view.

The last bits of today's crowd shuffled their way through the open doors of the theatre. They jostled one another as Sylvia, the door manager, collected their coin and waved them along.

The show would be starting soon.

Joan cut around them and sprinted toward the brown door nestled at the back of the building.

Not twenty paces from her goal, she slammed into another body and hit the ground with a thud, crown cracking against her hip as she landed on her bag.

Fury burst in Joan's chest. She shoved herself to her feet just as the bells at St. Mary Overie rang two o'clock. Joan growled, sending the man nearest her shuffling out of her way with a wide-eyed stare.

Whoever she'd run into disappeared into the crowds. Not that she had time to waste chasing him down.

She slipped through the thick crush of bodies and caught sight of two men leaning close together just to the side of the brown door.

Joan recognized the one with a pale face, sculpted brown beard, and a stocky form draped in the finery of Prince Hamlet—Richard Burbage, the company's lead actor. The other, a tall, thin man with a beautiful brown face and long dark ropes of hair, she'd never seen before.

But she did notice the faint glow shining from his skin that marked him as Fae. Harmless then, unless he made Master Burbage miss his cue.

Trumpets blared from inside the theatre. The show was starting.

Joan yelped and skittered past Master Burbage and the Fae keeping him so enraptured.

Burbage, even as the title character in today's play, still had time before he needed to appear onstage. Joan on the other hand—

She had to get inside.

She tore the door open with both hands and flung herself into the cool darkness of the tiring-house—the only fully enclosed portion of the theatre. She tried to catch her breath as the door slammed closed behind her, erasing all thoughts of Burbage and his Fae. This was where the actors prepared and waited between entrances and exits. Where they stored props, costumes, and stage weapons. This was the central hub of theatrical business hidden from the eyes of the audience.

Joan squinted as her eyes tried to adjust to the shift from bright afternoon sun to dim candlelight. The ominous timbre of drums and trumpets echoed down from the gallery two floors up, the sound distorting as it bounced along the wooden walls and rebounded through the corridors.

Nick swung down out of the darkness of the central staircase, his hands outstretched and eyes wide with urgency.

Joan jumped and frowned at him, her heart racing. "What are you doing? You'll miss your cue!"

"Can't break tradition." He shook his hands at her. "Hurry and I won't be late." The candlelight danced along his shiny hair, pulled back into a low ponytail and hanging over one shoulder.

"Joan," he hissed, "hurry. For luck."

Joan shook herself and nodded. "For luck." She slapped her palms against his, right then left. "Good show."

"Thanks!" Nick grinned at her and bolted back up the stairs to the stage, wood thumping under his every step.

She watched him go; pulse throbbing in her ears, hands tingling where they'd touched. They'd done the same before every show over the three years she'd worked with the company.

When had so tiny a thing started feeling so important?

Joan clenched her fists and sighed. She hated how easily he could distract her. She slipped up the short staircase that led to the main playing floor. She could hear the actors speaking just beyond the curtain ahead of her, knew exactly where the men would be standing onstage.

"I think I hear them.—Stand ho! Who is there?"

That was Nick's cue to enter as Horatio, Prince Hamlet's best friend. Joan ducked a bit out of sight as Nick threw aside the center curtain to walk onstage. He'd join the royal guards to await the appearance of a certain ghost currently in need of a certain crown.

"Joan!" Her brother called out in a hushed whisper and sprinted toward her in his queenly gown. Roz—one of the company's three tirewomen—trailed behind him holding tight to the bodice strings she was struggling to lace. "Where have you been? They're already doing the opening scene. Master Phillips is about to go on as the king's ghost—"

James didn't enter as Queen Gertrude, Hamlet's mother, until the next scene, so he had plenty of time to berate Joan, even though he'd been the one to forget to bring along the crown that morning.

Roz jerked her arms back, pulling the laces tight and cutting James off midsentence. She winked at Joan but didn't loosen her grip.

"Is she here yet?" a booming voice called from off to their right, a supernatural glow shining in the darkness near the stage. He was immediately shushed by the other actors around him so the audience wouldn't hear his outburst.

Phillips.

Joan reached into her satchel. "Right here!" She pulled out the ornate tin crown, bent and dented into a near-flat disk from when she'd fallen on the soft metal. Her stomach dropped.

"Master Phillips can't wear that!" James tugged at the long dark curls of his wig, his own crown shifting to one side.

Joan scowled, dropping the bag and taking the abused crown in both hands. "I know. Just give me a moment." She turned her back to James and Roz.

"Tush, tush, 'twill not appear." Another line from Nick carried all the way back to where they stood in the darkness of the tiring-house.

It was nearly Phillips's cue.

No time to waste.

Straighten out now. She thought.

The shiny tin of the crown warmed in her hands. With a gentle tug, she pulled it back out into a perfect circle.

James snatched it from her hands. "Thank you!" He sprinted off, ripping the laces out of Roz's hands. "Enjoy the show!"

Roz shook her head and followed after him.

Had Joan been fast enough?

She huffed but waited in the dim light, twirling her fingers around each other.

The bell in the attic sounded, its deep clang resonating loud enough to send the candles along the halls dancing.

If the action stopped, she'd know she'd missed her chance. She listened for a long silence.

"Peace, break thee off! Look where it comes again," said one guard.

"In the same figure like the King that's dead," said the other.

Joan felt her shoulders sag in relief. She could see it in her mind's eye. Right now, Master Phillips was making his way across the balcony in robes of eerie white, a stark silver crown atop his head. It was a sight to behold when it was done right. And by the hush throughout the theatre, she knew it had been.

She moved farther down the hallway so she wouldn't be accidentally revealed to the audience and leaned against the wall, letting the ache in her tired legs wash over her. She still had two hours of standing to do unless she paid money for a seat in one of the stalls. Or asked Mistress Woods, the bookkeeper, to let her sit for free.

She looked over to the open doorway that marked the older woman's office. Mistress Woods was no doubt going over the accounts, ready to note every penny that moved in or out of their company.

Joan remembered the last time she'd asked for a free seat. The look the woman had given could've burned the whole theatre down.

Frowning, she shook each leg out and turned the other way. Standing was best.

Joan crept forward, listening closely to make sure she wouldn't be caught crossing to the stairs when the stage curtain opened. Then she slipped down the stairs and shoved the door open with her shoulder.

"Excellent timing, Sands!" Burbage burst past her into the tiring-house, his face flushed. "Enjoy the show, lass." He disappeared up the stairs.

Joan shook her head and stepped out into the sunlight.

Applause roared from inside the theatre as Burbage took the stage, the crowd showing love for their favorite player. Outside, the road bustled with the mundane noises and acts of everyday life: vendors hawking their wares, shoppers haggling to keep their coin, workers eating their lunches in the mild afternoon sun.

The Fae man from earlier had disappeared. Joan wasn't surprised. Nothing could make Burbage miss a cue, not even a pretty face.

She let the door close softly behind her and circled around to the front of the Globe.

Sylvia sat at one end of the bridge at the theatre entrance, blocking the opening with her wooden stool and her body. She grinned when she caught sight of Joan, the long, pale scar cutting across her dark brown face crinkling.

"You done ol' Phillips's crown?"

Joan nodded. "How's it look?"

"Excellent. Like a professional. Your father teach you that all sneaky-like?"

Joan grinned. "Something like that."

"Bad luck he can't have you take over from him." Sylvia leaned in close. "Heard his apprentice is shite," she said conspiratorially.

Joan hummed but kept her opinions to herself. Henry's shoddy work was already tarnishing the shop's reputation. She knew her work could outshine Henry's with little effort but she couldn't do more than craft things her father could present as his own. She wasn't the apprentice, couldn't be—because girls got no such chances.

But no more of that now; it soured her mood.

"Well," Joan said, trying to keep her expression pleasantly blank, "I'll head on in."

Sylvia nodded as Joan slipped past and wound her way through the crowded groundlings, the people standing in the open courtyard surrounding the stage. They may have paid the least, but Joan still swore they had the best place to watch the plays. Closest to the action.

She pushed away all thoughts of goldsmiths, talentless apprentices, and marriage. Let herself be caught up in the troubles of the grieving Prince Hamlet and the doomed royals of Denmark. And for two hours, she'd do her best to forget what lay further ahead than that.

CHAPTER FOUR
Chilton Bromwell and the Hags

hilton Bromwell stumbled his way along the street, his purse clanging noisily with unspent coin.

He tossed the bag into the air and caught it on one pale, long-fingered hand.

He'd done well at the Bear Garden. The pit dog he'd wagered on swept a mighty and bloody victory. Three dogs and a bear lay dead as proof of the beast's ferocity.

Now drunk on strong wine and stronger luck, Chilton headed deeper into Southwark to try his luck with a Winchester goose or two. Or three, cheaply. Whatever number of working ladies his new coin could afford.

This wouldn't be his first time purchasing such company and entertainment, but it had been a while since his purse extended far enough to enjoy such pleasures.

And he'd been so long without a tumble. Good, bad, or otherwise.

The steady stench that made itself his constant companion kept any woman who could be plied by words alone well at bay. Today he'd search out one who'd ignore his foul smell for enough money.

Chilton doubted he'd have to look too hard.

Laughter echoed out of the Globe Theatre as he strolled past. Perhaps, if he was lucky, he'd have enough coin left to buy a seat at tomorrow's show. He should like to hear a play.

"You in need of company, sir?" a voice whispered.

Chilton turned to face the man who had spoken. His long ropes of black hair were decorated with shiny metal and sparkling gems, and his brown face was pretty enough to have drawn Chilton's attention if his inclinations went that way.

But they did not.

"And if I am?" Chilton said. He puffed up his broad chest in case the other man wanted trouble.

The dark-skinned man just smiled and crooked a finger at Chilton. "I know just where to find what you seek. Follow."

The man turned and slipped down a dim alleyway. Chilton frowned for a moment then shook his head.

The business he sought needed the secrecy of alleys and dark places. At an inn he'd pay double, so why not see what this pretty gentleman was about. He had the coin to spend but if he could get what he wanted for less, he'd not ignore that turn of good fortune.

Besides, if things weren't to Chilton's liking, he could always head to the Tabard Inn.

Deeply pleased with the thought of keeping more of his money, Chilton happily followed the man into the darkness between buildings.

Up ahead, three women huddled closely together, their thin shawls drawn over their bare shoulders to shield them from the sharp autumn chill.

Chilton grinned to himself, happy to avoid the trouble of seeking out more ladies and hoping to negotiate all three and still have coin left for more wine.

"Hags," the man said, grinning wide and bright, "I bring a tasty morsel."

Chilton frowned. The trio were far from hideous hags.

But he let his chest puff up at being called a tasty morsel.

The women turned as one when they approached.

"Enjoy," the man said and patted Chilton on the back.

Chilton nodded, glad for his help, and headed off to test his fortunes. "Good even, ladies," he said.

The three giggled and blushed and nodded to him.

"Good even, sir." The prettiest one stepped forward, letting her shawl slip down around her elbows. Her bosom hung nearly over the top of her bodice. "What need you?"

Chilton straightened his spine and struck a pose that presented his leg. He had a fine calf, firm and strong and more than enough to catch any lady's eye. 'Twas his only strength, really. "I've a bag full of coin and a mind to spend it with thee." He turned to who he thought was the second prettiest one. "Or with thee." He turned to the final one. "Or with thee."

Pretty looked him up and down, her tongue snaking out to wet her lips. "Aye, sir. You look to be the manner of man to satisfy us all three."

Chilton stamped down on his excitement lest it show on his face. "That is truth. How much for the pleasure?"

"No more than what you carry."

"That I'll gladly pay. For all three." It was more than he hoped to spend, but he'd drop the whole purse for all three. "Paid after the pleasure, if thou wilt."

Pretty nodded and smiled as the other two stepped forward to take one of Chilton's hands in each of theirs. Their grips were tight, but he didn't care.

This moment was for pleasure.

They guided him over to a narrow alleyway darkened by the shadow of two tall buildings. Chilton stumbled along in their wake, anticipating lying on a bed of willing women.

The trio stopped in the middle of the alley, the street a distant glimmer of light at either end.

"Hast none of you a room?" Chilton scowled and hiccuped. "I've no mind to be so exposed in public."

Pretty smiled at him as she pressed him against the wall. "We've no need of one for what we're to do."

She leaned in and kissed him. Her breath reeked, like spoiled meat. Not that Chilton cared—he didn't need her to talk.

She tilted her head to deepen the kiss. As soon as their tongues touched, Chilton's knees nearly buckled. He felt more pleasure than he ever had in his life. Vaguely he felt the other two chucks laying kisses along either side of his neck.

Pretty pulled away, her lips redder than before. He'd had a complaint about her mouth before but zounds if he could remember it now.

He heard a wet crunch sound and glanced to his right. The goose on that side tugged at his arm again, hard. The limb came away from the rest of his body at the shoulder and she lapped at the slow gush of blood that followed in its wake.

That felt nice. Chilton grinned at her.

The other woman slid down his body to rub her face against his calf like a cat. He watched her take a large bite out of his calf and chew it in rapture.

Somewhere deep in his mind, Chilton knew he should be saying something, but the thread of the thought was too far away and he felt too much euphoria to reach for it with any intention.

He sighed in pleasure. It had been too long since he'd felt a woman's touch.

Pretty still stood in front of him, red dripping from her lips. She took his left hand and brought it to her mouth. She slid his index finger along her tongue and bit it off with a crunch of bone. Her eyes met his while she sucked the blood out of his now bereft knuckle.

"We're going to enjoy you," she said before biting off his middle finger.

Chilton sighed in joy. Yes, they would. And he felt he'd enjoy them too.

CHAPTER FIVE
Everybody Dies in *Hamlet*

ake up the bodies. Such a sight as this / Becomes the field but here shows much amiss. / Go, bid the soldiers shoot."

Cannon fire exploded above their heads, shot from the window of the attic. Silence swept through the crowd gathered in the house. The bloody work was done.

The Danish royal family littered the stage in gruesome decoration—splattered here and there with pig's blood—as the living bowed their heads in respect. Hamlet lay dead in Horatio's arms, killed by the strike of a poisoned sword. Queen Gertrude's body draped the throne with the murderous King Claudius sprawled on the floor in front of her.

Then the trumpeter blew a trill from the gallery and the dead rose from their places. All around Joan, the crowd shouted and stomped along to the beat. Light streamed in through the circular opening in the roof, the afternoon sun casting a glint off the players' royal jewelry. Including Phillips's perfectly round, masterfully engraved crown.

Joan felt her spine straighten at the sight of her work.

She caught her brother's eye, his deep-brown skin standing out among the paler faces around him, and he grinned as he lifted his skirts above decent but below scandalous. She laughed as James shimmied his shoulders alongside Armin, the company's brilliant clown and the only player shorter than Joan and James both. Armin tossed his floppy cap into the air, spun James in a quick circle, and caught the hat again on the top of his head. His shaggy auburn hair flopped into his eyes. He blew it out of the way with a huff and twitched the thick red mustache that stretched across his pale face like a caterpillar. The audience roared with laughter.

Burbage's bellowing voice counted them down from his spot at the center of the stage, the newly risen Hamlet holding a different kind of court.

"FIVE, SIX, SEVEN, EIGHT!"

The players' dance began.

The groundlings went wild.

Joan joined along with the shouting mass around her, their pounding feet kicking up dust from the packed dirt floor. Even the crisp November air blustering in through the theatre's open roof couldn't dampen the people's excitement.

A man bumped her shoulder, catching her elbow when she stumbled forward.

"Sorry, lass," he shouted, floppy hat askew on his head. His pale face was the barely brown of one who spent long days in the sun. "'Tis my favorite part."

Joan grinned back at him. "Mine too."

He laughed and jerked himself around as one of the trumpeters blared out a particularly bombastic note.

Joan slipped out of reach of the man's flailing—she assumed it was dancing—and caught sight of the galleries, where the wealthy loomed over the crowd.

The gallery seats offered comfort and protection from the elements for those willing or able to pay a few coins more. But something diluted the spirit in the theatre by the time it reached those costly seats. Left to choose between a cushion and the pure, passionate experience of a play, well—

A woman grabbed Joan's hand and spun her in a quick laughing circle. Tory, one of the ladies who "did her best work upon her back," winked at Joan before flouncing off to find another dance partner.

Joan wished her luck.

A flash of silky black hair caught Joan's eye as Nick strutted across the stage, a half beat behind the music as always. Her stomach fluttered as he grinned out at the gathered crowd. He'd ripped the tie from his thick, dark hair and let it flow loose around his face in a silky curtain.

Joan preferred his hair down.

Although, when it was up you could see all the fine details of him: his thick eyebrows, the sharp angles of his lovely face, his long fan of lashes, his beautiful brown eyes—

Which now looked straight into hers.

His grin spread wide as he waved to her.

Joan flinched, having been caught staring like that. She tried to smile back, but her traitor body only managed a small convulsion, her hand flapping uselessly in his general direction.

God's wounds. Could she not look the fool in front of him?

She shifted her gaze away from Nick and saw James openly guffawing at her. She glared at her brother, then fled. She needed to meet the players backstage anyway.

Joan snaked her way out of the theatre, dodging flailing arms and flying drinks. Cheers and boos echoed from the Bear Garden over past the vacant Rose Theatre. Joan snorted. Her tastes never ran along the lines of watching wild animals fight to the death, but to each their own.

She had it timed perfectly: Leave during the closing dance and make it out before the mad rush to escape the Globe, and before the lingering fanatics—enamored of the players they'd just watched—blocked her way to the tiring-house door. The audience let her pass as they danced. Then she paused.

Every few paces, she noticed it. The faint glow of not human mingled with the average person.

Their presence at the theatre wasn't new. The Fae could be found throughout the whole city. But unlike most of the people around her, Joan knew when she stood shoulder to shoulder with the beings of magic.

There just usually weren't so many Fae in one place.

She thought of the man from earlier, the one cozied up with Burbage. Then she thought of Baba Ben and his pact. Did the Fae's presence at the performance have to do with a broken pact? Despite their larger numbers, the Fae around the theatre seemed to mean no harm.

But if Baba Ben had put himself in such danger to complete the ritual, that meant the threat was great. She'd finish her work here at the theatre, collect James, and together they'd figure out what this broken pact had released.

She took a step toward the door and then ducked to the side as the bare bone of a turkey leg flew past her ear—the audience was known to toss food while in the full throes of post-performance ecstasy.

Almost clear of the chaos.

She curved around a circle of dancing men and waved to Sylvia, still on guard in her distant archway. The ticket-taker nodded back.

As Joan approached the front doors, she noticed two dark forms moving in the shadows. A high-pitched giggle sounded, followed by a deep, masculine groan.

Joan snorted. "Not even waiting until the end today, Agnes?"

Agnes leaned her head into the light, the supernatural glow beneath her pale skin marking her as Fae. "'Tis a feast, dear girl, a feast for freedom." A grin spread wide across her face and her blue eyes glinted. "Best stay in come dark. All the nastiest nasties'll be about."

Danger.

The man wrapped in her arms nuzzled at her neck and gripped her back fiercely. Agnes's eyes rolled down to him hungrily. She raked her nails across his back, drawing blood across his nearly white skin. The man barely seemed to notice.

Danger!

Everything in Joan's body screamed the word, blaring it like an alarum bell.

Agnes often made meals of men nearby, feeding on their energy and letting them wander off exhausted but sated. But never had Joan see her look so . . . vicious.

Agnes reached out a hand. "Fly away, little bird, unless you want to come too."

A whisper, like a buzzing in her skull, drifted through her head. Her chest felt light. She took a deep breath, wondering at the sensation.

This wasn't fear, and it felt too calm to be panic. This was something new, a cold rush that straightened her spine and cleared her vision.

Whoever Agnes had in her clutches today wouldn't fare as well as the others. Joan was sure of that.

She shook her head. "Sir, maybe you shou—"

Spit flew from the man's mouth, splattering across the tips of Joan's shoes.

"Ain't ask for no Negress," he sneered. "My needs ain't that dire."

Joan's jaw clenched.

Agnes's face contorted into something grotesque as she glanced back over her shoulder.

"You'll leave me to it," Agnes said, "aye, Joan?"

Joan felt a twinge of guilt at the thought of leaving the man to his unknown fate. Until she looked at the globs of spittle still spread across her shoes.

No need to offer help where it—where she—wasn't wanted.

Joan turned and strode off.

—+—

Joan rounded the circular white walls of the building and slipped through the rear door just as a raucous cheer exploded behind her.

Timed. Perfectly.

The hungry look on Agnes's face flashed before her eyes.

She'd just left a man to die, she was sure of it.

Negress.

Joan shook her head. What was done was done. No way but forward.

She launched herself up the stairs and into the candlelit dimness of the tiring-house. She spotted Master Shakespeare's tall, slim form right as he noticed her. His angular features softened as a smile spread across his pale, tanned face and made his spiraling mustache twitch. He handed Roz his cap then headed straight for her, sword outstretched.

Joan met him halfway and took the blade from his hand.

"Were the fights to your liking, Mistress Sands?" He grinned at her and ran long fingers along the point of the perfectly sculpted black beard that matched his equally black mustache.

Joan frowned up at him—the playwright towered over her by a full head. "Burbage is a beat too fast on every move and doesn't commit to defense." She ran her fingers over the blade he'd given her, found the spot she was looking for. "I noticed when he chipped your blade here." She pointed to a spot on the sword with a tiny split in the steel. "You're lucky. If you'd done the fight as I taught it, you'd be breathing through a hole in your neck."

"SANDS!" Burbage's voice echoed through the backstage as he burst through the center curtain like a king. His broad shoulders sent other players and tirewomen scuttling sideways to avoid him. "What'd you think of today's battle?" He tossed his sword at her, blade barely clearing Phillips's white-haired head.

Phillips didn't notice his near accident as he loped along down the hallway.

Joan snatched it out of the air and kept the point down like a person with good sense. "You're too fast and you fight like a common brawler, not a Danish prince." She held up both swords. "And you keep chipping my blades."

Burbage flushed. "Now see here, Sands, I do every move just as you taught it me."

"You don't and you know it."

"Well." Master Shakespeare cleared his throat from beside her. "I think you do a fine jo—"

"A lie like that will have you headless next time, Master Shakespeare," she said. "You are the finest actor in England, Master Burbage, you needn't fight so hard. We'll have a pass when the playhouse clears. Both of you."

Shakespeare groaned, and Joan heard some other players snickering as she walked past. Her fastidiousness when it came to fights was well-known, as was her ruthlessness when it came to rehearsal.

She'd be lying if she said their fear didn't give her the slightest rush of pleasure.

Burbage's shoulders fell. "Have a heart, lass. You heard the line Armin snuck into the gravedigger's scene. He wants us to all meet over at Yaughan's alehouse for drinks." Burbage shifted his posture, perfectly imitating the aged crouch Amin used when he played the gravedigger in Hamlet. "*Get thee to Yaughan's and—*"

"*—fetch me a stoop of liquor,*" Joan finished and rolled her eyes. "Yes, I heard it but you don't pay me for heart, you pay me for honesty. I'll see you both onstage as soon as the crowd clears."

Burbage yelled, and Shakespeare cursed as she bounded up the stairs to the apprentice dressing area and ran directly into Nick's arms. They tightened around her waist, pulling her to his chest as she pitched backward.

"Whoa," he said and set her on her feet. "You all right, Joan?"

"Uh—" She shook her head, then nodded. She couldn't think beyond the easy way he'd lifted her off the ground. And the flex of his muscles beneath the hand she'd wrapped around his arm. And the brush of his soft hair against her face. And his smell of lilac and leather.

Why did he have to smell so lovely? It wasn't fair.

"Jooooooooan," James whined from his dressing area down the second-floor hall. "What's taking you so long?"

Nick pulled away, his lips tilted in a slight smile. "Sounds like you're being summoned. I should probably go see that Master Burbage's costumes are put away."

Joan smiled back, and Nick eased around her and down the rest of the stairs. She watched him go, clutching the swords to her chest to steady herself. Her face felt like it was on fire.

More and more, being near Nick felt like some puzzle piece slotting into place. It was completely overwhelming. Joan had no idea what to do with these urges, because being the wife of a player had no place in her plans for her future.

She froze.

The wife of a player? Where had that thought sprang from?

"Joooooooan," James wailed again.

She huffed out a breath and slipped around the corner. Her brother probably wanted her to help him untie his bodice or something. Roz liked tying complicated knots that James couldn't undo on his own.

The distraction would be welcome.

Joan pushed aside the curtain that gave the area some privacy. "What's the emergen— Oh."

A beautiful girl sat propped on the crate behind James's dressing curtain, her patchwork bodice accentuating her slim waist and generous bosom.

Joan swallowed and forced her gaze upward.

Bright brown eyes peered out from a pretty, pale brown face surrounded by a waterfall of curly black hair, the coils barely looser than Joan's own.

"Hello there." She smiled, a wide grin that spread her full rouged lips between sharp cheekbones. She swept her long hair over one shoulder and leaned back on her hands, crossing her legs at the ankle. "You didn't lie. Your sister is much prettier than you are, James."

Joan's heart thumped hard as their eyes met again. The girl licked her red lips and every thought flew out of Joan's mind.

This was not the distraction she'd been hoping for . . .

James appeared at Joan's side, and she tried not to flinch. Why was she even in his dressing room in the first place?

He still wore his complete costume from the show, wig and all. "Rose," he said, "this is Joan. Joan, this is my friend Rose."

Joan cut her eyes to James, wondering how he had a friend she'd neither heard of nor met.

"All right, Joan," Rose said. She smiled again, eyes crinkling at the corners.

Joan nodded and gripped the swords sliding through her suddenly slippery hands. "All right, Rose—" The words tumbled out of Joan's lips and splattered on the floor lamely. The swords clanged together in shame. She placed the damaged blades against the wall and discreetly dried her sweaty palms on her skirt.

"Right." James rolled his eyes at her. "So, Rose is friends with some of the working ladies here in Southwark, a few of whom have gone missing," James said.

That threw Joan back into herself. "Missing?" She stared at James.

James stared right back. "I want to help her out, so I told her we could meet tomorrow at six at the bridge and see what we can discover."

"I heard you fight well," Rose said, "and I wasn't sure who else would be willing to help us." She glanced at Joan, bit her lip, and sighed. "Look, you don't have to do this. None of it affects you, I know."

Joan frowned. She took in the different colors and fabrics sewn all over Rose's bodice, noticed a few more along her skirt.

Rose was poor, and there weren't many options for a poor Black girl in any sort of danger. "No, it's fine," Joan said as she smiled at Rose. "We'll absolutely help you."

Something in Rose's posture relaxed before she seemed to gather herself up again. She slipped off the crate and dusted off her skirt. "Thank you. Shall I see you tomorrow, then?" Standing, she towered over both of the twins. "I very much look forward to seeing your lovely face again." She reached out to clasp Joan's hand, her smile beaming directly in Joan's face.

A thrill shot straight up Joan's arm at her touch and raced down her spine to parts—unspoken.

Who was this girl and why was she so . . . everything? Pretty girls had left Joan tongue-tied before, but never like this.

Rose's gaze slipped away from Joan's eyes and down. Her grip tightened as she leaned close to Joan's ear. "Only fair I get a look too, yeah?"

Joan's mouth went dry. Maybe she could sneak a kiss; Rose seemed likely to be willing . . .

"Well met," James shouted suddenly in the silence, snagging the spare gray wool cloak from the hook in the corner. "I'm loaning you this, Rose. It'll keep out the chill." He grabbed Rose by her shoulders and guided her out through the curtain. "Until tomorrow, then."

Joan flexed the hand the other girl had shaken, her heart beating double time in her chest. She could still feel Rose's eyes scorching along her skin. But hadn't she felt the same when Nick had gripped her tightly earlier? Hadn't she been filled with this same heat threatening to burst through her skin?

She needed to sit down.

James slipped back around the curtain alone. He pulled the wig off his head and placed it delicately on a tall stand in the corner.

Joan wandered over and hopped onto the empty crate. "Rose—" She cleared her throat. "How do you know her?"

"She's been around the playhouse often."

Joan gave him a look.

He stuck his tongue out at her. "I can have friends that you don't know, sister." He reached for the strings tying his gown. "You and I are only together *nearly* every moment. That leaves me time for some private affairs. And we are the best ones to help her," He frowned. "Well, you are really. I just lend a hand where I can and look dashing." He struck a pose.

Joan shoved him backward with one foot. "And just what am I supposed to do?"

"Fight any brigands and villains of course." His hands scrambled at the laces at the back of his gown. "How the hell did Roz tie this?"

Joan smacked his hands out of the way and tugged the complicated knot loose. She slipped the dangling ends into James's searching fingers. "And you trust her?"

"Not completely, but I know not many others would care enough to help these women." James nodded to her and shimmied out of his costume, then passed her the two swords she'd left against the wall. "And I do trust you to keep us safe."

Joan smiled at her brother. His faith in her abilities warmed her heart, but there was still an uncomfortable knot in her chest, that insistent feeling of not-rightness that refused to leave her alone. She wondered if this too had something to do with Baba Ben's pact.

"Agnes was different today," she said.

"What do you mean, different?"

Joan shook her head, trying to put into words what she felt looking at Agnes with that man. The raw, brutal glee that had sent chills up her spine.

There was no way he would live through the night.

"There was a hunger on her face unlike any I've ever seen. She's Fae, and I think that pact breaking may have released something in her."

"And there were more Fae in the audience today as well," James said. "You're right, something has changed. Do you think Rose's problem may be part of this?"

"It's possible," she said, "but it sounds like the disappearances happened prior to today. This may be a different issue."

He nodded to her before turning to wipe his heavy makeup off in the small mirror on the crate in front of him. "We'll find out for sure tomorrow, so no need to worry that particular knot today. The rest, we'll discuss with Mother and Father when we get home this evening."

Joan watched him for a moment before she twitched her fingers, clanging the swords in her lap together.

Right—she needed to get to work.

She placed one of the weapons on the floor by her feet and laid the other across her lap. She ran her fingers over the blade, felt the steel warm at her touch. The split cried out for her to find it. She'd heard its song in her head since the final fight. It wasn't crying in pain—a sword couldn't feel that—but it was angry.

Metal was simple. It only felt joy or rage. Never anything troublesome like fear or anxiety or nerves. Not the nauseating gush of shame and embarrassment. Or that allover hot feeling of meeting someone too beautiful.

Shit.

She jerked her hand away and stuck her bleeding finger in her mouth. Found the break.

The sword's song brightened as its name slipped into her head, louder and more clearly than she'd ever heard.

Bia—

It thrummed. Joan felt the steady vibrations down deep, in her bones. She coaxed the metal along the broken blade and watched it repair itself before she'd even finished the thought, its edges sharpening to a fine point. Strange.

Frowning, Joan willed the blade to dull. She watched it blunt then go sharp again. It gave an impatient sigh.

That had never happened before. This couldn't be an ordinary sword.

"So, you're called Bia? If you keep this up," she hissed, "I'll turn you into horseshoes."

Bia hissed back but finally allowed itself to be blunted.

"Are you talking to the sword?" James slipped back through the curtain.

Joan shrugged. "There's something about this one. It's not normal. It demands. I've never felt that from a sword before."

"That can't be good for a play blade. Why'd you put it with the others?"

"I didn't." Joan frowned.

Looking at the sword, nothing about it marked it as any different from the rest of their mismatched collection of blades. The swept hilt was engraved with tiny dogs, but a glance showed nothing else of note.

Of course, Joan knew better.

She felt Bia settle in her hands, whole and dulled for safety. Joan pressed the blade to her lips and whispered, "Behave." She frowned, not sure what made her do that.

She placed the sword—Bia—near her feet and took the one James held out to her. It sang a name into her ear quietly just as every other sword did. *Alke*, it whispered.

But Joan could still feel Bia's vibrations from the floor.

She shook her head and found the break in Alke. "So, how friendly are you and Rose?" She set the metal flowing.

"Not so friendly as to block my dear sister's way into her affections." He grinned at her. "She's not my type."

Joan felt her whole face heat up but kept her attention on the sword. Must he always see through her like this?

James bumped his foot against hers. "I know I shouldn't get us tangled up in such things." He tapped out a steady beat. "But who else could someone like her go to for help?"

Joan nodded and bumped her foot back against his. "Don't worry. You did the right thing."

Whether he meant someone of Rose's profession or someone of her complexion, Joan knew it would be impossible for the other girl to get anyone to help her look for some missing prostitutes. Joan and James respected the women who worked in such a way as Rose would've known.

"And I can't help but think," James said, his foot stilling, "that Rose's problems may prove my morning's optimism wrong."

Joan frowned. "You think this is the work of the Fae?"

"As loath as I am to say that you're right—" James huffed out a breath.

"House's clear!" someone called from downstairs.

James jumped off the crate with a grin. "Incredible timing because you have to practice and now I need not say those dreaded words." He held the curtain aside for her. "Have fun with Burbage and Shakespeare."

Joan grabbed both swords and stood, ramming him with her shoulder as she passed. "Shouldn't you be helping Master Phillips with his costumes, apprentice?" She glanced back at him. "We'll talk later."

CHAPTER SIX
CRAP Out the Window

oan paused in front of the closed door to Master Shakespeare's private room and knocked. It swung open under her hand, revealing a disheveled and distracted Shakespeare on the other side.

"The house is clear." Joan raised an eyebrow at him. "Are you ready?"

He grinned at her, indolent as a cat with a mouse. "I'll be there anon."

"Will," a smooth voice cooed from within, "is it you or Burbage who plays the fairy king in *Midsummer*?"

"Ah, that would be me, fair youth." He winked at Joan. She caught sight of a glowing brown face and ropes of dark decorated hair behind him before Shakespeare closed the door on her.

The same beautiful man—Fae—from earlier, the one Burbage had been cozied up with outside the tiring-house. She frowned.

The two elder players' friendly rivalry never came to blows, but Joan thought they took it too far all the same. She was sure their long line of shared conquests would agree with her, especially if they realized their business was far from private.

Actors—

She had no idea how either of their wives dealt with them.

Joan shook her head and headed back down the hall to the prop storage area. She leaned Bia and Alke against the wall and wrestled her mass of hair into two long braids, twisting them into a knot at the back of her head. She held them with one hand as she tugged the green ribbon from around her head and used it to secure her hair.

She hoped it wasn't too crooked. It was always easier to use a mirror, but she'd forgotten to ask James to help her fix her hair before coming down.

No matter now; it was pulled back out of her face and that was good enough for this moment.

She snagged another performance blade from the storage barrel that held them between shows, did a quick count to make sure the other thirteen were still there.

She wasn't putting Bia in the hands of either Shakespeare or Burbage again if she could help it. They didn't have enough self-control.

She headed toward Master Burbage's room but caught sight of him as she passed the large double doors that opened onto the stage.

He stood center stage, looking like a king as he peered out into the empty theatre, thick arms akimbo as he surveyed the silent space. He cut an imposing figure even without his elaborate costumes and in just his shirt and trousers. It made it difficult to order him around sometimes.

But this was her job, and she'd be damned if she let one of them injure themselves because she found Burbage intimidating.

She took a steadying breath.

"Master Burbage," she called, "thank you for indulging me."

He whipped around. "Sands. I didn't mean to mess up what you taught me, lass. I swear it."

"I know, Master Burbage." Joan tossed Alke to him. Bia vibrated in her hand. "I think I know what's wrong. Once Master Shakespeare gets here, we'll run it twice through and be off to Yaughan's."

"Excellent," Shakespeare said as he strolled out onstage. He smoothed his black hair back down into a low ponytail, his shirt tucked haphazardly into his trousers.

Burbage squinted at the other man before turning to Joan. "With the lines, lass?"

Joan's grin broke across her face but her heart thumped hard in her chest. "Aye, with the lines. It would help both of you to show one expertise this day."

How could she say no to a private performance by Shakespeare and Burbage?

Burbage's broad laugh echoed through the empty playhouse, and Shakespeare grinned at her as they moved to their starting positions.

"Go half speed this first time." Joan placed her sword at her feet and girded up her skirt, tying the loose fabric at either side of her waist on the chance that she'd need to demonstrate some moves. You could never be sure with these two.

But Joan kept that thought to herself.

She snatched up Bia again and stepped toward the back of the stage, digging the sword's point into the wood floor. She laid her hands across the hilt. "To give you a chance to fix yourselves before I do it for you."

Both men snorted and squared off with each other. They held gazes for a long moment doing nothing, the air between them seeming to suddenly spark with a dangerous energy.

Joan frowned. "You can begin. Don't you want to get to the alehouse?"

"*Come on, sir,*" Burbage said.

"*Come, my lord,*" Shakespeare replied.

He swung for Burbage's neck—an opening move that Joan did not remember teaching them. Burbage leaned back, the blow whistling through the air where his neck had been before striking out with his own sword.

Shakespeare spun out of the way a second too late. Joan saw the split in his sleeve slowly turning red with blood.

"*One,*" Burbage said.

What was happening?

"Hold," she shouted. "None of this is what I taught you."

Burbage stabbed his sword at Shakespeare. Joan watched it catch the taller man along the stomach, ripping his shirt but not splitting the skin.

"*Judgment,*" Burbage shouted, speaking Hamlet's lines even as the two men fought in earnest.

"Hold!" she yelled. "Both of you, hold!"

Shakespeare ripped his blade along Burbage's arm. More blood drawn.

That was enough.

Joan lifted Bia and ran toward the two men. She slipped between them, knocking their swords away with two heavy blows.

"What's the matter with you? *Hold* means stop, or have you forgotten!"

Burbage stumbled a bit then stared straight at Joan. She tensed. His eyes shone like they had during the show, held a deadly glint he'd never aimed at her before today.

She glanced over at Shakespeare and saw a matching sharpness in his gaze.

So it hadn't been Bia pushing them after all.

Joan shifted her stance as they each took a step toward her. "Let's say that's enough for today."

Burbage charged forward, rushing into her space before she was ready. Joan dropped to one knee as his blade sliced the air over her head. She pivoted, swinging her blade up to parry his blow. The strength of it rattled her bones and sent her tumbling backward.

Shakespeare appeared above her as she hit the stage, his sword raised over his head. She threw herself to the side as the blow rang against the stage behind her.

"God's crown!" She scrambled to her feet, holding her sword out in front of herself and trying to keep both men in sight. "I said stop!"

"Judgment," Burbage said again.

"A hit," Shakespeare said, *"a very palpable hit."*

They rushed her, suddenly working in sync. She parried Shakespeare's cut, knocking his blade against Burbage's. She kept moving, rolling along Shakespeare's back and dancing out of range.

Burbage jerked forward, swiping at her wildly. His steps landed clumsily as he tried to keep up with her faster footwork.

Joan dodged a heavy blow; felt her heels slip off the edge of the stage and threw herself forward to keep from falling down into the dirt. She dove over a wild swing from Shakespeare and tucked her head, rolling across the stage. She let the movement push her to her feet smoothly and caught a glimpse of a slim man standing half obscured by one of the painted columns, his dark brown skin glowing.

"You," she growled, glaring at the Fae man. "How are you doing this?"

The Fae grinned at her and ran his fingertips over his lips. "A gift of my kiss."

Joan felt that sudden lightness in her chest again.

Not now.

She breathed deeply.

And just a moment too long. She twisted away from Shakespeare as Burbage's sword glanced along the back of her dress. It caught the ribbon securing her hair, sending her braids flopping down her back. She stumbled forward and watched the green pieces flutter to the stage.

Enough. She couldn't play defense forever, not with that Fae driving both of these men to kill her.

Joan spotted her opening as Burbage lunged toward her and tried to ignore the feeling growing in her chest.

She braced her feet as her sword slammed into Burbage's, put all her strength into blocking his blow. She surged forward, sliding her blade along his. She spun her sword around his and used Bia to lock Alke under her arm. She rammed her palm into the flat of the blade just above the guard. Burbage lost his grip and tumbled backward as she slammed her shoulder into his sternum.

Joan tilted her sword back and let Alke slide down into her left hand. She spun, crossing her swords to catch Shakespeare's in the air. She grunted and forced his blade up higher, leaving his belly open for an attack. She shoved her foot against his gut. His hand went limp as the air rushed out of his lungs. Joan tossed his sword to the floor as soon as he let go.

"That's enough," she said between gasps. "I'll not be forced to harm you."

That Fae stood ready to watch Burbage and Shakespeare murder each other. To murder her. That couldn't stand.

Joan felt as if her chest had suddenly filled with chilled air. She could hardly focus over the feeling of it. Her head went fuzzy, her vision darkening and narrowing around the edges.

She watched her body move as if from some far-off place. She tossed Alke high into the air. An iron spike formed in her free hand; she barely felt the cool flow of metal rush to her palm.

Things seemed to happen slowly and quickly at once, totally out of her control. She flung the iron spike forward then caught the falling sword before it hit the ground.

The Fae in the shadows threw himself to the side and the spike caught him across the cheek, opening a bloody gouge across his face. He screamed.

Joan jerked back as her head suddenly cleared and the cold lightness disappeared from her chest.

Where had that—

Had he been any slower, it would've struck between his eyes.

An instant kill.

Her stomach dropped to her feet.

James ran out from backstage, eyes widening as he spotted the Fae.

"Why is there screaming? I thought this was a mere practice?" Master Phillips strolled into the space and froze.

Joan turned back to where the Fae still stood.

He touched a hand to his bloody cheek then looked at his fingertips in wonder.

"We had a problem," Joan said, willing her voice not to shake because what had just happened? "But I'm handling it."

"Iron," the Fae mumbled. He rubbed his fingers across his wound again and again, sending blood oozing down his face. "The girl—controls iron—"

His eyes lifted to Joan's.

A chill ran through her bones and settled at the base of her neck. Her spine stiffened as a rushing sound clogged her ears.

And suddenly she was watching her body from some dark nothing place, far away. She screamed but had no voice. Tried to claw her way back out of the darkness.

What was happening?

"Enjoy your freedom now, faerie"—the words came from her mouth but in a deep voice, a man's voice—"before I return things to their proper order."

Joan gasped and stumbled as she fell back into herself. The roaring in her ears cleared.

She hadn't spoken, hadn't been the one to level the threat.

That had been Ogun. The Orisha had come through, possessing her to deliver his threat.

She glanced up at the Fae.

He watched her, his face ashen. "So you command his power—" He rubbed his bloody cheek again and stepped toward Joan.

She shifted Bia and Alke in her grip, sent iron flowing from her hand and out over Bia's steel blade.

The Fae froze at the glint of it.

Steel would hurt for a moment, but iron was deadly to the Fae.

They both knew that.

He bared his teeth at her. "You've spoiled my fun today, but you'd best hope we don't meet again, girl." Then he dropped down through the wood of the stage, almost as if he'd been made of water.

Joan rushed to where he disappeared and found nothing but the iron spike Ogun had used her to throw. She picked it up with shaking fingers.

Ogun had taken over control of her body. She'd seen this sort of thing happen to her mother, her father, other elders in their religion, but never, never had it happened to Joan herself.

She shivered and turned, her eyes searching for James. Her brother watched the spot where the Fae had disappeared before meeting her gaze. She glanced past him to Phillips, whose face was carefully blank.

Damnation.

"Why in God's name am I on the floor?" Burbage growled.

"Zounds," Shakespeare said, "am I bleeding?"

"You got a bit too energetic in your practice and some true wounds were given in jest." Joan jogged over to where they both were slowly stumbling to their feet. "But we're done, gentlemen. What say we go for that drink?"

She hoped they'd read the shaking in her voice as exhaustion. That they wouldn't see through her lies. That Phillips would play along.

That Ogun wouldn't feel the need to steal her control again.

Burbage laughed. "Indeed, lass? Told you I knew what I was about." He grinned at Shakespeare. "What's a bit of blood between we two greats, Will? To Yaughan's!"

Burbage threw his arm around Shakespeare's shoulders and the two wandered off together.

James held back for a moment before approaching Phillips, who turned his gaze to Joan, lips pressed together in a frown.

Joan stared back. She gripped Bia and Alke but refused to pull back the iron until Phillips turned away. Though he'd seen much of what had happened, there was no need to tell him more.

"Come along," Phillips said. "Armin'll be deep in his cups by now."

He turned and strode off, his glowing form disappearing back into the tiring-house. James glanced at Joan then jogged off after the old man.

Joan let out a breath she hadn't realized she was holding. She untied her skirt and shook it out as she moved toward the doorway to backstage.

She froze.

Something was there. She felt it like eyes on her back.

Fingers brushed against her neck and squeezed the tense muscles.

Joan spun, Bia screaming through the air behind her.

Nothing.

She stood alone in the empty playhouse.

CHAPTER SEVEN
Of Truth and Song

oan sat in a dim corner at the back of the alehouse, smushed in by James, whose foot tapped insistently against hers. The strange sword, Bia, hung around her wrist, thrumming in steady counterpoint to her brother's staccato rhythm.

The encounter at the theatre had shaken Joan, and she'd refused to leave the blade behind. But as a woman, she couldn't walk the streets with a sword on her belt. She'd shrunken and looped Bia to look like a thin silver bracelet.

No one would know she was armed, and the surprise of it would only help her should she need to draw the sword.

She'd not be caught unawares again.

Several people clustered by the front door yelled something incomprehensible and burst into raucous laughter. Joan glanced at them then away, taking in the scraps of paper plastered on the wall as decoration. Just over her shoulder, she glimpsed a few lines of a particularly filthy sonnet that slipped into the lewdest description Joan had ever heard of a particular act. One that sounded nigh on impossible for two people to work themselves into, but might prove enjoyable—

Nick's face and then Rose's flashed through her mind in quick succession.

She shook her head, hoping to dislodge those thoughts as her face blazed hot.

Phillips cleared his throat.

The old man took up the other side of the table and sipped his ale silently, like he hadn't dragged Joan and James over to this secluded nook as soon as their group had joined the rest of the players in the alehouse.

Joan watched him take slow drags of his drink and felt James squirm beside her.

As usual, Phillips's attempted intimidation only worked on her brother.

Joan could wait the old man out. Phillips was Fae, so he had to know of Baba Ben's pact. He may have questions for her and her brother, but she had her own to fire right back at him.

She focused her attention on her empty hand and breathed, deep and slow. She felt the tiniest shiver through her body as iron flowed like water up from her palm and formed a tiny disk. She pressed the edge of the disk against the table and spun it.

Over in the alehouse's main room, Armin, Shakespeare, and Burbage burst into song with Nick and Samuel banging out a clumsy beat on their table.

Joan watched them for a moment. Burbage had one foot up on the table, rattling it with each stomp. Armin stood in front of him, using the table's height to make sure everyone saw him as he invented new verses for the old jig and swung his long red hair back and forth.

Nick tried his best to keep time, his cheeks flushed each time Burbage urged him and Samuel faster or slower. His thick, black hair hung neatly over one shoulder, tied with a length of dark ribbon. Joan felt her lips curling up at his fumbling. She couldn't help but be charmed by even his lack of skill.

Armin waved a hand at Rob who slipped out of the crowd and grabbed two cups. He clanged them together with more grace. And rhythm.

Yaughan—the alehouse's boisterous, bald, and bearded owner—burst up from the basement, his usual wide grin splitting his pale face that was flushed pink with exertion. He pressed a stoup of ale into the hands of a customer then ripped off his apron, revealing his round belly and a shirt that must've been white at some point.

The other patrons cleared the way for him, shouting and cheering as he shuffled his feet and wiggled his shoulders in an intricate jig alongside his favorite customers.

Nick glanced up and caught Joan's eye. A crooked smile spread across his face and he jerked his head over toward the celebration.

Joan's coin clattered to the table as her knees bumped the underside. Shaking herself, she turned away from Nick and the rest.

Questioning Phillips was more important than joining their fun. She, Shakespeare, and Burbage had all nearly made pin cushions of one another at the pleasure of some strange Fae. Getting answers took precedence over all else.

She renewed her focus on her iron disk. If she pressed it gently, she could likely get it up to thirteen full rotations.

She heard Nick fall completely out of beat with the others at five, and Joan's coin hit the table at five and a half.

Damn.

Beside her, James was ready to vibrate out of his seat.

Phillips reached across the table to grab the fallen disk.

"No!" Joan shouted, James's voice echoing hers. She ripped the coin from the table and held it close to her chest.

Phillips frowned. "Tight-fisted with our money, I see."

James pressed against her side.

"That's not—" Joan clamped her mouth shut.

Should she reveal what they knew about Master Phillips and how they knew before he played his hand first?

There was danger in letting loose that secret. Was the risk of being the first to speak worth it? She glanced over at James.

Her brother chewed his lip but said nothing.

No help there.

Joan thought of the Fae from earlier who'd nearly made Masters Burbage and Shakespeare fight to the death. Phillips must know of him. Enough of the silence—she'd trade her secret for his and hopefully they could speak in earnest.

Joan breathed deep and said, "It's iron, sir." She watched his face carefully. "It'll do you harm if you touch it." She placed her hands in her lap and waited.

There, it was out in the open now. How would the old man respond?

Phillips narrowed his eyes but before he could answer Armin shimmied his way onto the bench beside him, Burbage sauntering over to stand beside James.

Armin grinned. "The mood here is too somber for our night of revels."

"I need to steal the young Sandses," Burbage said. He leaned across the table, pressing a hand to his face as if to whisper then didn't lower his voice at all. "Tooley and Crosse keep the beat poorly and they're soon to start hurling fruit should we leave them to it."

Phillips snorted. "Aye, aye. Those two have no sense of music. I'll make loan of my apprentice anon."

Burbage winked at them and strode away, barking at Nick to keep better time. Armin danced along behind him.

And still Phillips sat silent.

Joan walked the coin across her fingers where no one could see. Index. Middle. Ring. Pinkie. Ring. Middle. Index. Middle.

She'd tempted him with the reveal. He'd speak up soon enough.

Phillips sat back and crossed his arms. His bushy white beard twitched once.

Yes, he wouldn't last much longer.

But could they even trust anything the man said? How deeply did his loyalty to his fellow Fae run? Would his prejudices toward anyone darker than him allow him to lie with ease? She kept the coin moving, repeating the pattern to calm her racing mind.

Ring. Pinkie. Ring. Middle. Index. Middle. Ring.

James slammed his palms on the table. "We've known that you're Fae from the start, Master Phillips. But we've never told a soul. I swear it."

Clearly James didn't have her stores of patience. Joan could still wait, though. Let her brother talk.

Pinkie. Ring. Middle. Index. Middle. Ring. Pinkie.

"Your secret is safe with us," James said, "so please, sir, please keep me on as your apprentice."

Phillips turned to Joan.

Now they could talk. She palmed her disk.

"What do you have to say, Sands?"

James threw himself across the table with a wail. "I told you, sir—"

"Not you, boy. I'm talking to your sister."

James clamped his mouth shut and dropped back down onto the bench. Joan slipped her hand into his but kept her gaze level with Phillips. James's foot picked up its tapping again.

"We"—she paused, glanced around, leaned in closer—"can both see you true."

"You glow," James said sullenly. "Like a candle. All of the Fae do, I mean."

Phillips sat back and hummed. "Really, now?"

Joan squeezed her brother's hand but kept silent.

"And can I trust you both to keep this secret"—Phillips ran his fingers through his beard—"or shall I find a new apprentice?"

"Of course we'll tell not one soul!" James squeaked out. "Right, Joan?" He jerked hard on her hand, pulling her off-balance in his panic.

Joan scowled at him then looked back to Phillips. "Of course, we'll tell no one."

"Very well." Phillips nodded to them. "That confession and promise are all I sought of you two. Go save them before Tooley and Crosse lose their way any further."

James went nearly boneless beside her before leaping from the bench.

"A word more, Master Phillips," Joan said, delicately folding her hands on the table. "Please."

Phillips raised a bushy white eyebrow before settling back against the bench. He glanced at James. "We'll join you presently, my boy."

Relief smoothed out James's panicked face before he bolted, leaving Joan with Master Phillips.

He didn't even bother looking back.

Of course he didn't.

Phillips held his tongue until Armin belted out the first notes of his next song.

"Do you have any idea the danger you put yourself in today, girl?" he hissed.

"You mean besides being nearly killed by Burbage and Shakespeare while they were under some Fae's spell?" Joan scowled. "We were supposed to practice the fight, but they were really trying to cut each other down and they both turned on me when I stepped in. That Fae man at the theatre just now was controlling them somehow."

"That Fae man was—" Phillips suddenly clamped his mouth shut.

So he was feeling reticent. Joan would get him talking again.

"What does it mean now that the pact between mortals and the Fae has broken?"

"What?" Phillips jerked back, his eyes wide. "What do you know of the Pact?"

"Only that it may be no more."

Phillips blinked rapidly as his eyes shifted along the tabletop. "I had felt the change, but I didn't believe. But if *he* is here—"

His face paled to a ghostly white made more stark by his Fae glow.

Something had truly frightened him.

Joan shivered, suddenly colder in the dim corner.

"Master Phillips, tell me what's happening."

"I—" He huffed out a breath. "Be honest with me, lass. What can you do?"

Joan twisted her fingers around one another in her lap. The iron disk lay warm against her palm.

She knew Phillips's secret, so telling him the truth of herself was only fair. But could she trust him? She clenched her fist around her disk.

"What is the pact?"

Phillips stared at her, his gaze icy. Joan kept her eyes locked on his, refusing to back down. If he lunged for her, she'd grab his long white beard and wrench his head down toward the table. Once she'd thrown off his balance, she'd shimmy across the bench to the floor. The disk in her hand could easily become an iron spike. Or she could draw Bia and coat the sword's blade. One strike and he'd be—

Joan's heart leapt to her throat. Had she just planned how to murder Master Phillips? Her gaze dropped to her lap.

How easy it had been to imagine—

She felt sick.

"Joan—"

She looked up, sure that Phillips had somehow been privy to her terrible thoughts. She needed to know what, *who* had brought that terrible instinct out of her.

"I know—" She took a deep breath; steadied her voice. "I know you have your secrets, Master Phillips, but Shakespeare, Burbage, and I nearly died today—"

"Lass—"

"—and if you know anything about what happened, I need you to tell me."

She watched his face. His expression was set in a deep frown. She thought of what James would do, how he'd let his emotions slip to change people's minds.

Joan let loose all the fear she'd clamped down on so tightly. Her eyes watered, and she clasped her shaking hands, pressing them against the table. "Please, Master Phillips."

Phillips clenched his jaw as a realization passed over his face. "Lass, I—you—So you want to know about the Pact." He sighed and slumped as if the weight of all his years hung round his neck. "Nearly two thousand years ago, when this land was still wild, the Fae, all Fae, could do as we wished in the mortal realm. But when humans grew tired of being prey, things came to war and there was one among the mortals who was powerful enough to force the Fae to into an agreement to limit our power and reach. It trapped the strongest and most dangerous of us in Faerie and bound the rest to do no more than cause mortals mischief. That is the Pact."

Joan listened, her eyes wide. "Were you there all those millennia ago?"

"No, that was long before my time. I am a changeling, and we only live as long as the humans we replace before we're called back to Faerie."

She nodded and stayed silent, hoping Phillips would keep talking.

"All I know is that the Pact was brokered and sealed by a powerful entity called Ogun."

"Ogun?" Joan sat up so fast, she thought she heard her spine crack. "How do you know about Ogun?"

Phillips stared at her, eyes narrowing to thin slits. "How do *you* know about Ogun?"

This was the moment. She could reveal all to Master Phillips or—

She swallowed.

Master Phillips believed petty lies about people who didn't look like him, but he was also a man with a secret. A secret that would prove deadly if revealed.

Joan could trust in that to protect her, if nothing else.

She held out her hand and willed the disk to shift and change before Phillips's eyes. She paused for a moment. There was no going back after revealing this to him.

"I'm a child of Ogun. He's the Orisha who's blessed me."

She took a deep breath, imagined pulling the iron back into herself. Closed her eyes, feeling the cool flow of iron seeping back into her hand.

Phillips watched her with wide eyes. "And you can do this because of Ogun?"

Joan nodded.

"Did you wound with iron today?" His breaths came fast, his face open with fear.

"I—" She paused, thinking about the weapon she barely remembered forming, about Ogun taking control of her. "Yes."

Phillips need not know the rest.

He shook his head, pressing his palms into his eyes. "I knew you'd bring us trouble, lass, just not like this. Iron wounds don't heal. Auberon'll not forgive you that. See that you don't meet him again."

"Oberon? The character from the play?" She barked out a laugh. "Surely you jest—"

"Not Oberon, Auberon. The play's version of him is a watered-down buffoon Will imagined after getting me far too drunk one night and extrapolating on my wild ramblings. *Au*beron"—here he emphasized the difference in pronunciation—"is real and far more dangerous than that. I thought nothing of the differences because he—because *she* was trapped in Faerie, but now—" Phillips shook his head and pushed himself to his feet. "Enough. Come, lass. Let's join your brother and the rest."

"She? Who else from this Faerie should we fear meeting?"

"I've told you all I'll tell, child." He reached out for her hand, his shaking with a tremor of what might have been fear. "Come along."

"But Master Phillips—"

He glared at her. "Ask me no more."

Joan frowned but placed her hand in his and let herself be led over to the rest of the company.

She'd get no answers out of Phillips tonight, but she'd hold on to what he'd given her. Perhaps her parents would know more.

Someone had pulled out a tambourine, and James stood on the table clanging out an intricate beat with his hands and feet. He spotted her and grinned before tossing the instrument over. She snatched it out of the air.

"Come to show us how it's done, sister?"

A challenge, a dance, was just what she needed to lift her mood.

Joan laughed and banged the tambourine against her wrist. "If you must be schooled, I'll be your teacher."

The crowd around them cheered as James pulled her up atop the table.

"A jig?" James rolled up his sleeves.

"Double time, double time," Armin yelled from the back.

"Not for free," Shakespeare shouted.

Burbage's laugh carried over all other noise. "A double-time jig it shall be. Nick, gather the good people's donations."

Nick grabbed a hat off the table and grinned up at Joan. His gaze lingered, locked on hers, and the room suddenly felt too hot and too cold at equal turns.

Samuel elbowed Nick in the side and whispered something that made Nick duck his head, his beautiful hair hiding his face from view.

He slipped off, snaking his way through the crowd to collect coin. And Joan tried to collect herself.

"Show-offs," Rob shouted, but he grinned just as hard as the rest.

She snorted and winked at him. "Double time," she said.

James rolled his shoulders. "Easy start?"

"Of course. Try to keep up."

James gasped but Joan ignored him. She raised the tambourine, shaking it with one hand, then stomped her foot. One. Two. Three.

Off they went. James banged and shuffled out a beat, clapping his hands between the thumps of his heels on the tabletop. Joan matched him, catching the tambourine on her palm between his sounds. The beat was steady, a solid jig on the faster side of rhythms but nothing too challenging.

Joan could feel their audience getting restless. They'd paid their coin to see something fantastic.

She glanced at James who gave the smallest shake of his head.

Let them seethe a bit longer.

Joan smiled to herself and hit an extra flourish on the tambourine, banging it against her wrist then forearm and shaking it out to the side. She felt the shift. Someone in the back was getting rowdy, grumbling and hissing in dissatisfaction. Enough games. She tossed the tambourine into the air.

James stomped once and froze. The tambourine landed in her hands and they picked the beat back up, twice as fast as before. Joan laughed as she and James danced across the table switching places and tossing the tambourine between themselves.

At first a hush fell over the crowd, and then they burst out into cheers. She spotted Nick bobbing through the people to scoop up the coins they practically threw at him.

James nodded to Armin who picked up the beat with resounding claps. Others around him joined in, struggling to keep the rhythm. Joan ignored the rest and focused on Armin. James wouldn't let her forget it if she fell out of step.

James threw the tambourine back to her, and Joan banged it across her body. Palm, palm, shoulder, shoulder, wrist, hip, shake, hip, palm, throw. James caught it and Joan lifted her skirts to match his footwork. Stomp, shuffle, slide, hop, stomp, stomp, heel tap, toe tap, heel, toe, heel, toe.

The tambourine sailed through the air to Phillips, and James met Joan's eye. She grinned back at him and they doubled the tempo again.

Wonderful, steady Armin held the beat as they danced light steps across the tabletop. Joan could feel her ribs straining against her stays and knew she only had a little more left in her. James smiled and motioned for Phillips to give him back the tambourine. As soon as it dropped back into his hands he banged it against his palms and feet. Joan snatched the instrument from him on his third pass through and raised a challenging eyebrow at him as she jangled it against her fingers and the heel her palm. James laughed and nodded at her. They hit a few more quick steps and turns. Joan stomped three times and threw the tambourine in the air. She and James spun on one foot and Joan threw her arm up to catch the tambourine on her hand and let it slide down her arm until it clanged down against her shoulder.

All went silent before the crowd burst into shouts and cheers. James laughed and dragged her into a bow with a flourish. Joan let him pull her over then collapsed onto the table, trying to catch her breath, grinning between gasps.

The shrunken blade around her wrist pulsed. Every thought of the Fae and her earlier fight for her life flooded her mind in a jarring rush.

She glanced up, catching Phillips's eye across the crowd of people. Worry furrowed the old man's brow, a feeling she'd forgotten in the joy of their dance. Her laughter died on her lips as James, Nick, and Burbage quietly counted coins beside her.

They had no idea how deadly this day had almost been for all of them. Joan touched her fingertips to Bia, felt the disguised blade hum gently at her as she tried to calm the sudden fear squeezing her heart.

CHAPTER EIGHT
A Walk to Remember

hat did Master Phillips say to you?"

James strode along beside her, his hands tangled in the strap of his bag. Joan's own share of the coin they'd made from their impromptu performance hung in a thickly padded purse at her hip to silence the jingle of shillings and pence.

Joan snorted. "Quite a bit that I'd rather discuss once we've reached home."

The streets of Southwark were quiet and mostly empty this close to sundown and the closing of the gates. Only rogues and stragglers took to the streets after dark, and if you lived on the north side of the Thames, now was the time to start for home.

Joan and James had left Master Shakespeare at Yaughan's, drinking and carrying on with the other players who lived in and around Southwark. He'd find his own way across the Thames once he'd had his fill. He always did.

Up ahead, Joan could make out the turrets of the Stone Gateway, the entry to the south side of London Bridge, and the blackened heads of tarred traitors sticking up like grotesque trophies.

They crossed the bridge daily on their way to the Globe, but Joan didn't think she'd ever get used to the gruesome sight. She and James quickened their steps. They had to hurry or risk being caught when the gates closed for the night.

Neither of the twins wanted to explain to their parents that they couldn't make it home until after dawn because they'd lost track of time dancing for money at an alehouse on the south side of the Thames.

"He said the Fae at the theatre was *Au*beron," Joan whispered, carefully pronouncing the "Aw" instead of "Oh."

"Like from our play?" James raised an eyebrow at her.

She shrugged. "Yes and no? He said the play's Oberon is a buffoon compared to the real one."

"So, what? Are Master Shakespeare's characters coming to life now?" James snorted.

They slipped along with the few folks heading northbound, passing the homes and shops that lined London Bridge from one end to the other. Everyone was closing up and settling in for the night.

Joan tugged at her cloak, pulling it tightly around herself. She used the movement to discreetly check that her money hadn't been liberated by a thief.

The purse was still there and full but Joan refused to let her guard down even as they passed through Nonesuch House, the northern bridge gate, and turned west in the direction home.

"Shall we expect to meet Titania next? Or Nick Bottom? Which of us do you think will wear the ass's head? I hope it's Samuel, he could use a humbling."

Joan laughed along with James as they made their way toward Cheapside. The streets around them grew darker by the moment as the sun slipped below the horizon off to their left.

Lantern carriers bustled through the dim streets. The young boys huddled together in groups, calling out to any passing stranger who looked ready to hire someone to light his path.

She shook her head.

"That would be something," Joan said, then stumbled forward a few steps as she tripped over an uneven patch in the road. She took a moment to collect herself, turned back, and saw no breaks. "But what if it were true? You said yourself things feel off."

James frowned. "Yes, but what would that mean? That you faced off against the faerie king?" He grunted and tripped forward and, like Joan, looked down behind him to see what had thrown off his balance.

Again the limestone road lay smooth with no sign of anything that could've impeded their paths.

Strange . . .

Joan kept walking, trying to step carefully but quickly. "I don't know. He seemed so shaken."

She fell forward, nearly dropping to her knees before she could catch her balance. James seemed to gather himself as well, dancing his way out of a stumble. They stared at each other then looked back at the ground again.

The limestone paving held no cracks or splits, nothing to have tripped them up once, let alone three times.

"Well, that's unusual." James frowned.

"That it was." Joan's hand crept to where Bia still hung at her wrist. She thanked whatever instinct had told her to keep the blade close. "The lantern carriers are gone."

James scowled as he looked around the suddenly empty street. "So they are."

Bia slithered into Joan's hand, the blade vibrating at the thought of spilling more blood. Joan spread her stance and glanced around the empty street.

Nothing.

Something skittered across the stones behind James. Joan's eyes cut over to where she'd heard the sound, but neither of the twins moved. Something ran just beyond where she stood, a tiny glint of light barely larger than Joan's palm. James saw it too.

Suddenly, the papers in James's satchel began fluttering wildly, and then the entire roll of script pages popped out and flew off back toward the bridge. James cursed and sprinted after them.

"James, no!" Joan grunted and let Bia wrap back around her wrist. She grabbed a fistful of her skirts in each hand and ran after her brother.

Her head snapped back as someone snagged hold of her hair. Joan yelped, her neck aching from the force of the sudden stop. She batted around her head and her hand connected with something solid. She closed her fingers around whatever it was and brought it around to her face.

The small glowing form she held clutched in her hand hissed and spit like a caught cat. It looked nearly human except for its size and the luminous dark eyes that shone wide in the dimming light. Tiny feet kicked at Joan's fingers as its hairless head thrashed back and forth. A pixie?

"What is a pixie doing out before nightfall?" Joan frowned. "And why are you attacking us?"

The creature froze. "You dare question this one, mortal?" it said in a tiny voice like nails on porcelain. "This one is enraged." It renewed its struggle.

Joan shook her fist, and the creature shrieked. "I'll ask you again, wee one. Why did you attack my brother and me?"

"These ones do you mischief for your folly. Mischief for mischief done."

"Joan!"

Joan looked down the street where James had disappeared. She kept the creature in one hand and grabbed her skirts in the other as she ran over to him.

She found her brother snatching rolled pages off the ground and away from the tiny glowing pixies flying around him. Every so often, one would snatch a paper out of his reach and flutter about his head.

"Enough," James shouted. He glanced along the empty street quickly then brought his fingers to his lips as if to whistle. The air around them seemed to stop as if waiting for his next move.

He sucked in a deep breath and a sudden wind kicked up around him. It caught hold of every pixie with a stolen page and spun them in a tight circle.

Joan noticed a lone pixie creeping slowly past her, one of James's pages clutched in its tiny hands. She snatched it by one slim leg, pulled the paper from its grasp, and flung the page into James's vortex.

"James—" She held up her hand, the pixie she'd captured squirming in her grip. "They're pixies and they've come at us before dark."

He nodded and blew out a gust of breath.

Tiny shrieks echoed in the air around them as wind rushed out from around where James stood, sending the glowing creatures off in all directions. A few small screams and bright lights flew past Joan as the air dragged them away.

"Maferefun, Oya," James grunted.

Joan cursed under her breath. She couldn't remember if she'd offered the same gratitude to Ogun earlier.

Why couldn't the words come easily?

She thought of watching as the Orisha controlled her body from what felt like some faraway abyss.

And pushed it from her mind. Now wasn't the time.

James made his way over—his clothes were askew as he clutched a mess of papers to his chest. His eyes widened when he saw the pixie she held, then they narrowed.

"So, this"—he shook his loose pages in the creature's face—"is due to you and your friends, yes?"

"Mischief for mischief done," the creature screamed. "Mischief for mischief done. Mischief for mischief done. So he says and so shall it be."

James looked at Joan. "This is your fault."

"Let this one free! This one shall not go with you." The pixie thrashed and screeched.

Joan brought her hand up to her eye level and scowled at the creature. "'This one' has been captured and is coming home with us. Objections or no."

James fell into step beside Joan as they both headed toward home again. The sun had almost completely fallen beyond the horizon, and a lantern carrier ran along farther down the road brandishing a torch. Another followed along behind him as people came back out onto the street.

James clutched his script pages as if they'd break out running again at any moment. "I can't believe they stole my lines."

The sound of metal on metal, like the clanging of chains, echoed down the road just as a huge glowing figure loped down a side street farther in front of Joan and James. The creature stood twice as tall and twice as wide as any man she'd ever seen, its arms near as thick as Joan's waist.

"This must be another unleashed by the Pact," Joan groaned.

"The Pact?" James said, his face suddenly pale, "Baba Ben's pact has to do with this . . . monstrous thing?"

The pixie in Joan's grip giggled. "Our lord Auberon has sent his lieutenant jack."

"Lieutenant?" Joan said.

"His jack-in-irons," the pixie said in Joan's hand, "they're devourers and that one is our lord's right hand. He comes to feast on flesh at our lord's command."

"Feast on flesh?" Joan repeated. This hulking beast couldn't be allowed to do its master's bidding. "We have to follow it."

James grabbed her arm. "What? You can't follow after that thing like that."

She shot him a look. Hadn't he earlier volunteered them—volunteered her—to help Rose with some unknown danger? Why would he hesitate now when a monster stood before them?

"You'll need two free hands in case it attacks." He stuffed his script back into his bag and held out his hand. "Give me that pixie."

Joan gaped at him.

"Hurry, it's getting away." He shook his hand at her. "What? You know I'm not fighting that thing."

Joan rolled her eyes at her brother but gave over the tiny Fae. He was right. If it came down to a fight—and looking at the beast lumbering ahead of them, Joan knew that was inevitable—she'd be the one doing battle. And she would be ready.

CHAPTER NINE
William Cecil and the Jack-in-Irons

he last time William had heard his mother's voice, he'd been six years old and happy.

That night, the fire had crackled in their parlor, flaring too hot against his little body. He'd pressed his pale face into her skirts, the brocade scratching against his cheeks.

Mother had whispered a story of a greedy king who tried to make a deal with a monster, her dainty white hands shifting through his hair. The words didn't remain but William remembered shivering while his older sister Frances laughed.

Then Mother had crumpled. She'd laid limp in William's little arms until her ladies rushed to her side, shoving William and Frances away as they swarmed her like flies on meat. They whispered to each other about the new baby and midwives and doctors and then Mother was gone.

Frances had let him grip her hand while they sat alone in the antechamber. She'd squeezed back when Mother started screaming and let him tuck himself in close in the horrible silence of after.

That had been so long ago, the gap of nine years softening the memory's once-sharp edges.

But today, the voice he thought he had forgotten pulled him from his studies. It could have been a daydream brought on by too much reading by the dim light of the setting sun but—

Today he heard Mother call his name.

"William . . ."

Again. Just down the corridor from his bedchamber.

Frowning, he slipped away from his desk. He leaned against the door, letting his weight press it open in slow silence.

Father had come home early from work, his back more stooped than usual and the dark bruises under his eyes stark against his pale skin. He'd be in no mood to see William slacking on his studies.

He shivered, thinking of the disappointment and fury if his father caught William sneaking off before completing all his reading. There was no need to disturb him at present.

"William . . ."

William slipped through the open door and sprinted down the hall, sticking close to the wall to avoid creaking floors. Fifteen years of sneaking past his father's office had taught his feet exactly where to step.

He caught a glimpse of white at the bottom of the main staircase. One of the servants lay asleep along the side of the stairs, her pale profile almost glowing in the dying sunlight streaming in through the open front doors.

If father found her sleeping on the job, he'd dock her pay or worse. William hesitated, wondering if he should wake her and save her from his father's wrath.

"William . . ." his mother called from just outside.

His head jerked up. There was no mistaking it, not this close, this clear.

He burst out the front door.

His mother, Elizabeth Cecil, stood at the end of the long walkway haloed by the light of the setting sun. Her back was to him, but he knew it was her. She turned.

She looked just as she had all those years ago on that last day when he and Frances had sat at her knee. Mother smiled her most beautiful smile and reached out a hand for him.

"My William," she cooed.

William's heart beat hard in his chest.

"My beautiful boy. Come to me."

Tears blurred William's vision and he struggled to breathe around the lump in his throat. He'd never forgotten how much he missed her, no matter how deeply he tried to bury the hole in his heart.

He moved down the pathway toward her.

"William," his father called suddenly. "What are you doing out here?"

William turned back to the house and flinched at Father's look as he glared from the open doorway. A Negro man stood in the house looking out over Father's shoulder. The stranger's slim brown face was framed by long ropes of black hair dripping with ornaments.

"You should be—" Father stiffened as his gaze shifted to the form standing behind William in the road.

The Negro man's lips quirked into a smile. "Look upon your wife, Cecil, returned from the dead. See what gifts I can bring. Become my agent. Unite with me against our common enemy and I'll bring you so much more."

His father stumbled and clutched the doorjamb. "Elizabeth," he choked, his eyes wide and bright. "How have you—"

"Will you agree, Cecil?" the man said. "I can promise you, with my help, your king will not escape those who seek to harm him."

William smiled. "It's Mother. Or at least her spirit." He turned back to the apparition. She looked past him to Father.

"I'll not ask you again, Cecil," the Negro man said.

"Robert, my love," the spirit whispered. She turned to William. "Come to me, my boy. My sweet William."

William took a step toward her, reaching out to grasp her hand.

"You demon," his father spat, "as if I would ever stoop myself—"

William glanced back to see Father had turned deathly pale, the strange man's hand gripping his shoulder.

"Such venom," the man said and Father winced and cried out. "If only you had agreed to my most generous offer. Alas, this is what happens to those who oppose me."

"Come to Mother, my darling." Mother still reached for him.

"No, William—" Father's voice was a hoarse whisper. "Come back inside at once."

William shook his head and ignored him.

He reached out to grasp the hand of his mother's spirit. Her touch was solid but dry and icy cold.

"William, no," his father called. "Please, not my son. Please!"

"Too late, I'm afraid," the man said.

Too late for what?

William opened his mouth to ask when the hand holding his tightened. A chill rushed down his spine.

As she looked at him, Mother's beautiful smile shifted to something grotesque and inhuman. The color bled away from her eyes, her mouth widened, lips spread nearly ear to ear to expose long, sharp, pointed teeth.

Her body lengthened and thickened as heavy chains looped around her from neck to knees. William gasped as severed heads appeared dangling from the metal loops, their mouths open in silent, eternal shrieks.

William heard Father screaming behind him, loudly enough to draw out the entire rest of the household. To draw out all the neighbors.

But no one came.

Why did no one come?

He wished he could run back inside. To escape whatever held his hand in a crushing grip.

But his feet refused to move.

The creature stood twice William's height, its pale body nearly double William's slim frame. It tilted its head to one side, luminous white eyes seeming to rake over his face before it shrieked.

Unlike its touch, its breath was hot and moist. It stank like rotted meat and rang like an echo from hell itself.

William's heart seized in fear. The creature opened its gruesome mouth and lunged for his throat.

He closed his eyes and prayed death would be swift.

That Father wouldn't mourn him for too long.

Someone shouted as the creature screamed in pain, the sound high and tight, as a small hand pressed against William's chest and shoved hard.

He stumbled backward, tripped over his own feet, and slammed into the ground, teeth rattling with the impact.

A woman—no, a girl—stood before them, blocking the beast's path. Her wild hair and deep-brown skin showed her to be a Negro.

"Leave this boy alone," she said. She brandished a sword.

The thing rolled its head and glared down at her. It shrieked again.

William threw his hands up over his ears as the sound seemed to rattle his brain.

The girl held her ground, staring the thing down.

"Again, girl?" The Negro man who'd spoken to Father strolled out from behind them. "This is none of your affair. Leave now, and I'll grant you mercy."

"William! William!" Father's arms wrapped around him in a tight embrace.

"Mercy? I don't trust your mercy." The girl scowled and slipped into a ready stance, feet braced and blade raised to attack or defend. "I'm not afraid of you. Leave these people alone." Her sword glinted suddenly in the light.

"Well. I warned you. Jack"—the man laughed and waved a hand at the beast looming in the road, the one who'd cruelly worn William's mothers face—"kill them all." Then the man was gone, vanished into the evening air.

William felt his father stiffen.

The monster's lips spread wide as it advanced on the girl. She watched it move toward her then she struck. Her blade sliced across the beast's face then its torso.

It shrieked and reared back, clutching its bloody wounds.

"Iron?" it hissed, its voice slurred and shaky. "A blade of iron?"

"Leave," she said, then lunged at it again, sword flashing. The creature lurched out of her reach with a low keen. It slipped around her in a wide berth and loped off down the road in a cacophony of moaning and clanking chains.

The girl watched it go and didn't drop her sword until it was well out of sight. Then she turned. The light of the setting sun caught along her face, covering her in an ethereal light.

William flushed.

She was beautiful, with her dark brown skin, sparkling eyes, and full lips.

Had he been saved by an angel?

William's heart thumped in his chest. He felt Father dragging him back toward their house. But he couldn't go, not just yet. He jerked free and ran, grabbing her hand before she could slip away.

"Wait, please," he whispered. This close he could smell the sweet fragrance of her curly hair. He liked it very much. "Are you hurt?"

"No, no, I'm fine. Are you?" She smiled at him, and his breath caught in his throat.

"No, I'm safe thanks to you, beauty." He bowed low over her hand, like the gentleman he'd been trained to be, and laid a kiss across her knuckles. "Thank you for saving my life."

Her eye's widened. "Uh . . ." Her gaze shifted away from his.

"Her name's Joan," someone called from down the road. A Negro boy jogged into view, panting and clutching a satchel that shook in his grasp.

William nodded at the boy. "Thank you for saving my life, Joan. I shall not forget this." He smiled at her startled look then ran back to his father.

Her name felt good on his tongue, and he hoped this wouldn't be their last acquaintance.

"Where have you been?" William heard Joan hiss behind him.

"Making sure our other problem stayed handled, dear sister."

William turned and watched her disappear down the road alongside her brother. Then a hand wrapped around William's wrist as Father yanked him back into the house.

And drew him immediately into a desperate embrace.

"My boy," Father whispered as he squeezed William. "My boy. My boy."

Several servants huddled around something in the front hall covered in a white sheet. William thought he caught sight of a hand sticking out from beneath the fabric.

He turned away from the sight and closed his eyes, willing the girl's beautiful brown face to chase away the memory of rancid breath and sharp teeth.

He doubted it would work.

Nightmares always lingered.

CHAPTER TEN
A Most Unwelcome Guest

he bell at St. Paul's rang seven o'clock as Joan and James skirted the grand cathedral, headed toward home. Moonlight cast an eerie glow over the building, sending the bell tower's long shadow looming across the empty courtyard.

Following and fighting that jack-in-irons had taken them nearly to the other side of the city, but Joan couldn't regret it. She held the pleasure of saving that boy's life—tried not to examine the rush of excitement flowing through her after drawing the monster's blood—as she and James slipped through the dark streets. This close to curfew, they needed to avoid brigands and officers alike.

And rogue Fae.

Surely their parents would know what today's startling events meant. Hopefully, she and James could avoid any more . . . excitement until they made it safely home. Joan glanced over at the thrashing bag James held tightly in his grip. Yes, this, and the jack-in-irons, and the attack at the theatre all felt like more than enough to explain.

They finally rounded the corner onto Cheapside, and the lights lining their section of the street came into view.

Joan felt her body relax like it hadn't since she'd fought off Shakespeare and Burbage. Not for the first time, she said a tiny thanks for the torches that her father and all their neighbors along Goldsmith's Row had paid to have posted up and down the street. What usually felt like a boastful excess tonight proved its absolute practicality.

The sign for the shop—artful bright blue script declaring their father's name—swung in the dim light as Joan and James approached.

Henry swung open the front door, his long, pale brown face and bouncy black curls illuminated by the streetlights. "Well, if it isn't the wayward players finally come home. Now that you two are—" He paused, his wide grin slipping to a disgusted frown. "Joan, what has James gotten you into this time?"

"Nothing for you to worry about," James said curtly.

Joan clamped her mouth shut and let her gaze drift away from Henry's. She was sure she and her brother made quite the sight. James's sleeves hung loose from his doublet, untied and drooping down around his elbows as he clutched his bag to his chest in a tight grip. Joan's braids barely remained intact, her hair sticking out at all angles and half covering her face. And was that a slash of blood smeared across the front of her skirt?

Yes, that would be alarming, but they just needed to get inside.

"Joan"—Henry grabbed her hand in both of his—"you know it's dangerous for a lady in those playhouses. Don't let your brother—"

She pulled out of his grasp, every muscle struggling to keep the movement gentle and her face blank. "It's fine, Henry." She forced her lips into a smile. "You should head home. We'll lock up the shop."

Henry nodded, brow still furrowed, but stepped out the door and around Joan. "You don't have to follow James around like some—"

"Getting awfully close to curfew, isn't it?" James stood on the single stair leading into the shop so he was equal in height to Henry.

Joan laid a hand on Henry's arm—again forcing herself to be gentle when most of her wanted to shove him on his way. "There's no need for you to get into trouble being out late." She clenched her teeth and pushed the sides of her mouth up until her eyes crinkled. "Good night, Henry."

He gave Joan one last smile, glared at James, then turned and hurried down their street.

"You know he's only nice to you because he thinks he can marry you."

Joan sighed as she slipped past her brother and in through the door. "Yes."

"Sad you're going to turn him down." James snickered.

Joan kept silent as she bolted the locks behind them.

"Wait." James was suddenly close at her side. "Wait. You aren't. You can't. He's the worst."

James didn't understand. Time was running out on her freedom, and at least Henry could get her close to achieving her dream.

She shrugged. "I'll have to marry someone. When Henry owns the Partridge, as his wife I'd still be allowed to work here."

"Joan, you can't. What about the company?"

"What husband would allow me work at the playhouse?" She took in his silence. "As Henry's wife, I could at least keep something of what I love."

She slipped past him and headed toward the stairs leading up into the rest of the house.

"I won't let you marry him." James spun her to face him, his hands firm on her shoulders. "I forbid it."

Joan shook him off. "It's not your choice."

Her heart beat hard in her chest. She hadn't been this angry at her brother in a long time, but he had no idea what he was speaking on or how much she'd agonized over this very decision.

Because he was a boy and boys had options.

A shriek sounded from James's bag, now hanging loose at his hip. The pixie shot out into the open room and straight up the stairs into the main house.

Joan's wide eyes met her brother's. "Shite."

They both bolted for the stairs.

Nan came down from the third floor just as Joan and James crested the landing. "Thank the good Lord." She paused as she got a good look at them both. "What's all this?"

"Mischief for mischief done!" the pixie shrieked and snatched the white cap from Nan's head.

Joan dove forward. She snagged the cap and jerked it toward herself, catching hold of the pixie as it tumbled through the air.

"Jesus, Mary, and Joseph, is that a pixie? God's blessed mother," Nan stumbled back against the stairs, her right hand flying from her head to her chest to shoulder and shoulder repeating the sign of the cross. "What foolishness made you bring one of the Folk into this house, Joan?"

Joan scowled. "They attacked us."

"Mischief for mischief done. Mischief for mischief done," the creature shrieked.

"What does it mean 'mischief for mischief done'?" Nan paled. "God's teeth, you've angered the Folk. "

"They attacked us first, Nan."

"Mischief for mischief done. Mischief for mischief done."

"You've doomed us all. No prayers can save us."

"But they attacked *us*! Don't you think that's strange? Are you even listening to me?"

"Mischief for mischief done. Mischief for mischief done. Mischief for mischief done."

"ENOUGH."

The entire room went silent, the creature included, as Mrs. Bess Sands appeared at the top of the stairs. Her black hair was still piled immaculately atop her head in braids and twists dripping with gold pins. She wore only her chemise and a black robe embroidered with crimson roses. She'd obviously been getting ready for bed.

Joan glanced at James who looked slightly worried.

"What is all this?" Mrs. Sands said.

Everyone spoke at once as the creature picked back up its horrid screeching. Mrs. Sands watched the commotion for a while, face carefully blank.

"No," she said.

Her soft, firm voice cut through the cacophony and everyone went quiet. Even the pixie.

Joan admired that power.

"One at a time. What has been brought into my home? Nan, please stop wailing, the house is protected." Mrs. Sands descended the stairs completely and rubbed her hand along Nan's back until the younger woman choked her wails back into sniffles. "And why do my children look like they've run all the way here from Southwark?"

James and Joan looked at each other again then turned to their mother.

"We didn't run all the way here from Southwark—" Joan murmured.

James tried to retie his sleeves. "It was actually a brisk walk from closer to Westminster—"

"—on the Strand," Joan finished.

Mrs. Sands stared them down.

"What's this noise, then? Is Joan home? I need her to unknot this chain for me. It's giving me hell." Mr. Thomas Sands strode in from his study, fully dressed in a brilliant blue doublet and pantaloons over gray stockings. His hair was loose and his curls stretched out in long waves, the neat rows of braids he'd worn for the past month finally undone. A tangled gold chain hung from one hand. He pushed his magnifying lens up to his forehead. "Ah, you're home—what is that you're holding?"

Nan crossed herself again. "She's got a pixie, sir. And it's spitting mad, it is."

"No worries, the house is protected." Mr. Sands approached Joan, his gaze focused on the tiny form held in her fist. "Well, let's see it then." He hunched his big frame over and lifted Joan's hand up higher. "Hold steady there, Joan dear." He shifted his magnifying lens back over his eye and squinted at the creature.

The creature—pixie—stared back.

Her father nodded. "A pixie indeed. Good that they're harmless."

"Let it go," Mrs. Sands said.

"What?" Joan shouted, her exclamation echoed by James and Nan. She couldn't mean that.

"Joan—" Her mother raised an eyebrow, her face slipping into that familiar expression that always made Joan feel like a naughty child.

She meant it.

Joan felt her whole face heat up, but she uncurled her fingers. The pixie hovered in the air then took off, flying through the withdrawing room and up through the fireplace with a puff of displaced soot.

"By the tiny teeth of Baby Jesus," Nan wailed and crossed herself again.

"It's all right, Nan. It's gone." Mrs. Sands murmured.

Mr. Sands hummed. "Good thing that fire wasn't lit."

Joan shook her head in awe as her father finally dropped the knotted gold chain into her empty hand. "Mother, we should've questioned it before we let it go." Joan sighed and ran the chain through her fingertips, pulling it away fully straightened. "It could have told us more about the pact Baba Ben was trying to protect."

Her mother's face went hard. "When did Ben tell you about that?"

"Quite the eventful day we're having," Mr. Sands said, sending his wife a pointed look. "Let's take this conversation into my study, shall we? Excuse us, Nan."

Joan exchanged a glance with James before they trooped their way into their father's office as their mother calmed Nan and sent her off to bed.

"Now—" Their mother closed the door and moved to lean against their father's desk. "Why did you bring up the Pact?"

Joan glanced over at James who was hunched over leafing through his bundle of script pages and counting frantically.

No help there.

"I—" Joan pressed her fingertips against the sword curled around her wrist and found comfort in its steady thrum. "Baba Ben told me about it right before he was arrested." She watched her mother's face as she spoke but there was no change in her hard expression.

"Ben shouldn't have told you about that," Mrs. Sands said. "You're not ready."

"One problem at a time," her father said. "How'd you come into possession of this pixie?"

Joan frowned. "A swarm of them attacked James and me on our way home. Said it was 'mischief for mischief done.'"

Mr. Sands hummed and leaned back in his chair. "On your way home from the theatre or the Strand?"

"From the theatre—"

"From the alehouse," James muttered.

Their mother took a deep, steadying breath. "The alehouse, Joan? Haven't I asked you not to—"

"I went to ask Master Phillips what he knew," Joan said quickly. She didn't need this to devolve into a lecture about what a young lady of her stature should or shouldn't be seen doing. "He spoke of the broken pact as well."

Mrs. Sands's jaw clenched. "Enough of the Pact. What. Exactly. Happened, Joan?"

"Some Fae attacked Master Burbage and Master Shakespeare while Joan was practicing with them," James said. "Nearly made them kill each other, but Joan fought him off and injured him. And before you ask, no, I didn't see anything. I came in at the end with Master Phillips who had to know *something* about it all because he's Fae. He talked to Joan about many things, then we left to come home but we got attacked by a swarm of pixies as soon as we made it across the bridge and *then* we followed this giant, monster Fae to a house in Westminster and Joan saved a boy and his father from getting murdered by it and then we finally came home." James huffed out a breath. "So, can I go up to my room and study my lines for tomorrow's performance?"

Joan frowned. The way James described it made it sound like every step that night had been her idea.

It had been, but he needn't say it explicitly.

"No." Mrs. Sands said. She made pointed eye contact with her husband. "It's as we suspected."

Joan frowned. "So this is all connected to Baba and his ritual?"

Her mother signed deeply, shoulders slumping. "Yes. That's why I went to see Iya Mary this morning while your father searched for Ben."

James made a shocked noise. "You went to Stratford? Today?"

Joan's mind raced.

It took six days to travel from London to Stratford-upon-Avon where Iya Mary—their mother's godmother—lived, so they never paid a visit to her without purpose. Which explained why her mother had created a doorway this morning.

But connecting such a great distance came at a cost. Joan noticed the dark bruises beneath her mother's eyes and the unusual slump to her shoulders.

This added to the fear she'd seen in Baba's face yesterday and Joan's encounters today boded very ill times ahead.

They needed Baba back *now*.

Joan frowned. "Father, did you find where they're holding him?"

"No." Her father leaned his elbows on the desk and let his chin rest on his hands. "None of my usual contacts know where he is being held." He hesitated, scratched his nose. "I'll try again tomorrow."

"We need him to complete the ritual, he's the only—" Her mother's posture shifted; her spine loosened as she leaned back against the desk.

The air around them seemed suddenly thick. Joan felt her shoulders tense.

Elegua was here.

No matter how many times the Orisha possessed her mother, Joan never got used to the change. Used to the fact that the very spirits who blessed them, to whom they prayed, could command their bodies.

One moment you'd feel the Orisha's presence and the next moment you were gone. And who knows where you went when they took control.

Joan remembered that dark nothing that had engulfed her earlier, that feeling of being nowhere while Ogun possessed her. She imagined her mother there now, watching from far off, and a chill ran up her spine.

"Ago, Elegua," James and her father both said.

Joan echoed their words, late and hesitant, and prayed her father wouldn't notice.

"What d'you know of the Pact, girl?" Her mother's voice was simultaneously old and youthful. That was Elegua, both the old man and the child.

"I—" she started, shook her head, and took a breath. "I know it was made with the Fae and brokered by a child of Ogun nearly two thousand years ago. And that it's been broken."

Elegua squinted at her. "That it?" He barked out a laugh. "Your head is empty, child, and you must learn soon. Only the knife knows what's inside the yam. You must speak with Ogun soon or . . ." He let the words trail off with a shrug and a half grin.

Her mother trembled suddenly and slumped against the desk. Her father leapt up to take her by the elbow, guiding her to his empty chair. She sat heavily and leaned back with her eyes closed.

Elegua was gone.

Joan tucked her shaking hands into the folds of her skirt as Elegua's words ran through her head.

Speak with Ogun soon or what?

She and Baba Ben were the only two children of Ogun. The Orisha hadn't chosen anyone else in their community in decades.

"If we don't find Baba, I'll have to be the one to complete the ritual," Joan said, "won't I?"

Her heart raced at the thought of the Orisha taking control of her as Elegua had taken control of her mother. She'd felt the kiss of it earlier and that moment had been enough to fill her with fear.

"No," her mother said, voice fierce but tired. "You're not ready for something like that. We will find Ben."

James jumped up. "Sounds as though this has nothing to do with me, so may I go work on my lines?"

"No," said their father. He stood to his full height; eyes narrowed on both twins. "Now tell us everything from the beginning and leave nothing out."

Later, in the wee hours of the morning, Joan perched on her father's stool at his big workshop table. She ran her hands over another cluster of tangled chains and necklaces and tried not to dwell on Henry's ineptitude.

Here, alone and surrounded by metal, she could fully give in to the fantasy that this space belonged to her. She let herself feel as if the impossible could become true as she loosed each link and made order out of someone else's chaos.

Bia leaned against the table beside her, the sword thumping slow and deep like a heartbeat.

"I don't know how you came into my possession right when I needed you," she said to the sword, "but there's no way I'm giving you back to the playhouse."

Bia hummed back happily, the sound rattling in Joan's chest.

Joan smiled.

How could she give the blade up when it felt like an extension of her own arm? When Bia responded more easily than any other metal Joan had ever encountered?

"Don't get too excited. I can't carry you openly, so you'll have to stay hidden."

An angry bristle from Bia.

Joan sighed and let the last chain slither into place in the now orderly row. She reached over and pulled Bia into her lap, laying her hands flat across the blade.

"I know you don't like to hide, but there are laws, and I had rather keep you with me than leave you home."

"Is that sword speaking to you?"

Joan jerked upright, hand wrapping around Bia's hilt, until she met her mother's gaze. "Mother!" Relieved, she let the blade drop back into her lap. "Yes, it is."

"Does metal always speak to you this clearly?" Her mother frowned. "You've never mentioned it before."

"No, not like this. It's a very unusual sword." Joan cleared her throat and focused on the cool steel in her hands.

Never had she connected with a sword as she did with this one. She looked down at Bia's sleek blade, the delicate curves of her guard and hilt. The sword throbbed in her hand, the staccato beat slowing to an easy *ba-dum, ba-dum, ba-dum* in time with her heartbeat.

Mrs. Sands slid onto the high stool across from Joan and held out a hand. "May I?"

Joan nodded and passed Bia to her mother, hissing a quiet "behave" before letting go. A strange anxiety settled in her chest as her mother examined the sword, a sudden need to have it close to her pressing against her throat.

"Did you carve these black dogs into the hilt?"

"Uh, no." Joan hadn't considered them black, but the way the engravings had darkened did give that impression. And black dogs belonged to Ogun. Joan's eyes widened. "Do you think—"

"We'll ask Ben when we get him back," her mother said, handing back the sword. "Until then, keep it with you and take this."

She presented a small crimson sachet. "Clean with it and drop it at a crossroads tomorrow."

Joan let her mother place the bright red bag into her hands. It was small but heavy and the color seemed to sear itself into her eyes.

Crimson fabric wasn't cheap. Crimson fabric would never be wasted. Crimson fabric meant deep and heavy work.

If something so valuable was intended to just be dropped at a crossroads, that meant big trouble.

Her mother sat back, brushing her hands across the white apron she wore over her skirts. A flew splotches of deep red dotted across the fabric. Blood.

Deep and heavy work. It showed just how worried her parents were.

Clutching the sachet to her chest, Joan looked back up at her mother. Her face was even paler than it had been during their talk earlier; her usually luminous brown skin had taken on a gray hue, making the bruises beneath her eyes even more apparent.

She slid forward, grabbing her mother's hand. Mrs. Sands's fingers felt icy cold. Joan squeezed, sending her mother strength even as her own heart clenched in fear.

Mrs. Sands squeezed back. "I need you and your brother to stay out of this Pact business. This breaking has unleashed beings more powerful than we've seen in nearly two thousand years. We've no idea what or who will come through from the other side and I need you and your brother safe. Solving this crisis is beyond both of your abilities."

"Yes, if you don't find Baba then I—"

"We will find him." Her mother's expression hardened. "This responsibility isn't meant for you. Not yet. Know that your father and I will do everything within our power to keep you and your brother safe."

Joan felt the promise in those words wrap around her like an embrace. The truth there was near tangible.

She jerked her head in a half nod, half shake and hoped her mother wouldn't notice she'd never agreed. She swallowed any mention of her planned outing with Rose. Even though she'd been reprimanded heavily for yesterday's heroics, Joan refused to back out of helping the girl.

"Tomorrow, your father and I will speak with Yemoja and Elegua and figure out how fortify the house further," she said.

"Should I speak with Ogun, like Elegua said?" Fear clenched her heart as she remembered the empty nothing she'd drifted in when Ogun had taken control of her body.

Her mother's posture stiffened. "Not now, darling. What Elegua speaks of—" She shook her head. "That is for you to learn when you're a bit more spiritually mature."

The echo of Baba Ben's words made Joan frown. She knew both were right, she still had so much to learn, and she was still somewhat lax in her venerations of Ogun.

But what did any of that mean when Ogun had already taken control of her body? Was she working toward a future where she was expected to allow the Orisha to possess her? To give over control while Ogun took her over? To feel herself drift who knows where, a spectator to her own body's movements, and trust that she'd somehow be the same when she came back?

If she came back.

How could she stand it if that frightening nothingness lurked as a constant possibility?

It was more than she was ready to give.

Mrs. Sands sat back, releasing a sigh. "Is anything else troubling you, love?"

Ask her. Ask her about the feeling and the weapon. Ask her if I'm losing myself.

Ask her if Ogun can steal me from myself.

But the bone-deep exhaustion that hung round her mother like a heavy cloak gave Joan pause. She didn't need the weight of any more worry added to her burden now.

So Joan took a deep breath and shook her head.

Mrs. Sands smiled and nodded. She patted Joan's hand as she stood, then slipped out of the room.

Yes, no need to worry them further.

She unclenched her hand from around Bia's hilt, her knuckles aching with the released pressure.

She'd figure this out on her own.

CHAPTER ELEVEN
Some Shrewd Contents

"Why aren't you awake yet?"

Joan sat up, jerked from her sleep by the voice in her room, and saw James glaring at her from her bedside.

She groaned and rolled back into her blanket. "I only just managed to get to sleep." She'd spent another night tossing and turning, and clawing her way out of delirium was a struggle this morning. Besides, her body ached from all the real hits she'd taken yesterday. The bones in her shoulder released a loud crack as she curled up under her blanket.

"And I didn't?" James tugged at her covers. "I had to stay up to review my lines."

Joan kicked at his grabby hands. "That's a you problem."

"Get out of bed!"

"Just choose my clothes and go. I'll be up anon."

"Oh, if I had only done such a thing. Wait—" He tossed the heavy red gown into her face. "I already have." He sighed and slipped into the bed beside her. "Are you all right?"

Joan scooted over to make room for him. "No. How can you be?"

"I'm not." He shrugged. "But one problem at a time. All I can do for now is get up, get dressed, get you dressed"—he pressed his hand against her face, chuckling as she smacked it away—"and go to the theatre."

"That won't work forever."

"Ah, you only say that because you know how to fight. I, on the other hand, am only ornamental in the best way." He sat up and tugged at the scarf wrapped around her hair. "Now, out of bed. Remember, we're meeting Rose today and right now, you look awful."

Joan swatted his hands away as her face flushed. Although he was right. She needed—wanted—a little more time to do her hair.

James laughed and rolled out of the bed. "Thought that'd get you up. See you at breakfast."

"You've a message, love. Looks important." Nan handed the folded paper to Joan and frowned. "Are you going to finish your hair, dear?"

Joan stuffed a crust of bread into her mouth to avoid having to answer and gave the barest hint of a nod. The comb tangled in her hair smacked her in the face.

Nan shook her head and crossed herself as she wandered back to the kitchen. Mrs. Sands was still in bed, resting her body after yesterday's exertions, and Mr. Sands had already gone down to his workshop.

Joan flipped the letter over with her other hand. Her name flowed across the front in a formal hand, and the note was sealed with a wax crest on the back.

"What's that?" James said, leaning out of his seat to read over her shoulder.

She frowned and shoved his face away carefully and firmly. "I'm not sure."

"Is it a love confession, dear sister?" He snatched the letter out of her hand and danced around to the other side of the wide dining table. He flicked the seal open with one finger and unfolded it, then glanced up again. "What's with your hair?"

"Nothing." Joan sighed, aggressively ignoring the comb snarled in her thick curls. She'd already spent over an hour trying to pull it free to no avail. The more she tried to untangle the thing, the more it clutched and clung to her soft hair. She finally had to leave off or risk destroying her delicate curls. She'd try again after breakfast.

She pulled the softest parts out of her bread and jammed them into her mouth to help dispel her frustration. "Go ahead and read it then."

"I'll give you the best parts."

Joan sat back and watched as James scanned through the missive. His face shifted into a deep frown as he read.

That did not bode well.

"Well?" she said.

James looked up at her, then back down at the letter again. "I—it's from Robert Cecil, the secretary of state, thanking you for saving his son's life."

Joan sat up straight.

When had she saved anyone's son, let alone the king's right-hand man?

Then she remembered. Last night. Walking home with James. A pale, skinny boy in the clutches of a monster, Auberon's smug confidence, and the stricken face of the boy's father.

William from last night must have been the son of Robert Cecil. Which meant the small, frightened man in his doorway screaming for his son had been His Majesty's secretary of state, one of the people closest to King James himself.

And now that same man knew something of what she could do.

"Oh," she said, "that's kind of him."

The words felt hollow in her mouth. She hoped that was it. Gratitude and nothing more.

James shook his head. "There—there's more." He passed the letter to her.

Joan noted his furrowed brow as she took the paper. Her eyes immediately raced down the page to the signature at the end.

The Right Honorable, Robert Cecil, 1st Earl of Salisbury.

So that part had been true. She'd hoped James had been exaggerating. No such luck.

She scooted closer to the dining table, pushing her breakfast plate away and spreading the letter out in its place.

Her eyes sped over the slithering writing.

It is with deepest gratitude for the great service you have done my household in saving the life of my son this past night that I begin today. There exist not words to convey the true depth of my thanks and, simple and brief as it may be, this letter must do the deed justice. Your particular and peculiar talents may serve a higher and, while it may seem impossible, a much nobler purpose. A purpose that shall bring you into my direct employ. I have informed my messenger to await your acquiescence and bring you to my public office straight. Understand the import of the occasion that leads me to request this from one such as you and delay not your acceptance.

The Right Honourable Robert Cecil,
1st Earl of Salisbury

Joan collapsed against her chair. She was suddenly very glad that their parents hadn't joined them for breakfast this morning. She looked up, her eyes meeting James's across the table. "I have to say no."

"You can't say no to him." James blurted. "He's ruthless! Remember he had his wife's brothers executed for treason! Their heads are right there on London Bridge."

Joan blinked, her whole body feeling numb.

"If he'll do that to his family, what do you think he'll do to you, the Black daughter of a goldsmith?"

Her hands shook as she picked the letter up again. As a goldsmith, her father provided the family with a certain level of notoriety and wealth, but nothing so great as to challenge Cecil. "Maybe I can appeal to his gratitude? Because I saved his son's life." She didn't dare look up again, but she could feel James's stare burning into the top of her head. "The messenger who delivered this must still be here—"

"Joan—"

Joan pushed out of her seat as James did the same. Her heart raced in her chest as she made her way to the front hall. She glanced at the letter again.

Understand the import of the occasion that leads me to request this from one such as you—

The flowery language and delicate script did little to hide the insult of the words.

Whether his scorn was for her station, her sex, her age, or her complexion, Joan couldn't agree. God only knew what Robert Cecil wanted to use her for. How could she work for a man who likely thought of her as a tool instead of a person?

The messenger stood just beside the front door, his dark brown face stoic and his posture tall and stiff. Joan froze when she spotted him. She hadn't expected to see a face like her own. She cleared her throat.

He looked up. "I'm to escort you back to Lord Salisbury."

Joan glanced back at James before approaching the messenger. He towered over her.

She smiled at him. "How—How do you find it in your lord's employ? How does he treat you?"

The man's eyes skittered away from her as his jaw clenched.

Well, there was that answer. So there was only one she could give in return.

"Please tell Lord Salisbury"—Joan drew herself up as tall as she could—"that I accept his expression of gratitude with most gracious humility, but I cannot enter his employ."

The messenger's eyes widened. "Your answer is no?"

"My answer is no."

She felt all her energy leave her body with the words. But they were said, and she couldn't and wouldn't take them back. She locked her knees to keep herself upright.

The man's jaw clenched again but he nodded and turned away from the door.

It was done, and there was no turning back now.

oan scowled the whole way to the theatre, her awareness spread for any threat or danger, and comb still thoroughly entangled in her unruly hair. Every so often James would glance at her and burst into guffaws again.

"You need to be vigilant," she sneered at him, "instead of laughing at my misery."

James snorted. "How am I supposed to pay attention to impending doom when you look so ridiculous?"

Joan swatted at him but kept alert. The walk from their home in Cheapside to the playhouse in Southwark never felt as long as it did that day. Nor had the streets felt so crowded and so narrow. Everyone they passed stared at her, taking in the snarled mess of her hair and the wooden comb flopping along with each step. Too many of them glowed in that telltale way that marked them as Fae. Too many of them could mean a fight for their lives.

She struggled to hold every possibility in her head at once and felt an ache creep up along the back of her neck. A loud thump sounded just behind her. Joan spun, swords crashing to the ground as she reached for the shrunken blade wrapped around her wrist.

A young man with a sun-scorched red face lay sprawled on the ground. He'd tumbled head over heels after finding Joan's hair more interesting than the loose board jutting up from London Bridge.

Joan relaxed the hand that clutched the shrunken Bia as James snickered. She took a steadying breath, tried to calm her heart. There was no threat, only a boy paying too much mind to someone else's business. She let the sword curl back around her wrist and dropped to the ground to collect the dropped blades.

Part of Joan wished he'd fallen all the way into the stinky river's rushing water.

Actually, all of her wished it.

Gritting her teeth, she wrapped the swords back up in the thick canvas and gathered up the set in her arms again. As if anyone needed more reason to stare at her this morning . . .

"You know you could've worn a cap," James said.

Joan's eyes widened before she glared at him with the full force of her frustration, fury, and embarrassment. "Quiet, you."

He could've at least done her the courtesy of mentioning this most excellent idea before they'd left the house. If her arms hadn't been full of swords, she'd have already punched her brother. She shuffled her fabric-wrapped load, combat foils clanging against each other noisily. Maybe she could get a hand free. She only needed one for a moment.

As soon as he stepped within punching range, he'd feel her wrath.

But the opportunity never presented itself and, when they finally slipped through the backstage door, Nick peered out at them.

"Joan—what—" Nick stared at her, mouth agape.

Joan fervently wished she'd let Burbage and Shakespeare murder her the day before.

Anything to have been spared this moment.

Rob gave Joan a once over from where he stood just behind Nick. "Well, this is a . . . choice. Maybe use a comb with wider teeth next time? It's what I do with my hair." He ran a hand over his head of thick, luxuriant curls and grinned at Joan.

"Don't you have costumes to prepare, Apprentice?" She swung at him but he danced out of reach, laughing heartily.

She'd get him later.

Nick reached for the comb, then stopped himself short. "Sorry. May I? Perhaps I can—"

Joan nodded and he leaned over her, his lips pursed in a focused pout. His hands were gentle as he pulled and prodded.

She'd imagined Nick asking to touch her hair then running his hands through the soft strands and sighing at how they felt like so much velvet.

"It's like the harder I try, the worse it gets." Nick huffed and leaned away. "Sorry, Joan."

"Now this isn't a scene I expected to happen upon." Samuel said as he walked up behind Nick. "James, perhaps these two would like some privacy?" His expression shifted. "It's a wonder you didn't ask your own brother to help with such an intimate task."

Joan felt her face burning as she struggled not to make eye contact with anyone.

James grabbed her shoulders and shifted himself between Joan and Nick and Samuel. "She's trying a new hair technique, something people with straight hair like you both wouldn't understand."

Samuel snorted out a laugh as Nick flushed, looking ashamed. Joan opened her mouth to tell Nick it was fine. That he could touch her hair whenever he liked. He could touch more, if he so chose.

But Samuel would never give her a moment's peace over such a confession. She clamped her mouth shut as James pushed her past both boys and into the darkness.

"Of all the people to run into when I'm looking like this," Joan said. "I want to die."

"It's not that bad—" said James. "It looks like—"

Joan snarled, "Don't say another word."

She jerked away from James, trying to keep her head held high despite feeling the weight of the comb clanging against her scalp. She spotted Burbage descending the stairs backstage and made straight for him. His grin nearly split his face when she caught up to him.

"An interesting hair accessory you have there, Sands," Burbage said.

Joan huffed out a breath and thrust the wrapped bundle of swords out at him.

He leaned back on his heels, ignoring her offered parcel. "Is this a new thing the young women are trying?"

She stared at him, still holding the set of swords out with arms fully extended, and deeply regretted saving his life the day before.

"Should I take note"—he snorted before continuing—"for when I next play my Hamlet?"

Joan scowled and let the swords topple over her palms. Burbage snatched them up before they could hit the ground.

He frowned at her. "Come now, lass. There's no need for that. What's wrong?"

"Burbage, we need to get started soon," Phillips said, coming down the hall.

Joan's shoulders tensed as the old man approached them.

"In a moment, Augustine. My young Mistress Sands is in a foul mood and I've a mind to repair what vexes her."

She felt Phillips stop at her side and turned to look up at him. The old man ran his eyes over her hair and let out a deep sigh.

"Let me talk to the girl, Richard. You've no delicacy in situations such as this."

Burbage squinted at Phillips before glancing back at Joan. "Is that all right with you, lass?"

Joan nodded, only flinching a bit when the comb's handle banged against her skull.

She hated this. Hated it so, so much.

"Fine." Burbage tucked the bundle of foils under one arm. "Don't let old Augustine boss you around, lass. That's my job." He laughed his booming laugh at both of them and strode off down the hall. "Gentlemen, I bring our blades, courtesy of Mistress Sands. Take care."

The company's cheers echoed through the tiring-house.

"There's no swords in this one, Richard," Shakespeare shouted. "Don't give those out! Lowin, put that back!"

Phillips snorted at the commotion. Some days, he seemed the only one of the sharers with any sense of decorum. Not that it gave him any more ownership of the acting company than Shakespeare or Burbage held.

Joan chuckled to herself and shook her head. The handle of the comb smacked her in the eye.

"Shite!" Joan blinked hard and stared at Phillips through her one good eye.

"I assume hair this curly knots rather easily," the old Fae said.

Joan frowned. "It does, but never like this."

His indulgent look said he didn't believe her. Joan did her best to ignore it.

"I can't get this out," she said pointing to the comb wrapped up in her hair. She sounded like a petulant child but at this point she didn't care. She looked horrendous, and no one would take her seriously like this. She suddenly thought of having to meet Rose later this afternoon looking like a wild woman and her heart sank.

She'd look an ass in front of both Nick and Rose. She covered her face with her hands, trying to shove the tears back into her eyes with her palms.

The errant comb banged against her skull again.

The corner of Phillips's mouth lifted in the smallest of smiles. "I would imagine you couldn't," he said. "Not with that many faerie knots in your hair. They snarl even the loveliest of hair."

Joan bit her lip to stop herself from shouting in Phillips's face that her hair was in fact lovely. Conversations with him were always so exhausting.

Joan shook her head, flinching as the comb smacked her. "Faerie knots? So this is Fae doing?"

"Of course. Pixies love wreaking such minor havoc." He reached out a hand to touch the tangled curls and Joan instinctively leaned out of his reach. He pulled back, startled. She huffed out another breath and stared him down.

"Do you want this out of your mess of hair or not?"

Joan gritted her teeth and nodded, letting Phillips take hold of her hair.

She felt relief from the pressure on her scalp as Phillips worked his hands through her hair. Occasionally he'd pull a little too hard, but she again kept silent so he wouldn't stop. A little pain was a light price to pay to not look like a wild woman. Finally something gave, followed by a sudden lightness. Phillips placed the comb in her hands but kept working his fingers through her hair. Joan clenched her back teeth and let him keep going.

"Done," he finally said taking a step back. "It's much softer than I imagined it would be."

"Well it is hair, not fur." The words escaped Joan's mouth before she could stop them. She clanged her teeth together to stop any more insubordinate words from tumbling out.

Phillips stared at her for a long moment. "True."

Joan pursed her lips.

They both stood silently in the hall. Joan turned the comb over in her hands.

She looked up. "Than—"

"Don't." Phillips scowled and held up a hand. "Those words are admission to a debt owed and my kind will always collect on a debt. Be careful who you say that to."

"Yes, sir." Joan clenched the comb in her hands and bit her lip. "We were attacked by a swarm of pixies last night and then this with my hair this morning. It feels so childish."

"You are being toyed with, my girl." His white mustache twitched. "I'm on first."

"I fought a jack-in-irons last night," Joan blurted.

Phillips's face went white, his full attention on her again. "Zounds, girl, have you no sense of preservation? First Auberon and now his jack-in-irons? You're lucky you weren't strangled in your sleep."

"But—"

"Stay clear of Fae matters before you end up dead or worse."

He walked away from her then, signaling the end of the conversation. Joan scowled after him.

"Who knows how long I'll bear these petty inconveniences," she muttered. "I'd rather just fight outright."

"Fight what outright?"

Joan jumped and turned around to see Nick standing behind her. "Nick! Shouldn't you be onstage?" She placed a hand over her chest to calm her racing heart.

"I've come to see you." His lips quirked up on one side. "Is that not allowed?"

Joan's face exploded in heat. "Ah—yes—I—you—the scenes—"

He chuckled and stepped in close to her. "Who are you thinking of fighting and dirtying these lovely hands?"

Joan frowned. Nick snagged one of her hands in his and brought her wrist to his lips. He laid a gentle kiss along her pulse as their eyes met.

A chill shot through Joan's body straight to the back of her neck. Something in Nick's gaze was off. She snatched her hand away and stumbled backward. "Who—who are you?"

"Who are you looking at?" Not-Nick laughed and held both arms out.

"What but to speak of would offend again." Nick's real voice echoed down from the stage. Where the actual Nick was performing.

Something else was wearing Nick's form. Joan felt panic rising in her chest—this false form didn't glow.

Not-Nick pouted. "What inconvenient timing."

Joan scowled. "The truth, whatever you are."

"You need not know us—yet." Not-Nick's face twisted into a snarl. "Was that a promise, mortal? Will you truly fight those who'd harm you?"

Joan bristled. That familiar dull ache of Ogun's presence filled her chest.

Whoever, whatever this was with Nick's face was dangerous. She felt the threat rolling off them in waves.

It only made Joan angrier.

"If I'm challenged then I have no choice but to answer it," she said feeling the rage in her belly lighting fire behind her words. "I am no coward, I."

The creature pretending to be Nick laughed, a sharp edge cutting beneath the familiar sound. Joan clenched her fists.

A ripple floated over Nick's skin and his form seemed to melt away. A nude woman stood in his place, her brown skin glowing golden in the candlelight and her head bald.

Joan's face exploded with heat at the sight of the woman's ample curves. She'd never seen a naked body beyond her own. This woman was—Joan's eyes slid to a spot beyond the woman's head. Suddenly, her opponent disappeared from the edge of her vision. Joan jumped to attention.

A hand grabbed a fistful of Joan's hair and yanked her head back. Another wrapped around her throat, choking off her air.

"Never look away from your enemy, girl." The woman jerked Joan's face around and smiled at her, a row of perfect white teeth behind plump red lips set in an alarmingly familiar face. "I thought you'd at least know that."

This was the Fae from the Banqueting House, the one who had seen Baba Ben arrested. However quick Joan's glimpse of her had been, the memory of her was burned into Joan's mind.

Joan gasped for air and tugged at the Fae's arm. It was like trying to move stone. Black spots were starting to creep in around the edge of her vision.

Joan struggled to calm her mind. Cold rushed through her body as iron slid out over her palm. Joan touched it to the Fae's wrist.

There was a sound like sizzling meat and the Fae shrieked and pulled away. The skin on her arm blistered and smoked in the exact shape of Joan's palm, a wound they both knew would never heal.

Joan stumbled forward, gulping as much air into empty lungs as she could.

They stared at each other, but Joan struck first, swinging out with her iron-covered hand. Her head buzzed.

The metal surged into a deadly point, sweeping toward the Fae's exposed neck.

The Fae leaned backward. Joan's wild swing arced just above the tip of her nose. She snatched Joan's arm as it passed her and jerked her down, kneeing Joan in the ribs.

"So young you are." She smiled. "Young and foolish. But brave. It's been many seasons since we met one like you. We shall enjoy this."

The Fae faded away into nothing, leaving Joan alone in the hall, gasping for breath.

"Let mine own judgment pattern out my death, / And nothing come in partial. Sir, he must die."

Joan heard Burbage's voice echo down from where the men practiced onstage, none the wiser to their uninvited visitor. She ran her fingers along the place where Bia looped around her wrist.

Bia hummed at her touch, ready for battle.

There hadn't even been time to draw the blade.

She couldn't let that happen again.

CHAPTER THIRTEEN
Cyril Bendell and the Faerie Ring

yril Bendell needed only three more pennies before he'd be able to afford a sweet and a meal this evening.

Of course, he could always get the meal without the sweet. But where was the fun in that after a hard day's labor?

"Dannell"—he shoved his elbow into his work fellow's side—"got three pence for me?"

Dannell scowled and swatted Cyril's arm away. "I've naught for thee, boy. Where's my five pence from a fortnight past?"

"I suppose your five is with the pound I gave you—what's it been now—a month past?"

Dannell flushed and dug through the pockets in his coat. He dropped the three pennies in Cyril's hand with a grunt and mumbled as he shuffled away.

Cyril clutched the coins tightly. "I'll tally this against your debt, friend." He laughed as Dannell scuttled away down the limestone road.

Dannell never willingly paid back money owed, but Cyril wasn't one to drive a man to poverty over a debt. He'd watched his mother waste away while his father rotted in debtors' prison. They'd died within days of each other, leaving him to mourn as one soul called the next up to heaven.

Dannell could give over his debt a penny at a time before Cyril'd damn him to the Clink. No child should be forced into working off their parents' debts. The burden weighed on the mind, body, and heart.

He wondered what he'd feel like without the load. What it'd be like to be sixteen with both parents healthy and well. With any family at all.

Cyril crossed himself and kissed the fist clutching his money. Enough lingering upon melancholy memories.

To the alehouse!

He froze.

A young man stood off in the distance, his skin the same sun-caressed brown as Cyril's own. And by the Virgin Mary's blessed milk, he was beautiful.

Cyril cleared his suddenly dry throat. He had to speak to this vision, this angel in human form.

"Hello," the stranger said, his voice like music in Cyril's ears. The light caught on the stones and metal decorating his long ropes of hair.

Cyril hadn't noticed closing the distance between the two of them, but here they were face-to-face. This close, he could see they were about the same age.

Cyril extended his hand. "I'm Cyril, Cyril Bendell."

A smile bloomed across the young man's face. He clasped his hand around Cyril's, his wide palm and long fingers making Cyril's look dainty by comparison.

Cyril nearly swooned.

"Come along, then," the man said.

Cyril froze and dug in his heels. "Along where?"

The young man smiled again and pointed over to a circle of people dancing and laughing with abandon.

Cyril felt something inside him unclench. This was nothing menacing, just some small street fair. He barked out a laugh and let himself be dragged along.

Music blared as they crept closer to the action—horns and strings and drums all joined in a melody that should've been discordant but blended into smooth harmonies. The young man turned back again to smile at Cyril as they stepped over an odd line of mushrooms growing out of the packed dirt of the small street.

Two dancers snatched up Cyril's hands and swung him into the crowd. A hip bumped his. Someone spun him in a dizzying circle. He crashed back-to-back with a woman. She grinned over her shoulder at him and swayed from side to side, using her body to guide his with the movement. Hands on his again tugging him forward and into a man's burly embrace. Weightlessness as the man tossed Cyril into the air, caught him, and set him on his feet again. Cyril stumbled. A boy and a girl locked elbows with him on each side and danced him along sideways.

The boy let go. The girl spun Cyril in and shoved her chest against his, launching him back into the writhing crowd. He tripped over suddenly slow feet.

He was exhausted even though he'd only been among the dancers for a few moments.

Hands grabbed Cyril's just under his shoulders. He looked up. The beautiful young man from earlier smiled down at him. He heaved Cyril upright and into a stately pavane. The echoing music slowed to match the tempo of the dance. Cyril huffed and puffed, his breath coming fast now that he wasn't being tossed about like a leaf in the wind.

"What—" He took a deep gulp of air. "What's your name?"

The man smiled, not missing a step of the dance. "Auberon."

"'Tis an odd name."

"'Tis mine." Auberon yawned, sudden and wide. "I tire of these revels. Let us be gone."

Everything, music and dancers alike, stopped as one.

Auberon dropped Cyril's hand. "Farewell, mortal." He smiled and shoved Cyril away, his strength far greater than his slim frame suggested.

Cyril slammed into the ground, bright light flashing behind his closed eyelids. A cacophony of strange noises rushed into his ears. He grunted and opened his eyes.

His heart thumped heavily in his chest.

Glass structures surrounded him on all sides, towering over him like great sentinels. People in odd garments came and went through delicate-looking doors stuck into a wall made of the same fragile material.

Where was he?

This—this couldn't be London. Where were the shops? The houses? The steady odor of the Thames?

This had to be some dream.

He blinked and shook his head. But nothing changed.

He stood, staring at the glass structure in front of him. He let his eyes follow its sharp lines.

It flowed up, up, up. Stretched higher and higher until it stabbed into the very sky. It could be nothing but the seat of God himself. He stumbled backward, squinting as he tried to take in its peak. All around him the world screeched and hummed and shouted.

What dream was this?

Cyril's mouth opened and closed without sound. His mind raced. Where was his city? How had he ended up here?

Nothing made sense. He spun and ran. Tripped out onto a wide, black expanse he expected to swallow him up like tar. Something raced past him, blaring out a loud cry. The sound came at him again as a monstrous metal thing sped straight at him.

Arms wrapped around him and pulled him backward.

"Shit!"

The beast continued on through where he had stood without stopping.

A boy spun Cyril around, his hands patting Cyril down and straightening his clothes. "You good, bruv? You nearly died." His skin was a deep, rich dark brown and a luxurious purple jacket hung from his slim shoulders.

"Am I not yet dead?" Cyril murmured. "And here in hell or dreaming?"

"London can be shit"—the boy snorted—"but this sure ain't hell. Unless you're on the Central Line at rush."

Cyril jerked. London? This couldn't be London—

He remembered then. The beautiful young man—Auberon, he'd said his name was—the dancers, the mushrooms . . .

Cyril's knees buckled. A faerie ring. He'd fallen victim to one, had let a pretty face dance him right through a circle of mushrooms without a thought.

How many years had he spent dancing with the Fae?

The boy frowned and looked Cyril up and down. "You in a play or something?"

Cyril's head hurt.

CHAPTER FOURTEEN
With Two Evils

eems we had less of an audience today." James said, his script pages safely bound in his bag, as he slipped out the door and fell into step alongside Joan.

The groundlings had been sparsely spread out in the dirt around the stage, leaving great empty spaces where there was usually barely room to breathe. The glow of Fae, however, had increased once again, though Joan couldn't be sure if it there were more of them, or if it only seemed so because of the smaller crowd.

Measure for Measure never drew the largest audience. The story of a public official using his power to bully a novitiate into having sex with him had a distinct lack of sword fights. Besides, said public official never got punished in the end, and Joan was sure she wasn't the only person who hated that non-resolution.

Joan never understood why Shakespeare wrote such a powerful, persuasive speaker in Isabella, and then kept her silent at the end of the play. He should've let the novice announce that she was returning to her convent instead of receiving a marriage proposal from the duke without a word.

But that was merely her opinion.

The gallery had been just as full as always, but the lack of groundlings still bore some consideration. And after her earlier confrontation . . .

Joan kept an eye out.

Anything could happen. So much already had.

Her fingers traced along Bia where the sword hung round her wrist. She wouldn't be caught off guard again.

She and James made their way through the streets to their meeting place just beyond the Clink, the cries of prisoners begging for alms carrying across the wind to them. She slipped coins into as many reaching hands as she could as she passed, saw James doing the same just ahead. The sounds of desperation always dug deep and took hold in her heart.

Joan wished the place would collapse into dust every time she saw its stone walls. People who couldn't pay debts deserved better than a grim half existence confined by prison walls.

But that fight lay well beyond her abilities, though she wished it wasn't. Her hands twitched. She could bring down the prison's bars, send them melting away with a flick of her wrist. But what then? Watch the prisoners escape only to see them rounded up and locked away somewhere else?

James gently clasped her elbow and drew her away. Joan nodded and shook herself. Now wasn't the time. They were walking into who knows what sort of danger and she needed to focus. Which reminded her—

She pulled the crimson sachet from the purse hanging at her waist and dropped it just as they crossed the small street that ran alongside the prison. She wasn't sure what intentions her mother had placed on it, but Joan fully trusted it to work.

She only wished it had done something to calm her. She ran her fingers along Bia, the sword's anxious vibrations soothing her frayed nerves even as the thought of the sachet sent them spiraling again.

Then she spotted Rose, her head of curly black hair standing out in the distance. The tall girl darted through the crowds along the road, disappearing and reappearing in quick flashes.

Joan watched her approach. Rose moved gracefully, slipping around to avoid people who took special notice of her and shouldering past those who pretended she didn't even exist. She still wore the cloak James had loaned her; the heavy fabric wrapped around her shoulders hung short on her tall frame. She danced up to James, her smile widening when she saw Joan.

Joan felt her lips moving to match without even thinking it. She brushed her hands against her skirts, realized what she was doing, and froze the gesture halfway through.

"Well, if it isn't my favorite twins," Rose said. She gestured down Long Southwark, the main road leading away from the river. "Shall we?" She started off, then turned again, looking directly at Joan, her cheeks a rosy pink. "I like what you've done with your hair today."

Joan touched the complicated series of interlocking loops she'd done after spending her hours at the theatre sullenly twisting her hair. She'd hoped Rose would like it, but hearing the girl say it outright was . . .

She flushed. "Thank you."

"Enough, enough," James said. "Let's see to Rose's problem and then I'll give you two some privacy." He tightened the ties on his satchel and gestured for both girls to follow.

Joan groaned, ready to apologize to Rose for James's forwardness.

"Shall we hold him to that?" Rose said, gazing directly into Joan's eyes.

Joan felt her stomach flip even as the slow smile spread across her face. "Of course, it's only fair."

This time, Rose turned bright red and tugged at a curly chunk of hair. Joan found her rosy-cheeked embarrassment quite cute but kept that to herself.

A breeze swept up off the Thames and slid along the back of Joan's neck. Like a touch. She jumped and skittered forward a few steps, then jerked around to look behind her.

The small stretch of pathway was empty and nothing of the odd gust lingered but the stench of the river.

"You all right?" Rose said, reaching out to touch her shoulder.

Joan shivered but nodded. That awareness of Ogun's presence rose in her chest.

She took a deep breath, tried to press it down.

It didn't help.

It was just as it had been the day before in the theatre.

Someone was watching her.

Whether it was the Fae from earlier or Auberon or someone else completely, she couldn't be sure. Entirely too many had made attempts on her life in the past two days.

Joan hated it.

James stood farther down the road frowning, then doubled back to stand next to Joan. He wrapped her hands around his arm and tucked her in close along his side. She felt the tension in James's muscles.

They were both on edge. He must've felt it too.

Rose spun around ahead of them, walking backward as she talked. "Did you hear about the ferry accidents this morning? Made getting cross the Thames much harder today."

Joan glanced at James and he frowned back at her.

"No," Joan said, "we heard nothing of this."

"Some number of boats sank this morning and nearly all the passengers were lost." Rose shrugged. "No one knows why it happened."

"They must've hit something in the river," James said.

"Could have—but some say it was a thing like a horse that tipped the boats and ate all the people."

Bia hummed against her wrist, but the feeling was no longer calming.

Joan's heart skipped a beat. Yes, people lost boats and lives shooting the bridge, but unlike trying to sail between the pillars of London Bridge, the rest of the Thames posed no such danger.

It was the Fae—it had to be.

James stopped walking, glanced at Joan before looking back to Rose. "You believe that?"

Rose shrugged. "People say all sorts of things to explain away terrible happenings. Doesn't make it true."

"What do you think happened?" Joan asked.

"Doesn't matter what I think. I'm just some street chuck who wasn't there; my opinion means nothing."

Joan scowled. "You know better than most what really goes on in this city. So your opinion means a great deal to me. Truly."

Rose looked at Joan for a long moment, her cheeks flushing pink. "So it does."

Joan felt her own cheeks heat up under the other girl's scrutiny.

Rose hummed as her eyes darted away. "It'll sound strange, but the regulars haven't turned up."

"With this chill I'm not surprised," James says.

The air changed. Joan felt it, the shift and press of malevolence against her skin. The scent of something otherworldly floated beneath the usual stench of too many human bodies in proximity.

Bia vibrated at her wrist

Joan let James and Rose take the lead and softened her awareness to take in more of their surroundings. The street here was wide enough for several people to pass together, so an ambush was unlikely.

Still.

Joan touched Bia, letting the feeling of cold steel calm her mind.

"No," Rose said, "there's at least one man who comes faithfully. Some have two who will spite the weather for a night. Now they've all just . . . stopped."

They rounded a corner and came out into a wide, empty courtyard.

James chuckled. "Well, it seems that there are things even sex won't convince a man to risk."

Joan shaped her mouth into a laugh and forced the sound from her lips. It sounded like a bark, loud and harsh. She didn't care.

Something was close.

"Rose, is that you?"

There.

Joan, James, and Rose all turned as someone stepped out of the alleyway just beyond them.

Joan felt her blood run cold as the person came into view.

Rose huffed out a breath. "Christabell, where have you been? You had us worried sick."

"Who are your friends?" the creature replied. Whatever stepped out into the open was female, but definitely not human.

Fae. One with a glamour weak enough for Joan to see right through to its true form, just like the monstrosity they'd encountered the night before. But Joan had never seen a thing that looked like this.

Luminous red eyes peered out from a long face. Her thin lips spread nearly ear to ear to expose a mouth full of sharp, pointed teeth. Bright, oily, crimson hair hung around wide, bony shoulders limp and dripping. Her knuckles dragged along the ground even as she stood upright.

Had this thing been released by the broken Pact?

"What is that?" James whispered to Joan.

Joan shook her head. "Fae?"

"No, do you think?"

Joan nearly rebuked her brother until she saw the look he shot her way. She instead clamped her mouth shut.

"Christabell!" Rose smiled at the creature, "I brought these two to help."

Joan decided then she wouldn't let this creature drag Rose down to the same dismal fate as the woman it was pretending to be. She'd protect the other girl with everything in her power.

Shiny red eyes stared straight at them.

"This is not your friend, Rose," James said.

That's right. Where Joan and James saw the monster through the magic disguise, Rose would just see her human friend. She wouldn't know the danger.

Joan gave James the barest of nods and he stepped toward Rose. Joan eased around the other way, keeping her eyes on the creature as she moved.

"What do you mean?" Rose asked.

"This is why your friends and customers haven't returned," James said.

Joan felt a rage building. It blended with the heat of Ogun in her chest, too strong to calm this time. She felt it blaze forth.

"You've terrorized these women long enough, beast," Joan said, her voice deep and masculine as Ogun's words fell from her lips. "We'll see that you answer for that."

Her chest ached. She took a deep breath and tried to press the Orisha back down.

"Oh, you see her for what she is." Rose laughed. "Hear that, red cap," she said, "they can see through your glamour. They know your true shape."

James and Joan froze.

"You can see her true?" Joan whispered.

"Aye," Rose said, "as true as you do."

What?

"Traitor," the red cap sneered. "Oath breaker!"

Joan felt sick. "Are we betrayed?"

"I—" James held his hands out.

"No," Rose said. "She wears the blood of the women I called sisters. I owe the beast none of my loyalty."

Something prickled along Joan's skin. The sudden release of magic.

The red cap tilted her thin head to the side and smiled at Rose, wide and sharp. "You can join those mortals you love so much, hob-child." She dove.

Joan threw herself against Rose and braced as they slammed into the ground.

The creature sailed over them, claws gouging deep scratches into the dirt road as she landed behnd them. Joan rolled into a crouch and scrambled in front of Rose, sweeping her skirt clear of her feet.

"Kill her," Rose spat. "Chop off her head and don't let her wound you."

James shouted, and Joan's eyes darted toward her brother.

James danced around the red cap's wild swings. Each one came fast, nearly as soon as James moved.

Joan's heart thumped in her chest.

He couldn't keep this up. She had to save him.

"She's the red cap chieftain," Rose said, "so she's the strongest of her clan."

James stumbled and the red cap sprang toward him, jaw unhinged in a horrific scream.

No.

She couldn't reach him in time.

No!

The word burst through Joan's head like a shout. She threw her hand out, flinging a half-formed blade through the air.

The red cap shrieked as it hit and buried itself in her back.

James rolled to the side and grunted as the red cap's claws caught him along the arm. He staggered to his feet. Four large tears gaped in his sleeve, but there was no blood.

Still, that was the opening Joan needed.

More—

Joan ran at the beast as Bia sprang into her grip. She swung hard and missed, leaving herself open for an attack. Claws swept in and Joan knocked them away with the flat of her blade.

More—

The coolness of metal rushed out over Joan's fist, flowing over the sword. She swung her arm backward; felt bone shift beneath the blow as the heavy pommel of her sword smashed into the red cap's jaw.

Joan spun, blade held out ready to defend or strike.

The creature curled in on itself, keening horrendously.

Joan glanced back at Rose. The girl crouched against the wall, wide eyes locked on the red cap.

"You think you can kill me with your cold iron?" The gurgling voice pulled Joan's attention back to her opponent.

The red cap no longer sounded human, and it was clear why. Her mouth looked as if it'd been burned away, its teeth left exposed in a grotesque skeletal grimace.

"But you've brought me new blood," the red cap said. "Strong blood."

James cried out. He looked at Joan, his face pale and wet with sweat, and collapsed.

"What did you do to him?"

More.

Something screamed in Joan's head. Her brain felt too thick.

The red cap laughed. "Worry not, his essence is put to good use." She grinned as her skin knit itself back together.

Joan locked eyes with the creature, its vaguely human face stretched too thin across a large skull. The hair wasn't slick with oil but glistened with fresh blood, crimson droplets dripped to the ground as the strands were suddenly drenched in red.

The red of James's blood.

This was why her brother's wound remained dry despite its depth. This was red cap's power, a magic that strengthened the creature as it dragged James closer to death.

Joan needed to end this fight. Now. She dove forward, kept her first swing of Bia close and tight.

It missed, and she pulled her arm back then surged forward, slamming the guard against the red cap's chest.

The metal hissed when it touched white flesh, and the creature stumbled backward, startled and off-balance.

Joan's focus drifted . . . then nothing. She was surrounded by dark emptiness.

It was happening again. Ogun had overtaken her. Joan shoved against the pressure of the Orisha's presence with all her might and felt her awareness return to her body.

She held her knee against the red cap's back as her other foot pressed against its shoulder blades, holding it facedown in the dirt. One hand tangled in the bloody mass of hair and yanked its head back. Bia's blade—covered in a silvery sheen of iron—dug into the exposed throat.

Joan felt a moment of resistance. She grunted, throwing her weight behind the cut.

Flesh and bone yielded to the blade.

The red cap's severed head came away in Joan's hand and she tossed it over her shoulder. It hit the packed dirt walkway with a damp thump as blood surged out of the gaping neck.

Joan felt the warmth as the crimson fluid splattered over her face and clothes. Something like joy bubbled up inside her.

Good.

Someone called her name.

The world tilted and her knees buckled.

"I got you." Rose's arms wrapped around Joan as she fell. She eased both of them to the ground.

Joan lifted Bia. Blood, almost too red to be real, glistened wetly on the blade. She let go of the sword but the hilt stayed fixed to her palm. The blood sank into the metal of the blade, as if it was drinking, before the iron covering the sword seemed to melt and rush back into her hand.

Her heart still raced with excitement. Joan felt sick.

She glanced over at the headless torso, oozing red into the dirt, severed head lying just beside it.

She had done that.

"Joan—" James called.

She looked up. Her brother slowly pushed himself up onto his knees, hand clutching the open wound on his arm when it suddenly started gushing blood.

"That can't be good," James mumbled. "I really liked this shirt too."

Joan cried out and shoved herself out of Rose's arms.

She rushed to James, knees hitting the dirt hard as she dropped down beside him. There was so much blood, the red running over James's fingers. She needed to stop the bleeding.

"Hold still," she said. She tugged at his ruined sleeve, ripping it loose and using it to bind his wound.

"Joan, you're covered in blood."

She ignored him, tying the fabric tightly around his arm. "We need to get home." Her hands shook.

"How did you—"

"We need to get you home to Father *now*."

She looked up and her burning eyes met James's. She felt the tears fighting to fall, sniffled against the pressure of them in her nose.

His expression changed and he nodded. Joan let her gaze skitter away, fixing it on a point over his shoulder as she helped him up.

"That's a good idea," Rose said. "We should leave before more show."

They both turned to look at Rose who stood staring down at the body as it turned to black goop and melted into the ground.

"You killed the chieftain," she said, "and once the rest realize that, they'll come to avenge her."

Killed.

The thrill of the act filled Joan again and her stomach turned.

"And suddenly the mystery is so much less mysterious," James said. His injured arm hung limply at his side. "Excellent. You'll come along and explain all of this to our parents."

Rose paled. "I—"

"Joan just saved your life, both our lives. You owe her."

She turned to Joan, her eyes wide and pleading for something.

Joan looked away. She didn't have the fortitude to figure out what the other girl was asking. All she could think about was how she had killed. Of blood and the grind of metal cutting through bone.

And how good it had felt.

She swallowed, forcing down the push of bile in her throat.

Something in Rose's expression softened before she nodded. She walked toward James, but Joan slipped her shoulder under her brother's good arm before Rose could reach them.

"Come along." James smiled at Joan, leaning heavily on her shoulder. "Our parents will know what to make of all this."

Joan clutched him back and prayed that they would.

CHAPTER FIFTEEN
A Conference, A Confederacy

ell me again because I'm sure I misheard you," Mrs. Sands said. "Who were you fighting in Southwark after I plainly asked you and your brother to stay out of this?"

"A red cap," James said, his voice hoarse and tired. He lay across the top of their father's desk as Mr. Sands spread a salve on his wounds. "Joan killed the chieftain."

"Patients don't talk," Mrs. Sands scolded, and James clamped his mouth shut.

Joan wished she could somehow be swallowed by the hard cushions of the settee. Anything rather than face her mother's wrath. She tucked her shaking hands deeper into the folds of her skirt and stared at James's bloody shirt, tossed in a heap beside the desk.

With their father's care, James was sure to heal fine. As a child of Yemoja—the Orisha of the oceans and motherhood—their father had the ability to control salt water and knew all the secret ways to speed healing. And what he couldn't do himself, the salve he used would handle.

That should've been enough to cheer Joan, but it wasn't.

She had killed, had taken that beast's life as surely as it would have taken all of theirs. That she could make sense of, but the joy she'd felt in the deed . . .

"What do you mean Joan killed the red cap chieftain?" Mr. Sands's mild tone gave voice to the words but they echoed through Joan's head like a scream.

She felt her parents' eyes on her. It took everything in her to not turn in their direction. She didn't want to know what they thought of her taking a life.

A sob caught in her throat. She stopped her breath to contain it.

Mrs. Sands crouched in front of her and caught Joan's face gently between her hands.

Joan tried to breathe. Tried to speak. "Mother, I—"

"Hush, love." Mrs. Sands clenched her jaw. "You did what must be done. There's no wrong in that."

The truth of the words rang in the room but didn't reach Joan. She wished she could feel her mother's conviction, but it was all too much. The pressure of Ogun's presence, the weight of metal splitting flesh and bone and sinew, the rush of joy at the spray of the creature's blood . . . it all seemed too heavy a burden to lift with words.

She shook her head and tried to keep going past the crush of it.

"I'm sorry, ma'am," Rose said. She stood in the corner, her posture slumped. "It's my fault they were—"

Mrs. Sands's eyes whipped to Rose so quickly that the girl jumped. "And who are you?"

"That's Rose," James said.

Mrs. Sands held up a hand and James immediately went silent again. "Now, who are you? Or rather, what are you?"

Joan kept her eyes on her lap. Rose had known the danger she'd invited them into that could've ended them all. Rose had known, and she had lied, and Joan didn't know what to feel about that beyond anger.

"I—" Rose shifted in her seat, her eyes darting around the room. "I am but a maid who sought the help of your children."

"What are you?" Mrs. Sands stood.

Rose clenched her jaw. "A maid."

"We'll have no lies here. Are you Fae, girl? Is that why you nearly had my children murdered?"

Joan stared at her mother. "Rose can't be Fae, she doesn't glow." But Joan couldn't be sure even as she said the words.

The woman who'd been there when Baba had been arrested and attacked Joan at the theatre hadn't glowed. And what had that red cap called Rose? Hob-child? Joan's stomach turned.

How many lies had Rose told them?

"Let her answer for herself."

"She's mine." A person appeared in the middle of the room. Pale brown skin stretched firmly over an angular face. Long black eyelashes fanned out around gray eyes. A luxuriant spray of curly white hair tipped with purple exploded from a knot atop their head. A multicolored kirtle draped over their slim form and flowed out into billowing pants.

A person who was clearly Fae but didn't glow.

Joan leapt to her feet, Bia sliding off her wrist and shifting from bracelet to sword again in her grip.

Mrs. Sands held out her arm to stop her daughter. "Your disciple, Robin Goodfellow?"

"No, my child." This person—Robin Goodfellow—barely stood taller than Joan. They smiled, showing off brilliant white teeth. "You know me by sight, mortal?"

Joan's mother didn't back down. "Elegua knows you, and therefore I do too."

"A child of Elegua?" Their eyebrow raised. "Well met."

"Wait." Joan let Bia's point drop to the floor. "What's happening?"

"Zaza, please." Rose turned to Goodfellow, her eyes wide. "The girl saved me from Gorvenal."

Goodfellow jerked. "Gorvenal?" Rage washed across their face. "Then, aye," they said, "we'll answer your questions."

They beckoned Rose over. She glanced at Joan then followed Goodfellow to a corner of the room. The two spoke together but Joan could hear nothing.

"I feel like I can see the family resemblance," James said, his voice still quiet as he peered around their father.

"As can I," Mr. Sands said. "Around the eyes."

"Excellent," Goodfellow said and led Rose to the settee with a hand on her shoulder. Goodfellow then whirled into the center of the room. "I am Robin Goodfellow," they said with a bow. "Or Puck as I am so known by some."

James inhaled sharply and started coughing. "Again—like—in our—*Midsummer*?" He choked out between gasps.

"Oh, you mean the brainless, spineless, diminished version of me written by that mewling, milk-livered playwright?" Goodfellow laughed, the sound completely devoid of any warmth. "You wish I were truly so. Alas, I am far more dangerous."

Joan frowned. "First Auberon and now Puck?"

Goodfellow's eyes whipped to Joan. "You've met Auberon?"

"I— The king of the Fae?" Joan hesitated. "I've . . . met him twice."

"She wounded him too," James wheezed from the desktop. "Is Titania next? Or Mustardseed?"

"Auberon isn't a king," Goodfellow scoffed. "He has power and influence, but we have no kings. That said, you do not want his notice. Although you're unlikely to avoid it seeing how you killed Gorvenal, and the red caps have always aligned themselves with him."

"No, Joan" Rose blurted. "No—you shouldn't cross his path again. He wouldn't dare concern himself with one mortal girl." She looked up at Goodfellow pleadingly.

"That would be true were she a mere mortal girl," Goodfellow said, "but you are all children of the Orisha, yes?"

Joan nodded. She knew what Goodfellow would likely say about Auberon's interest in her but still dreaded it. How many more Fae creatures would she find herself fighting until Baba Ben could complete his ritual?

"Then he and his ilk shall seek to do you more mischief." Goodfellow sighed and ran a hand down their face. "Were the Pact still in place, they'd still be trapped in Faerie. A millennia and a half of truce between mortals and the Fae ended all because your new king took no action to uphold it."

"Mary's milky tits, Joan—"

Mrs. Sands scowled at James. "Language."

"Mother," James whined. "If ever there was reason to curse, this is it. If this pact was so important, why have we never heard of it?" He forced himself upright on the desk, his injured arm cradled in his good one.

"Because you're still too young to know such things," their mother said.

Goodfellow shrugged. "Aye, the Pact was made during the Roman reign to protect you from the most malevolent of Fae. One of your people and her Orisha, Ogun, oversaw its inception."

Joan's eyes widened. She'd known Ogun had brokered the deal but had assumed the Orisha had done so alone, without any mortal assistance. But he'd made the Pact along with one of his chosen then, and he'd need one of them to make things whole once more.

With Baba still missing and she the only other child of Ogun, had repairing the Pact become her responsibility? Perhaps that explained why Ogun's presence was suddenly so much stronger in her, and why he was taking control of her body when he'd never done so before.

But how could she complete a ritual she knew nothing about? And what would that mean for Ogun's power over her?

"Have you found Baba yet?" she asked.

Mrs. Sands scowled and squared her shoulders. "Not yet, but we will." She looked directly at Joan. "And he will help us fix this."

Joan nodded, but she wasn't comforted. The Fae had already put Joan's tiny circle of people in so much danger. Who knew what more was happening beyond her knowledge. The more time that passed, the more harm would come to everyone in this city. And what if the Fae managed to kill Baba Ben before he could renew the Pact? What if they killed her too? There'd be no hope beyond that. She couldn't let them fail.

But what was she to do?

"A family of Orisha children. What a crew you've aligned us with, Rosebud," Goodfellow said smiling. They turned to Joan. "Thank you, Joan, for protecting my daughter."

Rose's gaze jerked to her parent, and Joan's eyes widened,

remembering what Master Phillips had said earlier. "You're thanking me? Doesn't that mean—"

"Thank you," Goodfellow said slowly, "for saving my Rosebud. I am in your debt."

"We are in your debt," Rose said, and smiled her beautiful smile at Joan. Joan found herself smiling back.

"Now, Mother and Father Sands—" Goodfellow grinned.

Mrs. Sands leaned back against the desk. "Bess and Thomas"—her lips quirked up on one side—"please."

"Yes, no need for such formalities between friends." Their father slouched back in his chair and laid his clasped hands on his belly.

Goodfellow quirked an eyebrow. "No need at all. Call me Robin."

Dear Lord, were their parents . . . flirting?

Joan locked eyes with Rose who looked as horrified as she felt.

"And that's enough for us," James said loudly, limping toward the door. "Come, Joan, let us to bed. Rose, shall we see you out?"

The three adults stood close together, and Joan's mother let out a soft giggle.

Yes, time for them to leave.

"Ah—" Rose shook her head. "I have my own way." And then she seemed to disappear into the very air.

Their mother giggled again.

"Would that we could do that," James mumbled.

Joan just rolled her eyes and helped him out the door.

Sometime in the small hours of the night, Joan could hear the three parents singing bawdy songs and making toasts, and she prayed that this didn't bode as ill for their lives as it did for her sleep.

CHAPTER SIXTEEN
One Twin for the Other

oan gripped the knob on her brother's bedroom door, hesitated, then pulled back. James wouldn't be awake at this hour. The sun had barely risen. But still—

She scowled. There was no need to be nervous. James burst into her room all the time.

The door swung open. Joan jumped backward.

"No," James said. "You lurking outside my bedroom isn't creepy at all." His injured arm was strapped to his chest by a sling, and his skin was still a little ashen.

He'd lost so much blood from that wound . . .

Joan tried not to flinch each time the white bandage caught her eye.

He raised an eyebrow. "May I help you?"

"I—" Joan huffed out a breath, suddenly feeling very foolish. "I came to help you get dressed." Maybe she should just go back to her own room . . .

"You can only come in if you stop looking so maudlin."

"But it's my fault you're hurt." Tears burned her eyes.

James shrugged. "Well, my sister saved my life, so why don't you thank her from the both of us?"

Joan sniffled out a wet laugh as James opened the door wider.

"Come on, then. Let's see if you've learned anything from me."

Joan slipped into the room, heading straight for James's wardrobe. She shuffled through his clothes. She could feel the pressure of his eyes on her.

She could do this. It was only picking out clothes. She wasn't doing battle.

Her stomach flipped as she remembered the feel of her blade slicing through flesh and bone, the thrill, and blood, so much blood.

What kind of monster was she to have enjoyed that brutality?

Joan closed her eyes and took a deep breath to settle her nerves and shaking hands. She hoped James didn't notice.

A tan jerkin caught her eye, tucked between a blue one and yellow one. She pulled the garment free and held it out to James with a flourish.

The smile dropped off James's face. "Of course you pick the tan one. You've learned nothing." He raised an eyebrow. "No, I'm absolutely not wearing that. Try again."

"What's wrong with this one?" Joan scowled.

"Try again."

She huffed and turned back to the wardrobe. She'd never understand what her brother had against tan. Hopefully, his aversion wouldn't make them too late for breakfast.

When she pulled out a deep-gray jerkin, James actually screamed.

"The blue one is right there! Why are you like this?"

Joan resisted the urge to throttle her brother because he was injured, but it was a close thing. She reached past the brilliant blue jerkin to grab the dark, nearly black one just to spite him.

She dodged the pillow and comb he threw at her but couldn't hold back her laughter when the gust of wind he sent her way knocked her flat.

Because James was looking more like his usual self and less like he'd collapse at any moment, and that was enough for Joan to feel like she could breathe again.

✝

"You were attacked?"

Joan nodded.

She sat on a stack of boxes backstage in the tiring-house. James leaned beside her, the white bandages stark against his blue jerkin, the picking out of which had, in fact, made them late for breakfast.

Phillips loomed over both of them.

"By a red cap," James said.

"The chieftain," Joan said.

Phillips jerked to attention. "Gorvenal? Damn this bloody broken Pact, letting the likes of her through."

Joan shrugged.

"Well, she's not much to worry about now," James said. "She's dead."

"Dead?" Phillips paled. "How?"

James jabbed a finger in her direction. "Joan did it."

"By God and all the angels, girl."

Joan scowled. "I didn't—I couldn't—" She took a deep steadying breath. "She tried to kill James. How could I stay my blade when my brother's life would be forfeit?"

She said the words just as much for her own hearing as for Phillips's.

He clenched his jaw as his eyes cut to the bandages on James's arm.

"Master Phillips." James pushed himself to his feet. "You can glare at my sister as much as you'd like, and I'll go get ready for today's performance."

"Traitor," Joan hissed.

James stuck his tongue out at her.

"Absolutely not," Phillips said. "You can't use your arm."

Joan sat back. She'd watch her brother attempt to wiggle out of this. Besides, seeing James in trouble took her mind off other, more distressing things.

"Phillips. Sands." Shakespeare slipped through the curtain at the center of the stage. "We're waiting for you to begin rehearsal."

Phillips crossed his arms. "Sands isn't performing today."

"'Tis but a scratch." James shrugged one shoulder.

Joan scowled at him. "Shrug again, with both arms this time."

"You are not helping," James whispered.

"Now you know what that feels like," she whispered back.

"What's happening here?" Burbage burst out through the stage door. "Why aren't you lot ready?"

Joan gestured toward James.

"We've lost our Hermia," Shakespeare wailed.

"What?" Burbage shouted. He finally took a good look at James. "What did you do to your arm, my boy?"

James's mouth opened and closed like a fish.

"Accident," Joan said and left it at that.

"I can still play the part," James shouted. "Hermia doesn't need both arms!"

Joan frowned. "Yes, she does."

"For what? Snuggling with Lysander?"

"For fighting with Helena," Joan said. She banged her heels against the box. "Act three, scene two. *How low am I? I am not yet so low / But that my nails can reach unto thine eyes.'* Then you both fight."

Everyone stared at her.

"Right," James said. "What comes before that?"

Joan frowned. "What do you mean what comes before? The lines?"

James nodded, flapping his hand at her.

"How low am I, thou painted maypole?" she said. *"Speak."*

"My dear Mistress Sands." Shakespeare rubbed his hands together. "Have you this whole part memorized?"

Joan raised an eyebrow. "Aye, the whole play." Her heart leapt into her throat. "No, absolutely not."

Burbage grinned at her. "You know the whole thing, lass, and your brother is out today."

Her heart raced. She wasn't sure if it was from excitement or fear.

Not that it mattered. This could not happen.

"No." Joan scowled at the four men around her.

"You and James are near identical. Perfectly identical once painted and dressed." Shakespeare ran his fingers along his beard, brain already working through the possibilities. "No one will notice the difference."

Joan scrambled to her feet. "I'm a woman, it's illegal for me to be onstage! We could all be arrested."

Phillips snorted. "I wouldn't think you'd be one to back down in the face of a little danger." His lips tugged up into a smile.

Joan wanted to kick him in the chest. With an iron boot.

"What's the commotion?" Nick appeared just over Burbage's shoulder and handed the older man a cap.

"I'm injured so we're convincing Joan to go on as Hermia in my place," James said.

Joan shook her head. "Please tell them how ridiculous this plan is, Nick."

"Wait, you're to be my Hermia today, Joan? That's fantastic!"

All eyes turned to Nick, who flushed bright red.

"I mean—" Nick cleared his throat and fiddled with his long hair. "What a momentous occasion for all of us, yes? To play with Joan."

James raised an eyebrow. Joan's face burned as she tried to look anywhere but directly at Nick.

"Well—if that's all—then, ah, yes I need to go gather my props. I'll see you onstage, Joan." He beat a hasty retreat.

"That's settled then." Burbage laughed and slapped Joan on the back. "Our Mistress Sands will also be our Hermia today."

Shakespeare clapped his hands. "Most excellent. James, give her something to wear and get her onstage for rehearsal."

Her heart raced. She couldn't believe this was happening.

Joan slipped her shaking hands into the folds of her skirt. "Are we sure this is—"

"Men!" Burbage shouted, stomping his way back out onstage. "Prepare yourselves. Rehearsal begins shortly."

Shakespeare wandered off after him, muttering to himself.

"Seems it has been decided, lass." Phillips laid his hand on her shoulder. "You've faced down Gorvenal—this shall be easy. And hopefully less bloody." Then he was gone too.

Joan stood in the dim light trying to catch her breath. Was she tied too tightly? Her hands scrabbled for the strings of her bodice.

"Joan." James laid his hand across hers where her fingers tugged at her laces.

"James, you have to tell them— You have to make them— I—I can't do this."

James laughed. "Don't be foolish. Of course you can." His hand slipped up between her shoulder blades and he shoved, sending her stumbling toward the stairs. "Now, come along. Let's get you into some of my trousers. You're already late for rehearsal."

Joan wiped sweat-soaked hands off on the delicate layers of her borrowed costume. The cream-colored dress—made of at least five layers of gauzy fabric—was gathered at both shoulders before skimming down along her body to just barely brush the floor. Roz had figured out how to hide a bodice beneath it to support her breasts—something her brother never had to worry about.

Her hair had been quickly braided close to her head to better hide it beneath Hermia's wig. The straight black strands were pinned half up and half down. She looked as if she could've stepped off an ancient Greek vase, and it made her feel strange and beautiful.

The rumble of the crowd settled into Joan's chest. Voices raised to shout. Someone laughed heartily.

There were people and Fae out there. Waiting. And in this moment, Joan didn't know which caused her more fear.

Being pushed and pulled through rehearsal by the other actors—her fellow actors—Lord, the room just tilted before her eyes—was one thing in an empty playhouse. Doing the full show in front of an actual paying audience was another matter completely.

Not that she had reason to be so terrified. She knew her lines, had barely stumbled in the rehearsal. Hell, she'd been the one to teach fights to the rest of the players, knew them better than anyone else.

This deep, quivering fear she felt had no logical root.

And yet . . .

She breathed deeply and tiptoed over to the tall wooden doors leading out to the center of the stage. Gently, slowly, she pushed it open by the tiniest of cracks. No one would notice if she took a little peek. Just so the sight of the audience wouldn't surprise her when she first stepped out.

Beyond the wood planks lay a sea of heads. Expectant people, people she'd have to entertain.

People who could never know it wasn't her brother in Hermia's costume.

Her stomach dropped.

"Strange there's a smaller crowd than usual today. People love *Midsummer*."

Joan jerked upright, banging the top of her head against Nick's chin.

"I'm so sorry." She spun around and yanked the curtains closed behind her.

Nick rubbed his jaw and tried to smile down at her. "No apologies needed. I shouldn't have snuck up on you like that. I know how it can feel before your first performance."

Joan choked out a laugh that sounded more like a whimper. Her whole face went hot. "I don't think I can do this."

"Ah, yes. I said those exact words before my first performance. And before my second. And my third, in fact." Nick's face softened, his lopsided smile sliding across his face. "See, you fit right in."

Joan's heart picked up double time.

"And fear not," he said, placing his hands on her shoulders. "You'll be marvelous, and I'll be right there with you."

Joan grimaced. "I'm not my brother."

"Of course not, but that doesn't matter because we all have faith in you." Nick cleared his throat, redness creeping up from the collar of his shirt and over his ears. "And I—I think you're wonderful."

The smile burst across her face before she could control it. "I think you're wonderful too."

"Save it for the stage, you two." James shimmied his way between them and turned to Nick. "Off with thee, Lysander. And see that you take care of my sister."

Nick chuckled. "Of course." He met Joan's eyes over James's shoulder. "You'll be glorious, I know it."

"Thank you, Nick."

"Yes," James said, mimicking Joan's soft tone, "thank you, Nick."

Nick turned to leave then doubled back. "Nearly forgot. Can't break the tradition." He leaned around James and held his hands up to Joan. "For both of us this time."

"For both of us." Joan laughed and smacked her palms against his, right then left, as warmth bloomed in her chest. She suddenly felt a little less unsure.

But only a little. Her hands still shook.

Nick grinned and winked at James then jogged off to the other side of the stage.

James turned, eyebrow raised. "What was that?"

"Just something we do before every show," Joan said. She pursed her lips. "Why?"

"Oh, no reason." He tugged at Joan's costume and wig. "You know, you do look like a prettier version of me."

"Was that ever in doubt?" Joan let herself be primped and tried to calm her breathing.

"He's right, though. You will be marvelous."

Joan smiled at her brother. He gripped her hand in his single good one and squeezed.

"And I'm sure Nick will prefer kissing you instead of me today."

"Kiss?" Joan's whole body went cold then blazed hot.

"PLACES!"

She jumped. All around her, men hustled back and forth getting ready to start the show. Several hands patted her on the back and shoulders as the players passed her and wished her luck.

James raised an eyebrow. "That call was for you too, you know."

"When is there a kiss?"

"Act two, scene two." James grinned at her. "Are you ready?"

Rob and Samuel appeared on either side of her, Rob's grin so wide it looked ready to crack his face. Both boys wore their costumes, though only Samuel wore a man's clothes.

He squeezed Joan's shoulder. "Ready to make James look like an amateur and get your lips on the lovely Nick Tooley?" He puckered his lips at her and Joan swatted him away.

"There was no kiss in rehearsal," Joan blurted.

"Of course not," Rob said adjusting his elaborate gown. "We never rehearse the kisses. 'Tis a simple enough act."

Samuel winked at her. "Would you like a quick lesson before we begin?"

James huffed as Joan barked out a laugh.

"No, thanks." She flicked a finger against his nose. "You can ask your sister about how well I kiss."

They all burst into hushed laughter.

Samuel's smile turned genuine. "The audience'll love you, Joan. I'm sure of it."

She grinned back, feeling slightly better. Then both boys were gone, off to get ready for the start of the show.

The musicians struck up from the balcony above them.

This was it.

Joan felt the tremors start in her knees and creep up her body. "I'm not ready."

"Sounds about right." James laughed and shoved her toward the stage right entrance. "Off you go. Good show!"

CHAPTER SEVENTEEN
By th' Book

I t was like some beast waited beyond the doors. One with a great many heads who liked to throw rotted fruit when displeased.

"Hippolyta, I wooed thee with my sword / And won thy love doing thee injuries," Master Shakespeare—as Theseus, the Duke of Athens—said onstage. Rob stood beside him as Hippolyta, the Amazon Queen, decked out in furs, leather, and an artfully arranged blond wig. The couple flirted, announcing they were four days away from their impending royal wedding.

Joan took a deep breath and adjusted her own brown hairpiece.

It was hot. How did James stand it? She wished she could ask him if only to distract herself from her nerves, but he was already off to watch the show from some hidden vantage.

Was it too late to throw him into costume?

Phillips leaned in close. "Are you ready, child?"

She jerked a little and looked over at him. She managed a nod.

"—with pomp, with triumph—" Shakespeare said.

Samuel slipped up beside her. He caught her gaze and winked, his blue eyes shining in the dimness. Someone patted her on the shoulder. She glanced up and Nick smiled back at her. Phillips gave her an encouraging look and grabbed her wrist in a loose grip.

"—*and with reveling.*"

Their cue.

Phillips charged onstage, dragging her along. She stumbled out behind him, adding an extra misstep to look more reluctant.

She was Hermia—an Athenian girl—being dragged before Duke Theseus by her father. Joan heard the murmur of the crowd as they entered and felt the character's pain.

She blinked rapidly in the bright afternoon sun.

"*Happy be Theseus, our renownèd duke!*" Phillips said, pulling Joan into a bow.

Her knees jerked into a curtsy. Before her, a sea of people watched expectantly. A few leaned on the stage, wide-eyed faces propped up on elbows.

Her heart raced so fast, she thought it would burst.

Phillips tossed her hand away. She flinched and pulled her wrist close to her chest. She looked up at him and he glared back at her. Just as they'd practiced. Just as she'd seen James do dozens of times.

My father is angry with me, Joan thought, reminding herself of Hermia's state, *because I love Lysander and don't want to marry the man he's chosen—Demetrius.*

"*Full of vexation come I, with complaint / Against my child, my daughter Hermia,*" he sneered.

Ah! What would Hermia do?

Joan quickly averted her gaze, letting her eyes skitter down to the ground. She took another deep breath.

She could do this. No turning back now.

"What say you, Hermia?"

She looked up; eyes wide. Everyone watched her. Shakespeare, Phillips, Nick, Samuel, Rob, and thousands of expectant spectators.

Every word she had ever known immediately flew from her brain.

"To whom you are but as a form in wax—"

She clenched her fists, digging her nails into her palm. She was being absurd. She knew these words, this play, and no cluster of strangers would shake her confidence.

She zeroed in on her focus, tuning out everything but the men around her onstage. Where was Master Shakespeare in his speech? What was happening?

"Demetrius is a worthy gentleman," Shakespeare finished.

He'd said it was her father's right to bend her to his will, even with violence. He'd asked what she thought of the man her father had chosen.

She breathed. She answered.

"So is Lysander," she said.

Something inside her seemed to snap into place. Her heart still raced, but she knew.

She had this well-handled.

A held breath seemed to release itself across the stage as the players all relaxed. Joan doubted anyone in the audience noticed.

"In himself he is, but in this kind, wanting your father's voice"— Shakespeare turned his head away from the audience slightly and winked at her—*"the other must be held the worthier."*

"I would my father looked but with my eyes."

"Rather your eyes must with his judgment look."

Joan glanced over at Phillips and saw rage painted across the man's face. She let herself react honestly, flinched and looked away. Just like a girl cowed by her father's anger. But Hermia was determined, and love pushed her past her fear.

"I do entreat your Grace to pardon me. / I know not by what power I am made bold, / Nor how it may concern my modesty in such a presence here to plead my thoughts—" She raised her chin and let her voice ring loud across the playhouse. *"But I beseech your Grace that I may know / The worse that may befall me in this case / If I refuse to wed Demetrius."*

The lines flowed like water. Her actions suited the words. Her hands held steady, the fear a forgotten tremble.

She was here to play, and she would play well.

———✝———

Joan had made it through the first act without a stumble. James had showered her with praises as they waited backstage for her next entrance. The Rude Mechanicals—a group of bumbling actors led by Burbage as the boisterous Nick Bottom—gathered to rehearse a play they planned to perform at Duke Theseus's wedding. Meanwhile, Oberon—Shakespeare playing the fairy king—and Titania—Rob playing the fairy queen—argued over the mortal child in Titania's care. Oberon wanted the human boy as his henchman, but Titania refused as the boy was the orphan child of her dead mortal friend.

Joan had fought down a flinch at every utterance of the name Oberon. Now was not to think on those troubles, of that danger.

Her next scene was upon her. There was only time to act.

Hermia and her love, Lysander, had escaped into the forest outside Athens. The two planned to live with Lysander's aunt, leaving behind Athens, Demetrius, and Hermia's rageful father. But now they found themselves weary and lost in the darkness.

Joan trudged onstage, Nick's heavy footfalls letting her know he followed just behind her.

"Fair love"—Nick rushed to her side and gripped one of her hands—*"you faint with wand'ring in the wood."* He guided her over to sit on the floor near the tall wooden column on the far left of the stage.

She dropped down gracelessly as if she were exhausted and fanned herself with one hand.

"Be it so, Lysander. Find you out a bed." She stretched and spread herself out against the smooth wood pillar. *"For I upon this bank will rest my head."*

Nick slid in close to her, wrapping his arm around her and tugging her into his embrace—Lysander looking to take advantage of being alone in the dark without a chaperone.

Joan couldn't blame him. In this moment she was overwhelmed with Nick.

Her daydreams of being this close to him held not a candle to the reality of it. Her face fit right into the space between his neck and shoulder. She felt his warmth radiating against her skin. Strands of his thick black hair tickled her nose. He smelled of lilacs and leather.

She couldn't help herself. She inhaled deeply, holding it all, his smell, his feel in her memories.

He pulled away; eyes wide as he gazed at her.

Damn. He had noticed.

Why was he quiet? Was he disturbed by her? Too disgusted to speak? Or because it was her line and he was waiting for her to speak. Double damn.

"N—nay, good Lysander," she choked out. Laid a hand against his chest to push him away in opposition to her desires but according to her blocking. *"For my sake, my dear, / Lie further off yet. Do not l-lie not so near."*

Hermia needed Lysander away from her before their passion for each other drove them to do something improper. Joan barely needed to put effort into playing this scene, she understood Hermia's struggles intimately.

His lips spread into a slow smile. *"O, take the sense, sweet, of my innocence! / Love takes the meaning in love's conference."* He slid his hand along her cheek, his other clutching hers against his chest. His gaze traced along her face, lingering on her mouth. *"I mean that my heart unto yours is knit / So that but one heart we can make of it—"*

She felt his heart racing under her palm.

Oh.

"Two bosoms interchainèd with an oath—" He lifted her chin. *"So then two bosoms and a single troth."* He ran his fingers through a curl of her wig. *"Then by your side no bed-room me deny / For lying so, Hermia, I do not lie."*

Lysander's words—his pledge of love, his promise that their love was as true as a wedding vow and could be thus consummated—hit Joan as if they had been Nick's own.

Oh, but if they had been Nick's own, with him so close, surrounded by his scent, held in his arms, Joan would have refused him nothing, her future as a goldsmith be damned.

"Lysander riddles very prettily," she squeaked. She cleared her suddenly dry throat. *"Now much beshrew my manners and my pride / If Hermia meant*

to say Lysander lied." She swallowed, took a deep breath. Forced Hermia's second refusal of closeness past her lips. *"But, gentle friend, for love and courtesy / Lie further off in human modesty."*

Then she remembered the kiss.

The kiss in this scene between her and Nicholas Tooley.

The first time she'd be kissing someone since she'd caught Samuel's sister last year on the steps of the playhouse.

"Such separation—" How often had she of late imagined this moment? Imagined Nick's beautiful brown lips pressing against hers. *"—as may well be said, / Becomes a virtuous bachelor and a maid."*

Would they be as soft as they looked?

Her whole body burned hot. He had to hear her heart pounding against her ribs.

She tried to speak without stuttering. *"S-so far be d-distant; and g-good night, sweet friend."* She wasn't sure she'd ever fought a battle so hard. *"Thy love ne'er alter till thy sweet life end."*

His hand slipped around the back of her neck and pulled her in close. Their eyes met. He stopped; his brows knitted.

He was waiting for her permission because he couldn't be sure if Hermia's refusal mirrored Joan's own and wouldn't push her if it did.

Joan's stomach fluttered. If he knew how much she wanted him, there'd have been no hesitation. A mere word kept their lips from meeting in beautiful, blissful union.

In front of a thousand spectators.

The thought made her bold.

She pressed forward, closed the distance between them, and answered him with a kiss.

Nick moaned and pulled her closer.

She caught his full, lower lip between hers and sighed as he melted into her. The thumb of one hand brushed across her cheek and the other drew circles on her lower back.

Her heart stopped beating. She couldn't think.

Distantly she heard the audience whooping and hollering, but she couldn't be sure.

All she knew was Nick.

Nick's hand cupping her face. Nick's lips on hers. Nick's leg pressed along the length of hers.

She shivered.

He pulled back slowly, then surged in for one more quick brush of lips. His hand flexed against the back of her neck as he drew away. *"Amen, amen' to that fair prayer, say I—"*

Joan's eyes fluttered open. He still watched her and spoke like a man besotted. Breathless and awed.

The look shot straight to her belly. She thought she'd explode into flames in that moment; was sure she would if his gaze stayed on her like that.

"Do you kiss my brother like that?" she whispered as the crowd whooped and cheered.

"No," he said back just as quietly, chest heaving. "No, never like that. I—"

He swallowed. Joan watched the movement of his throat. Her eyes slid up to meet his.

He dragged himself away from her and crossed to his place on the opposite side of the stage. *"Here is my bed. Sleep give thee all his rest!"*

"With half that wish the wisher's eyes be pressed!" she said, Hermia wishing her love the same good night. Joan doubted anyone heard her, she barely had the breath to speak at all.

They lay down facing each other and pretended to sleep. Their eyes met again across the stage as Armin burst out onstage as Puck—who bore no resemblance to the real one Joan now knew—a leafy green crown circling his head. He'd come to do the bidding of his master, Oberon, and anoint the eyes of an Athenian boy with an herb that would make him fall in love with the Athenian girl he'd rebuffed. And Puck was about to stumble upon the wrong pair.

"Through the forest have I gone," Armin wailed.

Nick smiled, his face and the tips of his ears bright red.

"But Athenian found I none."

Joan smiled back, sure her face was equally crimson.

CHAPTER EIGHTEEN
Trouble at the Bear Garden

odge Rhode was used to the bloody business of the Bear Garden; he preferred to witness the brutality of battling beasts to the fluffy business of playmaking.

He had an eye for battle. Could peg the winner of a bout with no problem. He'd racked up enough winning bets to make him as despised as he was admired, especially given his youth.

The jealousy didn't bother him none, but the admiration felt like gold.

"Who we got today, Rodge?"

"Well." Rodge puffed out his chest and lay back along the bench like he was holding court. He felt the rough wood rub against his skin through the hole in his trousers. He ignored it. "Hephaestus's in the ring, so you know who my money's on."

The bear, Hephaestus, had yet to lose a match, be it against any manner of beast. Lion, dog, bull, or another bear would all fall before the beast's might.

Rodge'd never bet against the creature. Never was there a surer win.

"Heard he's goin''gainst a new'un," Garvin mumbled as he hobbled over. His pale pate shined with the memory of hair long gone.

Sykes snorted. "Yeah, a dog." He spat on the floor, the tip of his nose bright red against the rest of his paper-pale face.

"A dog?" Anders coughed out a laugh. He flapped a sunburned, four-fingered hand at the rest. "They puttin' a mangy ol' dog 'gainst Hephaestus?"

Rodge laughed too.

Hephaestus hadn't been defeated in twenty bouts against all manner of great beasts. No dog could break that streak, no matter how fierce.

"You never know, world's full of surprises these days."

Rodge and his crew turned to face the man who'd inserted himself into their gathering. He was tall and slim with a too-pretty face despite the ugly, barely healed scar cutting beneath one eye. He looked to be Black and, by his garments and ornamented hair, more suited for the playhouses than here among blood and battle.

Rodge ran his tongue across the gap where his two front teeth used to be. "You know something, stranger?"

The man smiled and shook his head. Rodge immediately averted his gaze. He could always tell a threat, animal or otherwise. And this man, despite his foppish appearance, was a threat.

"I say we go take a look at this new one," Anders said grinning, "and see what's got this knave making a fuss."

Rodge watched the other men shuffle off.

"Well," the stranger said, "aren't you going too?"

Rodge shook his head and refused to look at the man. "You go along with them, I'm fine right here."

"Oh, I think you should." The man's voice was suddenly very close. "I think you should go right now. With me."

Rodge felt the man's words shiver through his body like an icy touch. His feet moved without his permission, dragging him into step behind the man.

"That's a good lad," he said.

Rodge gritted his teeth and stopped moving. He hated when people called him "lad." At eighteen, he was fully a man, not some sniveling boy.

The other man turned around, rage in his eyes, before he let out an amused sigh.

"I must be out of practice after all this time," he said. "No matter." He stepped in close to Rodge and grabbed his chin. "You won't disobey me again, will you?" he cooed.

His lips caught Rodge's gaze. They looked dewy and soft. He wondered what they'd feel like to kiss. Rodge leaned in, pressing their mouths together quickly. Pulled back.

Rodge felt all the anger leave him as he looked into the man's eyes. Yes, there was no need to disobey him again. He had no idea why he'd even done it in the first place.

Strange.

He fell into step beside the stranger, who sported a wide grin across his face. They made their way through the bowels of the Bear Garden to the holding stalls.

Hephaestus the bear lay on the floor of his cell restrained by the massive chain wrapped around his neck. Hairless patches exposed the scars of battles past all over the beast's body. But that was no matter; he was still the Garden's fiercest competitor.

Rodge spotted his fellows farther down the walk, staring into another stall and falling all over each other in laughter. He approached them, just a step behind the tall stranger.

"Rodge! Rodge!" Garvin shouted. "You see this wee thing that ponce expects to beat Hephaestus?"

The men guffawed again as Rodge felt rage clench his fists. How dare they insult this beautiful gentleman? Such insolence needed to be punished. The man placed a hand on his shoulder and shook his head. The anger dissipated just as quickly as it had risen. Rodge stepped forward to look into the stall for himself.

Inside, a slim black dog glanced up at him from its place on the floor. Pointed ears swiveled around on its head, taking in all the sounds disturbing its rest. Fur so black it seemed to absorb the light fluffed out in all directions. Rodge felt a chill run up his spine.

"I think she has a chance," the stranger said.

The dog's tail wagged when she heard the stranger's voice. It thumped heavily against the floor. Rodge felt it boom in his chest.

Thump. Thump. Thump.

"But since you three find her so disappointing"—the man turned his gaze to Sykes, Garvin, and Anders—"perhaps you want to take a closer look."

Thump-thump-thump-thump. The excited wag of the dog's tail boomed ever faster.

The lads stood up straight. Anders reached forward and the stall padlock fell open in his hand.

Thump-thump-thump-thump-thump.

Anders swung the heavy gate open and walked into the stall right behind Sykes and Garvin.

Thumpthumpthumpthumpthumpthumpthump.

The gate swung closed with a clang, the lock in place as if it had never been touched.

There was a moment of perfect silence. Nothing moved. Nothing breathed.

The dog's first bite tore out Garvin's throat. He dropped to the floor with a gurgle as blood gushed down over his doublet. Sykes and Anders seemed to snap to attention at that and both sprinted back to the locked gate.

The dog was on Anders right as he turned. She grabbed a maw full of his hair and shook. The snap of his neck echoed all around them as his body suddenly went limp.

"Rodge! Rodge!" Sykes clawed at the bars as the wet sounds of a feasting beast raged behind him. "In God's name, boy, open the gate."

Rodge felt the slightest pressure of something. Took a step toward his shrieking friend.

A long-fingered hand held him back.

The stranger smiled at Sykes. "She doesn't look like much, does she?"

The beast growled and Sykes froze, all color draining from his face.

"But she is vicious."

Sykes jerked away from the bars as the beast dragged him back into her cell.

His cries went silent as she feasted.

The stranger suddenly turned to Rodge. He smiled, a harsh, venomous thing, and patted Rodge on the shoulder.

Then he was gone.

And Rodge was alone in a silence somehow louder than his friends' screams.

CHAPTER NINETEEN
'Tis Faerie Time

"I don't remember the kiss in that scene being quite like that," James sang in her ear.

Joan shushed him even as her cheeks blazed as hot as if she were sitting in front of a fire.

"*Good Master Mustardseed, I know your patience well. That same cowardly, giantlike ox-beef hath devoured many a gentleman of your house.*" A donkey-headed man flapped his hands at the gathered fairies. "*I promise you your kindred hath made my eyes water ere now. I desire you of more acquaintance, good Master Mustardseed.*"

The audience roared with laughter as the transformed Bottom—Burbage wearing a donkey headdress to signify the magical change—romanced Rob's Titania. The fairy queen had been dosed with love-in-idleness, a flower that made her fall in love with the first thing she saw. In this case, she first laid eyes on the bumbling weaver-turned-actor who'd been magicked to look like an ass.

Joan peeked out from backstage and grinned along with the audience.

"*Come, wait upon him. Lead him to my bower. / The moon, methinks, looks with a wat'ry eye, / And when she weeps, weeps every little flower, / Lamenting some enforcèd chastity.*" Rob, the cascading blond wig and gauzy gown marking him now as Titania, held up a hand. "*Tie up my lover's tongue. Bring him up silently.*"

Titania's fairies carried her and Bottom off to Titania's bed so the two could enjoy their love carnally.

Master Shakespeare took the stage as the devious Oberon, hoping to see if his revenge on his queen had been successful. "*I wonder if Titania be awaked—*"

Joan scowled and stepped back from the curtain and deeper into the darkness backstage. Oberon or Auberon, she had no interest in hearing about that character. She'd been so busy at the theatre, she hadn't had to deal with any Fae since her encounters yesterday. Though she knew it was unlikely, she hoped it meant they'd forgotten about her. That all this had gone away and she was deemed too small a combatant for much more notice.

But she wasn't sure that even the Fae were so fickle.

"Don't miss your cue."

She flinched and threw her elbow behind her. Samuel grunted as she caught him in his diaphragm.

"Sorry," she said. "And don't you worry, I haven't missed a cue yet." She turned to grin at him. He towered over her like Nick, and she could barely make out his face where he stood with light pouring in behind him. "Besides, I listen with my ears, not my eyes."

He said nothing.

She raised an eyebrow at him. "Are you going to tease me about the kiss? Did we execute it to your liking?"

Silence once again. Had she done something to anger him?

"Samuel, what—"

"—and the Athenian woman by his side / That, when he waked, of force she must be eyed." Armin's voice drifted back to them. Puck was reporting his success—really failure—with the Athenian youths.

Their cue. Joan looked at Samuel expectantly.

He turned suddenly and plowed out onto the stage. Joan squawked as she stumbled out after him.

She had no idea what had gotten into him, but she'd pay him back once the show ended. She wouldn't hurt him much, but it'd be no less than he deserved.

Onstage, the bright daylight blinded her for a moment but she kept her focus.

"Stand close," Shakespeare said. "This is the same Athenian."

"This is the woman, but not this the man," Armin said. For Puck had mistaken Lysander for Demetrius and had caused the other man to fall in love with another woman.

This scene would find Hermia begging her former betrothed—played by Samuel—to tell her where Lysander was, neither of them knowing the mistake.

Samuel spun, staring her down with rage.

Joan froze. This wasn't Samuel.

It hadn't been the light behind him backstage. The glow had been his own. An ugly, raw wound cut across Samuel's face, splitting the skin beneath one eye.

A wound she remembered delivering.

Her chest ached as Ogun made his presence known.

Auberon faced her now, wearing Samuel's form.

Damnation.

"*O, why rebuke you him that loves you so?*" Auberon spat the words from Samuel's mouth.

Joan's fingers slid to her wrist. She barely heard the lines he spoke as she reached for her weapon. And came up short. Bia wasn't there. The blade was back in James's dressing room where she had left it with the rest of her clothing.

How could she have been so foolish? They were doing *his* play. Of all the times for the monster to appear—

"*Lay breath so bitter on your bitter foe!*" he said with a laugh.

But no matter. He was here now before her. She'd face him with what she had. Even if all she had were her wits.

She glanced out at the crowd, none the wiser to the danger standing mere feet away. If they knew—

She couldn't risk raising one thousand people in panic. The show had to continue.

She squared her shoulders. "*Now I but chide, but I should use thee worse.*" She let her rage color her lines. Let Hermia give breath to Joan's own fury. "*For thou, I fear, hast given me cause to curse.*"

She glanced over at Shakespeare and Armin. Both men looked on, unaware. Neither had noticed anything unusual.

No help there, then. She was on her own.

"*If thou hast slain Lysander in his sleep,*" she said. Keep him playing the scene until she worked out a plan. "*Being o'er shoes in blood, plunge in the deep / And kill me too.*"

Auberon smiled. "All right."

Joan threw herself backward as he dove for her. She slammed to the stage just out of his reach and rolled to her feet.

So much for playing the scene.

Her head buzzed. She shook it and breathed deeply. Now wasn't the time to lose control of herself.

She needed to focus.

"Die by the hand of he that loves thee." He drew the sword that hung at his hip and cut through the air. The steel blade shrieked.

Double damn.

"This must be a new one," a woman in the audience said, "and it looks to be bloody."

Joan sincerely hoped it wouldn't.

"I like when they're bloody," the young girl beside her whispered back.

Joan cut her eyes to both of them for a quick moment. She doubted they'd find it entertaining if they knew she was in true danger. Although, knowing Londoners—

"If love be rough with you, be rough with love." Auberon advanced, sword tight in his grip. *"Prick love for pricking and you beat love down."*

He swung at her. She dodged to the side, and the wind from the blow brushed her cheek.

Her vision started to blur.

"Samuel," Shakespeare whispered as loudly as he dared in front of an audience. "Those lines are not in this play!"

"That's not Samu—"

Auberon brought his blade down on Joan's head.

She breathed deep and dropped to the floor, throwing up her arm. A metallic clang rang through the house as the sword caught on the iron that now coated her limb.

Auberon grunted and shoved his weight against her. She stumbled backward, heel catching in the fabric of her skirt. His fist slammed into her face.

Joan grunted and hit the stage hard. Her ears rang. She felt a wetness running down her cheek. She shook her head again, hoping to clear it; struggling to keep her eyes on her foe.

Her vision split. She tried to breathe through it. Tried to focus.

Focus.

Double Auberons shifted back to one solid form, but her head still ached.

He grinned back at her and ran a finger along his own wound, a raw and ugly red.

"Come, love," he cooed, "let me prick thee again."

He stepped toward her but a blast of wind knocked him off his feet.

Joan turned.

James stood panting in the wing; fingers still poised by his lips. He caught her eye and tossed something onstage. The object caught the sunlight as it arched toward her.

Bia.

Joan reached for it. The sword grew and unraveled in the air, hilt landing perfectly in her hand. She spun to her feet, slamming her blade into Auberon's. He stumbled to the side, knocked off course. She shoved her foot into his back and sent him falling onto his face.

Joan scrambled out of his reach. "Shall we make it fair?"

The feel of Bia in her grip settled her frayed nerves a bit. But still, that lightness in her chest, the buzzing in her head, persisted.

She tightened her hold on the sword.

Auberon growled as he pushed himself up. "Your death shall please me much, mortal."

He raised his hand and the stage shook. Joan struggled to keep her balance as all around them the audience gasped and applauded, thinking this some great new theatrical effect.

Not even Bia could hold off the feeling in her chest now. Her vision swam.

Someone rammed into her. Joan rolled across the stage and leapt back to her feet. A sharp wooden spike burst up through the boards right where she had stood.

Master Phillips held it in his bare hands, straining to push it back down beneath the floor. "Do you have any idea," he grunted, "how much it'll cost us to repair these boards?"

"You would betray me, Augustine? Betray your own kind for this mortal?" Auberon screamed. The shape of Samuel melted off him as if he'd been doused in water. The Fae stood as himself, brown skin and gold-laced braids. And still that unhealed scar.

Phillips growled, slowly moving the broken wooden board lower. "This child has my protection." He gritted his teeth. "You shall not harm her."

"You can't save her, Augustine, not from this." Auberon raised his arms and faced the audience, projecting out into the farthest stalls. "Here she is. Here is the girl who murdered your leader." He smiled directly at Joan. "Come. Take your bloody revenge."

Joan heard shouting from the house. Someone shoved their way toward the stage, cutting through the excited crowds.

Pure white skin stretched over a tall, skeletal frame and sharp teeth crowded together in a too-wide mouth. Brilliant red eyes glared out from the sallow face framed by hair oozing crimson liquid.

A red cap.

Another appeared at the other side of the house. Then another. And another. Then two more plowed through the writhing masses. Six red caps set to avenge the death of their chieftain, their arms long enough to drag their clawed hands along the ground.

The crowd parted around them, tittering excitedly that the actors were moving through the house. She could imagine the panic if they saw the Fae true as she did, the blood-drenched hair and carnivorous sharp-toothed grins. It was best they thought this all part of the play.

Joan let the iron slide down along her blade as the first red cap reached the stage, then vaulted up onto the boards.

"For Gorvenal," it growled.

Joan adjusted her stance and raised Bia. The sword sang in anticipation of battle. The odds were less than ideal, but she'd play this hand and she'd play it well.

She sliced Bia through the air. A sudden heat bloomed in her chest as her vision shifted and darkened around the edges. She felt her left hand raise of its own accord.

No, not its own accord. Ogun's.

Joan tried to breathe; tried to force herself back into control of her body. She stumbled and both arms dropped to her sides as her sight cleared. And in doing so, she left herself completely open to attack in the middle of battle.

She looked up too late and too disoriented to do anything but pray the incoming blow wasn't fatal. An arm slipped around her side, spinning her out of the way of the red cap's claws.

"Seven against one are unfair odds. I cannot sit by and watch." Shakespeare grinned down at her. He drew the sword from his sash. "It's dull, but it's a weapon still."

Joan stared, heart racing with blessed life. She touched her hand along Shakespeare's blade, watched it sharpen to a deadly point. His eyes went wide as he watched the metal shift at her command.

But that wouldn't be enough, Joan knew. Steel wounds healed. She took a deep breath and sent a coating of iron down the sword so he could hurt.

So he could kill.

"This—Ogun—" He blinked at her for a moment. "Of course you are—"

Joan stared at him. "How do you know that name?"

Shakespeare gritted his teeth and pushed away from her, and spinning into the fray. "Unto the breech!" he shouted and sprinted toward one of the red caps.

Joan watched him swing recklessly at the monster, confused. How did the playwright know of Ogun? Had he learned from Phillips?

"Don't let her wound you, Master Shakespeare," James shouted from backstage.

"I am for thee, beast!"

"Never turn your back on me, mortal."

Joan spun, throwing herself to the ground to avoid the claws swinging for her face.

Rose suddenly stepped between Joan and the red cap. The tall girl's hands gripped the monster's wrist, protecting Joan from their deadly cut.

"Not this time," Rose grunted. She shifted her feet and tossed the beast over her head. It smashed through one of Auberon's wooden spikes behind them.

Joan looked from the red cap to the girl who'd thrown it like it weighed nothing. "Where did you come from? How did you—" Joan ripped the crooked wig off her head and threw it at Rose. "Why didn't you do that yesterday when we nearly died?"

Rose sidestepped the errant hairpiece. "I couldn't because we hadn't officially taken your side yesterday. There are rules to fighting among our kind."

"So glad you changed your mind."

"How could I not for you?"

Joan flushed.

Something swung between them, slicing across the eyes of an approaching red cap. The creature stumbled backward, shrieking.

"Less talking, more fighting for our lives, ladies." Nick stood just behind them, dark hair tumbling around his shoulders and his performance sword at the ready.

"Nick, what are you doing?" Joan screeched at him.

"Protecting you." He smiled at her. "Isn't it obvious?"

Rose snorted on his other side. "We have this well-handled here." She stared pointedly at his dull blade. "Take your play sword and go hide."

Nick frowned at her. "Who are you?"

"Not the time." Joan shoved Nick back with one hand and knocked the red cap's claws away with Bia. The momentum sent it stumbling toward Rose who hefted it over her head.

Something slammed into Joan's back. She hit the stage hard, struggling to catch her breath. Bia clattered to the ground just beyond her reach.

A shadow shifted over her. "You're a tricky one, aren't you?"

Auberon.

Joan scrambled for her sword but Auberon caught her wrist under his boot.

"But not tricky enough." He pressed down, grinning when she cried out in pain. "Sad." He swung his sword back like a club.

"Have at thee, fiend!" Burbage dove into the fight, fist cracking across Auberon's chin.

The blow shifted him just enough for Joan to free her wrist and scramble toward Bia. She heard Burbage grunt.

"You mongrel bitch." Auberon jumped on her back. He drove his knee into her spine, fisted a hand in her hair, and ripped her head backward. "I'll slit your throat."

Thunder boomed in the air all around them.

"Who dares disturb the peace of my bower?"

Joan flinched as Auberon tightened his grip but managed to shift her gaze just enough to see the newcomer.

Titania stood on the railing of the balcony as musicians watched with wide eyes. Joan squinted. It wasn't their Titania. Rob was never that commanding.

"What are you doing here?" Auberon growled. His hand tightened again. Joan bit down on her shriek.

"Release the girl."

Auberon let go of Joan's hair. "This is no fight of yours, hobgoblin."

"Release the girl, Auberon." The not-Rob Titania stepped off the railing and landed delicately in front of them.

"You'd dare betray your king?"

The not-Rob Titania snorted, cascading blond curls melting away, revealing Robin Goodfellow. "I have no king."

"Nor I." Rose's foot slammed into the side of Auberon's face. He tumbled across the stage and landed in a heap.

Goodfellow reached out—still dressed in Titania's costume—and pulled Joan up with one hand. "Are you all right, Iron Blade?"

"I'll be sore tomorrow." Joan stretched her neck to either side. "But I'm alive. If you were playing Titania, where's Rob? Is he all right?"

Goodfellow smiled their devil's smile. "Oh, he's making himself useful."

A piercing whistle screamed across the stage from behind them. A squib struck Auberon in the back, exploding on contact.

Joan whipped around to see Rob, in his own Titania dress and no wig, and Armin readying another firework.

The audience broke into raucous cheers.

"You and your lot take care of these bloody biddies." Goodfellow cracked their knuckles. "I'll handle old Auby."

Joan nodded, still catching her breath. James and Nick struggled against a red cap, Nick desperately swinging his sword and James doing his best to dodge the claws with one working arm.

Rose grappled with another, each blow hitting with a jarring thud.

Shakespeare danced around yet another, slipping in and out of her guard to slice bloody trenches in her skin.

Burbage boxed with one. He evaded blows most excellently, but none of his heavy hits landed hard enough. He lacked Rose's supernatural strength.

Joan knew what to do. Now was no time to keep secrets, not with death so close.

"James," she shouted, flinging Bia through the air toward the boy. He snatched it and sliced across the face of the red cap reaching for him in one smooth move. Nick pulled James clear as another of Rob and Armin's fireworks rammed into the red cap.

"Master Burbage!" Joan ran toward where he was fighting. He turned at her call, fists still raised.

She called the iron to her hands, felt it flow over her palms like liquid, and clasped her palms over Burbage's bare knuckles. When she pulled back, his hands were covered in a gleaming layer of metal.

"See how she likes that," Joan said. A sudden wave of exhaustion hit her, and the world seemed to tilt beneath her feet. She locked her knees to stay upright.

You've given too much iron.

Joan shook her head, wondering where that thought had come from.

You've given too much.

Burbage looked at Joan in awe before a wide grin split his face. He spun, catching the red cap with a furious right hook. She screeched and stumbled backward.

"Well done, lass." Burbage flexed his fingers, watching as the metal moved along with him. "This I shall enjoy."

"Burbage. Burbage. Burbage," the crowd chanted.

You've weakened yourself.

Joan left Burbage to it and tried to pull herself together. She turned and came face-to-face with another red cap.

"Alone without your weapon, mortal?" the red cap sneered.

Joan stumbled backward. Everyone else was engaged, and James still had Bia.

You cannot win. But I will.

She felt Ogun's presence brush across the edges of her consciousness. Then she was gone, drifting in the dark emptiness.

The Orisha had taken over.

Joan felt herself drifting farther and farther away. Panicked, she tried to push herself back to the surface. Tried to regain control.

It was like trying to sprint through mud, but Joan shoved herself with all her might.

And broke through with a blade—an unfamiliar machete—buried in the red cap's gut, the creature's hot breath huffing past her ear. Joan grunted and drove the machete up, splitting red cap's body with ease. A gush of hot blood oozed down her blade and over her arm, and Joan felt herself smile.

As the creature collapsed, Joan saw it had lost an arm—the severed limb lay nearby on the stage—and several fingers, a few of which were scattered along the front of the stage.

When had she—

Auberon screamed and scrambled out from under Goodfellow, ripping his own arm off in the process. "Traitor! You filthy traitor. Does your mistress know you've attacked me like this?"

"Run." Goodfellow wielded Auberon's lost limb in one hand before tossing it to him. "Run, before I do worse than tear off your arm."

Joan watched as Auberon caught it and pressed the bloody end against the gaping wound in his shoulder. His fingers twitched and the injury healed as if it had never happened. Only the wounds she'd cleaved with iron remained.

"Run," Goodfellow growled. "Now."

Auberon flinched. "Retreat," he spat and seemed to melt through the stage floor like water.

All around them, red caps pulled out of their fights and hobbled off through the house.

The metal slipped back into Joan's palms and she was herself again. She dropped to her knees as the immense pressure of Ogun's presence slipped away.

And the machete in Joan's hand, where had that come from? What had Ogun done while he'd been in control?

Wood banged against wood as something struggled to push itself free. All eyes turned to the spot downstage right.

"I've never been built for battle," Phillips moaned as he shoved at the boards and spikes piled atop him.

"Augustine?" Burbage laughed and shuffled over to where the old man was pulling himself out of a pile of rubble. "You still alive, you old goat?"

"Blast you, Burbage, you windbag," Phillips said, grunting as he shoved at the heavy wood. "Help me."

Shakespeare, James, and Nick ran over to help Phillips. Joan shivered, her body still reeling from the weight of Ogun's presence.

How could anyone stand this possession? She wrapped her arms around herself, hands shaking and still covered in blood.

Silence hung heavy in the theatre. Joan looked out and froze.

A sea of expectant faces looked back at her, thousands of eyes waiting.

They still had an audience.

Shite.

CHAPTER TWENTY
A Grand Finale

h—" Joan said, as she locked eyes with a young girl standing up against the stage. The child gazed back.

"If we shadows have offended," Armin said, *"think but this and all is mended: / That you have only slumbered here while these visions did appear."*

Joan jerked to attention, her head whipping around to see Armin step out from backstage and assume the mantle of Puck again—his posture straight and his voice floating through the theatre like a spell.

"And this weak and idle theme, / No more yielding but a dream, / Gentles, do not reprehend."

He was delivering the final speech of the play as if the company hadn't just done battle with a group of malevolent Fae.

And as far as the audience knew, they hadn't. They watched Armin as he spoke, his eyes shifting through the crowd with each new line.

"If you pardon, we will mend. / And, as I am an honest Puck—"

Laughter as he winked at the groundlings and bounced his hip.

Joan's shoulders relaxed.

Bless Armin and his quick mind.

"—*if we have unearnèd luck / Now to 'scape the serpent's tongue, / We will make amends ere long. / Else the Puck a liar call. / So good night unto you all. / Give me your hands, if we be friends, / And Robin shall restore amends.*"

The musicians struck their chord, and the crowd burst into joyous roars. The final dance.

Armin grabbed Joan's hands and pulled her up. She stood on shaky feet, still thrown by the feeling of being possessed by Ogun.

Every show ended with the dance. All the actors, characters dead and alive, joined together in celebration of a job well done. The audience would expect it now.

"Dance, my girl." Armin grinned at her. "Let them think this was all in fun." He held her hand up and turned them both toward the crowd with a flourish. "One. Two. Three. Four."

Her heart thudded in her chest.

Because this was the one thing Joan had never taken the time to watch or learn.

The drummer kept time with Armin's quick counts, and Joan followed along as best she could.

She needn't have worried. Armin was the best dancer in the company. He led gently, twirling and lifting her to hide her stumbling steps.

Joan could hear the audience cheering and clapping along with them. She swung out of a tight spin and right into Shakespeare's arms. He slipped a hand around her waist and promenaded her across the stage.

"So," he whispered, "were you going to tell me you had this magic?"

Joan frowned then forced a false smile to her lips. "You'd have turned me out as a witch."

"Never." He spun her around to face him. "I would have never. My mother—" He glanced out at the audience, grinned, and swiveled his hips.

They cheered.

"Later," he whispered out of one side of his mouth before tossing her hand up into the air.

Nick caught her hand and pulled her close, walking them around in a tight circle. "Are you all right?" One of his sleeves had been ripped off during the fighting.

"Yes, are you?" Joan watched the pretty flex of firm muscles beneath his brown skin and did her best to keep them both on beat.

He grinned. "Yes, thanks to you. You were magnificent."

Joan flushed. Nick spun her away from him, ready to swing her back in when someone else grabbed her other hand and pulled her away. She smacked into a pair of soft breasts. Joan's face burned hotter than it ever had before as she looked up at Rose.

Damn her for being so much taller.

"Hello," Rose said and effortlessly lifted Joan over her head.

Joan squeaked and grasped the other girl's shoulders, laughing as Rose spun them both around. Distantly, Joan could hear the band building to a crescendo. As soon as Rose put her down, someone else grabbed her and tossed her into the air. She squealed as Burbage caught her this time. He locked his hand around hers and winked at her before running them both to the edge of the stage.

The rest of the company surged forward alongside them and the musicians sounded out an elaborate flourish.

Burbage threw their joined hands up as the drummer struck the final beat.

The audience exploded in cheers and yells. Joan didn't think her smile could spread any wider.

For all the time she spent with the King's Men, she'd never felt this—the pure adoration of an audience.

And she didn't know when she'd ever get to feel it again.

———†———

"Well, that was far more exciting than anything you've ever written, Will."

Shakespeare scowled at Burbage, who laughed in his face. Then the playwright's eyes lit up. "Although perhaps this means it is time for some rewrites."

They both watched intently as Joan laid her hands over Burbage's and called back the iron covering them. She locked her knees to stay upright.

"By God's lid, lass," Burbage whispered, "you've had real magic this whole time?"

Joan nodded, her lips pressed together. They could decry her a witch, have her burned. She glanced up a Burbage.

He grinned at her. "To our advantage then!" He flexed his bare fingers. "Fascinating. I may have need of this skill again, Mistress Sands."

Joan blurted out a too-loud laugh and nodded. Her shoulders slumped in relief and she sagged against the nearest wall. She was so tired, more than she'd ever been before, but there was still more to do. She glanced over at Shakespeare, who stood mumbling to himself. She needed to ask him how he knew of Ogun.

What he knew of Ogun.

He looked up and their eyes met. He frowned, opened his mouth to speak.

A chorus of shouting men's voices sprang up from outside the theatre.

"Here come the authorities." James jogged over with Nick and tossed Bia back to Joan. "Late as usual."

Burbage and Shakespeare glanced at Joan, still dressed as a decidedly disheveled Hermia. No one noticed that she'd barely caught the sword in fumbling hands.

Shakespeare paled and nodded. "Best for all of us they not catch on to our little switch today." He waved his hands at Joan and James. "We'll take care of things here." He looked pointedly at Goodfellow. "You'll see them home safely, of course."

"As if they were my own children," Goodfellow said. They looped their arm around Joan's waist and dragged her out of the open stage doors. Somehow, Joan's feet kept pace despite her exhaustion. Nick and James followed behind.

"Hold tight to me, Iron Blade," Goodfellow said. "I'll keep you under my glamour so none will see you."

As they wound through the dim backstage, a flash of white caught Joan's eye. She turned and there he was.

"No." She stumbled as Goodfellow pulled her forward.

Samuel's contorted body lay sprawled in a corner, his blue eyes barely open, breaths coming in short, panting gasps. Blood stained the front of his shirt as it oozed from the wound in his gut.

"Samuel!" Joan ripped herself away from Goodfellow and rushed to her injured friend. She heard the sharp rip of her costume as she dropped to her knees beside him.

He grimaced in her direction and whispered her name.

Tears sprang to Joan's eyes. She scrambled for a clean bit of her dress and, tearing it loose, pressed the white fabric against where she thought the wound was. He winced at her touch as the cloth near instantly turned crimson.

"Hold on, Samuel, just hold on."

She heard James gasp behind her, then he was at her side, eyes shimmering with tears. "Joan . . . he's—"

Joan cut across him before he could finish. "Stay with us, Samuel. We're here."

But she knew it was futile. James could feel the calm creep of death, and there was nothing any of them could do to stop it. She reached for Samuel's trembling hand, his skin nearly gray beneath the stains of blood.

"We're right—" The words stuck in her throat, choking her.

Nick lowered his tall form on her other side, and she felt Nick and James wrap their hands around hers, still holding Samuel's.

"Rest, friend," Nick said, tears streaming down his face. "Rest."

Her throat tightened. She couldn't breathe. This was her friend. Samuel was her friend and he was gone. There was nothing she could do to save him from this.

James laid a hand over Samuel's forehead and whispered a quiet prayer to Oya. Joan felt Samuel give her hand the faintest squeeze, then, with a rattling breath, he lay still.

Nick gently slipped the other boy's eyes closed. A sob burst from Joan's throat as James pried her hands away.

Her brother tried to pull her up. "Joan, we have to go."

She didn't move, couldn't move. Not with her friend's body right there.

"Joan, please. We have to get you out of here before the authorities see you." Rose tugged at Joan's other arm, forcing her up, forcing her forward. "He's already gone, there's nothing to be done for him now."

Joan felt her feet tripping toward the door but couldn't take her eyes off Samuel's body. Samuel, whose friendly teasing helped her hone her own wit. Samuel, who always took twice as long to learn the moves for a fight that he'd immediately forget.

Samuel, whose sister would be home waiting for a brother who'd never return.

Auberon had taken Samuel's life so callously. She remembered how easily the Fae had healed his own wound, shoving his severed arm back into place like it was nothing. The anger threatened to overwhelm her.

She couldn't see through her tears as rage burned her eyes.

Tucked against Goodfellow's side, she didn't need to see where they were going.

So she let the tears fall.

CHAPTER TWENTY-ONE
As Holy Pilgrims Do

 oan stumbled along under Goodfellow's cloak. This close, she could smell their clean, earthy scent. She tried to focus on that, let it calm her.

But all she could see were Samuel's eyes, wide and glassy.

She stumbled over the hem of her dress.

Goodfellow pulled her closer. "Keep in step, Iron Blade." They winked at her. "No need to show off your scandalous attire."

Right. She was still in Hermia's flowing dress. But she couldn't feel the cold air. That must've been Goodfellow's doing too.

"What have we just survived?" Nick said, eyes wide as he loped along behind them. "And Samuel, what—" His voice broke over the words.

Joan flinched.

Samuel was dead because of her.

Rose snorted. "Can you at least wait until we've gotten to safety before you have us spilling secrets?"

"We might have a problem." James froze beside her, his hand grasping Joan's tightly enough to grind her bones together.

Something buzzed along the back of Joan's neck and her head went foggy.

What now?

Goodfellow stopped too, pulling Joan even closer beneath their arm. "James," they hissed, "come close to me."

James dropped Joan's hand and slowly slipped to Goodfellow's other side. That's when Joan saw it.

Farther down the road was a woman, her pale brown face peeking out from under a dark hood with a long braid of dark hair hanging over each shoulder. She sat astride a splotch of nothingness, blocking their path.

No, not nothingness.

Two shining eyes peered out at them from that seemingly empty space and whinnied, the sound both familiar and foreign. It scraped against Joan's bones.

She shivered.

A horse. A horse made of darkness and its equally shadowed rider blocked their path.

"Who—"

"Hush, child." Goodfellow tucked James in close to their side. "Rose, see to the boy."

"I have him, Zaza." Rose held Nick's hand in one of hers and wrapped her other arm around his waist.

They were nearly the same height, Nick just barely taller than Rose.

Joan blushed and hated herself for getting distracted in this moment.

The dark horse let out a rumbling snort and thundered toward them with slow steps that echoed in Joan's chest.

Goodfellow's grip tightened painfully around her, but Joan bit down on her squeak of discomfort. Anything that frightened Goodfellow this much needn't be alerted to her presence.

"Keep quiet," they whispered, "do not make a sound."

The rider pulled back on the reins as she came up alongside where their group stood.

"Trickster." The rider's voice boomed and ground in Joan's ears. If a roaring fire had a voice, it would have sounded like this.

"Herne," Goodfellow replied.

"I did not think to find you here," Herne said. "You said you wanted no part in our revels now that the contract is broken."

Goodfellow chuckled. "Am I not allowed to change my mind, hunter?" They nodded toward Rose. "My child needs reminding that her Fae heritage holds the most power. What better time to teach her than now, when we are finally free?"

Joan held her breath. She reached her hand around Goodfellow's back, careful to stay beneath their cloak. James's fingers grasped hers from the other side.

This broken pact gave way to more horrors than she could've imagined.

"Will you ride this night, hunter?" Rose said. Her voice barely quavered. Joan admired that.

"Aye, Trickster's child. The Hunt and I have been commanded to find a mortal. Then we shall enjoy our new freedom."

Goodfellow turned, pulling Joan and James along with tense muscles. "Then we shall not hold you. Until we next meet, Herne the Hunter."

"Until we next meet, Robin Goodfellow." Herne's voice changed from a blaze to a smolder, but Joan could not see who she spoke to, didn't dare look. "Oh, hello there, dear."

Herne snapped the reins and the horse burst forward in an earth-shaking gallop. A cold wind kicked up behind it.

"Don't move," Goodfellow said, quiet and rushed. "And whatever you hear, do not look."

Joan tucked her head against Goodfellow's chest as the howling started. The sudden noise nearly made her peek through the opening in the cloak, but she remembered the warning.

And what she heard kept her obedient.

If the very gates of hell had opened and all manner of fiends ran amok on earth, their song could not have matched the cacophony they heard now. Her brain went blank, too horrified to even attempt to picture the nightmares lurking beyond the safety of Goodfellow's cloak. James's hand tightened on hers, and Joan prayed that he wouldn't be tempted to view the horrors racing past.

The sound rose, chaotic and savage. Laughter, shrieking, sobs, the grinding and splitting of bones, a putrid howl, and cries of bottomless despair all echoed cruelly, haunting enough to frighten the moon into hiding.

Every sound struck Joan in her chest like a blow.

Then silence.

Goodfellow loosened their grip. "We should hurry to your home. We do not want to be out when the Wild Hunt rides this night."

That hadn't been their worst? A shiver raced up Joan's spine.

"Zaza," Rose wailed. "Help."

Joan turned. Nick lay collapsed across Rose's arms, his brown skin ashen.

"Damn," Goodfellow spat.

Joan squeezed James's hand so tightly, she felt his knuckles knock together. "Is he—"

"Not yet, but if he looked upon the Wild Hunt, he'll be under Herne's thrall, near death but not dead."

Rose ran to Goodfellow, Nick jerking loosely in her arms. "Herne spoke to him." She stepped in close and pressed the two of them tightly against Goodfellow's back. "My glamour wasn't strong enough to protect him, Zaza. I'm sorry."

Joan felt Nick's arm flop against her and James's joined hands. James squeezed back.

"Hush, Rose. Now, hold tight to me," Goodfellow said.

The world around them faded to darkness. The blackness looked thick enough to touch. Joan reached one hand out. She couldn't help it. Whatever she touched pressed back against her outstretched fingers.

Then it broke like dawn, colors slowly easing into being before their eyes.

The tall brown timbers stamped between smooth white plaster. The great wooden door with the intricate carving done by their great-grandfather's hand.

Home. They were home.

"We need to get the boy inside," Goodfellow said. "Now."

Joan nodded and slipped out of their grip. She bolted up to the door just as it swung open. Her mother appeared in the glowing light of the front hall.

"Mother, we need—"

"Inside, quickly." Mrs. Sands looked off into the distance, beyond where the rest of their bedraggled number stood. "All of you. Now."

Goodfellow took Nick from Rose, cradling the boy's tall form like he was a baby as they all stumbled into the house.

Joan watched her mother slam the door closed behind them and drag over a nearby chair. She vaulted onto it; drew eight white lines at the top of the doorframe with efun. It looked like nothing more than chalk, but Joan knew the power behind those marks.

For protection. No malevolent spirit could cross that threshold as long as those eight lines marked their door.

Satisfied, Mrs. Sands slid the round into the pocket of her apron and dusted its white remnants off her hands. She jumped down from the chair and froze, taking in Joan's blood-covered clothes and Nick's limp form. "Lord, what has happened?"

Nick lay across a guest bed, his eyes wide open and unseeing. His chest rose and fell in an erratic rhythm, the only sign that he was still alive.

His hair spread loose across the pillow like black ink.

Joan perched on the stool beside him. She'd changed out of the Hermia costume and back into a simple blue dress of her own. She reached out and clasped one of Nick's hands in hers.

It was icy cold to the touch.

The chill slid all the way to her heart.

"Don't worry, Nick. We'll figure out how to fix this."

No response.

"I'm sorry." Rose slipped in through the door and closed it gently behind her. "I wasn't strong enough to protect him."

Joan sighed. "Will he be all right?"

"I don't know. I've never . . ." Something flickered across Rose's face before she folded her tall form to the floor beside Joan and let her back press against the side of the bed. "I know nothing of Herne or the Wild Hunt. Zaza never expected me to encounter them."

"Not even in"—Joan racked her brain for the right word—"in Faerie?"

"I've never been. I'm half mortal, and Zaza has been hiding me here since I was born."

Joan frowned. "Goodfellow could come freely into the mortal realm this whole time?"

"Of course, but only because they don't mean to do mortals any undue harm. That was a rule of the Pact."

Joan nodded, adding that information to the rest she'd learned of this deal.

"I barely know what my Fae blood means, what powers it grants me. But Zaza thought it best that other powerful Fae didn't know of my existence."

A quiet melancholy washed over Rose's face, and Joan's heart clenched at the sight.

"It must be very lonely to be detached from one whole part of yourself," Joan said gently. She reached for the taller girl's hand, squeezing it.

"It has been." Rose nodded and looked up, eyes locking with Joan's. "But sadness feels difficult now when it brought me to you."

Joan flushed and looked away, marveling at where she'd found herself. One hand holding Rose's and the other, Nick's. Caught between the two people who made her heart race—

And neither of them fit into her dreams for her future. The thought sat hollow in her chest.

She cleared her throat. "Is there anything we can do to help Nick?"

"Perhaps . . ." Rose frowned then raised an eyebrow. "How do you feel about him?"

Joan felt her face explode with heat at the question. "What?"

"I know of a possibility. Do you love him?" Rose watched her from her place on the floor, her arms resting across her bent knees.

"Love?" Joan jerked to her feet, dropping Nick's hand like it burned. The stool clattered to the floor behind her. Her face was on fire. "What?"

Did she love Nick? Joan knew she wanted to caress his strong arms, run her fingers through his silky hair. She wanted to kiss him again, possibly do more than kiss—

But Nick wasn't the only person she wanted that with—

"Kiss him," Rose blurted, her lips quirking up on one side. "That could bring him back. Isn't that what you want?"

"I—yes, but—" Every word suddenly left Joan's mind and all she could do was stare. At Rose. At Nick. At Nick's lips. At Rose's lips.

Why couldn't she think clearly?

Rose stood. "Look, I know you want to. You already kissed him earlier."

Joan flinched. "You saw that?"

"I wasn't going to miss your stage debut." Rose's smile widened. She stepped around and placed her hands on Joan's shoulders. "Just one kiss to bring him back. It wouldn't hurt anyone."

"No, that's not appropriate." Joan tried to step back but Rose held her fast. She looked at Nick's face again. His wide-open eyes still stared at nothing and a gray pallor faded the golden glow of his tan skin.

Just one kiss. It wouldn't be their first. Her first.

But this wasn't onstage.

This was real life.

And he was barely here.

"Are you going to let propriety and manners keep you from saving Nick's life?" Rose whispered in her ear.

She was too close. Joan couldn't gather her thoughts with Rose so near her. Whispering to her to kiss Nick. Again.

One kiss. One kiss and Nick would come back to her. To them.

Joan dropped to the edge of his bed. She glanced at his lips.

Just one kiss.

She leaned over. She could still feel Rose's fingertips pressing into her shoulders. A distraction. Why was Rose still holding on so tightly? Joan could feel the heat of her hands through her chemise.

Just one kiss.

Joan remembered the feel of Nick's body against hers, his smell of lilac and leather, the silky whisper of his long hair, the caress of his touch on her cheek.

Gently, softly, she pressed her lips against his forehead. Joan pulled back.

Nick's eyes stared forward, seeing nothing.

"That's not what I meant when I said you could cure him with a kiss."

Joan jerked out of Rose's hold. "I'm not going to kiss him while he's asleep."

Rose snorted.

"I would never violate his trust like that." Joan leapt to her feet. Rose towered over her, but Joan barely noticed. "Never."

"Are you that noble, or just afraid to make your intentions known in front of me?"

Joan flinched. "What?"

"If you think I'm jealous of him"—Rose flung a hand out toward Nick on the bed—"know that I feel no such thing."

Joan sputtered, her words catching in her throat again.

"I see how you look at him, how you look at me." She smiled again, tracing along Joan's chin with soft fingertips. "I only wish I too had some way to feel the touch of your sweet li—"

Joan threw her arms around Rose's neck and pulled her down to her level and kissed her. Their lips pressed together, quick and firm and resolute and perfect.

She pulled away, eyes searching Rose's, then she surged forward again. Rose met her halfway, pulling their bodies flush against each other. Joan moaned and slanted her mouth over Rose's, sliding her tongue across the seam of her lips. Rose's tongue darted out and tangled with hers in the most delicious way and she couldn't help but grip her closer.

She couldn't get enough of her lips, couldn't get enough of Rose. Joan forced herself to pull away, and Rose's lips tried to follow.

"Wait," Joan breathed. The tips of her ears burned and her hands shook.

Rose choked out a chuckle. "Stop thinking of what's proper"—her hand ghosted along Joan's cheek and slipped around the back of her neck—"when you can have both of us."

Both? Hopeful curiosity bloomed suddenly in her chest.

Was such a thing truly possible? Could she find her happiness with both Nick and Rose?

"No." Joan pressed a hand to Rose's chest, holding her back. She untangled herself and stepped away, ignoring the painful clenching in her chest.

Rose reached for her again. "What's wrong?"

She'd already dragged Nick into this danger with her nearness. And even if he awoke and every part of this Fae threat disappeared, was this desire for him, for both of them, worth tossing away her plans? She could already feel her resolve to marry Henry and take over the shop cracking under the pressure.

"I—" Joan pulled back. "I can't—"

Yes? No? Yes?

Thoughts came too quickly for her to grasp. She needed a moment. She needed to breathe.

To leave.

She ignored Rose's shouted "Wait!" and bolted out the door.

CHAPTER TWENTY-TWO
An Offer She Can't Refuse

oan grabbed hold of the banister and swung herself around. She didn't dare look back to see if Rose followed her.

James flapped his hands frantically at her and pointed at their receiving room. She hesitated and slipped down the first step. Both her hands wrapped around the wooden post to keep her from tumbling down the staircase and braining herself.

Joan dropped to a seat on the stairs and watched James strain his ear toward the other room.

Voices drifted faintly up to where she sat. One was the rumbling bass of her father. The other was unfamiliar. She could barely make out the words, but the tones were clipped and direct.

"What's going on?" Rose whispered near Joan's ear.

Joan jumped but managed to strangle her yelp into a quiet squeak. She shushed Rose and pointed toward James at the bottom of the staircase. Rose grimaced and sat beside Joan. The parlor door opened and Joan's mother slipped out into the hall. She pulled the door closed behind her and whispered something to James, who pointed up the stairs to Joan.

Joan flinched at the fear in her mother's face. Not much on this earth frightened the fierce Mrs. Sands.

But whoever lurked in their parlor was enough to shake her. Joan didn't like that one bit.

"What happened?"

Joan and Rose spun around. Nick stumbled down the hall toward them. He'd nearly reached them when he pitched forward.

"Nick!" Joan dove forward to catch him. She struggled under his limp weight until Rose came to steady them both. "It worked. I—" Joan met Rose's eyes over Nick's shoulder, but the other girl's face was carefully blank. Rose hadn't lied about waking Nick with a kiss, despite her cruel delivery. Joan felt something unclench in her chest.

"There she is. Today's unlikely star." A man stood at the base of the stairs, small and pale and flanked by royal guards on either side. The crisp white ruff around his neck stood stark against his otherwise black doublet, black breeches, black stockings, and black boots.

The last time Joan had seen this man, he'd been cowering with his son at the feet of a Fae monster.

Then he'd written her a letter, gratitude dripping with threat.

This was Robert Cecil, first Earl of Salisbury.

Here in her home, after she had refused him and returned his letter. Shite.

Joan's stomach dropped to her feet. She felt two sets of arms tighten around her. She tried to let Nick and Rose's presence steady her. But one look at her mother's tense posture and fixed smile erased all that.

"Come, child." Cecil beckoned her with one hand. "You and I shall have words."

Joan doubted she'd wanted anything less in her life.

"Lord Salisbury," her mother cooed, "is it really necessary for Joan to sit through your discussions with her father? She's but a girl."

Cecil kept his eyes locked on Joan. "An exceptional girl. I'm sure she'll have no problems speaking with me after addressing an audience of thousands. I am but one man." He smiled, his eyes crinkling around the edges. "Besides, she saw fit to break the law; she can sit through the negotiations happening on her behalf."

How did he— He couldn't have known unless he'd been at the Globe today.

And Cecil would've known to find her there after she turned away his messenger.

Joan's knees buckled, but Rose kept her standing.

"That was me at the theatre, my lord," James blurted. "I'm afraid that she and I look too much alike."

"I'll ignore that blatant lie, boy." Cecil looked pointedly at James's bandaged arm before glancing back to Joan. "Will you join us, child? Or shall I send one of my men up to escort you?"

Her eyes jumped between the faces of his two guards, neither of them Black and both of their pale faces cold and blank as marble.

No, she'd not take her chances on them handling her gently.

Joan swallowed. "I come anon, my lord." She pulled away from Rose and Nick, hoping they'd at least keep hold of each other. She drew her shoulders up and slipped into a brief curtsy.

She descended the stairs, one hand gripping her skirts and the other catching sweatily as it slid along the banister. Cecil held his elbow out to her when she reached the bottom of the stairs.

She looped her arm through his and allowed herself to be led into the parlor. She noted the man was barely taller than her.

His guards closed ranks behind them, but Joan didn't even attempt to turn around.

"It seems your lovely daughter will be joining us after all, Sands."

Her father sat back on the settee, his posture relaxed and non-threatening. Joan met his eyes as they walked in. He smiled at her. "I see you're feeling better, love."

"Yes, Father." Joan kept her hand soft on Cecil's arm. "Thank you for giving me time to recover my strength."

Cecil sneered. "Enough of this farce." He shoved her toward Mr. Sands.

Joan stumbled forward and caught her father's outstretched hand. He helped her sit beside him, his grip tightening for a moment before letting her go.

Joan understood and settled in to play the obedient daughter.

Cecil flopped onto the chair behind her father's desk. The candlelight cast stark shadows across his pinched face, highlighting the bruise-like circles beneath his eyes.

He looked exhausted.

Joan felt Bia vibrate against her wrist and ran her fingers over the blade, hoping to calm the rage in them both.

"Do you know how easily I could have you all arrested?" Cecil lifted the mermaid figurine from her father's desktop. He tossed the delicate statue from one hand to the other. "And I do mean all. Not even His Majesty's players are above the law."

What's stopping you?

Joan strangled the words in her throat. She had no power here. Silence was her only option.

"We understand the severity of the offense, my lord," her father said, voice low and cloying. "Only something so important would bring one so high as His Majesty's secretary of state to our humble home."

Joan hated to hear her father's voice sound like that. But she knew the importance of it just the same.

Cecil looked up. "Indeed. I've come to offer clemency. In return for a service."

A chill raced down Joan's spine.

"Indeed, my lord," Mr. Sands said. "If it is within my power—"

"Not from you, I'm afraid." Cecil locked eyes with Joan. "From the young lady player."

Joan's father tensed beside her. "My lord, my daughter—"

"I understand you killed one of the Fae in Southwark, girl, after you fought one off at my home two nights past. And then again today at your playhouse. Creatures that should only exist in stories we tell to scare naughty children by the fire. Creatures that, if the repeated reports I've received of late are to be believed, are running amok in this very city.

"My earlier offer was delivered with some patience. But let me assure you, that magnanimity has expired."

Joan kept her posture straight, proud that she didn't allow her fists to clench.

"My lord," her father said in that slick, placating tone, "I must insist—"

Cecil smashed the mermaid statuette against the desk. Joan flinched, but her father did not.

"The girl will speak for herself." A trickle of blood slid across his hand and dripped onto the shattered remains of the figure. "Unless she wants me to have her dragged off to the Clink. If she wants to play the whore, I will see to it that she's treated as such."

Joan shoved her shaking hands into the folds of her skirt. Her heart raced. "Aye, Lord Salisbury. I faced down such creatures."

"Excellent. See how easy it is to speak up." Cecil sat back. One of his guards rushed over with a handkerchief. Cecil snatched it and dabbed at his bloody hand. "And now, my offer."

Joan's jaw ached as she ground her back teeth together.

"I shall see fit to pardon the whole lot of you if you would bring the one known as Auberon to heel."

She squeezed her lips closed on the scowl trying to slip across her face.

"He's made himself known to me as their king," he said, simply and plainly, "and I want you to kill him."

Joan felt too many things at once to do more than stare. "My—Pardon my presumption, my lord." She mentally congratulated herself on not choking on the words, "With your myriad of resources, why would you need me, a mere girl, to—"

He held up a hand. "As much as I enjoy your struggle to speak proper words, I have neither the time nor the patience. Speak plainly."

She kept her clenched fists tucked away. "Why me?"

Free never meant truly free to a man like this.

"I have other business that demands my attention. Business that is of the utmost importance and requires my deft mind. The Fae respond to your natural brutality, as was proven at my home. What say you, girl? Will you come under my employ for a full pardon?"

She said nothing.

Cecil hummed and rose from her father's desk. Joan and her father jumped to their feet as he stood. As was proper for a man of his station.

She hated the performance this man's presence forced them into.

Bia vibrated hard enough to rattle the bones in Joan's wrist. She let the feeling ground her.

"I shall allow you this night to ruminate on my request, young Mistress Sands." Cecil flicked his hand at his guards, who swung the parlor doors open. "It is a kindness born out of the love I bear my only son that I make this request a second time. Do not expect that good will to extend much further."

He reached into his pocket and pulled out a well-creased slip of paper. He let it dangle between his fingers as he held it out to Joan.

On the other side of the door, Joan's mother glided into view, James at her side. The front hall was otherwise empty. No sign of Rose, Nick, or Goodfellow.

That was likely for the best.

Joan took the paper, calling on all her strength to keep her from snatching it out of his grip.

Cecil pursed his thin lips and turned to leave.

"Lord Salisbury, we thank you for gracing our home with your presence." Joan's mother smiled at him, her entire body draped with the lie. She led Cecil and his retinue down the stairs and through the darkened shop. She swung the door open, her face frozen in a pleasant mask.

Cecil bared his teeth at them as he moved toward the door, flanked by his guards. "I shall expect an answer tomorrow, girl. I encourage you to agree. It would not be in your best interest to cross me again."

He and his guards marched out into the street, and then he clambered up into the waiting coach.

Their mother closed the door as Cecil's coach clacked off down the road.

Silence lay thick and heavy throughout the house. Bia still pulsed at Joan's wrist. She focused on that, tracing her fingers along the metal.

"Where's the boy?" Her father sounded exhausted.

Joan felt the same bone-deep weariness.

"Goodfellow and Rose took him home," James said. "Goodfellow said they'll call on us again tomorrow."

"What did the king's secretary want with our Joan?" Their mother demanded. She slipped her arm around Joan's shoulders.

Joan stared down at the paper in her hands and the address scrawled across it. "He wants me to kill Auberon for him. He came to make the request—demand—in person after I refused him yesterday morning."

"Kill Auberon?" James jumped in front of her. "On your own?"

"Refused him yesterday?" Her mother paled. "Joan, why didn't you—"

James shook his head. "You can't accept. There's no way."

Joan met his gaze. "I don't think I have a choice." The weight of everything felt heavy enough to crush her. She slid to the floor, her skirts pooling around her.

"We're running out of time. We need to find where they're holding Ben," her mother said. "Joan, you cannot seek out this Fae."

Joan pressed her palms into her eyes. Nick was alive but Samuel was dead. Auberon had come for her at the theatre, and Cecil had invaded her home.

She'd been possessed, shoved out of her own body by her Orisha.

Her father stood at the base of the stairs, his brown face pale. "I used nearly every resource I have but . . . love, I'm afraid Ben may be gone. We need to prepare ourselves, prepare Joan."

"No, Joan isn't ready for this." Her mother shook her head fiercely. "We will find Ben."

"Bess—"

Mrs. Sands crouched down and gripped Joan's hands. "Joan, promise me you'll stay out of this."

"Mother, Lord Salisbury won't stand for that." Joan sighed. "And I can't risk him harming our family. He's too dangerous."

She suddenly found herself wrapped up in her mother's tight embrace. Joan let herself sink into the hold and wished with all her heart that things could be different.

INTERLUDE

CHAPTER TWENTY-THREE
The Wild Hunt

erne sat astride her stallion, watching as the sun drowned along the horizon.

The time was nearly upon them.

Behind her, the Hunt churned, savage and restless. When was the last time they had been allowed to ride free?

No matter. The Hunt rode tonight.

The last bit of sunlight bled out over the city, casting the sky red before being swallowed by inky darkness.

Herne snapped her reins—the sound a call to arms to every horror and nightmare at her command. They answered in a joyous yowl, the noise a calamitous symphony.

Herne listened and rejoiced and, as night folded the city of London in her shroud, the Wild Hunt soared.

Guy Fawkes jabbed at the logs slowly burning to ash in his fire. The wood blazed but his room still held a chill.

He scowled and wrapped his blanket around himself like a cloak. He was from the north; this weak southern cold shouldn't be able to shake him.

And yet.

It was as if he had never been this chilled in his entire life.

Weak.

He shivered.

Weak.

He threw the blanket off his shoulders. How could he call himself a true man of York if he was brought low by this flimsy London nip? How could he light the fires of justice and bring down this false Protestant king if he couldn't brave the weather?

Thirty-six barrels of gunpowder sat beneath the House of Lords awaiting his flint. He was man enough for Catesby and Percy to trust him with the most important step of their plot and he was man enough to handle some womanly chill.

Let none ever call Guy Fawkes a mewling welp.

He ripped his shirt over his head, tossing it somewhere behind him, and threw the windows open into the night air. Bare-chested, he screamed into the darkness.

"Come at me, you chill London air! You'll never have me!"

"Is that a challenge, mortal?"

Guy stumbled backward, choking as he inhaled a glob of spittle. His back slammed into the floor.

A specter of absolute darkness blotted out the stars as it loomed in the window. Whatever it was stepped over the sill and slipped into his room. Guy shivered as it moved silently across the floor toward him.

"Wh-what a-are—"

A gash of white appeared somewhere near the top of the darkness. Teeth, Guy realized, sharp teeth bared in a gruesome grin.

His heart stopped, then picked up double time.

"Worry not what we of the Hunt are," the deep voice said, rattling his bones. "Your last thoughts in this world should not be wasted thus."

Guy felt dizzy. "Wha—"

Shrieks from the bowels of hell itself bombarded his ears as shadowy unspeakable things exploded through the window behind the beastly darkness. They engulfed him, swallowing his screams.

And then there was nothing more.

Feet pounded on the stairs, and the door rattled as someone pounded against it.

"Master Johnson?" a woman called. "Master Johnson, are you all right?"

The Fae now wearing Guy Fawkes's form sat up jerkily. His eyes slid up to the towering shadow of Herne, who nodded at the door.

Not-Guy stumbled to his feet and toddled toward the door like a babe. He was unused to moving in mortal flesh, walking on two legs. He tripped and slammed into the door before clumsily pulling it open enough to peek his face out. His beard—waxed and groomed to a sharp point—caught on the doorframe before flicking outward. He watched it with interest then gazed up at the person who'd come knocking.

An older woman stood holding a candle in one trembling hand with her other fist raised to bang on the door again. "Are you all right, Master Johnson? I heard such a terrible commotion up here."

He spread his lips in a smile. Devouring the mortal had given him all of the man's memories. He knew the landlady and the false name by which she called him. "Apologies, Mistress Whynniard. A commotion outside caught my eye and I responded a bit too enthusiastically. All is fine."

"Bless." Mistress Whynniard laid a hand against her chest and huffed out a sigh. She frowned at him. "Please try not to wake the whole of the house with any more excitement."

Not-Guy smiled at her and watched as she descended the stairs. Once she and her candle faded out of sight, he slipped the door closed and turned back to the hunter's shadowy darkness.

"They plan to destroy their king in fire with the gunpowder they've stored beneath somewhere called the House of Lords."

"Indeed?" Herne said. "Maintain this form and await further orders."

Not-Guy nodded and stumbled over to the bed to make himself comfortable for the night.

Herne grinned her tiger's smile again. "Come, my Hunt, a wide night still awaits us." She threw herself out into the inky darkness.

The Hunt streamed back through the open window, following their leader to ride until the sun rose.

The shutters swung closed behind them as if they had never been.

Tomkin Leef stumbled out of Devil Tavern, arm slung across the shoulders of Buckley Isley. Both men barely kept the other on his feet. Someone bumped them, grunting out a curt "Sorry." Buckley reached out, catching the stranger by his collar and dragging him back over.

"How about," Buckley sneered, "you give us back our purse?"

The boy, for that's all he could be with nary a speck of hair on his face, batted at Buckley's hands. "I ain't got no purse save my own," he spat.

Tomkin leaned over, staring the boy in his eyes. The boy looked away and Tomkin flicked his wrist. The blade he kept hidden in his sleeve slipped easily into his palm.

He pressed the tip against the boy's throat. "We ain't the types you should lie to, boy."

The boy's already pale face went white. His hands fished around in his jerkin, and then he pulled out Tomkin's purse. Tomkin knew it by the slipshod patch his late sister had sewn along one side.

The coins inside it clanked noisily as the boy dropped it into Buckley's hand.

"We're not the ones to steal from, hear?" Tomkin kept his knife against the boy's neck and poked around in his purse with his other hand. He pulled out a coin and slipped it into the boy's pocket. "From one scoundrel to another."

Buckley shoved him and they both watched as the boy sprinted noisily down the road.

"Well, now I'm upsettingly sober," Buckley said. He stuffed the purse into Tomkin's pocket and tucked one of the other man's braids behind his ear. "What say we have another?"

Tomkin burst out laughing. "How can I say no to that saucy look?"

Buckley grinned as they turned back toward the tavern.

Behind them, the boy stumbled his way to a crossroads and paused to catch his breath.

The ruckus from inside the alehouse drowned out the rumbling scream of approaching danger as Tomkin swung the door open.

But the boy, standing alone in the dark street, heard.

A cheer rose up in Devil Tavern as Buckley and Tomkin jostled their way back in for another round. The doors swung closed behind them.

Outside, beyond that warm safety, the boy with the coin in his pocket looked up. Shrieking darkness overtook him, silencing his scream before it could leave his lips.

· 4 NOVEMBER ·

CHAPTER TWENTY-FOUR
Our Revels Ended

ou're so quiet," James said.

He walked with both arms wrapped around his satchel and the strap hooked tightly across his body. Thanks to their father's treatments, James had healed enough to remove the sling this morning.

Joan nodded. "I'm on guard."

She wore Bia around her wrist again but had extended the shrunken hilt to rub against her palm. She wouldn't be caught unarmed as she had been twice already. She slid her fingers along the metal and felt the sword vibrate at her touch.

"But you don't have to be so quiet," James said. He knocked his knee against the back of hers and sent her stumbling forward a few steps.

Joan turned, scowling at him. "Stop, this isn't a game."

"Don't you think I know that?" James sighed. "We nearly lost our lives yesterday. Samuel—" He swallowed, blinking back sudden tears. "Samuel is dead. I know what's at stake."

Joan lowered her eyes. James was right and had been by her side through this whole mess.

He knew the severity of things better than anyone.

"I'm sorry. I'm just—"

"Scared?" He grabbed her hand, squeezing it. "Me too, but you don't have to face this alone."

Joan nodded, her throat tight.

"Please, don't shut me out now. I couldn't bear it."

Joan swallowed her tears and forced out a tiny smile. She kept hold of his hand for the rest of their walk.

As they rounded the corner, just skirting past the Bear Garden, banging and thumping echoed from down the street. Joan spotted a group of royal guards fastening planks of wood over the windows and door of a small house. She shifted her gaze away, throwing up a quick prayer for the people being barricaded inside their home.

The plague was a hell of a way to die.

She thought of Samuel, the wound slowly bleeding his life out over her hands.

The white walls of the theatre came into view first, a small cluster of players huddled around the rear entrance—Shakespeare, Burbage, Armin, Phillips, Rob, and Nick.

Relief swept over Joan at the sight of Nick upright and well. He turned, eyes lighting up when he saw her. He broke away from the group and ran toward her.

But Shakespeare reached them first. He swept Joan and James up in his long arms, hugging them tightly. "Thank God you're both safe."

Joan wrapped her arms around him and felt everything she'd been hiding, all that she'd been stuffing down deep inside so she could just keep moving come rushing up.

She felt it right there, pressing against her teeth, ready to burst free.

She took a deep breath. Shoved it all back down within herself and eased out of Shakespeare's hold.

She wouldn't break down weeping. Not now.

"You didn't have to wait out here for us," James said. He swiped his hand across his eyes, wiping away tears.

Rob slipped up beside him. "While we are overjoyed to see you two whole and healthy, we had no choice but to wait outside." He tangled their hands together, and James gave him a watery smile.

"That's right," Burbage said. He laid a hand on Joan's shoulder and squeezed gently. "No shows today. We've been shut down because of the plague."

Joan felt a chill.

Cecil.

He was making good on his threat to force her hand.

"Come, let's speak inside." Phillips waved the others toward the backstage door.

Joan hung back, forcing a smile when James looked back at her, a question in his eyes. "I'll be in soon. I just need a moment."

James frowned but let Rob drag him inside. Burbage, Shakespeare, and Armin followed but Nick lingered. He stepped up to Joan and took both her hands in his.

"You're all right," they said as one.

Nick flushed, his grip tensing and relaxing. Joan felt her own face grow hot. She was overjoyed to see that the color had returned to Nick's beautiful brown skin.

"What happened last night? With that lord?"

Joan frowned and shook her head. "A discussion." No need to worry him with Cecil's offer; she'd figure out how to handle it. "Who delivered the message that we'd been closed?"

Nick groaned. "There was a post nailed to the door. Are you sure you're—"

"I have to go." She slipped her hands out of Nick's. She knew where she had to go. She had stared at the paper Cecil had left her last night until the address was burned into her brain.

Nick looked at her, eyes full of worry. "Where are you going?"

"To run an errand." She smiled and waved Nick away. "I'll return shortly."

He held her gaze for a long moment before he went to join the rest in the theatre. Joan waited until he disappeared through the dark wooden door. She spun on her heel and stomped off, letting her anger overpower her fear.

Shakespeare and the rest depended on the money they made through the playhouse.

Their families depended on the money.

She couldn't allow them to suffer because of her. One person, one girl, shouldn't be the ruin of the entire company.

Cecil trusted this act would fully bring her to heel. Joan wished she could've proven him wrong, but with the fate of the King's Men in her hands, how could she do anything but agree to Cecil's demands?

Joan tried to breathe through her fear and rage as the severed heads on top of the Stone Gateway came into view.

If this was how she was rewarded for saving Cecil's son from Auberon's jack-in-irons, how much worse would he do if she refused him one final time?

How else would he harm the people she loved?

He'd surely destroy everything with nary a care, and Joan refused to let that happen. Even if what he asked of her was too much.

She couldn't risk bringing more danger to the company.

Joan swallowed, thinking of Samuel and the hole in his chest; the murder Auberon had committed right under their noses while they'd been playing.

Her hands shook and she tucked them into her skirts. She needed to get control of her emotions before she faced Cecil. She couldn't afford to give him another weakness to exploit.

CHAPTER TWENTY-FIVE
A Deal with a Gentleman

 oan expected to be left to wait once she reached Cecil's offices. Instead she near immediately found herself sitting in front of the man.

"I see you aren't a complete fool," he said, leaning deeply into his chair.

He looked even more haggard than he had the evening before, his eyes sunken and bruised, his complexion chalky and damp. Like he'd known no rest for years.

Joan couldn't manage to drum up an ounce of sympathy.

"Why do you want me to kill Auberon for you?" she blurted. She had no desire to spend more time in this man's company.

Cecil's lips slid up into a smirk. "Impertinent. How old are you, girl?"

"Sixteen." Joan clenched her jaw and held his gaze.

"Truly a child. I'm sure you remember nothing of Her Majesty Queen Elizabeth's reign."

She kept silent, her back rod straight.

"Peace, prosperity, your own precious players flourished under our great queen. Many gave their very lives to usher in England's golden days. My own father was one such dedicated citizen.

"You would think these hard-won times would last for decades to come, but reality is seldom so kind. Certain forces have become—unruly and beyond our control."

Joan's eyes narrowed. "He offered you something that night, didn't he?"

Cecil's expression darkened. "What did you say, girl?"

"I—" Joan flinched. She'd said too much.

He reached beneath his desk, eyes narrowed at her.

Joan tensed.

He placed an ornate, gilded crucifix on the center of his desk. "Pick it up."

What? Would this be how she died at his hands? Killed by a tool of the church?

"Pick. It. Up," he growled. "Now."

She stared at him. Wrapped her fingers carefully around the cross. Her senses felt nothing but plain gold.

Tension flowed from her shoulders.

It wasn't poisoned. But—but what was its purpose?

Cecil nodded. "Very well. Had you any Fae blood, that cross would have revealed you. Such godless creatures are harmed by such holy tools." He pointed to his desk.

Joan placed the crucifix down and slid her hands into her lap. She doubted the item could truly protect him. His faith seemed more strategic than true belief, and such weak sentiments rarely held power.

"As I said, you are to eliminate Auberon. Once he's gone, I suspect the rest of these creatures shall fall in line once again."

Joan knew that wasn't true. Auberon, dangerous as he was, didn't bear that much power over the rest of the Fae. But Cecil would never believe her if she said as much. Men like him only trusted their own knowledge, no matter how it may be lacking.

"Why can't you arrange for his elimination on your own?" she said instead.

"I am. You seem to have some magic that these beasts fear. So I confront one abomination with another." He sneered the word *magic*. Cecil shuffled through the papers piled on his desk. He pulled one free and tossed it to her. "I assume your parents taught you to read."

"As is proper for one of my station, my lord." Joan clamped her teeth shut around the retort she truly wanted to give and scanned the words hastily scrawled across the page.

My Lord, out of the love I bear to some of your friends, I have a care of your preservation. Therefore, I would advise you, as you tender your life, to devise some excuse to shift your attendance at this parliament; for God and man hath concurred to punish the wickedness of this time. And think not slightly of this advertisement, but retire yourself into your country where you may expect the event in safety. For though there be no appearance of any stir, yet I say they shall receive a terrible blow this parliament; and yet they shall not see who hurts them. This counsel is not to be condemned because it may do you good and can do you no harm; for the danger is passed as soon as you have burnt the letter. And I hope God will give you the grace to make good use of it, to whose holy protection I commend you.

Joan's head jerked up. "What is this?"

"A member of Parliament received that warning. As a threat to our sovereign king," Cecil said, "this deserves my full attention."

Joan nodded, placing the letter back onto the desk with shaking hands.

"Therefore, you shall eliminate Auberon using whatever devil-craft you command."

"I—"

Cecil slammed his fist onto the desk. "Defy me, girl, and I will put an end to everything you hold dear. Know that nothing is more important to me than the prosperity of England, and I've ended lives of far more value for her sake."

Yes. He'd seen his own family executed in defense of the crown. Even now, the severed heads of his wife's brothers stared out at the world from atop the Stone Gateway of London Bridge.

"Do you agree to my terms, girl?"

What was she to a man capable of that?

"Do you agree? I'll not ask you again."

Joan wondered why Ogun didn't rise to take on this man, didn't push at her consciousness to fight.

Was it because, even as he threatened to end her life, Cecil was still only human?

Not that she would let the Orisha take control of her, even to take on Lord Salisbury. The memory of floating in that cold nothingness as her body moved at the command of another sent a chill down her spine.

Joan cleared her throat.

"Yes," she said through gritted teeth.

"Excellent. His Majesty opens Parliament the fifth of November. You will handle this before that time."

"But that's tomorrow."

"Then you'd best hurry," Cecil sneered. "You are dismissed."

Joan jumped as the door flung open behind her. "Wait!" She gripped the arms of the chair, refusing to be moved until she'd had her say. "I'm doing as you've asked, so what about the theatre? You must allow the company to perform again."

"I'm afraid the Globe has been closed due to an outbreak of the plague." Cecil shrugged as he shuffled through the papers on his desk. "It is for the safety of our population."

Her stomach dropped as she remembered seeing the men nailing that house shut on her walk to the theatre. The threat of the plague was the surest way to close the Globe, and there was nothing to be done for it.

She'd just agreed to risk her life for the promise of nothing.

He pulled a folded page loose from the stack of papers on his desk and handed it to her. She grabbed it from him and glanced at the wax seal holding it closed. King James's seal.

"The theatre is closed, but the King's Men shall perform at court for the queen this evening." He shooed her off with a nasty smile. "Best hurry and deliver that to your players. You wouldn't want them to be late."

A guard snatched her by the arm and dragged her out of the office and through the building before tossing her out into the street.

The door slammed behind her.

CHAPTER TWENTY-SIX
A Dismal Display

oan kept her face carefully blank as she followed Burbage into the Banqueting House. Her muslin-wrapped collection of swords clanged and jangled with every step no matter how tightly she held them.

Too many thoughts raced through her mind. How could she find Auberon before tomorrow, and what was her plan once she did? Could she kill the Fae even if it meant allowing Ogun to use her as the Orisha saw fit?

If her parents found Baba Ben, he could restore what was broken and explain why and how Ogun could control her like this.

But they hadn't found him yet. She feared nothing would be that simple.

Shakespeare stood at the center of the playing space directing the placement of props as men set chairs and benches on surrounding scaffolding. James and Rob handed out costumes under Phillips's watchful eye.

Samuel would've been helping them if—

Joan pushed that thought aside with all her might. Like Shakespeare said, she couldn't take responsibility for Samuel's death. The weight was too heavy to carry.

But how could she put it down when Auberon had murdered Samuel while trying to kill her?

She clutched the swords tightly, muslin slipping against her sweaty palms.

Despite the company's worry and sorrow, a buzz of excitement flowed through the room, bouncing like lightning from player to player. Because in just a few hours, they'd gone from a closed theatre with no prospects to being summoned for a royal showing.

A performance for the queen in Whitehall Palace was no small thing, and that also meant no small fee. The company would dine well tonight, their wallets fatter and their reputations loftier.

Joan took it all in. Tried to feel that thrill, that anticipation. But she couldn't reach, couldn't grasp it. The weight of what she'd promised to get them here dragged her down.

Tomorrow. She had until tomorrow to find and eliminate Auberon. She would help the King's Men get set up for today's performance, help James get ready, then she would go hunt down the Fae.

It was the only solution.

Besides, she hated this play, *Othello*. Hated the disparagement of black skin. Hated seeing Burbage with his face painted black. Hated seeing James covered in white paint and powder. It turned her stomach and soured the play's poetry in her ears.

But no matter. Her Majesty Queen Anne had requested *Othello*, so the downfall of the Moor they would play.

It was a gift they were free to play at all when they could be keeping company in the Clink. So she swallowed her displeasure, stamped down her fear and worry, and prepared with the rest of the company.

—————+—————

"How can you stand doing Othello?"

James shrugged as Joan dabbed chalky white paint across his face and chest.

"I don't have much choice," he said. "I am but a lowly apprentice and I must speak the speech as Master Shakespeare would have me speak it. The only feelings I can have about dear Othello are Desdemona's." He shifted and raised his arms to be painted. "It's not like they'd notice anything that would offend us."

Joan scrunched up her nose. "Because in their eyes, we're different from the Moor."

"So, I let them have their fun." He winked at her. "And I try to steal every scene from Burbage."

Joan choked out a laugh and snorted as James chided her for smudging his paint.

A commotion sounded just beyond the curtain that blocked them from view. She and James turned as Rob swung his head around it, his white-painted shoulders bare and his corset, Emilia's costume, hanging loosely laced around his waist.

"Joan—" He paused, cleared his throat, and tried again. "Joan, you've been requested to attend Her Majesty."

"The queen?" Joan's stomach dropped to her feet as the sponge fell from her hand. She glanced at James who looked back with wide eyes.

Why was the queen of England requesting an audience with Joan? How did Her Majesty even know who Joan was? "But . . ."

Rob looked as flustered as she felt. "She asked for you specifically."

"She'll be along anon," James said. He smiled at Rob as the boy nodded and took his leave. The curtain fell closed and James ripped a gilded ribbon from the top of his cosmetics kit. He flapped a hand at Joan.

Numbly she turned around and immediately felt James's hands tugging her hair out of its neat but plain style. She snorted. "I'm glad I didn't paint your hands yet."

"Indeed."

Shakespeare threw the curtain aside. "Joan's been summoned by the queen!"

"We know." James grunted as he worked to unbraid and rebraid Joan's hair. "I'm trying to make her look like a proper lady."

"Sands! Saaaaaaaaands!"

Joan frowned. "Was that Burbage?"

Shakespeare ducked, and a heavy bolt of burgundy brocade and silk smacked Joan in the chest.

"Here's the dress, Will. I know you'll not shame us, Joan! Burbage, his face painted pure black, yelled then strode out of sight.

Shakespeare nodded. "Get your sister dressed and send her off. Joan"—he clapped his hands together—"good luck."

Then he was gone.

"What happ—" She glanced down at the fine gown in her arms.

"No time," James said, pulling at the laces of her bodice. "Let's get you dressed."

The curtain burst aside just as the garment dropped down around her waist.

"I heard Joan is to appear before the queen." Nick grinned, hair flying wild around his face. His gown—Bianca's costume—clung to his form and his face, neck, and chest already bore the white paint for the show.

Joan shrieked and clutched her loose bodice to her chest. She knew exactly how little the light fabric of her shirt concealed.

"Nicholas Tooley!" James tossed something at the other boy. "You can't just barge in on my sister!"

Nick's eyes went wide and he spun around, jerking the curtain closed behind him. "Sorry. Sorry. God's wounds—I—I'm sorry. I didn't—"

"It's fine," Joan said, her face on fire. How much had he seen? Would he want to see it again? To see more?

Her entire body went hot at the thought. Hadn't she already decided to let him go?

James raised an eyebrow at her. "What lewd imaginings have you so flushed?"

Joan shoved him away but didn't answer.

"I'll stay out," Nick mumbled, "but I brought along this." He reached his hand through a small opening in the curtain. A delicate golden necklace hung with a blooming flower pendant dangled from his closed fist. "It's always brought me luck, so I figured I'd loan it to Joan. The occasion calls for it."

Oh, but this . . .

"Nick, it's beautiful." Joan caught the necklace—real gold, she could feel it—and brought both hands around Nick's. She squeezed. "Thank you."

I could have both.

"You're welcome," he said, voice soft.

The sound settled in Joan's chest. Warmed her.

Henry and the shop be damned if I could keep this feeling—

Nick slipped both his hands through the curtain. "For luck?"

"For luck." Joan grinned, heart beating fast, and slapped her palms against his. Right. Left.

Could stoke this warmth into more. So, so much more.

"Enough." James tugged her back by her strings. "Thank you, Nick, but off with you. Both of you need to get dressed."

Nick's hands disappeared back out through the curtain. "Ah, yes—right."

Let this heat I feel for them blaze into an inferno.

Joan heard his footsteps retreat as she clutched the necklace to her chest. The temptation to call him back again washed over her. She'd hold on to this moment of warmth as tightly as she could and carry it with her through whatever came next.

———————+———————

A guard met Joan at the archway leading out of the performance space. She wiggled a little in her burgundy gown. James had pulled her bodice tighter than she was used to. She'd nearly protested before she caught a glimpse of herself in the mirror: the flat front swept up and pressed against her bosom, exaggerating their swell.

Shallow breathing was a small price to pay for the stunning look her brother had managed. She'd curse her vanity for overruling her good sense, but now was no time to think that far. She just breathed carefully and tried not to overexert herself.

James had twisted and spun her hair until it flowed out in beautiful spirals and curls. The gilded ribbon weaved in and out of the braid that framed her face. Looking like this, she wouldn't stand out among the other ladies of the court.

She hoped. Still her heart pounded in her chest. Her last encounter with a member of the peerage had ended poorly.

Tension seized the back of her neck as she remembered Cecil and his demands. There wasn't time to meet the queen when Joan had to find and kill Auberon. But there was no refusing a royal summons.

Joan resisted drying her sweaty palms on her heavy silk skirt. Bia hung subtly around her wrist, the disguised sword's quiet hum doing little to calm her nerves.

The guard led her along corridors and twisted and turned through halls until Joan knew she couldn't have found her way back to the company alone no matter how hard she tried. She didn't much like that. The royals had nothing to fear from her. She hoped she could count on the same safety but knew she could not.

Finally they approached a blond girl with a pale, barely pink complexion posted outside a door. She was draped in brilliant emerald brocade and velvet, her wispy hair pulled up and pinned with pearls and jewels.

She couldn't have been much older than Joan.

"My Lady Clifford," the guard said in deep, clipped tones, "the girl is here at Her Majesty's request."

Lady Clifford smiled brightly at Joan and held out her hand. "I shall take it from here. Mistress Joan Sands, yes?"

Joan nodded and reached out to take her hand. Her pale grip was soft as a rose petal. Joan flushed and tucked her own calloused hand into the folds of her skirt as soon as Lady Clifford let go.

"Most wonderful!" Lady Clifford politely pretended not to notice Joan's gesture and turned to knock once on the door. "Her Majesty will be very pleased to meet the King's Men's woman."

"Ah," Joan said lamely. She dare not speak more at risk of damning herself.

The door swung open, and the cloying smell of roses assaulted Joan's nose.

Lady Clifford turned to her, lips pushed out in a pout. "If I may be so bold, Mistress Sands, how old are you?"

"Sixteen, my lady."

Lady Clifford waved a hand at her. "Ah! We have but one year between us."

Joan forced her lips into a smile and mumbled out an agreement. She felt off-kilter and out of her element. Never was she so desperate to go back to her rowdy company of actors. But it was too late. Lady Clifford dragged her into the flowery room.

Pale ladies sat perched on pillows and divans around the room like a flock of colorful birds. And there, in the center of them all, her flaxen hair piled high on her head and pinned through with sparkling gems, sat Her Majesty Queen Anne herself. Joan felt many eyes burning into her as the door clicked closed behind her.

"Your Majesty," Lady Clifford said, "may I present Mistress Joan Sands."

Joan dropped into a curtsy, letting one knee touch the floor.

"My dear Lady Clifford." The queen's voice was high and grating. "You didn't tell me she was a Negress. How charming!"

Joan clenched her jaw but kept her gaze down so no one would see, because of course she'd have to deal with this.

And there was no easy escape.

Joan held completely still as the queen's ladies flitted around her. Two ran their hands along the skin of her arms.

"It's a wonder the brown doesn't rub away," one said. Joan called her Lady Foul-Breath in her head. "I had half hoped it could be cleared off like in the masque Ben Jonson wrote for us."

"Nonsense," the other said. This one was Lady Snort for her stuffy, nasal voice. "We'd need bleach for that."

They both tittered with laughter. Joan's jaw ached with the strain of keeping silent.

"Penelope," the queen called, "come, show me her palm."

Lady Foul-Breath nodded and jerked Joan forward by her arm. She flipped Joan's hand over once they were close enough for Her Majesty's view.

Lady Foul-Breath gasped. "'Tis pale. 'Tis pale as ours!"

A chorus of exclamations burst round the room, and soon Joan was surrounded on all sides. They pulled and poked at both her hands as they chirped at each other like a flock of gulls.

"I thought as much," Her Majesty said. "The next time we play Negroes, we need not paint the palms of our hands." She smiled brightly. "We shall save ourselves from such a mess."

Joan tensed her shoulders, pressing down on the tremors of rage with every ounce of her will. She could never let it show. Not here, not in this company. She breathed deeply and continued making up cruel names for each of them in her head.

Her gaze drifted between the heads of two ladies. She spotted Lady Clifford standing off to one side, her lips pursed in a frown.

Someone knocked at the door and the woman Joan called Lady Goose Neck flounced over to speak to them. She spun back into the room with a wide smile.

"The players are ready, Your Majesty."

"Most excellent!" the queen said. "Let us attend them." She stood and strode toward the door, the rest of her retinue following after. She paused at the door and turned back. "Lady Clifford, dear"—she waved a hand at the girl—"bring along the Negress; she shall sit with us."

Joan's stomach plummeted. She didn't know how much longer she could stand this treatment. She felt Lady Clifford step up beside her.

"Of course, Your Majesty."

Satisfied, the queen continued on in the company of her ladies. Lady Clifford gave Joan a tight-lipped smile. Joan said nothing and followed the rest out into the main hall.

Her Majesty Queen Anne had a special viewing area set up for herself and her ladies upon the highest scaffold in the Banqueting House's main hall. Several gilded chairs clustered together around a gaudy throne of gold and crimson velvet.

The perfect spot to see and be seen.

The queen took her place as Lady Foul-Breath, Lady Snort, and the rest arranged themselves around her. Leaving one empty chair. Joan stood awkwardly beside Lady Clifford, willing her imagination silent. She tried to expect nothing.

"Fetch me a cushion," the queen shouted into the room.

A boy appeared and placed a tufted pillow at the queen's feet. She nodded at him and he disappeared just as suddenly.

"Come, girl," she said, "you shall sit here."

Joan jerked forward, keeping her eyes low. When the pillow slipped into her view, she slowly lowered herself to the floor. She arranged her burgundy skirts neatly around her legs before placing her hands in her lap and facing forward.

Someone gripped her hair, jerking her head back.

"My word," the queen said, "'tis soft."

Instantly a flock of hands pawed at Joan's head as the queen and her ladies tittered about how soft her hair was.

Her eyes burned.

Joan touched Bia where the sword looped around her wrist and shaped it into a dull point. She took a breath then jabbed her finger against the tip, hard enough to hurt but not so much that she'd draw blood.

The sudden soft pain dried her eyes.

Good.

She pressed her finger against it again. She'd focus on that feeling. She'd focus and she'd get through this.

She stabbed her finger again.

She would.

"Greetings, Your Majesty."

Joan flinched at the familiar male voice. His shoes came into view first, but Joan doubted she'd ever forget his flat, nasal tones.

She glanced up and met Cecil's dispassionate glare. His eyes drifted away from her as if she were nothing.

Joan clenched her jaw and stared straight ahead. That thrice-damned man had given her a day to do his bidding and here she was forced to waste most of that precious time planted at Her Majesty's feet while the queen pulled and tugged at her hair.

She stabbed her finger with Bia again, hard, and looked down expecting to see blood. There was none, but Joan eased up on her jabs nonetheless.

"Salisbury," the queen sneered. "Come to nose about the court again?"

"Like a weasel?" Lady Foul-Breath muttered.

"Or a rat," Lady Snort said.

The ladies tittered with laughter. Joan looked up at Cecil from beneath her eyelashes.

His haggard face was pleasantly blank; none of the bite he had in front of Joan showed itself before the queen. "I am merely here to hear the play, Your Majesty."

"Tell me, girl," the queen jerked Joan's head back by her hair. "Shall Master Burbage be playing today?"

Joan swallowed her yelp of pain. "Aye, Your Majesty. He shall play Othello himself." She watched Cecil's shoes shuffle off as the queen ignored him.

She almost, nearly, barely felt a twinge of sadness for him.

But no.

"Oh, wonderful! My dear Lucy is quite enamored of him. Aren't you, Lucy?"

Lady Snort blushed bright red as the women around her giggled.

The musicians struck up and a hush fell over the crowd.

"Speak not to me until the play is done." The queen jabbed the toe of her shoe into Joan's spine. "Be sure you do not make a sound. I'll not have this ruined with your distraction."

Joan stabbed herself in the finger and wished again that she was anywhere but here.

———+———

"That handkerchief / Which I so loved and gave thee, thou gavest to / Cassio," Burbage thundered, his face painted all over in black.

"No, by my life and soul!" James, painted and powdered with white, cowered in the pile of pillows and throws that made Othello and Desdemona's bed. *"Send for the man / And ask him."*

Joan hated this ending. Watching mistrust brew between two people as in love and suited to each other as Desdemona and Othello always broke her heart.

"How monstrous a Black brute is he," Her Majesty sneered.

Joan felt her teeth grind together with the struggle to keep silent.

James hung from Burbage's robes. *"O, banish me, my lord, but kill me not!"* The blond curls of his wig tumbled gracefully over his shoulders even in his desperation.

"Down, strumpet!" Burbage kicked James away.

The audience gasped, someone even booed loudly.

"Kill me tomorrow, let me live tonight."

"Nay, if you strive—"

"But half an hour!"

"Being done there is no pause—"

"But while I say one prayer!"

"It is too late."

Burbage snatched up a pillow and dove on James. He seemed to press it against Joan's brother's face, smothering his cries.

"Of course the foolish Moor murders the poor girl," the queen whispered behind Joan. "I have heard that their brains are smaller than ours."

Joan's jaw ached from the effort of stifling her thoughts for the three-hours traffic of the play. She jabbed herself again in the finger.

Sad though the scene may be, it meant that the relief of the performance's end was nigh. Joan could barely contain her relief.

Let them all die and be done with and let me be free of this detested admiration, Joan thought.

One by one they all fell. Desdemona died smothered by her husband, Othello. Her maid Emilia—played by Rob—perished upon the sword of her own husband, Iago—acted by Shakespeare himself. And finally, Othello stabbed himself in the heart.

Joan doubted she'd ever felt so much relief seeing Burbage collapse to the floor.

"*Myself will straight abroad,*" the actor hired to play Lodovico this performance said, "*and to the state / This heavy act with heavy heart relate.*"

Silence. Then the trill of a flute, the bang of the drum, and—their heavy work complete—the players gathered as one to dance.

"Bravo, Master Burbage! Bravo!"

The queen's shouts were joined by a chorus of her ladies and surrounding subjects as they heaped praises upon Burbage and his coal-smudged face.

He, always a fan of cheers, added an extra flourish when he took center stage. Joan noticed his extra shimmy and rolled her eyes.

She glanced through the rest of the company until she found James's white-painted face. Their eyes met as he straightened from his bow. She tried to convey everything she couldn't speak with her gaze and saw his fists clench.

And then the players were gone.

"How beastly was Master Burbage's Othello," the queen sneered. "Expected of one of his complexion." She stabbed her toe into Joan's back again. "Are you such a brute when angered, girl?"

Joan closed her eyes and choked down the sour rage clogging her throat. Pressed her finger against her iron spike.

"It's merely a play, Your Majesty," Lady Clifford said with a laugh. "I'm sure dear Joan is as gentle as any of us."

Joan glanced over at her. The other girl's wide smile didn't reach her eyes.

"Indeed?" The queen hummed. "We have learned much today. Girl, you are dismissed. Anne, return her."

Lady Clifford leapt from her seat. Joan struggled to her feet on tingling legs. She turned, giving an ugly, clumsy curtsy, her legs numb from sitting on the pillow for three hours.

"It was a pleasure attending upon Your Majesty today," Joan said. Her voice pitched high as the gratitude struggled from her mouth. She jabbed her finger again.

She was surprised she had yet to draw blood.

The queen hummed, rose from her seat, and disappeared through the hall's doors. Her ladies followed behind her, leaving Joan and Lady Clifford behind.

Joan willed Bia to wrap smoothly around her wrist again. She glanced down at the bright red sore spot at the center of her finger.

"You did well, Joan." Lady Clifford smiled tightly at her. "I could not have taken so much in silence."

"Thank you, Lady Clifford." She dipped into another stiff curtsy. "May I ask if I am dismissed?"

Lady Clifford nodded, frowning. Joan straightened and turned to leave.

"Joan?" The girl grabbed Joan's arm tightly, her gaze hard. "Such disgraceful behavior will not happen again. I swear it."

Joan felt an odd chill at the force of the words. "Th-thank you for your concern, Lady Clifford."

The sharp presence of Ogun burned in her chest.

But why now?

"Is that thanks sincere?" Lady Clifford's eyes lit up.

Joan blinked at her. "Yes," she said slowly, something about the radiant joy in the other girl's face unnerving her.

"Most excellent. I shall hold you to that."

Lady Clifford pulled away and exited through the door that the queen and her ladies had used. Joan watched her go. The other girl's sleeve slid up and Joan caught a glimpse of some redness on the pale, unblemished skin of Lady Clifford's forearm. Joan squinted at the mark. It seemed almost in the shape of a palm.

Joan's heart thumped, racing double time. She'd given such a wound in the dimness of the Globe's tiring-house. She remembered it now. The struggle backstage, the naked woman she'd barely fought off. The taste of her own death on her lips as the woman nearly strangled her before Joan forced her away by burning the woman's arm with iron.

She remembered the joy on that same woman's face as Joan's godfather was dragged away.

Bia vibrated at Joan's wrist as Ogun pressed for dominance over her consciousness. Joan took a deep breath and forced herself to keep control.

Lady Clifford smiled at her from the open door. "I so look forward to our next meeting." And then she was gone.

Joan stood for a long moment, staring at the dark wood through which the disguised Fae woman had gone.

Should she follow? Reveal her to someone of authority?

Joan stepped toward the door.

She remembered hands in her hair, touching her skin, treating her like a pet. A thing. A novelty.

No one who behaved like that would listen to anything Joan had to say, especially about one of their own.

Beneath whatever stolen form she wore, Joan knew that woman, that Fae, bore the same dark skin as she. Had surely felt each prod and barb as sharply as Joan had. And she had promised Joan justice, truly. Joan felt the weight of the words that Lady Clifford had spoken.

And yet, this same woman knew something of Baba Ben's disappearance. How could Joan trust the Fae who'd helped vanish her godfather? What more did that woman have in store for Joan herself?

Joan turned and made her way back to the company. The royals had their own protections, Cecil included. The risk of accusing, of attacking, one of the queen's ladies loomed over her. Joan was no good to anyone, least of all Baba Ben, if she was sent to a cell right alongside him or worse, executed.

These secrets would have to wait until she dispatched Auberon. Joan just prayed there would be time enough to discover them.

CHAPTER TWENTY-SEVEN
The Faerie Rade

anceen Dock tossed the rancid contents of the chamber pot out into the streets and groaned as her back cracked in protest.

"That the last of 'em?" Gussie Kilner slipped into the room. She pressed the door closed behind her with a soft click.

"Aye," Fanceen said as she slipped the ceramic bowl back under the young mistress's bed. The young mistress who was barely a year younger than Fanceen and Gussie.

Fanceen straightened as Gussie crossed the room and clasped her cheeks with both hands. "I'd touch you but I think I've got shite on my hands."

Gussie barked out a laugh and kissed her until she could scarcely breathe. "Wipe it on the brat's sheets and let's be gone." She pulled away. "Ferry still ain't running, so we'll have to walk."

Fanceen rubbed the grime from her hands on a corner of the young mistress's bedsheets. The child wouldn't notice; she already kept questionable hygiene unchecked.

Fanceen followed Gussie through the house and down into the kitchen, untying her apron as they went. Both women nodded at the steward as they draped their aprons over the hook by the back door.

She slipped her wrap over her shoulders and lifted her chin as Gussie tucked the fabric more tightly under her neck. Over Gussie's shoulder, Fanceen could see the steward shaking his head. She raised an eyebrow at him and watched as he hobbled off back into the main house.

"Jealous old coot," Gussie grumbled.

Fanceen just smiled and followed her out the door.

They walked in silence, hands occasionally brushing together. Fanceen fought a grin every time their fingers tangled. The towers at the north end of London Bridge had just loomed into view when she spotted him.

A magnificent man sat astride a mighty buck so white it seemed to glow in the fading sunlight. Jewels blinked and twinkled as they dripped all across the ornate saddle and looped around a mighty pair of antlers nearly as big as Gussie was tall.

Fanceen's eyes drifted along the starlight sparkle of stones until she saw his face. Her heart thumped in her chest.

No gem could match the majesty of that face. Fanceen had never seen anyone so beautiful.

"What's your name?" he said, his voice soft as a caress wrapped around her loudly and clearly.

"Fanceen," she whispered back.

A tug at her hand.

"From where have you come, Fanceen?"

"My employers, Lord and Lady Saunders."

He smiled at her and she knew, if she could, she'd follow him forever into eternity and beyond.

Another tug, harder this time.

"Have they a daughter?" he cooed.

"Aye," she said. Never had a man made her feel this way. "One named Olivia."

His beautiful face shifted into a scowl then, and Fanceen had never felt a wound cut her as deeply as that look. She felt her heart break; would do whatever it took to have him smile upon her again. Would throw herself into the depths of the Thames if only—

Something stepped into her way, blocking her view of heaven's most magnificent creature. Fanceen's head whipped to the side, her cheek aching as that something slapped her.

No, not something. Someone.

She shook her head. Gussie gripped both her shoulders, eyes wide and frightened as she stared into Fanceen's face.

"Love," Gussie said, "what's wrong with you?"

Love.

Something in the word knocked Fanceen back into herself. She felt her shoulders sag as her sudden enthrallment flew from her mind. She looked up into Gussie's face, her wildly bushy eyebrows and crooked nose from a break when they were children.

This, this was the most beautiful face she'd ever seen. How could she have forgotten? How could some man, however handsome, make her forget her Gussie?

"You slapped me," she said.

Gussie snorted. "I wouldn't have if you'd just answered me instead of acting all possessed."

"There was a man—" Fanceen turned, but the mysterious rider was gone.

Gussie barked out a laugh. "You noticed a man? Must've been a specter of some sort for that to happen." She twined her fingers with Fanceen's and pulled her along toward London Bridge.

"No, it was—"

"Don't. Let's just get home before dark, eh?"

Fanceen clamped her lips shut. She felt the tremors in Gussie's hand and the tight way the other woman gripped her fingers.

So she had seen it too. Whatever it was.

Fanceen tried to smile, forcing the corners of her mouth to twist up. "Yes," she said, "let's go home. I must be more tired than I thought."

Gussie nodded and the two quickened their pace.

Two streets over, Hannalee Chamberlain let her velvet skirts drag through the mud and filth with nary a care. The beautiful man wanted her to follow, and she'd go with him anywhere.

She reached out a hand to brush along the tail of his stag. The creature twisted its majestic neck around and flashed sharp teeth at her.

Hannalee felt a sting then sudden wetness. The stag pulled back, its mouth stained liquid crimson.

"Oh dear," Auberon said. He patted the buck on the neck.

His voice was just as glorious as the rest of him. It flowed through her ears like music, and Hannalee's heart swelled with love.

He smiled at her. "He despises being touched by mortal hands. Don't try again unless you want to lose the other one."

Hannalee looked down at herself and found a bleeding stump where her right hand used to be. All at once, the pain hit her. Her breath shuddered.

"Girl," Auberon said.

She looked up and her eyes met his. He leaned close, so close that pressing up to kiss him was easy.

His lips were sweet as nectar, and suddenly nothing else mattered again. No pain. No blood.

Nothing but him.

"Come along."

She nodded and began to walk behind him. If each step became more of a struggle and the world seemed to tilt and shift before her, she noticed not. She only had eyes for her beautiful man. Someone bumped her shoulder. She whipped her head to the side. Another woman had fallen in step beside Hannalee.

Auberon turned and jerked his stag to a stop when he saw this new woman. He stared at her, his eyebrow raised. "What's your name, mortal?"

"Nan," the woman said smiling up at him.

"Tell me, Nan, from whence have you come?"

Nan blushed. "From my employers, my lord."

"Call me king. And who are your employers?"

"Master and Mistress Sands, my king."

Hannalee squirmed as Auberon's face lit up with joy. She felt blinded.

"Is this the one I seek?" Auberon seemed to ask the air beside him.

"Yes," the air answered in a tiny voice like the tinkling of a bell. "This one serves in the house of the Iron Blade."

Strange that the air should speak, but Hannalee expected no less from her majestic lord. Her heart swelled with adoration again.

"The Sands," he said slowly, "have a daughter, do they not?"

Nan nodded. "Aye, my king. One named Joan."

He slipped from his elaborate saddle and walked toward the two women.

Hannalee felt her heart quicken as he approached.

"Joan Sands," Auberon laughed. He reached out, hooking a finger under Nan's brown face. "Joan Sands, how delightful." He pulled Nan in close, waited until she pressed her lips to his. Smiled. "You truly are the prize I've been hunting for this wide night. Come, my dear, you ride with me."

He guided Nan over to his stag and lifted her into the saddle. He swung up behind her and pulled her to lean against him. "I have a task for you, my Nan. Let us return to your employers."

Hannalee hurried up beside him. "And me, my king?"

He looked down at her. "You—" He nudged her away with his foot. "You shall walk."

She stumbled backward, eyes slipping closed in rapture.

Never had she felt a kiss that held in it such bliss as the touch of his foot. She sighed and followed behind him, even unto oblivion.

CHAPTER TWENTY-EIGHT
Merely Players

nother round for the company!"

A cheer burst forth from the King's Men as Yaughan poured ale liberally in Burbage's direction. Rob and James tried to teach Nick a complex sequence of dance steps as Shakespeare watched, clapping and laughing.

Joan observed the celebrations over the rim of her tankard. She took a sip as Burbage and Armin toasted each other sloppily, Burbage still painted that false black.

The weakened ale soured on her tongue.

The people loved Burbage's Othello, and Burbage loved the people's attention. It didn't matter how it made anyone feel beyond that; the adoration was loudest, and that's what mattered.

Joan sighed. That insult alone was enough to turn her mood, but so much more weighed upon her mind.

Seeing Cecil again made her promise sit in her stomach like a stone. She couldn't escape her task. And she only had until tomorrow to accomplish it.

To kill Auberon.

No one seemed to notice her tucked into the dim corner. Joan couldn't decide if that was a bad thing or not.

Goodfellow appeared at the inn and draped themself next to Joan as Rose slid in across the table.

"Tell me, Iron Blade," Goodfellow said, "did the company come by this royal summons by way of a certain spymaster?"

Joan sighed and nodded miserably.

"And do they know this, in all their revelry?"

"No." She looked up at Goodfellow, eyes pleading. "Don't tell them. I don't want them to know."

They nodded, lips pursed.

Rose scowled. "I doubt you could get a single word in with any of them now."

"Of course not," Goodfellow said. "They're actors."

"Let them have their fun," Joan said. Goodfellow and Rose both turned to her. "Playmaking is hard work."

"And being tasked with killing Auberon isn't?" Rose raised an eyebrow.

Joan shrugged. "If Cecil hadn't caught me using my powers, I wouldn't be forced to do his bidding now."

Rose hissed. "You think Auberon is the only one you need to worry—"

Goodfellow held up a hand and Rose clamped her mouth shut.

"Cecil knows how dangerous Auberon is," Joan said. "That's why he chose me. Either I succeed and solve his problem, or I die trying and he loses nothing but a lowly Negro girl." She took a deep breath. Air caught tightly in her chest. She ran her fingers over Bia, wrapped around her wrist. "It's best that I face this alone. I can't—" Samuel appeared in her mind, his face pale and slack as blood poured from a wound they couldn't suture. "I can't lose anyone else."

"If this is the path you've chosen, then you've no room for doubt, Iron Blade," Goodfellow said frowning.

It felt as if the floor had dropped out from under her.

All she had was doubt. How could she possibly . . .

Joan thought of that feeling, of losing herself to Ogun, of not being in control of her own body. Of disappearing into the dark abyss as an Orisha bent her to his will.

She shivered.

This was too much.

She felt Goodfellow's eyes burning into her skull like the sun focused through a lens. They huffed and threw a hand up to signal someone.

James jogged over to their table. "What has you lot looking so gloomy? We had a royal—"

"Go gather your master and your playwright. We have a . . . task." Goodfellow waved him off.

Joan scowled as she watched James wrangle Shakespeare and Phillips. She glared at Goodfellow as the men approached the table. Goodfellow ignored her and gestured for the men to have a seat.

"What's all this?" Shakespeare said as he plopped down. "Joan, why are you hiding over here?"

"Gentlemen," Goodfellow said, "we have a crisis."

Shakespeare scowled. "Does this have anything to do with our troubles yesterday?"

"Or our troubles this morning?" Phillips said.

"It seems that Robert Cecil is excellent at keeping his promises." Goodfellow looked pointedly at James.

"Wait." The information traveled across James's face as he put the pieces together. "Joan, tell me you didn't."

"I—" She clamped her mouth shut, unwilling to lie to her brother's face.

Shakespeare frowned. "Cecil? The king's spymaster? Why would he visit our Joan?"

Goodfellow snorted. "He wants her to kill Auberon."

Phillips's pale face drained of all color.

"You told him yes, didn't you?" James scowled at Joan. "That's where you disappeared to this morning."

Joan could barely breathe. They weren't supposed to know.

"Hold, hold," Shakespeare said. "What has she agreed to and what does Oberon have to do with it?" He turned to Goodfellow. "And I never did catch your name—"

"That's Robin Goodfellow," Phillips said.

Goodfellow nodded to him. Joan saw the moment the name registered on Shakespeare's face. She'd have chuckled if she could actually catch her breath.

This was going all wrong.

"And it's *Au*beron, not *O*beron," Phillips continued. "The Pact between the Fae and the English monarchs has been broken. There's nothing holding any of us back now."

Shakespeare turned wide eyes to Phillips. "Broken?"

"You know of the Pact?"

"Yes, my mother told me." Shakespeare shook his head.

Phillips frowned. "Your mother? She's Fae?"

"No—" He hesitated, breathed deeply. "My mother Mary is like Joan."

Joan's mind raced. Shakespeare's mother was a child of the Orisha? Then that meant—

"Your mother is Black? Like us?" James blurted.

Shakespeare held up a hand. "Aye, and we'll speak more of my mother later. There are things more pressing." He pursed his lips and looked to Goodfellow. "Why has this task fallen to our Joan?"

"She saved his son," James said. "From a jack-in-irons. And this is how he repays her."

"Stop talking about me as if I'm not here," she hissed. "I had to do it. Cecil would have destroyed everything if I hadn't agreed to his demands."

She felt her eyes burn and swallowed the lump in her throat. She'd been so good at holding the weight of all this back. But now . . .

If she just breathed through this, she wouldn't cry. She couldn't. Not in front of them.

If only she could catch her breath.

"He would've arrested us all," she said carefully. "He closed the the-atre, and that's what he was going to do next. Put us all into prison. How could I let that happen—because of me? How could I let you all come to ruin because of me?"

She felt it coming and she couldn't stop it. Her throat pinched closed, her nose clogged, and she couldn't hold back. Tears spilled down her face. She shoved her fists against her eyes, willing them to stop; she felt the wetness pouring over her hands like defeat.

"Hush, Joan, hush." Shakespeare swept her into his embrace, his voice rumbling against her face. "What's done is done, but we'll not let you take this burden upon you and leave us out." He squeezed as she sobbed into his shirt. "You're not alone, Joan. Know that."

Joan couldn't see, could barely hear through the pounding of blood in her ears. She hated being so weak. Knew it wouldn't help her in the coming fight.

But she didn't have more in her. Not now.

"None of our company should have to stand alone," Shakespeare said gently.

Joan felt her heart hiccup and struggle to keep pace as hope bloomed in her chest.

She'd have to face Cecil's challenge, but she wouldn't have to face it alone. She felt her shoulders relax, easing down from where they'd bunched near her ears.

"So, what's our plan?" Phillips said as several suspicious gazes turned to him at once. He huffed out a breath. "Don't eye me so. If it's Auberon we're after, then I am with you all. I may be Fae but I owe him none of my loyalty."

"With the whole company, we'll have numbers on our side," Shakespeare muttered before grinning. "Aye, that's the plan. We take him on together, just as we did yesterday."

Goodfellow snorted. "Numbers are all well and good, but only Joan has the ability to do any real damage."

"I can arm them," Joan said, wiping the wetness from her face. She pulled away from Shakespeare to address their whole group. "I'll fit the blades with iron, enough for the whole company."

Yes. With her whole company behind her and with a plan, she'd come out on the other side of Cecil's challenge victorious and, most importantly, alive.

Joan sat on her father's workshop stool and focused on coating the blade in her hands in a layer of iron. She felt exhausted. The day had brought so much: her meeting with Cecil, an audience with the queen, Shakespeare and Phillips agreeing to rally the company to her defense, and now preparing these weapons.

She'd never produced so much iron; had already coated some thirteen-odd swords. It felt like the metal was being wrung out of her very bones. But she couldn't stop. Not until every member of their group was well-armed.

"Joan."

She looked up, squinting in the dim candlelight. James stood close, frowning at her.

How had he gotten so near without her noticing?

"You need to sleep," he said.

Joan shook her head. "Not until this is done. Everyone must have adequate arms."

"And you're no good to anyone tomorrow if you exhaust yourself tonight." He knelt before her and gently pulled the sword from her hands. "You've done enough."

"If anything happens, it's on me. If anyone else—" She took a breath, tried to steady herself. "I can't let anyone die because of this."

"You've done enough. You must sleep."

Joan looked at her brother. She knew he was right. Never had she felt this worn down and nearly empty. If she kept this up, she'd be useless in a fight. She nodded, and James smiled and squeezed her hands.

He stood. "Come on, let's get you to bed."

Joan paused, hands clutching her skirts. She couldn't move, not yet. A thought still troubled her.

"Are Mother and Father here?"

James frowned. "Not yet, but you're not staying up to wait for them. Look at you. You're practically asleep right here."

"That's not—" Joan shook her head. "James, does Oya ever—has she ever taken control of you?"

"Once in a ceremony but mostly I feel her presence here." He placed a hand over his chest. "Especially when I perform."

"Has she possessed you in any other times?"

James frowned. "What do you mean?"

"When I—" She took another shaky breath. "Both times fighting the red caps, I—I wasn't in control of myself. It was Ogun. I had his power and strength, but it was like I was watching myself from far away."

"Like you were in the heat of battle?"

"No, he— I had no control over myself. All I could do was watch as he moved me like a puppet."

James's eyes widened. "What? Joan, why didn't you say—"

"What becomes of me if he takes me over completely and I can't get back?"

"I don't think that's—"

Hinges squeaked as the shop door swung open and Nan slipped through. Joan held a hand to her chest to calm her racing heart. James snorted, pretending he hadn't been caught off guard as well.

"Nan, we thought you'd gone," he said.

Nan looked up at them with a distracted smile. "Ah, young master and young miss. It's past the bells so I had best stay here for the night."

Joan nodded to her. Nan's blackness made her an easy target for any patrolman out to catch someone after curfew. She often stayed for the night if the roads seemed unsafe.

"Rest well, Nan," James said.

Nan nodded and headed upstairs, leaving them alone in the workshop.

"I don't think you'll lose yourself, but let's talk with Mother and Father in the morning." James pulled Joan to her feet and into a hug. "They'll find Baba and all the rest of this will be repaired. You'll see."

Joan nodded, feeling more worn out now that she stood. She swayed a little.

"You need sleep, dear sister. Let's get you upstairs to your bed." James looped her arm through his to take on most of her weight.

Yes, sleep was imperative. She smiled at her brother and let him lead her out of the shop.

She'd get her answers tomorrow.

CHAPTER TWENTY-NINE
Labors Lost

oan awoke shivering in the early morning darkness. Across the room, the fireplace sat cold and dark as if no one had ever lit it.

Joan scowled and sat up, remembering James stoking the flames to blazing after helping her into bed.

"You'd think after one thousand five hundred and sixty-two long years held prisoner to that Pact"—the form of a man stepped out of the shadows lurking along the edge of her bedroom—"I'd finally be able to enjoy having the freedom I deserve."

She sat up, and Auberon was on her, pinning her to the bed. His sharp knees dug into her shoulders. Joan took a deep breath to scream.

His hands wrapped around her throat, strangling the sound before she could make it.

"No," he said. "No help. It's just you and me now, girl."

Joan bucked against him. He barely shifted.

She felt the scarf unraveling itself from her hair as she struggled. Her vision darkened around the edges.

Auberon leaned in close, the gems and trinkets in his long hair scratching against her face. "You have been a thorn in my side since I first laid eyes on you."

He loosened his grip.

Joan gasped and coughed. Her mind cleared.

"But you can be of use to me." His fist tightened around her throat again. "Before I end your life."

No breath. Her fingers clawed at the sheets.

"Although I'd love to watch the life leave your eyes like this." He leaned in closer, touching his nose to hers. "It would be delicious."

Her head went light. Her hands dropped limply to the bed.

No. She refused to die like this.

Her arms were pinned but her legs were free.

An iron blade formed on her knee, taking shape far faster than she'd ever managed before. Her body bucked and she drove it into Auberon's back. Skin and sinew gave way, then the hot rush of blood.

Auberon's eyes widened and his mouth flapped in shock.

The wet thrust of the blade sounded like justice.

She struck again. And again.

Suddenly she could move. Her arms swung around, knocking his hands away from her throat.

Auberon let out a strangled gurgle and she shoved him away. He thudded against the floor. Joan leapt from the bed, flinging the blankets behind herself.

Joan felt Ogun's presence creeping into her mind, fire and fury. She tried to focus but her chest burned.

A chill rushed through her, sudden and stark. Then she was surrounded by that cursed nothingness as the Orisha shoved her aside and her presence disappeared from this plane.

Fear clenched Joan's heart deep in the darkness where she floated, helpless. She felt like screaming but how could she with no mouth, no throat, no lungs?

No, I don't want this. Give me back my body.

Joan couldn't lose herself like this. She tried to focus through the panic, through the fear. Tried to claw her way out of the terrifying abyss and back to the surface.

Let me go. Give me back my body.

Desperate, she thought of things to ground herself in herself. The cool press of metal, the chill morning air in her room.

Give me back my body.

The soft shift of her nightgown against her skin.

Give me back my body.

The icy floor beneath her bare feet.

GIVE ME BACK MY BODY.

She shoved with every ounce of will within her to drive her way out of the darkness. The world shifted into sudden bright focus as she fell back into control of her own body. It felt like bursting through the surface of an icy lake.

Sudden awareness flooded her senses. Her foot pressed down onto Auberon's chest, holding him down with a strength beyond her own. A machete of pure iron kissed his exposed throat, drawing the thinnest sliver of crimson blood. The villain gasped for breath and for the first time, Joan saw fear in his eyes.

She hesitated for a moment too long.

Auberon growled and batted her away.

She slammed into the wall with a thud. The machete clattered to the ground. She shook her head, trying to clear the flashes of light from her vision.

Joan grunted and struggled to her knees. Her throat ached and she couldn't stop shivering.

"A mistake," Auberon panted, stumbling toward her. "Sparing me was a mistake."

"I won't make it again," she spat, voice rasping and raw.

"Joan!"

Her bedroom door swung open and James tore into the room. He threw himself at Auberon. They both tumbled across the floor.

Joan reached for the machete. Her fingers brushed against it, and it vanished. She jerked her hand away.

"You'll do, boy," Auberon said from somewhere behind her.

She spun, ready to tackle the Fae unarmed, but the room was empty. Auberon was gone and James along with him.

"James!" she screamed. She turned her palm up and tried to call the machete to her again.

Nothing.

She closed her eyes and turned all her focus inward, listening for singing of metal, for Ogun's voice, for anything.

Silence.

Her stomach clenched. She commanded iron to flow into her hand.

Nothing.

No.

No, no, no, no, no.

She crawled across the floor, snatching Bia from where the blade leaned against the wall.

The sword lay silent in her grip. Not a hum. Not a whisper. Nothing.

She collapsed on the floor.

Had Ogun forsaken her completely? All because she didn't want to be possessed?

"That's not fair," she whispered, tears burning her eyes. "I need you to help me save James." She focused on the blade, listening for something. Anything. "You can't abandon me. I need you."

But there was nothing, because she'd driven away Ogun, and he'd taken her powers as punishment.

And what was she to do with nothing?

How could she defeat Auberon with nothing?

She gripped Bia until her knuckles cramped.

Her mind raced. She hadn't covered the sword in iron last night because she'd been exhausted and sure she'd be able to do it before she faced down Auberon. But now, that confidence looked like foolishness.

One problem at a time.

She needed to get her hands on one of those thirteen blades she had prepared for the other players. She'd grab the blades and gather Shakespeare and the rest.

Then they'd take down Auberon and rescue James and she'd worry about her powers and Ogun once everyone was safe.

One problem at a time.

She needed those swords.

She scrambled to her feet and flung open her door.

"Joan!"

Her parents stumbled toward her, her mother bloody and half draped across her father's back.

"Mother!" Joan screamed. Bia clattered to the floor. She slipped under her mother's other arm and helped drag her over to the bed. A warm wetness seeped into Joan's chemise from somewhere around her mother's waist.

"Where's James?" her father said. "We need his help."

Joan looked up at her father, her eyes welling with tears. "Auberon—he was here. He attacked me and James—" Her voice broke over the words. "He took James."

Her mother moaned in pain and her father cursed. He ripped open the fabric covering her mother's torso, revealing a long gash sluggishly oozing blood.

Joan recoiled.

"He got through our protections," her mother grunted. "He shouldn't have been able to get through—" She winced and groaned. "Someone let that damned Fae in."

Her father placed his hands over her mother's wound and pressed down. Her mother moaned then gritted her teeth. This had to be done so he could heal her.

Joan stumbled back away from the bed. She'd heard enough. James could still be alive in Auberon's clutches. She couldn't bear to think of anything else. She had to act.

She held her hand open, calling for the metal once again.

Nothing.

All this time, she'd been afraid of Ogun taking her. Of the Orisha swallowing her up until there was nothing of Joan left. But now . . .

Now, without him, without the powers he granted her, how could she ever hope to win?

No. She still had the swords, thirteen of them down in the workshop. With those, the fight wasn't hopeless.

She looked up at her father working to stop her mother's bleeding. She couldn't ask them to help her. This would have to be her fight.

"I have to go." She laid a kiss on her mother's forehead and locked eyes with her father.

He nodded at her and turned back to his work.

"Wait, Joan," her mother whispered, grasping for her hand. "We found Ben."

Joan froze. "Where?" Hope filled her heart.

Baba would know what to do. He'd complete the ritual and tell her how to regain her magic. Help her save James.

"He's in the Tower," her father said, not looking at her.

Despair washed over her.

The Tower of London was the most secure prison in all of London. If Baba was being held there, then he was as good as lost.

Everything was falling to pieces.

One problem at a time.

She gripped her mother's hand to try to stop her own from shaking.

One problem at a time.

"I'll bring James home," she said. "Then we can figure out the rest together."

One problem at a time.

She gently released her mother's hands and nodded to her father before rushing to her closet.

She tossed on the first skirt and bodice her hands touched and, with Bia in hand, sprinted down the stairs. She bounded off the final step, sprinting through the still-dark store when a light in the workshop caught her eye.

Joan stopped then raised Bia as she crept into the other room, ready to strike whoever or whatever she found there.

Nan stood in front of the furnace, the roaring fire casting her in silhouette. She reached beside herself and tossed something else onto the blazing flames.

"Nan," Joan said, dropping Bia's point to the ground. "Nan, you need to go upstairs and help Father. Mother's hurt and James is in grave danger."

Nan tossed something else into the furnace. "I'm doing as my king asked."

Joan froze. Her king?

"Nan, what are you doing?"

"As my king bade me." She tossed another thing into the flames.

A sword.

"No!" Joan raced to where she'd left the iron-coated swords. The basket was empty.

Nan tossed another sword into the fire.

A sword covered in iron. A sword Joan couldn't remake without Ogun's blessing.

"Nan, stop!"

"It's as my king bade me," she said, tossing in the final blade.

Joan grabbed her arm. "Do you have any idea what you've done?" She spun the older woman around. "You've doomed us all. Those swords were our only hope."

"I've done as my king bade me." Her eyes gazed out at nothing.

"It was you. You're under his control. You let him in."

"I've done as my king bade me."

Joan looked into the woman's glazed eyes. "I'm sorry, Nan. Hopefully, you won't remember this." Joan brought Bia's guard down on the back of Nan's head.

The woman dropped like a stone, silent and unconscious.

Joan grabbed a length of nearby rope and tied Nan to the heavy worktable.

She prayed it would hold as she sprinted out into the early light, the barest fringes of a plan forming in her mind.

One problem at a time.

She had to end this today. Even if she had only her wits to rely on, she'd finish Auberon and rescue her brother.

Or die trying.

CHAPTER THIRTY
Fair Terms

 rumpled, bleary-eyed Shakespeare met her in his parlor. He yawned as he looked her over.

"What in the name of Mary's milky tit has you calling so damn early?"

"I need you to get me an audience with Lady Clifford. Immediately."

The poet snorted. "It's a little early to call on one of Her Majesty's ladies." He smiled at her. "Can it not wait until after we've at least broken our fast?"

"No." Joan clenched her fists and tried to keep her voice level. "Auberon attacked my home this morning and tried to kill me and my family." Her voice broke but she forced the words out. "He has James. It is imperative that I speak with Lady Clifford."

Shakespeare jerked forward in his seat. "What? That's—" He jumped up, his jaw set. He strode over and pulled paper and a quill from a table drawer. He scribbled something across it and folded the note closed. He looked up at Joan. "Allow me to get dressed and I'll take you to her straight."

He disappeared out the door.

"I sent correspondence ahead of us so she should know we're coming."

Joan struggled to keep up with Shakespeare's long strides as she followed him through the streets. She trusted him to know his way to Lady Clifford's home.

He'd loaned her a belt so Bia could hang at her waist. The sword banged against her thigh with every other step. She took small comfort in the feeling of that weight.

Shakespeare glanced back at her over his shoulder. "Are you sure about this, Joan?"

"No." She smiled at him. "But it's a chance I'm willing to take."

They turned a corner, and Goodfellow and Rose stood in the middle of the road.

"What have you gotten yourself into, Iron Blade?"

Joan laughed. It sounded watery even to her. "One hell of a mess. He has James."

"Shite," Rose spat.

"We don't have much time," Goodfellow said. They beckoned Shakespeare and Joan over. "Come along, quickly now."

Shakespeare held out a hand. "We can't. I'm taking her to meet—"

"I know," Goodfellow said. They walked up, placing a hand on Joan's and Shakespeare's shoulders. "I'm your escort."

Escort? How—

She stared hard at Goodfellow, but they wouldn't meet her gaze.

"Joan, just trust us." Rose laid her hand against Joan's back. "Please."

Joan let her eyes slide closed as the sounds of dawn on the London streets faded to silence.

"Joan, we had hoped we would see you again, but did not think it would be so soon."

Her eyes shot open.

Lady Clifford sat before them in indolent repose, blond hair loose and hanging around her shoulders.

"All this time you've been working for her?" Joan jerked away from Goodfellow and Rose.

"Joan, it's—" Rose reached out for her, face falling as Joan jumped away. Goodfellow looked stricken.

Lady Clifford laughed. "Do not blame dear Puck or their delightful little girl. There are no traitors here."

Her form shifted, the pale, blond Lady Clifford sloughing off like water to leave behind dark brown skin; a smooth, bare head; and high, naked breasts.

Joan flushed, her eyes skittering down and away.

Shakespeare hummed, his gaze steady on.

Joan noticed three thick, leather-bound books on a shelf flanked by flickering candles, far away from the woman's nakedness.

"My queen," Goodfellow sighed, "your magnificence dazzles the child."

Queen?

Joan glanced up, caught sight of nude, brown flesh. She looked away from the woman's bare skin and instead inspected the two damask sofas facing off over a low, dark table.

"She'll be fine," Shakespeare blurted.

A single, lonely thread poked up from the soft rug beneath Joan's feet as she studied it intently. A much more—less—interesting detail than a beautiful, naked woman.

The woman's rich laugh echoed through the room. "We have always liked you, poet, but we would prefer dear Joan attentive to our words and not our assets. You can look now, child."

Joan lifted her eyes. The woman was draped in crimson, purple, and gold fabric. She remained impossibly beautiful, but was thankfully no longer naked. Joan's cheeks still burned too hot.

She cleared her throat. "Goodfellow called you queen—"

"They did indeed address us as such."

Joan glared at Goodfellow. "I thought you said you had no monarch."

"Zaza said no king," Rose said, expression surly. "Those who follow Auberon are outliers. Titanea is our true queen."

Titanea's grin turned sharp. "Dear Will does us no favors in his little play."

"My apologies, Your Majesty," Shakespeare said bowing low, "but how could I ever hope to catch such magnificence with my shallow words?"

Joan's mind went silent as too many things raced through her brain.

A king was not a queen, so that hadn't actually been a lie. The Fae who'd nearly killed her backstage and the one who'd watched her be manhandled in the presence of Queen Anne was the real ruler of the Fae?

"We shall deal with you later, playwright. Our dear Joan, what have you come to ask of us?"

"You tried to kill me," Joan blurted.

Titanea smiled gently. "We did indeed." She held up her wrist, the red blister burned bright against her smooth brown skin. "But what is a bit of blood between warriors? What is your desire, favorite?"

Joan felt her shoulders relax, barely. Titanea held a calm to her menace, like Goodfellow. She wasn't sure if she could trust either of them, but for now she had no choice.

James needed her.

"I need you to kill Auberon."

"No."

"No?" Joan's stomach plummeted to her feet. "But he has my brother and he wants me dead. Please."

Titanea snorted. "Typical. But we cannot kill him for you. It is not within our power."

"But—"

"And what makes you think"—Titanea leaned back in her chair indolently—"that we will allow you to end his life?"

Joan's heart sank. "I—"

"Fret not, favorite, you'll have your fair revenge. There is no love lost between ourselves and that filth." She grinned. "We shall grant you this boon: all who we command will not harm you this day. Give him our regards as he breathes his last."

"All but Auberon?"

Titanea stared at her. "All who we command. Is it not well?"

Goodfellow clamped a hand down on Joan's shoulder. "You are fair and just, my queen."

Joan shook them off. "Tha—"

"Come, we must find your brother, Joan." Rose interrupted as she stepped up on Joan's other side.

Joan started, letting the rest of the words die in her throat.

Her heart raced.

She'd nearly thanked Titanea, here where gratitude was a vow and not just courtesy. She dropped into a deep curtsy instead. "Your Majesty."

"Stop, we have not yet dismissed you. Puck—"

Goodfellow jerked to attention, their face suddenly blank. "Yes, my queen."

"Do you think we do not know that you confronted Auberon directly? You and your daughter, who you've hidden from us for these years." Titanea bared her teeth. "Stay. We will discuss this further with you and your seed. The rest of you may go."

Rose clutched Joan's arm and pulled her in for a hug. "I'm sorry I couldn't tell you about this. I wanted to, every moment I wanted to reveal all to you."

"I believe you." Joan sighed, squeezing the other girl tightly.

"Be careful." Rose pressed her lips against Joan's in an all-too-brief kiss.

Joan tried to take all of her in—the smell of flowers that clung to her skin, the brush of her curls against her face. Then it was over.

"A kiss before battle," Shakespeare snickered. "Seems you've learned well of me."

Joan's face heated so fast, she was surprised she didn't burst into flames.

"Enough, hob-child. Let them go on their way and come so we may know you better." Titanea grinned sharply, crooking a finger at Rose as the blond form of Lady Clifford washed over her again. "Good luck, dear Joan. We should like to see our favorite again." She stared at Shakespeare. "You, we shall deal with later."

Shakespeare's eyes widened before he folded over in a deep bow. "Ah, yes. Of course, my lady—ah— Your Majesty. Anything at your pleasure."

Titanea, again as Lady Clifford, squinted at him. She sliced her hand through the air.

Joan was back on the same street again with a still-bowing Shakespeare beside her. Beyond them, the horizon was just pinking with the approach of the dawn.

She took a deep breath that did nothing to calm her racing heart.

Today this would end.

She turned, striding through the still dim streets.

"Joan," Shakespeare called. He jogged up alongside her, his longer legs keeping pace easily. "I—What—" He huffed out a breath. "Where are our blades? We can't fight the Fae without iron weapons."

Joan ignored him. "We need to meet the others at the theatre as we arranged. We need to tell them James was taken."

"Joan, we need those blades. Shall we retrieve them—"

The north gate of London Bridge peeked over the rooftops ahead.

A large form stepped out from the shadows.

"I end you here, mortal," the red cap growled, inky blood dribbling from her cap and down her face. "In the name of Gorvenal."

"Uh," Shakespeare said eloquently, "protection?"

"Not if they've sided with Auberon," Joan spat.

The red cap charged, sending them scrambling in different directions. Joan stumbled over her long skirts, Bia tangling in her flailing legs. She hit the dirt hard.

"Don't let her draw blood," Joan screeched. She scratched at the ties on her skirt. "It only makes her stronger."

She couldn't fight like this.

The strings knotted around her fingers.

A foot caught her below her ribs. She rolled across the dirt, gasping for breath as her belly cramped and fluttered.

"Get up and fight, bitch," the red cap growled.

"Apologies—" Shakespeare slammed a length of wood into the red cap's face. "We have another engagement."

He grabbed Joan's hands and dragged her to her feet. "Come along, love. We need—"

Joan shoved him away as a clawed fist swung down between them. She threw herself out of the way of the next hit. Fabric from her skirt wrapped around her heel. Her tail bone smacked the ground as Bia finally sliced through her strings. She used her momentum to roll backward, ripping her legs free of the skirt. She jumped up, the morning air cold against her bare legs.

The riverbank lay behind her in a steep drop. If she angled this the right way . . .

The red cap dove. Joan swung Bia, slicing across the creature's eyes. She screeched and stumbled a few steps as Joan danced out of the way of her wild swipes.

She glanced behind herself.

Just a little bit farther.

The Fae paused and pulled bloodstained hands away from her face. Joan watched as the red cap's eyes slowly repaired themselves until the creature stood unblemished.

Joan's stomach dropped.

That's right—she had no iron now. Her strikes were useless.

She sprinted off, the red cap's steps thundering behind her. Up ahead she saw a spot where the murky flow of the Thames scraped high against the shore. She leaned into her run. Her chest strained against the shallow breaths allowed by her bodice.

She heard the red cap close behind her.

Near enough.

Joan spun. Bia flashed out. Right. Left.

The red cap gurgled as blood poured from her eyes and the open gash at her throat. The attack wouldn't end her, but it would disorient her. She stumbled toward Joan.

Joan grabbed one of the creature's arms in both her hands. She threw her weight backward and planted her feet in the red cap's pelvis. She shoved.

Splash!

Joan rolled over, eyes scanning the fast-moving river. Downstream and far out of reach, the red cap bobbed to the surface. She flailed and sputtered before a wave rushed over her head and dragged her beneath the rushing water. Another caught her as she surfaced and she disappeared again into the dark river.

"Are you all right, Joan?" Shakespeare said, pulling her up and tossing his cloak around her shoulders. "Let us take our leave before we are forced to entertain more guests."

She nodded and let him bustle her toward London Bridge.

She clutched Bia close, the sword still silent in her grasp, and tried not to think about what that meant for the fight ahead.

It would do her no good now, anyway.

CHAPTER THIRTY-ONE
Dear Friends, Once More

he gates were closed at London Bridge, all the windows of Nonesuch House shuttered and dark. They'd forgotten. At this hour, before the full light of dawn, none were allowed to cross.

"We'll have to take a wherry," Shakespeare called and headed off toward the closest dock to argue with the lone boatman posted along the northern shore.

Joan took a breath and hurried down the embankment to meet them. The boatman raised an eyebrow at her makeshift cloak-skirt but otherwise kept silent as he ushered them onto his tiny boat.

"Lucky I'm still here," he mumbled. He shoved away from the dock with his oar and set to rowing them across. "Most wherries is scared to make the trip. Claim something's hunting on the river."

Joan caught a shadow drift by them from the corner of her eye. Her head whipped around to follow it.

Nothing.

Shakespeare smiled stiffly at the man. "Fascinating story."

Something hit the wherry with a low thump, and it rocked side to side. Joan turned to the southern shore. They weren't even halfway across. She smiled at the boatman. "Might I trouble you to row a bit faster—"

"I row fast as I'm able." He scowled at her.

Another thump. The wherry listed to one side, taking in a splash of icy water. The boatman's frown deepened.

Joan gripped the side of the boat. "Can you swim, Master Shakespeare?" Joan said, meeting the other man's wide-eyed gaze.

"Yes, I—"

The wherry flipped over sideways. The icy water hit like a slap to the face as all three went under.

Joan kicked her way to the surface, gasping and shivering as she broke through, glad she'd already lost her skirts. The heavy fabric held water and would've dragged her down into the depths with ease.

Something large brushed against her leg.

"Swim for the shore!" She strained, pushing her body to keep moving in spite of the cold water.

Shakespeare came up beside her, his long arms reaching and legs kicking furiously against the water. A scream sounded behind them. They turned.

The wherryman clung desperately to his capsized boat as something tugged at his leg. A head, like a horse covered in slime and seaweed, lurched out of the water and snapped its teeth around the man's head in an explosion of blood.

Joan threw herself back around, paddling furiously for the north shore. The rocky ground grew closer with each pull, almost like she was being propelled. Shakespeare kept pace with her, a look of concentration on his face. She prayed they wouldn't meet their ends in the murky waters.

The creature brushed against her leg again. She swam harder. It bumped her roughly, launching her out of the water. Joan gasped as she hit the icy river again. She drew Bia, the motion slowed by the water and the cold.

She couldn't see. The beast could be anywhere, could come at her from any angle and she wouldn't know it. She held the sword high, out of the water, and waited.

It surfaced on her left side. Joan spun her blade, jabbing the point through the beast's eye. She pulled back and slashed across the other eye, then slipped under the water and kicked her way back up, sputtering and gasping.

"Swim, Master Shakespeare!" she shrieked.

He frowned but pushed his way toward the shore. "But you've killed it."

"Won't hold. It'll heal and be on us again soon."

"How soon?"

It sprang up ahead of them. Lunged for Joan. She swung Bia up, and the beast stopped. It lifted its head above the water, the long face the grayish-green of a drowned horse. A long black mane hung in limp, wet hunks and draped down into the water. Shining black eyes blinked at her.

"Dear God," Shakespeare whispered.

The creature's lips curled back, showing a mouth full of razor-sharp teeth. Teeth she'd seen bite a man's head clean off.

Teeth that would devour her and Shakespeare both with no trouble.

It dipped its head back down and snorted, blowing bubbles that splashed water in Joan's face. Joan sputtered, too shocked by the playful move to take another swing, but then the beast swam off in the opposite direction.

Joan caught Shakespeare's eye and they both paddled frantically back toward the north shore. They dragged themselves up onto the rocks, sputtering and shivering.

"Well, I didn't expect to have a morning swim." Shakespeare shoved himself to his knees, coughing out water. "Ugh, tastes like shite and smells like shite. Remind me to never do this again."

Joan rolled onto her back, gasping for air. "Yes, never again." She glanced over at her right hand to make sure her numb fingers hadn't dropped Bia into the icy river.

"Must've been one of Titanea's if it let us be."

"Aye." The sword glinted in Joan's grip, silent.

She lay there looking up at the sky and shivering in the cold air. The early kiss of sunrise was just starting to stain the inky night sky a pale blue. It blurred before her eyes.

"That's twice you didn't cover your blade in iron and now's not the time to hesitate—"

"I can't."

"What?" Shakespeare's face appeared over hers, but she couldn't see him clearly.

She rubbed a hand across her eyes. "I can't make iron anymore." Her fingers came away wet.

She was crying and she couldn't hold the tears back because all was lost.

"I can't make iron, I can't control metal. I can do nothing because"—she tried to breathe but everything came too fast—"because Ogun abandoned me. I—I refused him and he's forsaken me when I need him the most. Without him I'm nothing."

"No." He laid a hand on her shoulder. "The Orisha don't abandon their children. That's not how this works."

Joan frowned at him. "Did your mother face this?"

"No, I did." He squeezed Joan's shoulder. "I'm a child of Oshun. I gave up on speaking to her when my son died and I couldn't save him. But when I saw how Ogun blessed you, moved with you—I prayed for the first time in nearly ten years, and Oshun spoke to me. I felt her here"—he laid a hand against his chest, tears welling in his eyes—"just as I always did so long ago."

Joan tried to keep breathing, hope and despair choking each pull of air in her chest. "But I can't hear him, I can't feel him."

"That doesn't mean he's gone." Shakespeare grabbed her hands tightly in his own. "We've been claimed, Joan. We are their children. Orisha are always there. Ogun is always there. You just have to reach for him."

Joan felt the sob well up in her chest and pressed it down. Now wasn't the time for crying. She had to find James and save him.

Something in the air shifted, and she swayed, dizzy and light-headed.

"What's that?" Shakespeare whispered, pointing over to the west.

Joan turned. There, in the distance, a cluster of dark clouds churned in a swirling mass. The rising sun peeked through a circle of clear sky at the center, sending a column of light shining across the buildings over which it loomed.

"Is that—a hurricane?" Shakespeare said, pushing himself to his feet. "A hurricane in England?"

Joan leapt up beside him. "It's James."

"Oya—" Shakespeare shook his head. "Of course, James is a child of Oya."

"He's telling us where he is."

"Then there's no time to waste." Shakespeare jerked his head toward the stairs leading up from the riverbank. "Let's go."

Joan nodded. She slipped Bia back into the sheath at her hip and sprinted after the tall man. Her heart raced as she and Shakespeare bounded up the stairs and back into the street, thankfully leaving the foul river and its even fouler inhabitants behind.

James—brilliant, brave James—was using the wind to speak to her, had called a hurricane to lead her to where Auberon held him captive.

All she needed to do was follow.

"We need to get west, Master Shakespeare." She started jogging off in that direction, doing her best to ignore the cold air against her skin.

James was out there in danger. She needed to hurry.

Shakespeare grabbed her arm. "Wait. You'll never make it in time on foot. Or looking like that."

She looked down and flushed. She'd forgotten she was soaked and barely dressed, with Shakespeare's damp cloak the only thing keeping her from exposing her legs and womanly parts to the world. She'd be arrested for indecency before she made it halfway across the city. But there was no time for her to return home for clothes. Who knew how long James could keep conjuring the hurricane?

She turned to Shakespeare and over his shoulder spotted a gangly boy yawing as he led a horse down the road. She grinned. "Here's our solution."

Joan ran toward the boy, Shakespeare close behind her.

"Boy, I need your horse."

He looked up and scowled at her. "Ain't giving you my horse for free."

"And your clothes," Shakespeare said, "if you'd be so kind."

"Definitely ain't giving you my clothes for free," he snorted.

Joan reached into her bodice and tugged at the secret pocket stitched inside. Four gold coins clanked together noisily as they tumbled out into her palm. She held them out to him. "That enough?"

He snatched the coins and pressed his teeth against one. Grinned brightly as the gold bent under the pressure. "He's all yours," he said as he shoved the reins into Joan's hands.

"And the clothes?" Shakespeare said, his smile both bright and dangerous.

The boy flinched but nodded.

Joan shook her head. "Just the trousers and the jacket are fine."

The boy flushed.

"Quickly," Shakespeare cooed—part placation, part threat, "please."

Joan swung herself up onto the gelding's back, the wool of the boy's trousers scratching against her legs. She'd secured them around her waist using the belt that held Bia's scabbard.

"Joan," Shakespeare called to her.

She looked down at where he stood and leaned over in the saddle to grab hold of the hand he reached up toward her. She hoped he didn't notice how hard she was shaking. Tried to feel some confidence, because despite the silent sword at her side, there was no way she was leaving James to Auberon.

They both looked up to where the clouds kept their tight circle. They'd already thinned, letting more sunlight through.

James couldn't keep this up forever.

"Iron wench!"

Joan turned to where an enormous pale creature loped toward them, twice as tall and twice as wide as a human. Chains crisscrossed its body, severed heads hanging from them in eternal screams, and gleaming white eyes peered out at them. Two raw red wounds showed through the beast's white skin. This was the same jack-in-irons she'd scared off from Cecil's home.

"A friend of yours?" Shakespeare asked.

Joan scowled. "Of a sort. I gave him those wounds."

"Your life is mine, mortal," the jack growled.

Joan's heart raced. There was no time for this, not when she had to get to James.

Shakespeare stepped between Joan and the Fae. "I'll take up that challenge, beast."

"No!" Joan shouted.

Shakespeare held up a hand. "You have other matters to attend to. Besides"—he flashed a dazzling smile over his shoulder at her—"I've kept Oshun out of this battle for too long."

He held out his hands, eyes slipping closed as he moved. Joan heard the sudden churning and rushing of water. A column of river water burst up into the sky before slamming into the Fae creature, knocking it off its feet. It gurgled and shrieked as it tumbled down the road, pushed along by a blast of rank water from the Thames.

"See, we haven't lost our touch." Shakespeare turned to her again, his brow furrowed in concentration and beaded with sweat. "Go show Auberon your mettle, Joan Sands. I'll catch up when I'm done here." Then he turned back to his fight.

Joan's hands clenched the reins, but she was wasting precious time. Time Master Shakespeare may have just bought her with his life.

She had to move.

"Yah!" She jerked the reins and dug her heels into the horse's sides.

The horse snorted and took off, galloping west down the still mostly empty dirt road.

She followed James's storm through the city. Let the sight of the black clouds anchor her as she sped west.

West toward her brother.

West toward her fate.

West toward Auberon.

CHAPTER THIRTY-TWO
Bloody Noses & Crack'd Crowns

oan slipped off the horse.

James's hurricane had led her far west, all the way to Westminster, near the House of Lords and the House of Commons. The center of the government.

Auberon had to be somewhere near here. She was sure of it. Her brother's life depended on it. Hell, who knew how many lives depended on her finding Auberon. He'd done so much harm to those closest to her—murdered Samuel in cold blood and nearly killed Joan's mother. Joan knew others had fallen to prey to Auberon's casual violence, that countless more would suffer if she didn't stop him.

And yet—

And yet, some small part of her feared facing this Fae.

She followed her brother's trail along the road to a gathering of large stone buildings. She frowned. This was the House of Lords, where the queen used to meet with the rest of her government. Where the new king would meet with his own.

Why had Auberon chosen to hide here?

Only one of them would walk away today, and Joan hoped beyond hope that it would be her.

But how could it be her when she had no power?

The Orisha don't abandon their children.

Her hand clenched at her side and she stamped down doubts and fears. She had to do this, and she had to win.

Iron may not heed her call, but she could still fight.

And she would give Auberon everything she had.

Joan peered at the sky, looking for the strongest shaft of light in the swirl of clouds. She followed where it pointed, creeping around the north side of the gathering of buildings.

It was early enough that the random collection of shops and the like scattered around the courtyard were still shuttered, their owners only just awaking to start their day. Joan was thankful for that as she crept through the narrow spaces between buildings. She came upon a long alleyway between the imposing House of Lords and another building leading to a short set of stairs that ended at a wide door surrounded by darkness.

She looked up to see James's storm clouds fully dissipating over her head. She prayed that didn't mean he was—

She shook her head.

Joan looked around again. No one was near. She jogged over and crept down the stairs. The heavy door sat half propped open, a slash of dark red splattered across its front.

Joan ran her fingers across it and the crimson came off at her touch.

Blood. She did her best not to think of whose it was.

This was it. Behind this door Auberon held her brother.

She wasn't—

Her hand still shook when she thought of the give of flesh and sinew. The scalding rush of fresh blood.

And she had no—

She couldn't—

She flexed suddenly stiff fingers.

She wasn't ready for this. But there was no doing otherwise.

Not when James needed her.

She pushed through the door and into the long, dim cellar beyond.

"Couldn't wait for me to kill you, girl?"

Auberon materialized before her; his torso circled by sloppy bandages dyed deep burgundy with old blood. The wounds she'd given him with iron hadn't healed.

"Funny, seems like I won our last bout." Her voice held steady with feigned confidence that she hoped would bleed into reality.

Auberon laughed, the sound ending in a hard cough. "That cheek shall be your downfall, mortal."

"Where is my brother?"

Auberon flung out his hand and James tumbled across the dirty ground, bloody and bruised but alive.

Joan thanked heaven for that.

"Damn you," James grunted. "This was my favorite nightgown; now it's probably ruined."

Auberon kicked James in the gut. Joan flinched as her brother cried out in pain.

"Your brother couldn't do what I asked of him," Auberon said, "but now you will, girl." He gestured over his shoulder. "Now move those iron bars."

Joan looked at where he'd pointed and saw nothing but the empty expanse of the storage cellar.

"I—"

"Move the bars, girl! Move them now!" Auberon screeched. He kicked James again.

"Don't touch him!"

"Then do as I say, girl. Move those iron bars."

Again Joan could see no iron bars around them. She glanced at James, her heart racing as he coughed once then lay still.

"Don't ignore me, girl." Auberon's fist cracked across her face as he smacked her. "Has she already gotten to you? Is that why you refuse to obey me now?"

The metallic taste of blood filled Joan's mouth. How had he gotten so close so quickly? "She who?"

"Stop playing the fool!" he screamed, spit flying from his mouth. "I know you are Titanea's. Do you think she won't kill you even if you help her plans succeed?"

His eyes looked wild and feral, some unseen fear driving him.

Fear of Titanea. The realization hit Joan suddenly. Auberon was afraid of the Fae queen. Didn't he know Titanea refused to attack him outright? Joan wouldn't be the one to inform him otherwise. Let him believe she attacked him now with Titanea's full help. The fear would make him sloppy, and Joan needed any and every advantage she could discover.

"She sends you her worst regards," Joan spat and watched his eyes widen. She pulled the still-silent sword from her waist.

She'd hesitated once before; it would not happen again.

"You'll die here." He stepped toward Joan, hands outstretched. "I'll rend you limb from limb before I let her have your power."

She shifted Bia in her grip.

Even if she couldn't hear, couldn't feel as she once did, she would figure out how to end this. Or die trying.

"Come, beast." The air around Bia shrieked as she whipped the sword through the air. "I am for you."

Something flashed sharp in Auberon's grip and he was on her far faster than she expected from someone suffering from three gaping stab wounds.

Joan threw herself to the side, barely dodging the strike. It caught her along one cheek. She hissed, swung Bia, and missed.

Auberon laughed. "You're slow today, girl. That's dangerous." He flung out a hand. The ground trembled as sharp stone burst up through the dirt.

She spun out of the way and sprang forward. Joan rammed her shoulder into Auberon's side, jabbing her fist into one of the bloody spots on his bandages.

He groaned and crumpled as she used her momentum to roll to her feet. His back was to her.

She lunged. Felt flesh and muscle resist the push of her sword before giving way. Her stomach lurched. Bia's hilt hit Auberon's back, the point of the sword sticking out of his chest.

"From behind?" Auberon coughed, bloody flecks of spittle coloring his lips. "How ruthless." He jerked away from her, Bia sliding out from his body with a slick smacking sound as he pulled himself off the sword. He stumbled a few steps.

Joan held her breath, Bia still ready in her grip.

Her head was silent. No vibrations from her sword, no ghost of something pressing against her awareness. No Ogun.

She was truly on her own.

Auberon straightened. His shoulders shook before he threw his head back in harsh laughter.

Her heart dropped, but she shifted her feet into a ready stance.

He grinned at her over his shoulder. "You think to kill me with that mortal weapon?" He ran at her, hand outstretched.

Joan swiped Bia through the air. Auberon's hand hit the dirt floor with a thunk. His smile widened.

"A trifle," he said. He picked up the severed appendage and held it against his bloody wrist. It reattached as if nothing had happened. He flexed his fingers. "Where's your iron, girl?"

Joan gritted her teeth. Bia trembled in her hold. She tightened her grip, knuckles turning white with the force.

And still she felt nothing.

"Where's your iron, you filthy mortal?" Auberon shrieked. "You'll not kill me without iron."

He sprang at Joan again.

She thrust Bia at him, sword catching in his gut.

He grunted as it pierced his stomach and pressed forward, driving the blade straight through.

Joan jerked her arm backward too slowly. Auberon caught her wrist in one hand and wrapped the other around her throat.

He squeezed, grinding the bones in her wrist together. She screamed. He cut the noise silent as he throttled her.

"Stupid, stupid girl," he hissed in her face. He shook her once, snapping her head back then forward again. "I'd admire your cheek if you hadn't been such a thorn in my side." He tossed her across the floor.

Joan hit hard, agony shooting through her sword arm. She could barely move it. It had to be broken.

Useless.

Auberon grabbed Bia by the hilt and dragged the blade from his gut. He held it out in front of him. "No more dangerous than a twig, now." He snapped the blade across his knee.

Joan cried out as the sword broke. She watched him toss the pieces away, her heart racing.

If she died here today, she wouldn't be dying on her own. Auberon would surely murder James and probably the rest of her family too.

All because she'd been too afraid. All because she couldn't fully accept what being chosen by the Orisha meant. What being chosen by Ogun meant.

She remembered Shakespeare, calling upon Oshun after so long.

The Orisha don't abandon their children.

And for the first time in a long time, Joan prayed. Prayed for that connection she'd taken for granted. Prayed for herself, for her family, for her friends.

Prayed for forgiveness.

The silence, the emptiness within her ached like an open wound. She could barely feel the agony of her broken arm for the ache of it but still she prayed.

"This is the end of you, girl," Auberon said. He kicked her shoulder, forcing her flat on her back for an easy attack. He dropped his knee onto her chest.

She gasped as his weight forced all the air from her lungs. The fingers on her right hand twitched, reaching for a sword that wouldn't come and sending bolts of pain shooting up her broken arm.

And then . . .

She felt a spark inside herself, a pressure, a heat, familiar but faint.

It ignited deep in her chest.

She wouldn't die here. She refused.

The fire inside her burned hotter.

Ogun.

Her arms felt hot and cold at the same time. She could barely breathe beyond Auberon's weight on her chest. But she still felt that brightness, the touch of the Orisha's presence. The one she thought she had lost forever.

Ogun was still with her.

Her head felt light.

Would she accept what she could do, what Ogun gave her? Embrace it with her whole self?

Auberon leaned in close. "I shall take my revenge on your family when I am done with you."

Yes. Yes, she would.

Joan waited to be shoved back into that dark abyss as she allowed Ogun's presence to overtake her. But as that familiar pressure overwhelmed her senses, her awareness stayed. She felt a shiver rush through her body. It vibrated her bones. Surely Auberon could feel Ogun's power surging through her, sudden and free.

The Orisha's energy filled her with a scorching heat, the powerful sensation just on the edge of pain and more beautiful than anything she'd ever felt. This was what she'd been running from, what waited on the other side of her fear. Not control but completeness.

A deep satisfaction washed over her then, her own and a matching feeling so ancient and deep it could only be Ogun. The cold, familiar heft of iron ran down her arm like icy water and gushed out from her left hand.

Yes.

Joan smiled, but Auberon was too close to see the spread of her lips.

Yes.

The weight of the fully formed blade tilted in her grip. The press of it heavy like the embrace a long-lost friend.

Yes.

The machete flashed in the cellar's dim light as she drove it straight up and through Auberon's exposed throat.

Auberon looked down at her, his eyes wide and mouth gaping open as blood oozed out over the blade and down Joan's arm.

Her smile widened in the face of his terror and she drove the machete sideways, feeling the gentle give as the sharp blade sliced through his spine.

His head tumbled from his shoulders, thudding against the dirt beside her. His body loomed over her before it collapsed limply.

Joan grunted at the impact and tried to catch her breath. The warm heat of the Fae's blood felt like victory as it scorched her skin and it soaked into her clothes. She glanced to the side. Auberon's head lay facing her, eyes dim and lifeless.

The work was done.

This time, when the rush of joy hit her, she let it wash over her whole body without shame. She watched as the machete drank up the blood coating it before recalling the iron blade back into herself.

"Joan . . ."

She rolled over.

James limped toward her, one hand clutching his ribs. Relief rushed through her, so strong she could barely breathe.

"Joan, are you—"

"I'm fine," she croaked, her voice more haggard than she expected. "Think my arm is broken, though." She pushed herself up as James collapsed into the dirt beside her. She wanted to weep. She wanted to hug him close and never let him go. "You look like shite."

"At least we're both in better shape than that bastard."

Joan glanced over at Auberon's unseeing eyes. She shook her head. "Infinitely better shape."

She waited for the regret to rush in after saying those words.

Didn't know what kind of monster it made her when it never did.

"I'm glad you're safe." James laid a hand on her shoulder.

She choked out a laugh. "I'm supposed to tell you that."

"You took too long."

They fell into each other's arms. Her wrist throbbed but she just hugged her brother more tightly. She'd nearly lost him.

"I love you," she said.

"I love you too." He pulled back, eyes shiny with tears.

Joan tucked her uninjured shoulder under James's arm and they pushed each other to their feet.

James looked her over and frowned. "Those cannot be my clothes."

"I bought them off of a stable hand on the street." Joan groaned.

"Clearly . . ."

Joan ignored him and looked around the room. She spotted Bia where the broken sword had been thrown aside.

She hobbled over to the snapped blade and dragged the two pieces close together. She felt the faintest thrum from the metal. She held the broken ends together in one hand and concentrated.

She nearly cried when she heard the familiar song of flowing metal.

Bia throbbed sudden and strong in her grip, the steady thump keeping time with Joan's heartbeat.

God, she had missed that feeling.

"Maferefun, Ogun," she said.

She pulled her hand back. The sword was whole once again.

"You fought well, friend." Joan smiled to herself and touched the blade gently to her lips. She focused again, and Bia shrunk down and wrapped around her left wrist like a bracelet.

The sword hummed against her skin.

"So what was that bastard so interested in?"

She looked up. James stood near a long cluster of iron bars piled against something. Joan frowned.

The bars must've been hidden behind a glamour. Without Ogun's blessing, Joan hadn't been able to pierce the magic.

Joan waved, pushing the iron bars off to either side and uncovering several large barrels. She looked to James who shrugged and approached the nearest one. A plug stuck out about halfway up its round side.

"You think this is wine? Doubt they'd mind if we had a sip." James grinned at Joan before pulling it free. "We both could do with a little wine right now." A fine black powder spilled out from the opening.

"God's teeth," James whispered, "it's gunpowder."

"Gunpowder?" Joan did a quick count of the kegs huddled together against one wall.

Wait.

Joan thought of that letter that Cecil had shown her in his office.

They shall receive a terrible blow this parliament; and yet they shall not see who hurts them.

A blow to Parliament. These barrels of gunpowder planted beneath the House of Lords, the very place where the heads of the government would meet.

"Should be thirty-six." A deep, rumbling voice said from the darkness. "Was that your count, girl?"

Joan jerked to attention, a machete forming instantly in her left hand. James hobbled over to her as quickly as he could, but Joan stepped in front of her brother.

"Who's there?" Joan said.

The shadows formed themselves into a woman, one who Joan last remembered barely glimpsing astride a horse made of darkness.

"Herne," Joan whispered.

Herne the Hunter laughed, like steel on glass. "Thank you for moving that iron, girl. You've made our task much easier." She glanced down, dark eyes widening as she spotted Auberon's severed head. She looked up at Joan. "Is this your doing?"

Joan's hand tightened on her machete. Her injured arm hung limp and useless at her side.

Auberon might be dead, but that wasn't the end. The Pact remained broken, which meant the Fae still ran unrestrained.

Joan breathed deeply. She prepared to fight with all she had because the danger still lived and she couldn't let it stand.

The door burst open, flooding the dark cellar with blinding daylight as the sound of feet filled the cellar around them.

"Stop where you are," a man shouted.

Hands grabbed at Joan's broken arm. Her vision went dim as someone dragged James out from behind her. The machete faded back into Joan's palm.

"Don't move," another man screamed.

James cried out as they threw him to the ground.

"Quiet!" A guard planted a knee in his back.

Joan jerked against the man holding her despite the pain in her arm. "Don't do that! His ribs are broken."

The guard glared at her and pressed his foot down harder. James groaned and coughed.

"And why do I find you here, girl?"

Joan scowled. She'd know that grating voice anywhere.

Cecil had made his appearance.

CHAPTER THIRTY-THREE
All Met, Ill Met

oan's vision finally adjusted to the sudden illumination. Uniformed guards streamed in through the door and crowded around the cellar. Herne watched them gather, her lips quirked in a slight smile.

An impeccably clean pair of shoes stepped into Joan's field of vision. She glanced up and locked eyes with Cecil. "Our deal is done. Auberon is dead. Let my brother and me go."

"Am I to just take your word for it? To trust you?" He scowled at her as another group of men rushed in behind him.

Joan frowned at him. If he wanted proof, well, she had it, just near her foot.

"My word and this," she said. She kicked Auberon's head across the floor toward Cecil. It banged against his shins, dripping blood onto his shoes, then rolled backward before settling face up. "It should serve as sufficient proof."

Cecil froze. He looked up at her, eyes wide as if seeing her for the first time.

Good. Let him handle Herne and her gunpowder. Joan's debt was paid.

"Sir." A guard slipped beside Cecil. "We've found nothing."

What?

Joan looked up. Herne waved to her from where she leaned against a barrel of gunpowder.

Cecil glared at him, "What do you mean you found nothing?"

"This cellar is empty, my lord."

Color drained from Cecil's face. "Th—that cannot be. Search again! Guy Fawkes is here. I know it."

A glowing man strode out of the darkness to stand beside Herne. His face was pale and pinched beneath his long, pointed black beard. He tipped his black hat at Joan.

What did they mean the cellar was empty?

Joan frowned as the guards scrambled around.

Several men ran back and forth. Past Herne, past the man with the pointed beard. Past each of the thirty-six powder kegs.

Almost as if they couldn't see any of them.

Joan's heart leapt into her throat.

Because they couldn't see through Fae glamour.

"Cecil," Joan called, "there are—"

Her head whipped to the side as Cecil backhanded her.

"You'll address me as Lord Salisbury or you won't address me at all, you insolent brat."

Joan spat a glob of blood on the ground. Her lip throbbed and wetness dripped down her face where the slice across her cheek had started bleeding anew.

She took a steadying breath. Stamped down the rage boiling in her gut.

"Lord Salisbury," she said carefully, "there are—"

"You." Cecil pointed to the guards holding Joan and James. "Take them to my office, make sure they do not leave."

"Lord Salisbury, you must listen—"

He kicked Auberon's head toward another man, who flinched. "You, take this as well."

"Lord Salisbury—" Joan jerked against the man holding her, breaking free of his grip. "There are barrels of—"

The guard hooked his arm around her throat and squeezed, choking off her words.

"Get them out of here," Cecil sneered. "The rest of you, search the grounds. There must be something here."

The retinue of guards shuffled and shoved their way out of the door just as suddenly as they had appeared.

Cecil glared at Joan one last time as she was dragged out by the throat. She batted at the guard until he twisted her broken arm.

Pain silenced her brain.

The guard hauled her out into the morning sunlight. She blinked as it burned her eyes.

Damn that man for not listening.

———✝———

Joan refused to give the guard manhandling her an easy job of imprisoning her in Cecil's office. She twisted and fought and dragged her heels and made his every step away from the compromised cellar a battle. They'd barely made it to the edge of the open courtyard when a voice stopped everyone in their tracks.

"What hideous scene have I stumbled upon this morning?" Queen Anne herself descended from her elaborate carriage.

Lady Clifford followed after, face stormy as she looked at the scene before her. Two more ladies accompanied them, heads bowed.

"That's the girl who attended you at the play not a day ago, Your Majesty," Lady Clifford said. "Why is she here? And covered in blood?"

Joan locked eyes with Lady Clifford—Titanea. She felt herself relax.

Here was an ally.

Here was help.

The queen frowned. "Indeed, it is that Negress child. Who is in charge here?"

"Your Majesty." Cecil slithered out from behind one of the nearby buildings and bowed low to the queen.

Queen Anne groaned. "I should have known it was you."

"It is not safe for you to be here right now, Your Majesty." The smile froze on Cecil's face. "If you'll let my men and me continue our work and return later—"

Joan wished she could enjoy the man's discomfort, but she still had a hand clutched round her throat.

"What work are you doing? And why do you have that girl, Jane—"

"Joan," Lady Clifford said.

"Joan being handled in such a manner? And why is she covered in blood?"

Cecil paled. "Ah—well, Your Majesty—"

"You." The queen pointed directly at the man choking Joan. "Unhand that girl immediately."

Nothing happened.

Queen Anne's mouth pinched together as her face turned an unhealthy shade of purple. "Did you not hear the command of your queen?" she said through gritted teeth. "Unhand the girl. Immediately."

The man let Joan go, and she stumbled forward, gasping for air. She glanced up as Lady Clifford whispered something into the queen's ear.

"The boy too." Queen Anne flapped her hand toward where James was being held.

Cecil scowled. "With all due respect, Your Majesty—"

"No one asked you to speak. Unhand the boy."

The guard holding James up let him go. With no support, James pitched forward weakly.

Joan rushed forward, throwing herself beneath him to break his fall.

"I hate that Cecil bastard," James whispered into her ear.

Joan held him close. "Me too."

The queen waved over the two ladies. "Lady Clifford, have them see to these children before you join me within."

Lady Clifford and the two quiet women bowed low as the queen made her way past the guards and Cecil, who all fell into step behind her. Joan allowed herself to be bolstered by the ladies as Lady Clifford led them out into the courtyard and toward the queen's carriage.

"Are you two all right?" Lady Clifford said quietly.

Joan shook her head distractedly. "What are you doing here?"

"Parliament meets today, and Her Majesty wished to inspect the Hall of Lords"—here Lady Clifford rolled her eyes—"to ensure that her choice of dress didn't clash with the decor of the space." She looked over Joan. "Is this your blood?"

Joan shook her head. "It's Auberon's. I killed him."

Lady Clifford jerked back, eyes wide. Slowly, a smile spread across her face. "Well done, dear Joan. Well done indeed." She leaned in close. "We hope you enjoyed your kill. He was a menace."

"I—"

"I, on the other hand," James choked out, "am in a great deal of pain and would love any assistance you can offer, my lady."

Lady Clifford looked him over. "Of course." She nodded at the women. "Bandage their wounds here and await our return. We must attend the queen."

"I'm glad to see that you live, Iron Blade." One of the other ladies dropped down beside Joan. The woman's features rippled, her face shifting into Goodfellow's.

The lady who knelt on the other side shifted into Rose, wrapping Joan up in her arms. "We're here to take you home."

"Rose—" Joan said.

Rose pulled away, grabbing Joan's face in her hands and pressing their lips together.

Joan sighed and leaned into the kiss, happy to be alive, happy to feel Rose's touch again. Rose leaned back, touching her forehead to Joan's.

"Rose," Joan said, the danger lurking below them rushing back to her. "Rose, quickly, we have to—"

Goodfellow placed a hand on Joan's head. "Quiet, child. We're getting you two home."

Joan's heart beat double time. She thought of Cecil's letter, of the two disguised Fae waiting with thirty-six barrels of gunpowder. "No, you can't go in there."

Lady Clifford frowned. "Why ever not?"

"It's Auberon. He put powder kegs under the building and has two Fae waiting to light them." Joan shook her head. It all made sense now. "That must've been his plan all along, to kill the royal family. I saw the letter Cecil acquired. You have to get the queen out of here."

Lady Clifford barked out a laugh. "Auberon's plan? Puck, Hob-child, get these two youths out of here. We'll see to the mortal queen."

"But my queen . . ." Goodfellow leaned forward, ready to stand.

"Do as we say, Puck."

Goodfellow shrank back, as cowed as Joan had never seen them. Lady Clifford jumped to her feet, hands clutching her skirts as she sprinted down the narrow road between buildings where Joan could barely make out the entrance to the House of Lords.

Joan held her breath, hoping her warning hadn't come too late.

But with thirty-six barrels of gunpowder beneath them ready to explode, none of them were safe yet.

"Joan! James!" Shakespeare skidded to the ground beside them. "Goodfellow, you're here—and Rose too. Is it done?"

"What are you doing here?" she hissed.

James shifted in her arms. "Who's here?"

"I've come to help. Is this your blood?" Shakespeare touched a hand to her face.

"No, it's Auberon's," Rose said.

He grinned. "That's my girl—"

"Master Shakespeare," Joan said, "we have to—"

"Joan, Will!" Burbage rushed toward them along with Phillips, and Armin, and Nick, and Rob. The lot of them brandished pans, pokers, and what looked to be horseshoes.

Joan's heart raced.

"The battle's won, men," Shakespeare said.

They couldn't be here.

Phillips shook his head. "Done? Child you are amaz—"

"God's holy hand, what happened to you two?" Armin said.

They were all in danger now. Not even the courtyard would survive an explosion with that much fuel.

Joan shook her head and tried to speak over the gathered players. "We all need to get out of here. There's—"

"The queen," Rose shouted.

Joan turned as tiny form of Lady Clifford appeared again in the doorway leading a frowning Queen Anne back out into the morning light. They started down the small staircase, whispering fiercely to each other.

Relief rushed through Joan, dread following close on its heels.

Then the world exploded.

A searing heat and incredible pressure blew Joan backward. She tumbled across the ground, rolling to a jarring stop on the stones. Her ears throbbed and her arm, her whole body ached. She coughed. Tried to push herself up.

All she could hear was ringing.

James hit the ground beside her. He convulsed and rolled over, curling in on himself. He groaned in pain. Hurt, but alive.

Where were the others?

At the end of the narrow road, Joan could see that the explosion had crumpled the front entrance to the House of Lords to a pile of rubble. The bodies of several of Cecil's guards lay strewn about as plumes of smoke snaked their way up to the sky.

Cecil himself rolled to his hands and knees, screaming and directing his remaining forces. Men ran forward, struggling to clear away the fallen stones under which lay the queen of England.

The ringing in Joan's ears tapered off, replaced by shouting and the sound of alarums ringing. She coughed and sputtered, smoke and dust catching in her throat. Using every bit of strength she had left, she shoved herself shakily to her feet with her good arm.

She had to find the others.

There. Shakespeare rolled onto his back, coughing and groaning. Rob stumbled toward them covered in dust, a bloody gash on his forehead but otherwise unharmed. Phillips braced himself as he pulled Burbage up from his sprawl on the ground. Armin sat up nearby, shaking his head and blinking rapidly.

A distant flash of color caught her eye and Joan saw Rose beside Goodfellow, both digging frantically through smoking pile of wood and stone.

"Joan," Nick's hoarse voice called.

She spun and there he was, safe but dusty, coughing but blessedly whole. All of her people accounted for—

She took a step toward Nick and collapsed in his arms.

"Here," a voice shouted. "Someone's alive here!"

They turned as the many rescuers converged on a single place, hauling away debris rapidly. Someone whooped in triumph as a woman was pulled from the smoldering ruins, her gown dusty and singed.

Joan prayed for a glimpse of blond hair and the familiar face of Lady Clifford—of Titanea.

"It's the queen," another called. "By heaven, the queen's alive!"

Titanea was gone. Joan's best lead for rescuing Baba Ben lost to Auberon's final attack.

Rose looked up suddenly, her eyes meeting Joan's across the destroyed courtyard. Their gazes held for a moment before Rose's face crumpled in sadness. Goodfellow grabbed their daughter's arm suddenly and dragged her away, both disappearing into the gathering crowd.

Joan felt her knees start to buckle. Nick pulled her close, keeping her upright.

She looked around as shocked people flooded out of the surrounding buildings, all of them miraculously standing save for some blown-out windows. Somehow, the damage had been concentrated only on the House of Lords, precisely where the queen and Lady Clifford had unfortunately been.

Auberon's last act had been far, far too effective.

But he was dead and Joan's people were all alive, despite being on the precipice of catastrophe. Even the loss of Titanea couldn't destroy the hope that bloomed in her heart because those she loved still breathed.

That hope would be enough to carry her through whatever happened next.

CHAPTER THIRTY-FOUR
Nelwyna Musgrove and the Kelpie

elwyna Musgrove sighed as she collapsed onto one of the benches laid out across the wherryman's boat. Little Elma plopped down between her mother's feet and leaned her tiny, dark brown face into the full fabric of Nelwyna's skirt.

"NORTHWARD, HO! the pale-skinned boatman shouted. His thick arms pulled at the oars as he rowed his few passengers across the icy river.

All around them boats large and small launched and landed. London Bridge had yet to open at this lean hour, so anyone looking to make the crossing could only rely on wherries and ferries. Less crowded than the bridge, but much closer to the river's stench.

Nelwyna tangled her fingers through daughter's ample curls as the boat jerked from its mooring and started its drift across the Thames. She held a handkerchief scented with rosewater to her nose with her other hand. No matter how many times she crossed the river, she would never grow accustomed to the pungent odor.

The sun barely pinked the horizon at this hour. If Nelwyna had it her way, she'd still be asleep. She and Elma would be curled up snug under furs and blankets with a bed warmer.

Would that Mrs. Goodspeed's bread could bake itself—

Elma slipped out from under Nelwyna's hand, and Nelwyna jerked upright, eyes open and alert. Her daughter was still within reach. Little Elma had only turned a little to look out over the dimly lit water. Nelwyna relaxed back into her seat but kept her eyes on her daughter.

"Horse," Elma said.

Nelwyna smiled. "We'll see the horses when we reach the other side, love."

Elma pointed out at the water to where another boat made its lazy way in the opposite direction.

"Horse. Horse."

"There aren't any horses in the river, love." Nelwyna squinted in the direction her daughter pointed. There was *something* in the water. Like a log. Only it moved against the current and toward the other boat.

Nelwyna couldn't breathe as she watched the dark shape slink closer to the wherry, no one on the vessel any wiser. She knew she should shout, call out, wave, anything—but her whole body felt like lead. She could only watch.

Watch when the craft jerked suddenly. Watch when it seemed to bounce up out of the water. Watch the silhouetted passengers spring into sudden motion.

"We—we need to get to shore."

She barely heard the words she'd spoken herself; there's no way the boatman had heard the whisper. A couple other passengers had noticed the commotion happening upriver and squinted out into the semidarkness. Nelwyna gripped the back of Elma's dress and started praying.

"Hail, Mary, full of grace, the Lord is with thee—"

"Whazzat?"

A man leaned over past Nelwyna but she ignored him.

"Blessed art thou amongst women and blessed is the fruit of thy womb, Jesus."

The sun finally crawled its way up over the horizon, casting the whole river in a hazy and golden light. And there it was. A horse's head cut through the water, its skin gray-green as if it had drowned, but it swam far better and faster than that creature should be able. It circled the other wherry, bumping the boatman's oars.

"Kelpie," the man beside her whispered and crossed himself frantically.

People around her were shouting now, trying to warn anyone on the other boat.

Nelwyna let them try and kept praying. "Holy Mary, Mother of God—"

There was a sound like an explosion and the distant boat launched into the air. Far-off screams sounded as people splashed down into the icy river. No sooner had they bobbed to the surface sputtering and shouting did they disappear under again. Snatched by a creature that shouldn't exist outside faerie stories.

"—pray for us sinners, now and at the hour of our death. Amen."

"Get us to shore! It'll come for us once it's eaten all of them."

"Hail, Mary, full of grace—"

Another man had grabbed one of the boatman's oars and frantically pulled for the east bank.

"—the Lord is with thee—"

They were close, the dock was in sight. Elma whimpered and Nelwyna pulled her into her arms.

"Blessed art thou amongst women—"

Something bumped their boat. Everyone screamed. They were so close to the shore.

"—and blessed is the fruit of thy womb, Jesus."

Another bump.

Nelwyna shuffled Elma around onto her back, felt tiny arms lock around her neck. "Holy Mary, Mother of God—"

The dock was so close now, but the boat would never dock. But maybe Nelwyna could reach. "—pray for us sinners"—she gathered up her skirts as high as they could go and planted her feet—"now and at the hour of our death."

The boat took another hit and Nelwyna launched herself forward. She hit the end of the dock hard, catching the edge with both arms and one leg.

Behind her the world exploded into screams as the boat and all its passengers flipped into the cold water of the Thames.

Nelwyna felt herself slipping backward, Elma crying hysterically in her ear. Suddenly she felt hands on her, pulling both of them up and away from the water. She was dragged forward, off the dock and onto dry land. Her legs buckled beneath her and her knees cracked when she hit the ground.

She barely noticed the pain because she was alive. Elma was in her arms and they were alive.

"Miss. Miss. What happened? What happened to the wherry?"

Nelwyna's eyes drifted up. A man knelt in front of her, his hands on both her shoulders.

She coughed out a sound and took a deep breath. "Attacked. Something attacked it."

They both turned to look down at the river.

The current drifted past jauntily, sparkling in the bright rays of the now risen sun.

Gentle waves flowed along smoothly, alerting none to the monstrosity that lurked in its murky depths. As the city awoke, the beast prepared to devour again.

It would eat well this day.

CHAPTER THIRTY-FIVE
The Feast and the Epiphany

he sixth of January was Joan's favorite day of the year, and not even the troubles looming over her—the broken Pact with the Fae, her still-missing godfather, and the explosion at the House of Lords—could keep her joy for the day from bubbling up within her as she sat down to breakfast with her family. Joan let the smells of their celebratory meal—junket flavored with rosewater with sweet, crumbly shortcakes to dip into the creamy custard—fill her nose and reveled in the feeling of being alive.

Today marked her and James's seventeenth birthday, a day she'd feared they wouldn't see only two months ago.

"Thank you, Nan," Joan said as the woman laid a plate of sausage on the table. Joan would of course give it over to James in exchange for a second helping of shortcake as she did every year.

Nan nodded, refusing to meet anyone's eyes as she skittered back into the kitchen. Though the entire family had forgiven Nan for allowing Auberon entry into their home, Nan had yet to forgive herself.

Silence settled around the table as Joan slid her plate over to James. He rolled her sausage onto his own plate, dropped two slices of shortcake down in its place, and shoved the whole thing back to Joan. She snagged the treat with a grin, glimpsing her father's smile from the corner of her eye.

"I still don't like you going to the palace today, Joan," her mother said.

Joan bit her lip but stayed silent. Her mother was both right and wrong in her worry. The family had only just recovered from the events of two months prior. But Joan understood. The sight of her mother pale and weak, blood staining everything crimson and the devastation in her father's eyes as he struggled to keep her alive wouldn't leave Joan's mind. She was sure the sight of her children battered, broken, and covered in blood and ashes similarly haunted her mother.

Not only had Joan faced down a powerful Fae, but the explosion that followed had nearly ended the queen's life—had killed young Lady Clifford, Titanea—and collapsed one entire wall of the House of Lords. Joan, James, and the rest had been lucky to make it out alive at all when so many closer to the blast had not.

The official report stated that a group of Catholic dissidents, led by a man called Robert Catesby, had set forth the plan to murder King James.

But Joan knew better. Auberon had been the power behind their attempted coup, and when she'd killed him, everything had fallen apart. Still, Joan doubted it would be long before Catesby and the whole lot found their heads upon Traitor's Gate alongside Cecil's brothers-in-law.

James sighed. "Mother, the King's Men perform for Twelfth Night at Whitehall every year."

"But must you this year?" Here she looked directly to Joan. "Surely Cecil will be in attendance. He's forgotten about you for this long, why tempt him now?"

Cecil had also survived the explosion at the House of Lords, though he'd lost a quarter of his forces in the blast and—based on what Shakespeare had gleaned from court gossip—lost the explicit respect of King James. With Auberon dead and his own reputation in tatters, the secretary of state's priorities lay elsewhere.

Joan smiled gently, placing her hand on her mother's. "It's fine. I'll be with the company's tirewomen and well out of his notice." She took a steadying breath and glanced at James. "We also think this is the perfect time to try to find more information about Baba Ben."

"That's right," James said nodding. The two of them had discussed the possibility over the past several days, finally agreeing this morning that this opportunity couldn't be missed.

Today was to be a triple celebration: the Feast of the Epiphany—the final night of the Christmas season; the marriage of Lady Something and Lord So & So—the children of two noble families; and Queen Anne's full recovery—finally healed enough after her brush with death for a public appearance. The courtiers, loose-limbed with drink and revels, would be easy to ply for secrets. Freeing Baba Ben was worth any risk, even facing down Robert Cecil again.

"Surely there is another way—"

"Bess—" Mr. Sands's quiet voice cut gently across his wife's. "It's all right. We can trust them to do this."

Mrs. Sands smiled, her eyes glossy. "Of course, you're right." She delicately dipped a bit of shortcake into her junket. "And you'll have to be home at a reasonable hour this evening if you want to receive any of your gifts."

"When have we ever missed out on receiving gifts?" James snorted around a mouth full of sausage, choking when some went down the wrong way.

The entire table burst into laughter as their father slapped a coughing James heartily on the back.

"Everything will be fine, Mother," Joan said smiling. "I'm sure of it."

Candles dripped wax in nearly every corner of the Banqueting House. Banners skipped from beam to beam. A breeze blew in past the stone-painted fabric walls in a flickering, waving chill. Soft strains of music echoed out from within Whitehall Palace, where among food and fires the royal court awaited tonight's entertainment.

Joan, arms laden with costumes, appreciated the excess. Darkness came so quickly in winter, so the bright illumination from so many tiny flames made the room feel less harsh.

She laid the costumes out across a wide table and picked through the pieces.

Her Majesty had requested the King's Men perform *A Midsummer Night's Dream*. Joan was thankful that she hadn't asked for an encore of *Othello*.

She pulled Hermia's white dress free from the rest. It had been reconstructed, since the one she'd worn had been completely destroyed fighting Auberon at the Globe. Her stomach clenched as a memory of his dead eyes flashed in her mind.

"Ah, Joan. There you are."

She turned, cheeks burning as Nick ran up to her. He stopped just shy of standing too close and smiled his beautiful smile.

That was truly unfair.

"I—ah—I—" He ran a hand through his hair as his eyes glanced at everything except her. "I wanted to give you this." He reached for her hand and pressed something into her grip, closing her fingers around it. "Happy Birthday."

He placed a gentle kiss on her wrist and, holding eye contact, pressed his lips against her skin.

"Thank you," she said, feeling her entire body go hot.

"My apprenticeship ends soon, you know." His gaze shifted away before he took a steadying breath and met her eyes again. "I— When it's done, I'd like you to know it's my intention to court you."

Joan's heart thudded in her chest.

"You need not answer now and I'll seek your parents' blessings first, of course, but this is—" He tugged nervously at the end of his ponytail and took another deep breath. "I wanted to tell you first."

She stared as he turned and walked away. She felt numb all over as excitement and terror warred in her heart. A small, cold weight pressed against her palm. Slowly, she opened her hand.

It was a pendant, iron from the way it sang to her. Something looked to be carved into the smooth surface.

She lifted it higher, squinting at the inscription.

To My Sweet Hermia, now and always.

Joan didn't think her face could burn any hotter. She wanted to call his name, throw herself into his arms, and kiss him. But she held back, hands tightening around the pendant.

Could she accept Nick's suit? Her heart screamed yes but—

What would her life look like as the wife of a player? And what of Rose?

The tall girl's smiling face suddenly appeared in her mind.

Stop thinking of what's proper when you can have both of us.

The words wouldn't leave Joan's mind. But Rose couldn't really mean both; it wasn't possible.

"Joan, I have news."

Joan jerked back to the present and slipped the disk into her pocket as James strode up behind her. "What is it?"

"It's about Baba Ben." He glanced around then leaned in conspiratorially. "Master Shakespeare was able to glean some more information about his arrest from a courtier close to the queen."

Joan rolled her eyes even as her heart beat double time. "Of course he was. What is it?"

"A royal order is what put Baba in the Tower."

Joan jerked away, staring at James, willing him to drop his jest. He stared back in horrible confirmation.

A royal order could only come from someone close to the king but why would anyone with that much power command that Baba Ben, who by all appearances was a mere tailor, be held there? The Tower of London was reserved for the most important prisoners, like those responsible for the explosion that had nearly killed the queen. Joan's godfather had done nothing that demanded he be sent to such a place. It made no sense.

"Joan." James's voice cut through her panic as he squeezed her shoulders. "It isn't hopeless. We now know where he is and, with some luck, someone at the celebration tonight will be able to get us in to see him. Worry not."

She took a deep breath and nodded. "Yes, you're right and he's safest there under such careful watch."

Besides, with Titanea gone, there were no Fae close to the crown. A mortal threat to her godfather was frightening but far better than a Fae one. This was the only joy Joan would take in Titanea's demise, and the sudden feeling of relief made her head spin.

"Exactly." James grinned then glanced down at her hands and pursed his lips. "So you can stop strangling my dress now."

"Sorry!" Joan flinched and loosened her grip on the costume, draping it over her arm to smooth out the tiny wrinkles she'd caused.

James raised an eyebrow at her. "Would you like to have another go at Hermia? I'm sure Nick wouldn't mind tasting of your lips again. You could give me a rest for my birthday and Nick can give you kisses for yours."

"Very funny." Her cheeks burned at the memory of their last kiss. She scowled at James before shoving the costume against his chest. "I'll not be doing your duties today. Not getting the company arrested is my gift to the both of us. Happy Birthday."

James laughed in her face.

"Joan!" Burbage jogged toward them, a deep blue gown clutched in his grip.

Joan's heart raced.

Not again.

He reached them, grinning broadly as he shoved the gown at her. "Her Majesty has requested you attend her again, my dear. You must've made quite the impression."

She let the weight of the dress fall against her arms and tried to smile. She hoped her distaste didn't show on her face. Not here and definitely not in Her Majesty's presence.

James laughed and it sounded hollow. "Come, sister, let me work my magic on you once again." He slipped his arm around her back and guided her toward his dressing space. "At least you'll not have to sit through *Othello* this time," he whispered in her ear.

Bia hummed against her wrist. Joan let the feeling comfort her.

She could make it through this once again. After all, facing the queen and her ladies was surely easier than murder, and she'd done both before.

———+———

Joan couldn't be sure if this was the same guard who'd guided her through the mazelike halls before. They all looked the same with their pale faces glaring out from stiff uniforms.

Not that it mattered much; she just wanted to escape this encounter with her dignity intact, and no guard would ever be her ally.

"You there. Allow me to speak to this girl for a moment."

Joan froze as Cecil strode down the hall toward them. The secretary of state, though impeccably dressed with nary a string out of place, looked more haggard than he'd been when they'd last met. His eyes were sunken in and wild, the lines around his frowning mouth so pronounced that it seemed he wore no other expression.

His star had truly fallen since the attack. Joan tried her best not to enjoy his obvious misfortune. The struggle was mighty.

"Her Majesty the Queen has requested the girl's presence," the guard said. He shifted a bit under Cecil's glare.

Coward.

"Then you'd best allow me to speak with the child so you can deliver her without too much delay. Leave us."

The guard bowed his head to Cecil and disappeared back around the corner.

Joan scowled and met Cecil's eyes. "I've done all you asked of me, Lord Salisbury."

He flinched and his face twisted in rage. "You impudent girl. I could see you hanged."

"Yes, but the last time someone wanted me dead . . ." Joan smiled at him, sickly sweet. "Well, you still have his head as a trophy, do you not? And he had magic." She bared her teeth. "You're only mortal."

Cecil's whole body seemed to vibrate before he went suddenly still. "Witchcraft is an abomination against God and nature, one His Majesty the King particularly abhors." He moved past her, leaning in close to her ear as their shoulders met. "Cross me again and I'll see you burn, girl." He smiled at her. "Guard, you may deliver her to the queen."

The guard seemed to reappear from nowhere. He saluted Cecil and gestured Joan forward. She turned, watching Cecil's smiling face until they disappeared around another corner.

Joan wiped suddenly sweaty hands against her skirt. She hadn't thought Cecil could frighten her after she'd defeated Auberon. Clearly, she'd been wrong. She tried to will her hands to stop shaking. Soon she'd have to face down the queen and her ladies, and she'd need all her wits about her to make it through that.

She thought of Titanea, disguised as Lady Clifford, and her promise that she'd not let Joan be treated like an exotic creature the next time she found herself before the queen. But Titanea was gone.

The Fae queen had been caught up in Auberon's plot and had paid the ultimate price.

Joan was on her own in this snake's den.

She took a deep breath as they rounded the final corner to the royal chamber. This time, Lady Foul-Breath stood outside the door.

"Mistress Joan Sands to see the queen," the guard said.

"I remember you," Lady Foul-Breath said. She gripped Joan's arm with audacious familiarity and dragged her forward into the room.

This time, the smell of flowers wasn't as cloying. It blended with a woody undertone. Joan tried to focus on the pleasant scent.

"Mistress Joan Sands," Lady Foul-Breath said.

Joan dropped into a curtsy and discreetly let her eyes scan the faces in the room. She wished Lady Clifford's round face and blond hair would pop defiantly out of the assembled ladies. But Titanea was dead.

Joan's heart sank as she turned her eyes to the floor.

"Welcome, Mistress Sands," the queen said. She lounged on an abundance of pillows and cushions, slightly paler than before but otherwise looking radiant.

Joan kept her eyes down. "The pleasure is mine, Your Majesty."

Someone tugged at Joan's hair, jerking her head to the side and knocking her off-balance.

"Look at how tightly she braids her hair."

Another hand on her head pulled it the other way.

"How does she get such knotted hair so tamed?"

Joan breathed deeply and forced her hands to stay limp at her sides.

"Ladies!" the queen bellowed. "Unhand Mistress Sands."

Joan froze as the hands snatched away from her. She glanced up.

All eyes in the room focused on Queen Anne as she frowned out at them.

"She is here as our guest," the queen said, "and will not be fondled so."

The ladies mumbled and muttered apologies as Joan slowly rose from her curtsy.

What was happening?

Queen Anne held out one dainty hand. "Come, child. Sit."

Numbly, Joan crossed the room and dropped down onto one of the cushions nearest the queen.

"Penelope, pour our guest some wine."

Lady Foul-Breath pursed her lips but rose to get Joan's drink. She scowled as she approached Joan with the full goblet. Joan could read the intention all over the other woman's face and prepared for her borrowed gown to be ruined. She wondered how much it would cost to replace the beautiful blue dress.

Queen Anne plucked the drink from her lady's hands and gently passed it to Joan.

Joan's brain skittered to a stop. She shook her head and took the wine. "Thank you, Your Majesty."

The queen smiled brightly at her. "Catherine," she snapped at Lady Goose Neck. "Fetch some musicians. We shall hear some songs before we hear our play."

Lady Goose Neck rose and rushed to the door and slipped out into the hall.

Joan just watched and sipped her wine, hoping to find some sense in the bottom of her cup.

———✚———

"If we shadows have offended, / Think but this and all is mended: / That you have only slumbered here while these visions did appear." Armin stood center stage, dressed in Puck's fine costume.

Joan remembered the last time she'd heard him deliver this speech and the rush of applause that followed.

"So good night unto you all. / Give me your hands, if we be friends, / And Robin shall restore amends." Armin held out his hands to the audience, his attention focused up where Queen Anne and her ladies sat upon the highest scaffold. He winked at Joan, who occupied a place of honor in the chair just beside the queen's.

A tambourine clanged, a drum thumped, then the horns sounded. The full company of King's Men flooded the stage.

"Wonderful! Most wonderful!" The queen rose from her seat to applaud the players.

Joan rose alongside her. Lady Foul-Breath struggled to stand from the cushion at the queen's feet. Joan thought about tired legs tingling with nerves and pretended she didn't see the woman stumble.

The company bowed again. James caught Joan's eye as he stood. He tilted his head and Joan shrugged back. She had no clue as to Her Majesty's sudden kindness and generosity. And it wasn't something she'd question now.

"Lovely." The queen sat back in her ornate seat, the rest of the ladies drifting down like butterflies around her. "Although I doubt the fairy queen would be so easily tricked." She turned. "What do you think, dear Joan?"

Wait.

Joan looked up, her eyes meeting the queen's. Something in her tone made Joan's heart leap into her throat. "Y-Your Majesty?" she choked out.

It couldn't be—

The queen laughed. "Our Joan agrees and is speechless."

The ladies tittered along with her.

Joan couldn't breathe.

The kindness, the generosity, it all made sense if this were—

But it couldn't be—

"Dear Joan"—the queen grabbed one of Joan's hands in both of hers—"there's been a hole in my heart since the loss of my dear Lady Clifford in the attack that nearly killed me."

Joan's heart raced.

"Your presence today has lightened that burden." The queen's grip tightened. "You'll allow us to call on you again, yes?"

Joan looked into the queen's eyes. Brown bled through, overtaking Queen Anne's bright blue gaze for a moment before turning back.

This—this was Titanea.

Joan's mouth opened and closed dumbly as a gush of relief flowed through her body.

Titanea was alive. She had survived Auberon's attack.

"Of course, Your Majesty." Joan smiled at the queen—no, at Titanea—and gripped her hands back. "It would be my pleasure."

And Joan found she meant it. A thought crossed her mind. With Titanea, a friend, in this place of power, perhaps Joan could convince her to see Baba Ben released from his imprisonment in the Tower. She'd already asked so much, but what was one more small request? Hope swelled in her chest.

"Most excellent," Titanea said. She leaned in close to Joan, whispered in her ear. "Were you worried, dear Joan? You shouldn't have feared, favorite. Now that the Pact is dissolved, we shall wield our true power soon enough."

Joan froze, her mind racing.

"Your Majesty, my godfather, Baba Ben—"

"Nearly two centuries is a long time, even for one such as we," Titanea said, cutting off her words. "We were done being trapped, and that man threatened to keep us imprisoned. But he is still alive, worry not."

A sudden rage bubbled up in Joan's chest. "What did you do?"

"Auberon was a thorn in our side we could not remove, but did you know Herne is one of our faithful?" Titanea leaned back and smiled. "And the rules, as they were, would not allow us to sit before you in this realm or in the shape of this mortal queen."

Joan's heart beat double time.

Herne the Hunter had been the one guarding the explosives that day. Joan had spoken to her before being dragged away by Cecil's guards. Joan had thought vicious Herne was part of Auberon's side, but all this time, the hunter had been Titanea's agent.

Joan's eyes met Titanea's. "It was you. You planted the gunpowder to kill the real queen."

The Fae queen's smile shifted into that tiger's grin of hers. "What loyalty did you have to her—a woman who treated you worse than an animal? Be grateful we are here while you curry our favor, dear Joan. Do not make us regret our love for you and remember"—Titanea leaned in close, tapping her finger on Joan's cheek—"you twice over are in our debt."

Never had Joan felt so much like prey. She remembered now, the hasty expression of gratitude offered in a moment when she'd felt raw and vulnerable and again today because she'd never considered Queen Anne being anything more than mortal. Two promises she couldn't take back.

Damnation.

And here, before the might of the crown wielded by an impostor, bound to a seemingly benevolent power, Joan smiled back at the false queen of England as Bia sang at her wrist.

A NOTE ON HISTORY

Introduction

While this novel is a work of historical fiction, it was born from a place of historical fact. Several of the characters we meet were real people alive in 1605, and while there were narrative liberties taken with the timeline, most of it is true to life. Although the existence of the Fae in England at this time is debatable, the presence of non-white citizens and queer people is not.

The King's Men

A group of actors who worked and performed together from 1594 to 1642, with William Shakespeare as a member from their inception to 1613. All acting companies of the time needed a patron—a person of wealth and status under whose household they were employed. Without one, actors could be arrested and jailed as vagrants. This particular company had three patrons with a name change under each one. They were known as the Lord Chamberlain's Men with Henry Carey—Lord Chamberlain and in charge of entertainment for Queen Elizabeth's court—from 1594 until Carey's death in 1596. His son, George Carey, took over their patronage from 1596 to 1603 and they became Hunsdon's Men until George became the new Lord Chamberlain in 1597, giving the company back their old name. They became the King's Men when King James I took over their patronage from 1603 to 1642. At this time, acting companies had levels of membership: sharers—those who owned portions of the company's assets; apprentices—boy actors in training who usually played the female roles; hired men—those brought on for roles in specific shows; and musicians—self-explanatory. All the members mentioned below were real people and part of the King's Men in 1605.

James Sands, or Saunders according to some records, was an apprentice under Augustine Phillips in 1605. Not much more is known about him besides the fact that Phillips left all his instruments to him in his will.

William Shakespeare was an actor, playwright, poet, and the member of the King's Men you're most likely to recognize. He's noted as having performed with this same company of actors from 1594 until his retirement in 1613. Historians still debate his sexuality—he was believed to be a lover of the Earl of Southampton—he was married to Anne Hathaway and they had three children together: Susanna, Hamnet, and Judith. He had no connection to the Orisha in real life.

Richard Burbage was the most famous actor of his time and a sharer with the King's Men. Records of the company's performances note him as having played most of the main roles in Shakespeare's plays, including the title roles in *Hamlet*, *Othello*, *King Lear*, and *Macbeth*.

Robert Armin was a principal actor with the King's Men and the company's clown. He's believed to have played the Fool in *King Lear*,

Touchstone in *As You Like It*, and Feste in *Twelfth Night*. He took over after William Kempe—famous for his acrobatics and ability to make up songs on the spot—left the company sometime around 1600.

Augustine Phillips was a sharer with the King's Men and the master actor under whom James Sands apprenticed. He died in May 1605 and—according to his will—left forty shillings and three musical instruments to his apprentice, James Sands.

Nicholas Tooley was a principal actor with the King's Men. Not much is known about him.

Robert Gough was a principal actor with the King's Men. Not much is known about him.

Samuel Crosse was a principal actor with the King's Men who died sometime after 1604. Not much is known about him.

The Court of King James I

The following are real members of the royal court under King James I—England's first non-Tudor ruler since 1485.

Robert Cecil was the secretary of state and royal spymaster from 1596 to 1612. He inherited the spymaster job from his father, William Cecil, who had worked himself to death in 1596. Robert proceeded to do the same and died in 1612. When Queen Elizabeth I died without leaving an heir to take the throne, Robert had already arranged for the king of Scotland, James VI, to take her place. Robert was not well-liked in court but was excellent at his job. He rooted out multiple assassination attempts, including the 1603 Bye Plot—perpetrated by his brothers-in-law—and the 1605 Gunpowder Plot—which was completely unsuccessful in real life.

King James I was the king of England and Scotland from 1603 to 1625. He was the first king of England to be named James and the sixth king of Scotland with that name. His parents were Mary, Queen of Scots—beheaded for treason in 1587 by Queen Elizabeth I—and Henry Stuart—who died suddenly and under mysterious circumstances in 1567 after having Mary's lover executed. James is known for uniting England and Scotland under the name Great Britain and for commissioning a translation of the Bible known as the King James Version.

Queen Anne was the princess of Denmark and the wife of James I. She was an avid supporter of the arts and performed in several private court masques. One was *The Masque of Blackness* by Ben Jonson, where the queen and her ladies played the daughters of the sea god Neptune on a quest to "clean" their dark skin. It was done in blackface—the performers all painted their skin with dark or black makeup to mimic brown skin.

Lady Anne Clifford, Lucy, Catherine, and Penelope were all ladies-in-waiting to Queen Anne. Lady Anne Clifford was the fourteen-year-old Duchess of Clifford and a favorite of the queen.

—┼—

The Orisha

This novel contains a fictionalized version of the very real tradition, Orisha veneration or worship—which was born in West Africa, mainly in the area we now know as Nigeria. While certain aspects may be familiar to practitioners, this is not a true reflection of the religion and should be taken as fantastical.

My personal knowledge of the Orisha is through Lucumí (commonly known as Santería)—a branch of the practice from Cuba. It was born when enslaved African people blended their traditional religion with the Catholic practices forced on them by the Spanish. The cover of Catholicism helped them worship as they wanted without punishment.

For the religion as Joan and her family practice it, I asked myself, what would things look like if the religion came to England without being shaped by the cruelties of the slave trade? I also added the idea that the Orisha give you magical powers.

If you'd like to know more about the Santería religion or the Orisha, I recommend *Black Gods: Orisa Studies in the New World* by John Mason and *Finding Soul on the Path of Orisa: A West African Spiritual Tradition* by Tobe Melora Correal, but ultimately the best resource is an actual practitioner or priest.

ACKNOWLEDGMENTS

It's hard to believe that my first novel is here in the world and in our hands. What a journey, from the NaNoWriMo bones of this to my first draft in 2019 to this beautiful book in 2023! So many folks helped me get this story from the pictures in my head to the page, and I am eternally grateful for everything they've done.

Thank you to my editor, Maggie Lehrman, for seeing the book of my heart and helping me polish it to this brilliant shine. The work was hard with real babies and book babies, but we made it to the finish line! Your passion, excitement, and insights are more than I could've hoped for in an editor, and I'm thrilled to build the rest of Joan's adventures with you.

Thank you to the rest of the fantastic team at Abrams and Amulet Books: Amy Vreeland, Maggie Moore, Jenna Lisanti, Megan Evans, Mary Marolla, Trish McNamara O'Neill, Gaby Paez, Emily Daluga, and—the man in charge—Andrew Smith. Thank you for all your hard work. You've made me feel appreciated and I'm so glad I put my debut into your capable hands.

Thank you to my copyeditor, Shasta Clinch, and proofreader Margo Winton Parodi for catching all my punctuation and grammar mistakes, because 60 percent of my school English lessons have refused to stick, and for those tiny plot goofs that were trying to sneak through. Your eyes were so sharp, and it was a gift to have you both reviewing my work.

Thank you to my cover illustrator, Fernanda Suarez. I've been a fan for years, and the life you breathed into Joan was nothing short of incredible. Thank you to my cover designer, Chelsea Hunter—you got my baby looking right, and I love it so much! And thank you to my map artist, Jaime Zollars, for giving me the map of my dreams that captures the multiple vibes of this book so perfectly. All of you are incredible.

Thank you to my early readers! To Cavan Scott for making sure my Brits were British-ing appropriately. To Tracy Deonn for shaking some loose strings out of my plot and letting me send you rewritten chapters and art and snippets so I'd have someone to squeal with me. To my beloved Carrie McClain for reading my draft and me with such a loving and shrewd eye. To my agency sib Sonora Reyes for your fantastic insights and wonderful enthusiasm. You all taught me so much through your skill and generosity, and I am forever grateful.

Thank you to my team at Writers House. To the foreign rights team: Cecilia de la Campa, Alessandra Birch, and Sofia Bolido, you have been such fierce advocates for my niche book baby and have worked such magic. I couldn't ask for better supporters.

Thank you to my incredible, wonderful, outstanding, absolute rockstar of an agent and friend, Alexandra Levick. You've fought so hard for this book, this story at every step and it has paid off in ways I'd barely imagined. Thank you for pushing me to find the outstanding book within the good one and helping me stay true to the heart of my story. Thank you for your notes, for the calls to talk me out of publishing panic, for your incredible enthusiasm, and your belief in me. There is no better book champion in the world, and I'm so blessed to be able to work with someone as brilliant as you.

Thank you to my friends who supported me through this process. To Clinton; Amy & Paul; Leigh; Jalisa; Ron & Leslie; Jonathan, Resse, Ashley, and my Arena Players family; Nicole, Leslie, Izetta, and Carrie, my Taco Tuesday, Womanism Every Day group chat; Will, Omar, and the rest of my Black Nerd Problems family; all my beautiful, chaotic geniuses in the Black Nerd Problems Discord; my hilarious and supportive D&D squad; and Soni, Zoulfa, and the rest of my Agent Siblings. I wouldn't be here without y'all, thank you for making all the hard work a little bit easier on my heart and mind.

Thank you to my wonderful family. Thank you to the whole Williams/ Johnson/Cook clan for always being my biggest cheerleaders even when you only halfway know what I'm talking about, the love I have for you all knows no bounds. To my brother, Eric, for being the best early birthday gift a kid could ask for, for growing up to be so much cooler than me, and for giving me the most adorable niece. To my baby sister, Ericka, for being so smart and way cooler than any of the rest of us. To Mom & Dad Older and Malka, Lou, and the kids, thank you for loving me and welcoming me into the family with such warmth and generosity. To my wonderful Grandma for believing in me harder and longer than anyone in this world and cheering me on in everything that I've done. None of this is possible without you.

Thank you to my love, Daniel. Words could never capture how much your presence, your love, your generosity, your kindness all mean to me. I could wax poetic for pages and still only skim the surface. I love you with all of my being and thank you for always seeing all my brightest and darkest parts and holding them all in your heart.

Thank you to Tito for being born. I love you more than anything. We've both grown so much through this process, and being your mommy is the greatest gift I've ever been given. Love you, my baby.

Finally, thank you to every single one of you who bought, requested, read, shared, or talked up this book. The writing was solitary, but the publishing is a group effort and I appreciate you joining us on this journey. Thank you all from the bottom of my heart.

LL THE WORLD'S A STAGE,
and Joan's story has just begun!

Read on for a glimpse of her next adventure

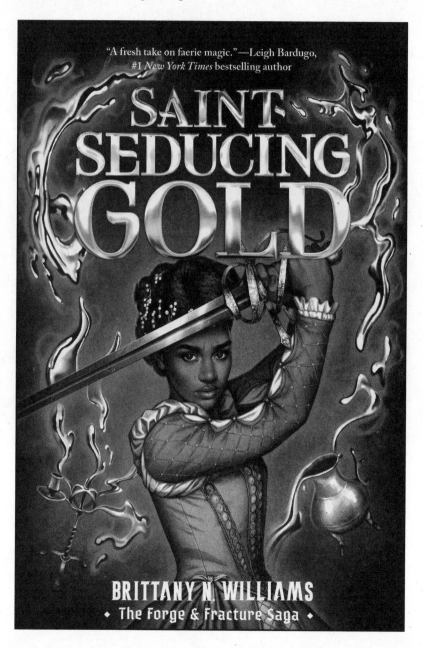

"A fresh take on faerie magic." —Leigh Bardugo,
#1 *New York Times* bestselling author

SAINT-SEDUCING GOLD

BRITTANY N. WILLIAMS
◆ The Forge & Fracture Saga ◆

CHAPTER ONE
Fortunes Made & Marred

he queen is dead.

Joan Sands had expected Twelfth Night to go smoothly. She and her twin brother, James, would celebrate their birthday over a lovely morning meal with their family then spend the rest of the day at court with the King's Men. In the afternoon she'd help him and the rest of the players prepare for their royal performance. They'd pack up and end the evening eating royal delights, until Master Shakespeare and Master Burbage got drunk enough to take each other for an indecent turn on the dance floor. The day followed that exact pattern from the first time she'd attended the Feast of the Epiphany celebrations with the King's Men four years ago and every time since.

She'd been a fool to think the mayhem and bloodshed of last November wouldn't ripple chaos through this day and the royal court.

The queen is dead, and an imposter sits on her throne.

The breaking of the Pact between the Fae and the children of the Orisha released chaos upon mortal London. The only person with the knowledge of its sealing—Joan's godfather, Baba Ben—rotted in the Tower of London. Joan had killed Auberon, depriving the worst of the Fae of their leader; and Titanea, the Fae queen, had been killed by the explosion that decimated the House of Lords.

Or so they'd believed.

The quiet of the last two months seemed to prove they'd averted a greater crisis. But what did it mean now that Titanea was alive and wearing the face of the mortal queen of England?

More than that, she was the mastermind behind the broken Pact. She'd had Baba Ben arrested and imprisoned in the Tower of London. She'd orchestrated the explosion that had killed the true Queen Anne and so many others.

Titanea, who smiled as she lounged on England's throne and wore the form of its dead monarch.

Joan sat on the edge of her own gilded chair placed beside Titanea's on the highest scaffold. The rest of the royal guests spread out before their platform and along the sides of the hall; a sea of festive courtiers perched on row upon row of benches bordering the central playing space.

Joan had never felt more exposed in her life.

The warmth of Ogun's presence burned in her chest, the pulsing heat seeming to encourage her along with the persistent thrum of Bia, the sword she'd worn hidden around her wrist as a bracelet from the moment she'd laid hands on it. No other blade seemed so attuned to Joan's senses. Even now, its steady rhythm beat in harmony to Ogun's fire.

Titanea patted Joan's cheek. "Do not make us regret our love for you, and remember you twice over are in our debt."

Joan's heart raced at the memory, a shiver shooting down her spine as fear and regret overpowered even Ogun's burn. Her thoughts had been so overtaken first by her mistreatment at the hands of Queen Anne and her ladies and then at the queen's abrupt good grace, that Joan had offered her gratitude without hesitation.

Strike . . .

What a fool she'd been. Now the Fae queen held two chances to command Joan's absolute obedience to any request she may have. Two magical boons, which Titanea could use to compel her at any time to any purpose.

The potential in such unmitigated power was terrifying.

Strike.

Joan shook her head as if to dislodge the thought that she knew wasn't her own. She cut a look over her shoulder, certain that the women around them had heard every word. The queen's ladies faced away from the two of them, not a bit of attention paid to Joan. They twittered idle gossip like an obnoxious flock of birds, speaking eagerly to each other as if willed to do so by some force. A glance at Titanea's knowing smile told Joan they had been. None of them realized who they served in disguise, though Joan doubted they'd care so long as they continued to curry the monarch's favor.

She wondered if the difference mattered to her. She swallowed the uncomfortable lump in her throat when she couldn't give a simple answer even to herself.

Yes, Titanea had had Baba Ben arrested, but he was alive and unharmed—if she was to be believed. She'd caused the death of the true queen, but she'd also aided Joan in her greatest time of need. Titanea had given Joan the opportunity to rescue James by telling all under her command to stand down. Whatever dismay Joan felt over the loss of the true Queen Anne was hardly strong enough to drive an attack on its own, let alone when weighed against Titanea's aid.

Strike.

Ogun and Bia held no such doubts. The sword at her wrist pulsed so intensely that she feared Titanea could feel the vibrations. Her chest blazed with Ogun's pressure, the scorching heat urging her, driving her to attack the Fae queen though she'd done no harm in the time since the explosion.

Strike.

Ogun's command echoed firm and sure within her, but Joan didn't feel the Orisha's certainty. The doubt she held in her mind stayed her hand. She couldn't attack Titanea if any remained, refused to gamble with the lives of her loved ones. The stakes here loomed too high to allow any such errors.

Now. Strike now.

Joan took a shuddering breath, forcing the demand down and trying to calm the fire within her. Moving to murder Titanea now was not only unprovoked but rash and unwise. However much Bia and Ogun compelled her to attack, Joan knew she could not. She needed to be sure.

"Why have you done this?" Joan said, even as the insistent whispers raced through her mind.

Strike.

Titanea smiled indulgently and squeezed Joan's cheeks. "Know us better and you will understand the why, dear Joan."

Joan gritted her teeth but held the smile on her face. The vague response along with Ogun's pressing made her head swim. Joan hadn't expected a direct answer to her question, but Titanea's face held genuine affection. There was an advantage to be found in that. She only needed to press it.

"I would like to, Your Highness," Joan said, exaggerating the deference in her voice. She cast her gaze down demurely. "But your star lies so far above my own that we may find no more opportune moment to speak than this." She frowned and lifted her eyes. "A mere merchant's daughter could hardly hope to meet with Queen Anne once. Twice is unprecedented and I fear any more time together would be impossible." The sad resignation she forced into the words would've made James proud.

Had her brother been in her place, he'd have cajoled a full confession out of Titanea as easily as breathing, but he stood with the actors in the tiring-room, the lot of them completely unaware of the queen's true identity. Joan prayed her own playing moved Titanea to make even a small admission, anything to help Joan plan her next action.

Strike.

Joan watched the Fae queen's expression shift from comprehension to dismay to a sudden sly satisfaction. She released Joan's face and leaned back on her throne. "If it's time you want, dear Joan, then time you shall have." She patted Joan's hand gently, her grin shooting apprehension through Joan's gut.

Strike!

The Orisha's voice screamed in Joan's head, and she found herself fighting against the familiar haze of Ogun's possession. Her vision darkened around the edges.

Strike!

She'd wavered for too long, and her indecision left her conflicted mind open for Ogun to overtake her. He'd attack where she wouldn't and damn them all to traitor's deaths.

She tried to resist but felt herself drifting, a numbness overwhelming her as her consciousness was shoved away from her physical body. Ogun pushed through and left her to see and feel with no control of her actions.

It played out in her head. She'd grab the front of Titanea's chemise, wrenching the Fae queen forward as she called forth an iron blade. One jab through the woman's throat would finish her with a wound she couldn't hope to heal.

A quick, clean kill before a room of spectators and an assured death for Joan and every single person she loved.

Her fingers twitched when the cool rush of iron flowed down her arm toward her palm. She breathed deeply, exerting all of her will to force the Orisha back. Her hands tingled with the effort, her movements nearly her own again. She shifted forward just as someone seized her wrist. She spun and met Cecil's fierce gaze. Terror surged through her, slamming full awareness back into her body with a cold clarity.

"His Majesty the king approaches," he said to Titanea, eyes slipping from Joan's face to her open palm, and then to her other hand still clasped within Titanea's. His scowl deepened. Did he know what she'd been about to do under Ogun's control?

"Cross me again and I'll see you burn, girl."

The memory of the threat he'd hissed earlier in the hall rushed back into her mind. Even Cecil's own family wasn't free from his wrath. She passed the heads of Cecil's own in-laws, tarred and perched atop London Bridge as gruesome trophies, each time she crossed the Thames. If he'd seen her attempt . . .

Titanea raised one blond eyebrow. "We shall prepare space for the king."

She snapped her fingers, and a flurry of activity burst around them. Two servants brought up another throne, larger and more ornate than the queen's, and placed it beside her. Her ladies scrambled to their feet, Lady Foul-Breath stumbling up from her cushion on the floor. Their idle chatter flooded Joan's ears. Lady Goose Neck attempted to shoulder Joan out of the way. Joan planted her feet and let the woman ricochet off her.

Cecil's nails dug into Joan's skin. "Shall I return this child to her players?" He spoke the words lightly even as he attempted to draw blood with his hold.

Damn that man. But she was herself again and Ogun's voice had gone quiet.

"Your Highness," Joan blurted, squeezing Titanea's hand even as she felt Cecil's grip on her other wrist tighten. "If I might have your ear for one moment more."

Cecil jerked her backward. Joan stumbled, her attention on Titanea the only thing that allowed the weaker man to move her even slightly. The Fae queen scowled and laced her fingers through Joan's, holding fast.

"Have we dismissed her, Salisbury?" she said, her voice sharp with command.

Cecil paled.

"Oh my," a voice said from behind them, their tone gleefully scandalized. "It seems Lord Salisbury has soured Her Highness's happy mood."

"You'd suppose that after his last failure nearly killed my queen, he'd tread more cautiously before her," another replied.

Joan twisted over her shoulder to see the tall, pale form of King James ascending the stairs to the raised dais. Clusters of flickering candles on polished gold candelabras cast shifting light and shadow across his imposing form, playing over his sculpted blond hair and beard. A striking young man barely older than Joan herself stood just behind the king, his equally flaxen hair secured with an ebony ribbon at his nape and pulled over one shoulder.

His gaze shifted from Joan's face to where Cecil held her wrist before sliding over to where Titanea's fingers intertwined with her own. A sly smile spread across the young man's face as he leaned toward the king. "It seems this girl has caused some strife between our queen and Lord Salisbury. I'm surprised he has the temerity to so challenge Her Highness."

"How impertinent," the king grunted before dropping comfortably onto his throne. "Erskine? Remind the Earl of Salisbury of his place."

Cecil froze as a tall man approached from behind him, candlelight dancing over sharp features set in a pale but handsome face. His short fair hair was combed carefully to one side and brushed against his bushy blond beard. He wore the crimson uniform of a yeoman guard, well-cut and bearing a host of medals and embellishments. A sword hung at his waist, shiny and well-made, but Joan could see the worn leather of the grip that spoke of its frequent use.

Erskine—for that must be his name—raised a bushy blond eyebrow. "I doubt the maid deserves such rough treatment." A heavy Scottish accent colored his deep voice, making the words sing. He placed one gloved hand casually on the hilt of his sword.

Cecil dropped Joan's wrist as if she'd burned him. She stumbled with the sudden release, and only Titanea tightening her grip kept her standing.

The young man slipped into place behind the king and leaned across the high back of the chair with an ease that spoke of comfort and frequency. A series of servants scurried around them, placing the brightly colored standards bearing the royal Stuart crest all around the dais before disappearing discreetly.

King James's gaze swept over Joan. "A blackamoor?" He raised an eyebrow. "Is she so special?"

"She is indeed, my lord," Titanea said, squeezing Joan's fingers again. "After the loss of my dear Lady Clifford, I've found myself quite comforted by this girl's presence." She sniffled, and one of her ladies dropped a delicate handkerchief into her other hand.

Joan fought the urge to snort as she watched the woman dab at dry eyes. The king smiled indulgently at Titanea, his expression gentle and affectionate.

"Of course, my queen," he said. "What would you have done with the girl?"

The queen is dead, and a Fae imposter sits on her throne.

Titanea cast a grateful look at the king, then turned to Joan, her expression sharp with glee. "I want her as my lady-in-waiting."

"What?" Joan blurted. Shock shoved any sense of propriety from Joan's mind as she boldly locked eyes with Titanea.

The Fae queen jerked her close to whisper in her ear. "You wanted time, dear Joan, and time you shall have."

Long live the queen.

THE STORY CONTINUES IN
Saint-Seducing Gold . . .

ABOUT THE AUTHOR

Brittany N. Williams is a classically trained actress who studied musical theater at Howard University and Shakespearean performance at the Royal Central School of Speech and Drama in London. Previously, she has been a principal vocalist at Hong Kong Disneyland, a theater professor at Coppin State University and has made appearances in *Queen Sugar* and *Leverage: Redemption*. Her short stories have been published in the *Gambit Weekly*, *Fireside Magazine*, and the *Star Wars* anthology *From a Certain Point of View: The Empire Strikes Back*. Learn more at brittanynwilliams.com.